FALLEN

*"Taut, page-turning suspense and heart-stopping romance:
Leslie Tentler is a rising star of romantic suspense."*

- NYT Bestselling Author Allison Brennan

PRAISE FOR BOOKS IN
THE CHASING EVIL TRILOGY,
ALSO BY LESLIE TENTLER

"A smooth prose style and an authentic Big Easy vibe distinguish Tentler's debut … the shivers are worthy of a Lisa Jackson."

- Publishers Weekly, Midnight Caller

"From the turn of the first page, Leslie Tentler hooks the reader and holds them in the palm of her hands."

- Examiner.com, Midnight Fear

"A compelling plot, thick suspense, a cunning villain, a shattered cop and a victim who wants answers at any cost place Tentler in the same category as bestselling authors Lisa Jackson and Beverly Barton."

- RT Book Reviews, Edge of Midnight

FALLEN

Leslie Tentler

To live in hearts we leave behind is not to die.

— *Thomas Campbell*

PROLOGUE

—▶)•●•(◀—

"I'M SORRY I'M late." APD Detective Nate Weisz glanced at the digital numbers glowering at him in luminescent green from the car dashboard. He moved his cell phone to his other hand, pressing it against his ear as he made the sharp cut into the parking garage of the Midtown Atlanta condo building. "We arrested four prostitutes on Ponce tonight in a sting. I got caught up in paperwork."

"It's after nine already, Nate. Those tickets were hard to get."

He could hear the irritation in Kristen's tone. It would be a long night, the perfect ending to another shitty day. "If it was so important, why didn't you just take your sister?"

"Because I wanted to go with *you*. You're my husband. Or doesn't that matter to you anymore?"

He sighed in the sedan's darkened interior before shutting off the engine and pushing the door open. "I'm in the parking garage now, all right? I'll come up, change clothes and we'll go somewhere else. Maybe catch a movie at Atlantic Station—"

Kristen's voice floated on a wave of petulance. "No. It's too late."

She disconnected the call without saying good-bye. With a muttered curse, Nate shoved his phone into the pocket of his suit coat. As he got out and closed the door, his anger reignited at the scratch that remained visible on the driver's side. He chirped the key fob and headed toward the elevator, the sound of his dress shoes echoing off the deck's concrete walls. He only hoped he didn't smell like booze. The last thing he needed was another knock-down, drag-out with Kristen. There'd been too many of them lately, and frankly, he was too goddamned tired. Eight years as a Narcotics and Vice detective, and to Kristen his excuses had become interchangeable—a drug bust, a prostitution ring, a warrant to serve on an illegal gambling operation. Any of them could be that night's culprit behind him getting home late.

So could a few drinks, he admitted, but he'd needed to unwind.

Above him, the lighting in the garage ceiling flickered. The condominiums were getting old and needed renovation, but the location was excellent, with easy access to I-85 and the zone five precinct near Centennial Olympic Park. They were also less than ten minutes from the high-rise where Kristen worked. Still, she'd been nagging him about moving to one of the newer, fancier—albeit smaller and pricier—loft apartments stacked along Midtown.

The fluorescent panel hummed, emitting an electrical crackle before leaving Nate in darkness. Grumbling, he pushed the elevator button and stared through the deck's steel barriers at the IHOP building that was now an all-you-can-eat Korean buffet. He waited impatiently as the mechanical coffin rumbled its way down to him, nearly drowning out what sounded like the faint approach of footsteps. He turned and peered into the grainy darkness.

Nothing. He was alone.

The garage gave him the creeps. He'd talk to the super tomorrow—he didn't want Kristen down here in the dark. Despite the city's enthusiastic PR spin, crime inside the Perimeter had only continued to worsen. There were muggings, robberies and car-jackings these days even in the best parts of town. Not to mention, criminal activity always got worse in the summer heat. As the elevator neared his floor, the overhead light winked back to life. The convex curve of the security mirror to the right of the bay caught Nate's attention. A human form, clad in an oversize hooded sweatshirt despite the muggy night, was visible in the mirror's reflection.

He saw the gun.

Nate whirled. He extracted his weapon from his holster, losing his grip on the .38 as the blast hit him. He staggered and fell to the concrete floor. Surprise gave way to a screaming pain.

The light flickered off again as the hooded form inched closer. In disbelief, Nate pushed away, kicking clumsily with his feet like a wounded sand crab. *You?* His gun was out of reach, lost somewhere in the deck's shadowy recesses. Behind him, the elevator doors slid open. His frantic pulse thudded in his ears. Nate tried to locate his cell, pawing at his coat pocket, but his fingers had grown numb and useless. His voice croaked out a cry for help that ended in a wet cough. He tasted blood.

Outside, Atlanta's North Street was a barrage of honking horns and car engines, radios turned up loud on a Friday night. Noise that had masked the gun's discharge, not that it had made much sound. Even in the encroaching haze, Nate's trained mind noted the silencer on the barrel.

The barrel that remained pointed at him.

His body convulsed at the entrance of the second bullet. This time he felt no pain, just a slicing coldness and a pressure in his chest like a ten-pound dumbbell had been dropped onto his sternum. He wanted to speak to Kristen, tell her he loved her and beg for her forgiveness. Weakly, he raised his hand, attempting to bargain.

No, don't. Please.

God help me.

The third bullet sent him hurtling into darkness and the unknown.

CHAPTER ONE

---◄)•●•(►---

"GSW, TWO MINUTES out!" Jamaal Reeves made the booming announcement from behind the ER admittance desk at Mercy Hospital. His words put medical personnel on alert, including Dr. Lydia Costa, who stood in the jaundiced glow of the light box, reviewing chest films for an eighty-two-year-old with suspected pneumonia.

"It's a ten-double-zero, people," he added, using police code that over time had slipped into the level one trauma center's vernacular.

Officer down.

A momentary hush fell over the staff before the beehive of activity resumed, leaving only Lydia frozen. Gunshot wounds were always nasty injuries, but it was the ten-double-zero that caused anxiety to pool in her stomach. There were hundreds of police inside the city, she reminded herself. Still, leaving the X-ray hanging, she shouldered her way through the scrubs-clad crowd. Reaching Jamaal's desk, she asked, "What else do you know about the incoming?"

He slurped from a Varsity cup. "Multiple bullets to the chest and abdomen, intubated by paramedics on scene—"

"Do you have a name? A precinct?"

"What? Uh, uh—didn't ask." Jamaal shrugged, his eyes returning to the stack of paperwork in front of him, information forms for the three dozen or so coughing, vomiting or otherwise miserable-looking people who waited in rows of vinyl-covered chairs for treatment.

"Plainclothes, though," he murmured as an afterthought, scribbling directives onto one of the forms.

Lydia felt her knees weaken. Still, her inner voice spoke to her, pointing out that she was one of the attendings on a busy Friday night. She moved briskly toward the automated, sliding glass doors that led inside from the ambulance bay, joining the assembling team and preparing to take charge of whatever faced her with the paramedics' arrival.

"Get trauma room three set up," she ordered, raising her voice to be heard above the din. "We're going to need an echocardiogram. Have a crash cart and thoracotomy set ready."

All the while, a mantra repeated inside her head. It was more like a prayer, if she believed in such things. She used to, but didn't anymore.

Please don't let it be him.

Behind her, she overheard Roe Goodman, one of the senior floor nurses. "You're a jackass, Jamaal. Her ex-husband's a cop. A detective."

"Notify OR to stand by!" Lydia shouted as the flashing

red lights of an ambulance stained the vestibule's walls. Her heartbeat quickened, dread filling her as she stood with the rest of the waiting staff, watching as the paramedics opened the vehicle's double doors and removed the gurney, snapping its legs into place and rolling it into the building. The back of one of the emergency workers obscured her view, making it impossible to get a look at the victim.

"Multiple GSWs, two to the chest and one to the abdomen. Only one exit wound," Ravi Kapoor, the lead paramedic, rattled off as he strode in at the head of the gurney. "Systolic is down to sixty-two, pressure's been dropping in the rig. Probably has a bad internal bleed. Worsening acidosis, hypoxia—"

"Blood type?" someone asked.

"O-negative."

"Type and cross-match," Lydia said, finding her voice. "Call up to the blood bank and tell them we need six units of O-neg, stat."

She nearly stopped breathing as the victim came into view. He was cyanotic, his skin bluish and pale, the ventilation bag's mask concealing his features. But one look told her it wasn't Ryan on the gurney, his shirt ripped open and blood covering his chest. The victim was stockier, his hair inky black, where Ryan's was a light brown. Lydia nearly went limp with relief.

But that relief was fleeting. Lydia *did* know him. Nate Weisz. He was a colleague of Ryan's, from the same precinct, although Nate was a Narcotics and Vice detective, while Ryan worked Homicide. Lydia knew his wife, Kristen, from APD picnics and softball tournaments. Events that were no longer a part of her life.

Shrugging off the shock, she snapped into action. "Get him into trauma three."

Lydia jogged alongside the gurney, knowing it was a matter of minutes before the ER would be swarming with blue uniforms. News about the shooting was no doubt already infiltrating the ranks, spreading down from zone commanders to captains, detectives and beat cops. The turnout from the zone five precinct in particular would be heavy. There would also be television news crews on the scene.

"Coming through!" Ravi shouted, bumping into a staggering male in a gold and black Georgia Tech T-shirt. The man—more of a lanky kid, really—appeared intoxicated and held a wad of gauze against his bleeding forehead.

Lydia called to an intern as they passed. "Lonigan, get that guy out of the hallway! He's got a head lac and needs sutures."

They moved into the trauma room, wheeling the gurney around until it was parallel with the table.

"On my count. One-two-three," Lydia instructed. The trauma team made the transfer to the table, the room becoming a well-timed choreography as lead wires and sensors were attached, IV poles and drips set up.

"Let's get a pulse ox—"

"Where's the O-neg? We need a central line, now!"

"I'll do it, Dr. Costa," an eager resident offered.

"I've got another run. Good luck, Lydia," Ravi said, knocking three times on the door well's metal frame. His eyes met hers through her safety glasses as the paramedics receded into the corridor.

"Blood's here, Doctor." A nurse hurried into the room with a bag of platelets.

"Hang it. Let Radiology know we're going to need a C-spine, chest and belly films." Lydia frowned as the heart monitor sent out a sharp, electronic wail. She studied the EKG lead, her stomach dropping. *Damn it.* "We've got v-tach! Power the paddles and start compressions."

A second-year resident, a large male named Kevin Rossman, stepped forward and began pumping Nate's chest hard enough to crack ribs. It had to be that forceful to work. Lydia felt a trickle of perspiration roll down her back as she took the paddles. "Charge to two-sixty."

A few seconds later, the defibrillator's high-pitched whine filled the room. "Clear!"

Rossman halted the compressions and stepped back, palms lifted. Lydia pressed the paddles against Nate's chest, his body jerking with the electrical charge. Her eyes moved to the monitor. No change. "Two-sixty again! Stand by!"

Come on, Nate.

"Clear!" The second shock regulated the heart rhythm. Lydia suspected the reason for the ventricular tachycardia. "I need a ten-blade."

Someone handed her the surgical scalpel. Counting between the ribs, she made a careful incision into the pleural cavity. Blood spurted out, staining her scrubs as she pushed the chest tube through the opening to re-inflate the lung. Air hissed from the tube, followed by more blood and fluid.

"Give him an amp of atropine, an amp of epi. Turn him over and we'll close the external bleed. As soon as he's stable enough he's going up to Radiology and then surgery." Lydia knew they didn't have much time. He was losing blood through the exit wound, and Ravi was right—probably through internal perforations. Bullets had a way of ricocheting around inside the body, creating a vicious path of destruction. "Alert Dr. Varek that we're on our way up."

Several minutes later, Lydia and Rossman accompanied the gurney down the hallway toward the elevator. A small group of law enforcement had already begun to gather, a handful of uniforms and men in suit pants and dress shirts.

"Lydia."

She heard Ryan's voice. Turning but still moving down the hallway, she looked into his handsome, somber face. He appeared tired, his blue eyes troubled and questioning. He glanced at Nate's still form, at the blood on Lydia's scrubs, then followed in the gurney's wake. "Is he going to make it?"

Lydia didn't reply, her gaze communicating the severity of the situation. Ryan shoved his hands into his pockets. The sleeves of his dress shirt were rolled up, his tie loose and hanging around his neck. He wore a shoulder holster, his shield clipped to the belt at his waist.

"Where's Kristen?" Lydia asked.

"She's the one who found him. They wouldn't let her in the ambulance. A unit's bringing her in now."

She gave a faint nod. His eyes held on to hers as the elevator bell chimed. Lydia helped roll the gurney inside. She felt emotion engulf her after seeing Ryan. It always did. Once the doors slid closed, she looked again at Nate. Rossman pumped air into his lungs with the manual vent as they made the journey upstairs. The only chance was to get him on a rapid infuser, find the bullets and try to repair the damage.

It could have been Ryan, Lydia thought. No matter what had happened or the time they'd been apart, the realization still tore at her.

APD Det. Ryan Winter sipped lukewarm, bitter-tasting coffee from the hospital vending machine, part of the growing sea of law enforcement milling around outside the closed doors of the surgical ward. Except for Nate's partner, Mike Perry, and the zone five precinct captain, the private waiting room across the hall had been left open for arriving family. The air around Ryan hummed with low conversation centered on Nate.

He was a colleague and friend, one of their own. They all knew the job had its risks, but things like this never got any easier.

Leaning against the corridor wall, Ryan could see inside the room that contained upholstered chairs and two couches, as well as laminated end tables topped with fanned-out stacks of magazines. Kristen Weisz sat huddled in one of the seats, red-eyed, clutching a tissue and looking as if she was barely holding it together. Ryan's heart tugged. Lydia sat with her.

"Lydia cut her hair." The statement came from his partner, Mateo Hernandez, who had been pacing the hall before finding a spot next to Ryan against the wall. He also stared into the room. "It looks nice."

"Yeah," Ryan agreed quietly. He'd been watching Lydia since she had entered a few minutes earlier. She was talking to Kristen, her hand placed comfortingly on the other woman's back. Lydia's dark hair that had once been below her shoulders was now cut in a shorter, blunt style that fell just past her jawline. Ryan had been surprised to see the new look, but he had to admit he liked it. The hairstyle set off her delicate features and worked well with her petite frame. She looked up, her cocoa-brown eyes meeting his as she saw him outside the room. Ryan's hand tightened imperceptibly on the foam cup, and he lifted it to his mouth, taking a sip.

"I just talked to Darnell. He's in charge of securing the crime scene," Mateo said, referring to Darnell Richardson, another detective with the APD. "There's no security camera in the condo's parking garage, and so far no one's claiming to have seen or heard anything."

Ryan scowled. "No one heard a gunshot in a busy area? No one heard *three* of them?"

"My guess is a silencer." Mateo scratched his cheek. "He still had his wallet, so it doesn't appear to be a robbery."

"It could have been a collar, looking to get even." Nate had more than a few enemies, they all did. It came with the territory. Some recent arrest or an ex-convict Nate had helped put away. There was any number of possibilities.

"Here's the thing." Mateo touched Ryan's shoulder, guiding him a few feet away from the crowd of police. He lowered his voice. "There was an off-duty uniform shot dead six weeks ago outside a package store on Howell Mill Road where he moonlighted as a security guard. He had just gotten off for the night and gone around back to his car. *Also not a robbery.* He worked out of the zone two precinct—"

Ryan remembered. "John Watterson."

Mateo nodded. "Darnell looked at the shell casings from the parking deck where Nate was shot. They're from the same type of bullets as the ones used to kill Watterson. Coincidence?"

Ryan pressed his lips together. "I don't know. Maybe."

"It's something to think about though, right? I'm going over to the scene as soon as we get some word on Nate."

"I'll go, too." Briefly, he massaged his closed eyelids with his fingertips. It had been a long day, and he'd been on his way home when he had learned of the shooting. He had turned the car around and headed toward Mercy Hospital, feeling the need to stand vigil with his fellow officers. But he'd also been aware that Lydia might be here, since she often had the Friday night shift. Ryan reopened his eyes as a staccato of high-pitched beeps came from the waiting room. Lydia checked her beeper, then embraced Kristen before departing.

"Lydia," Mateo called in greeting as she walked toward them on her way back to the ER. He stepped forward, wrapping her in a bear hug.

"It's good to see you, Mateo. How are Evie and Carlos?"

"They're great. You should give Evie a call sometime. She's working part time now that Carlos is in kindergarten. You should see him. Riding his bike around, no training wheels like a real daredevil—"

He stopped, an awkward silence replacing his words. Ryan was familiar with the uncomfortable pauses. He knew Lydia was, too, although he still saw the faint shadow of pain in her eyes. But her smile was genuine as she touched Mateo's arm. "Give them both my love, okay?"

"How is he, Lydia?" Ryan asked, halting her exit. He'd noticed she had changed her scrubs since he had seen her taking Nate upstairs, trading the blue, bloodstained ones for mint green.

She shook her head and lowered her voice. "Not good. One of the bullets lodged in the left chamber of his heart. He has a bowel perforation and damage to his spinal cord. He's still in surgery. It's touch and go right now."

"What about Kristen?"

They glanced back into the room. A woman Ryan guessed was Kristen's sister had taken the seat Lydia had vacated.

"She's beating herself up pretty badly," Lydia said. "She and Nate had been fighting on the phone."

Her beeper went off again. She checked it with a soft sigh. "I have to get back. I'll check in again soon."

She turned and went down the hallway. He watched as she waited several seconds in front of the elevator, then took the stairwell when it didn't arrive.

"Christ. Sorry, man," Mateo offered, looking repentant. "My mouth's two steps ahead of my brain."

"Don't worry about it."

Ryan pretended not to feel Mateo's gaze on him, evaluating his reaction to seeing Lydia again. The truth was, he *did* see her from time to time. She came by the house on occasion to drop off insulin and syringes for Max, their eleven-year-old diabetic tabby that had stayed with him in the Inman Park bungalow after the divorce. And he'd called her a few times, mostly regarding some leftover business aspect of their marriage—tax payments, mail ending up at the wrong address. Mostly, though, he had wanted to hear her voice.

"Spinal cord damage," Mateo said in disbelief.

All cops considered the possibility of being taken down in gunfire—during a robbery, a hostage standoff, a violent domestic disturbance. But Nate had been shot in the parking garage of his own building, apparently caught off guard while waiting for the elevator to take him upstairs for the night. A place where he'd believed he was safe. Ryan thought about the last time he had seen Nate. He'd been outside the precinct house yesterday afternoon, involved in a tense conversation on his cell phone. Nate had seemed antsy, nervous, and he had stopped speaking altogether when he noticed Ryan within earshot, on his way to grab some lunch.

You do that and I'll fucking kill you.

It was the one thing Ryan had clearly heard Nate say. He wondered now to whom he'd been talking.

CHAPTER TWO

"I THOUGHT I should tell you first. You know most of them out there."

Lydia stood inside the surgery suite with Dr. Rick Varek, head of cardiothoracic medicine.

"What happened?" she asked.

He sighed, running a hand through his salt-and-pepper hair. He wore scrubs, and he'd removed his surgical cap, although his mask still hung around his neck. "The bullet basically ripped up the left ventricle, leading to pericardial effusion and cardiac tamponade. We administered electric shock and internal compressions longer than we probably should have."

Rick peered at her. "You okay, Lydia?"

She nodded, not speaking. It would be impossible to explain what she was feeling. Seeing the gathered police, the situation in general, it had all touched a raw nerve.

"Who do I need to speak to?"

"His wife, Kristen. His mother's there, too. She's elderly, Rick. In her seventies—"

"I'll use my best bedside manner," he said seriously.

"I'll go in with you. My shift's over. I just need to sign out downstairs."

Lydia began to walk away, but he caught her hand, pulling her back toward him. "You're off tomorrow. I checked the schedule."

She shook her head faintly in hesitation. "Rick …"

"There's a new restaurant in Phipps Plaza that's getting great reviews." He smiled charmingly. "I was thinking we could have dinner tomorrow night, then go see the new Renoir exhibit at the High Museum—"

"It's not a good time. I mean, with Nate and everything," Lydia explained. She felt guilty using Nate's death as an excuse, but she wasn't up to agreeing to a night out, not now. She and Rick had been on a handful of dates, and so far he had respected her request to take things slowly. She'd accepted his invitations, primarily because she knew it was something she *should* do. Get on with her life. At least, everyone kept telling her so. She was thirty-six and not getting any younger, as her little sister, Natalie, had bluntly pointed out to her over the phone just yesterday. Most of the female physicians and nursing staff considered Rick Varek a catch— refined, successful, a highly respected surgeon at the top of his field. A few of the ER nurses thought he looked a little like Richard Gere.

"I understand." Rick seemed to take her refusal in stride. He indicated the darkened operating room where Nate's body remained. "I can tell you're upset, Lydia. You knew the deceased well?"

"Through police functions. It's a pretty close-knit group—"

"He's out there, isn't he? Your ex-husband?" Her face must have given him his answer, because he added, "I thought so."

Rick turned and pushed through the swinging doors that led deeper into the suite. "I'll get an intern started on closing the chest. The family will want to see him. Go sign out, Lydia. Then we'll talk to them together. It's going to be a tough crowd. I can use your help."

Five minutes later, they walked down the corridor and into the swell of midnight-blue uniforms. The horde parted, the hum of conversation dying as Lydia and Rick moved toward the waiting room. As she went past, her eyes locked with Ryan's. She saw his jaw clench and he cupped the back of his neck, his shoulders slumping under his blue dress shirt.

He knew her too well, could tell by her expression the news she had come to deliver, Lydia realized.

She felt the almost possessive touch of Rick's fingers against the small of her back as they entered the space where Kristen Weisz now sat with her mother-in-law. A spate of other family members—siblings, cousins, aunts and uncles, Lydia guessed—had also arrived. Her face paling at their appearance, Kristen reached for her mother-in-law's finely veined hand.

"Is Nate going to be okay?" a man asked, stepping forward to take charge. He bore a resemblance to Nate, similar dark hair and eyes, and was probably his brother. Lydia felt the hard beat of her heart inside her chest.

She closed the door to the room. "This is Dr. Varek, head of cardiothoracic medicine. He operated on Nate."

Lydia sank onto the vacant chair on the other side of Kristen, who had begun to weep softly. Rick took the seat facing them. He leaned forward, his hands templed together between his knees.

"As you know, Nate arrived in the ER with three gunshot wounds, two to his chest and one to his abdomen," he explained gently. "In surgery, we found extensive damage ..."

Empathy welling inside her, Lydia felt tears threaten behind her eyes. She held a box of tissues out to Kristen as Rick continued. "The injury to the left side of his heart was especially bad. We performed CPR with internal paddles for over forty minutes—"

"I don't understand," Nate's mother interjected. She looked around at the faces of her family, frightened and confused.

"Just tell us!" Kristen sobbed, turning to Lydia. "Please, I can't take this!"

Lydia swallowed hard and placed her hand on Kristen's thigh. She hated this part of her job, and her personal involvement this time made it especially difficult. It also brought back painful memories she worked hard, every day, to push aside. Her trained mind reminded her to be direct and concise.

Still, her voice shook. "I'm so sorry. Nate died."

＊

The group had begun to disperse, everyone leaving for their homes or to have a solemn drink together in Nate's memory before the downtown bars stopped serving at two a.m. A few others had filtered down to the hospital lobby to hear the chief of police's statement to the waiting media, sound bites that would be the top story on the news. Ryan was one of the few who had remained behind, wanting to talk to Lydia before meeting up with Mateo at the crime scene in Nate's parking garage. For now, she was still behind the closed doors of the waiting room with Nate's family and a member of the police chaplaincy unit.

"Detective Winter?"

The surgeon who had gone into the room with Lydia strode toward him. He was dignified looking, probably in his early fifties, with a full head of graying hair and designer wire-rimmed glasses.

"I'm Dr. Varek." He extended his hand, and Ryan shook it. "I performed the surgery on Detective Weisz. We did our best. I'm very sorry for your loss."

Ryan nodded. "Thank you."

"Despite the unfortunate circumstances, I wanted to take the opportunity to meet you and introduce myself." Varek smiled congenially. "Lydia and I have become good friends. You should know she speaks very highly of you. High praise from the ex. That's unusual in cases of divorce, don't you think?"

"I suppose so." Ryan felt tension creep into his

shoulders. The nuanced wording hadn't escaped him. Varek had said *good friends,* not colleagues or co-workers. He'd also noticed his hand on Lydia's back as they'd entered the waiting room.

"You're new?" he asked casually. "Because I used to know most of Lydia's co-workers."

"I'm the new head of cardiothoracic medicine. I moved here to take the position a few months ago. I was on staff at Mass Gen previously." Varek shifted slightly, allowing two uniformed officers to pass by them in the hallway. "Lydia's been invaluable in helping me get acclimated to the staff here, as well as a new city. Atlanta's a universe away from Boston. She's an exceptional trauma doctor and a good person, but I'm sure you know that."

He paused heavily before adding, "I'm also aware she's had to deal with her share of tragedy. You both have."

Ryan's throat tightened, but he met Varek's gaze. "We've gotten through it."

The surgeon's eyes were sympathetic. Just then, the hospital's intercom system sent out a page for him. "I'm afraid I have to go. Nice to finally meet you, Detective Winter."

As Varek traveled away, Ryan couldn't help but feel defensive and territorial. But at the same time he knew he had no right to be. The divorce had been final for nearly a year. Who Lydia spent time with, who she confided in about her personal life, was no longer his business. He wondered if she and Varek were really just good friends or if he had used the phrase as a euphemism for something more. It was an unsettling thought.

We've gotten through it.

It had been a poor choice of words. It was true they'd both survived Tyler's death, had managed to go on breathing and living somehow, but they hadn't gotten through it *together.*

The loss had torn them apart.

Ryan stared at the closed waiting room door. He wasn't sure if waiting to see Lydia was such a good idea, after all. In the end, it would probably only do him more harm than good. He had begun walking down the hallway when he heard her call his name. Stopping, he waited for her to catch up to him.

"Kristen's going to stay with family for a while," she said, falling in step beside him.

"That's good. She doesn't need to go back to their place alone right now."

"No," Lydia agreed.

"Thanks for being there for her." He pushed the button as they reached the elevator.

"How's Mike?" she asked, referring to Nate's partner.

"Pretty broken up. He left a little while ago. He's being put on paid leave for a while. It's department protocol when something like this happens."

She looked at him, concerned. "What about you, Ryan? Are you all right? You knew Nate pretty well."

He felt grief as well as anger spark inside him. "I just want to find the bastard who did this."

"Is it your investigation?"

"I wasn't assigned to the crime scene tonight." Initially, however, it hadn't been a homicide. "No matter who catches the case, the entire force is going to want to take part. I'm going now to meet Mateo at Nate's condo building."

The elevator opened, and they stepped inside. He asked, "What floor?"

"Two."

He selected the second floor and then the lobby. "It's the second cop shooting in six weeks."

"I know," Lydia replied solemnly. As the primary public hospital downtown and a top-rated trauma center, most police injuries passed through Mercy's ER doors.

Ryan looked at her before saying, "I like the new style."

She touched her dark hair self-consciously. "Thanks. It saves me time in the mornings."

He wanted to ask her about Varek, but didn't. It certainly wasn't a question he could just blurt out. Besides, after the trauma of the past few hours, he wasn't sure he could handle it if she confirmed what he believed Varek had been trying to imply, that they were more than just friends. "Are you headed home?"

"I just have to get my things from my locker."

"I'll wait for you and walk you to your car."

She didn't refuse his offer. Ryan got off at the second floor with her and stayed in the hallway while Lydia went into the physician lounge. She returned a few minutes later wearing a sleeveless top and denim capris, a backpack slung over one slender shoulder. Ryan thought she looked more like a pretty college co-ed than an attending ER physician with a half-dozen residents under her charge.

They had both come a long way. Lydia had been a first-year resident when they'd met, and he'd been a uniformed cop. Since then, he had obtained his master's in criminal justice and been promoted to APD detective, then moved up in the ranks to lieutenant detective, first class. Neither he nor Lydia had come from privileged backgrounds. They'd both worked hard to get where they were.

It was his dedication in particular that had cost them everything.

Leaving the elevator, they made their way past the remaining camera crews that were still in the lobby, pushing together through the plate-glass doors. Outside, the nighttime air was warm and humid, a sharp contrast to the hospital's air-conditioned interior. It was mid-June, and the city was experiencing record heat.

They reached her car—the same silver Volvo—in one of the garage levels reserved for staff. It was after midnight, and the deck was dark and shadowed, with only a few anemic overhead lights. Ryan thought about where Nate had been shot, and he didn't like the idea of Lydia walking out here alone. He wondered if Varek ever escorted her.

"I thought it was you tonight," she said softly, surprising him. Her brown eyes were liquid and troubled. "All I knew was that a plainclothes had been shot—"

He shook his head, gently scolding. "Lydia."

"I'm glad it wasn't you, Ryan. I ... I hope you know that."

A heavy silence fell between them, until he finally opened the car door for her and took a step back. He felt the hard thrum of his pulse. Lydia tossed her backpack onto the passenger seat and got inside. A short time later, she looked at him once more through the car's window and started the engine. Hands shoved inside his pockets, Ryan watched as she drove out of the garage toward her home.

He'd had to let her go. As much as he had been hurting, he'd known her pain was worse and that he'd been responsible. The divorce was what she wanted. Ryan hadn't fought it.

He had deserved to lose her, he realized.

CHAPTER THREE

RYAN STUDIED THE grim, cordoned-off crime scene lit by mobile lights from Forensics. Although the parking deck had been kept clear until the area was processed, several members of the APD's cross-precinct Major Crimes division still lingered, unwilling to leave the place where one of their own had been gunned down. Small yellow cones marked the locations where shell casings had been found on the garage floor, and a puddle of blood, now brownish and thick, remained in front of the closed doors of the elevator. A gruesome smear on the floor indicated where Nate had apparently pushed himself along the concrete slab, trying to escape. The image was disturbing.

"Where was Nate's gun?" Ryan asked, a pain inside his throat. He carefully sidestepped a pile of bloodied gauze pads and empty, plastic vials left behind by the paramedics.

"The orange cone." Mateo nodded to a marker different from the others. "The weapon wasn't fired. According to the evidence techs, blood spatter and trajectories indicate the first shot was made from about twenty feet away. The bullet exited through Nate's body and pierced the elevator door."

"And the other two?"

Mateo moved to the blood pool and stood directly over it. Still wearing latex gloves, he pointed his finger downward in a gun-like motion, demonstrating. "The shooter was basically standing over him."

Ryan recalled their earlier conversation. "What about Watterson? The cop shot behind the package store?"

"Same thing," Det. Darnell Richardson answered as he walked from a gaggle of law enforcement to where Ryan and Mateo stood. A heavyset, middle-aged African American, he typically handled armed robbery and assault. He was in charge of the crime scene and had been the one to alert Mateo to the same type bullet being used in the two different police slayings.

"The first shot was fired from a distance to take Watterson down, the next two at close range," Darnell said. "It's suspected a silencer was used, since the package store was still open and no one heard anything. How you doin', Ryan? Mateo said you were on your way over here."

"Good to see you, Darnell."

Darnell actually hugged him. It was an unusual gesture, but emotions within the force were running high. "I saw your baby brother tonight. He's on duty, said he'll probably catch up to you tomorrow."

Ryan nodded. He and Adam sometimes took part in

pickup basketball games in Goldsboro Park on Saturdays, if neither was working.

"Damn shame about Nate." Darnell shook his head sorrowfully. "So what do you think? Is it open season on cops?"

Alone, the shell casing was common and could be purely coincidental. But Ryan had to admit the similar MO—three shots, two at close range and the possible use of a silencer—was troubling. "I think we need to wait on ballistics to see if we're looking at the same gun."

Darnell nodded. "Either way, it's not going to be my investigation. It's a homicide now."

Ryan stared past the crime scene tape blocking the entrance to the garage deck. A uniformed cop was stationed there to keep out news crews and curious passersby, and to direct the building's residents to a public lot across the street, where they would have to park temporarily. The cars already inside the garage were currently inaccessible to their owners and would remain so until the cleaning crew came in to do its job sometime in the next few hours.

"If it wasn't an armed robbery, it was a hit. An execution," Mateo pointed out, glancing up as the light panel in the ceiling flickered, making a buzzing sound.

Ryan thought again of the argument Nate had been having with someone on his cell the day before outside the precinct. It was worth looking into. They would need to get a writ for Nate's phone records from the wireless carrier— or ask Kristen for his personal effects from the hospital, which probably included his cell. He didn't want to bother her any more than necessary.

"I can tell you this—I can think of two dozen or so punks who wouldn't mind putting a bullet in me." Darnell checked his wristwatch. "It's damn near one, way past my bedtime if I can get any sleep at all after this. We're going to keep a guard unit here overnight. A news van from Channel Two's still parked across the street, but if they think they're getting in here, they're SOL."

"If it bleeds, it leads," Mateo grumbled under his breath.

"Where's Nate's car?" Ryan asked.

Darnell had already begun walking away, but he turned and pointed to the last row. "Forensics went through it already. Nate was a neat freak, so the interior's as clean as a preacher's sheets. The exterior has a key scratch, though. A nice long one on the driver's side."

Gang members in particular were fond of keying cops' vehicles. As a Narcotics and Vice detective, Nate had dealt with a number of them. Ryan called again to Darnell, who had already ducked under the crime scene tape. "What about Watterson's car? Anything similar?"

"I'll check into it."

Ryan looked at the pool of blood on the deck's floor. Anger tightened his chest.

"I want this case," he said quietly.

"Be careful what you wish for." Mateo stood beside him. "Thompson called me on the way over. He wants

Homicide at the precinct at eight a.m. I told him I'd let you know."

✳

It was after two in the morning, but Lydia found herself still unable to sleep.

She stood at the floor-to-ceiling window in her high-rise condominium, looking down at Buckhead's sprawling Lenox Square and Peachtree Road. From her eighth-floor view, Atlanta appeared quiet and peaceful, a cityscape of twinkling lights.

It was all a façade.

Around the city, car accidents were occurring— robberies happening, people being shot. Someone was dying from a heart attack or cancer. The possibilities were endless. As an ER doctor, Lydia carried this knowledge inside her. She grasped the thin stem of her wine glass, taking another sip. Nate's death, his grieving family, seeing Ryan within the confines of the hospital … it had all reopened old wounds.

Tragedy could happen to anyone.

"There's a child being brought in, a submersion victim." Abe Solomon, the ER's chief of staff, had taken her aside. He'd spoken in his quiet, fatherly tone, sympathy and dread lining his face as he laid a hand on her shoulder. *"Lydia, I … have bad news. It's Tyler. Your husband's in the ambulance with him. They're on their way."*

The words hadn't seemed real to her. Sometimes they still didn't.

The wail of a police siren on Peachtree below pulled her back to the present. Absently, Lydia watched as the flashing blue lights sailed around the other vehicles, the squad car running through a red light and disappearing down the street. Turning from the window, she glanced at the framed photos on a nearby bookshelf. They were cherished images of her life *before*. Magnetized, she moved closer, her fingers touching the silver frames one by one. In her favorite photo, Tyler grinned back at her, a green four-leaf clover painted on his cheek by a street artist at the city's annual Dogwood Festival. A beautiful boy, he'd inherited her dark hair and Ryan's nearly startling blue eyes. In another photo, she, Ryan and Tyler were on the beach in Hilton Head. The sun had been setting over the ocean behind them, the water on fire with orange and gold. Ryan held Tyler against his chest, his arms around him, their smiles identical. Lydia's head lay on Ryan's shoulder, her with her two men.

It had been their last family vacation.

She closed her eyes, trying to fight off the memories.

"Three-year-old male, unresponsive. Water aspiration leading to hypoxia and LOC—"

"Sustained apnea after cardiopulmonary resuscitation on scene and en route—"

Lydia had run alongside the paramedics' gurney, grasping Tyler's small, limp hand. He'd appeared so still and pale. Bluish. They'd put an endotracheal tube down his throat, which meant he wasn't breathing on his own.

Oh, God. Tyler.

She'd sobbed, pleaded with him to open his eyes, until

Abe and an orderly had blocked her from entering the trauma room. She'd had no choice but to watch helplessly through the observation window as physicians and nurses—the men and women she worked with every day— fought to save him. Her world had faded to gray.

"Get an arterial blood gas, chest X-ray, CBC—"

"Test for renal and liver functions—"

"Get Patel in Neuro down here now!"

Each phrase, each snippet of medical jargon, had been like a scalpel slicing away at her insides. This time, it was her child, her son.

Tyler.

It had taken awhile for her to become aware of Ryan's presence. He'd been standing in the hallway a short distance away. His eyes were red, face ashen, hair and clothes wet. Shivering, he made a weak gesture with his hands, his throat convulsing.

"How long?" She advanced on him. *"How long was he down there?"*

"I-I don't know. Five minutes—"

Even now, Lydia could still feel the sting against her palm, the jarring numbness in her wrist. She'd struck his face hard, needing to lash out, to focus her pain somewhere. Ryan had appeared stunned, on the verge of collapse. Tears had rolled down his cheeks as she'd beaten at his chest and then shoved him away.

She finished the wine and went to the kitchen, where she poured herself another generous glass, hoping it might dull the activity inside her mind. The condo was achingly quiet. She hadn't even turned on the television, she realized. Around her, the kitchen appliances were stainless steel, framed by honey oak cabinets and granite counters. The floor was Italian tile. It was beautiful but also sterile, lacking any real warmth. Lydia thought of the cozy Craftsman bungalow in Inman Park, the one she and Ryan had worked so hard to renovate together, to make into a home.

He had bought her out as part of the divorce. Lydia couldn't bear to live there with the memories, and the real estate market had gone soft along with the economy, making it harder to sell. But the market was getting better now.

Sometimes she believed he remained there to punish himself.

She'd gone into therapy after Tyler's death. Taken a leave of absence from work to return home to New Orleans, to be with family and friends. Time had passed, allowing her grief to ease somewhat and along with it, the need to blame someone for the terrible thing that had happened.

It had been a freak accident. Tyler could have drowned on her watch, just as easily as Ryan's. She was able to admit that to herself now. They had been two busy people juggling too many tasks. But it didn't quell the emptiness in her heart.

Finishing her second glass of wine, she'd become unsure of how long she'd been standing there, just staring off into space. Leaving the empty goblet on the counter, Lydia went into the bathroom to prepare for bed. She took a sleeping pill, too, aware of the dangers of mixing it with alcohol. Turning down the comforter, she slid under the sheets and turned off the bedside lamp. The hazed glow of the city outside was her nightlight.

As she drifted to sleep, Lydia wondered what she always did—if Tyler had struggled, been afraid. If he'd felt any pain as his lungs filled.

His cries sometimes still woke her at night, the ghost sobs of a child who didn't exist anymore.

CHAPTER FOUR

———————⟫•●•⟪———————

A POPULAR HANGOUT with police, McCrosky's was a pub in a renovated brick building near Olympic Centennial Park. Entering the cool tavern, Ryan spotted his brother seated at one of the tables in back, near a windowed wall overlooking the park's plaza and lawn.

"Could've used you on the courts today," Adam said as Ryan slid onto the wooden bench across from him. Adam was thirty-three, younger than Ryan by five years and a uniformed police officer in another zone. However, he was currently dressed in basketball shorts, high-tops and a T-shirt emblazoned with the logo of a popular sporting goods manufacturer.

"Cops versus bucket boys," he continued, referring to the traditional rivalry between police and firemen. He took a sip of his beer. "We got our asses kicked. It was a tragedy."

"Sorry, I had to work."

Adam's expression turned serious. The brothers had similar features, but the younger Winter had inherited their father's decidedly *Black Irish* genes. Where Ryan's eyes were blue, Adam's were a deep amber that complemented his dark hair. "You were assigned Nate Weisz's murder?"

"Mateo and I are taking the lead," Ryan said. In fact, they'd requested it despite an already full caseload. "But you know how things like these are. It's pretty much a precinct-wide investigation. IA's involved, too."

The tense morning meeting had turned into an all-day event. After being briefed by Forensics on crime scene evidence, Ryan and Mateo had returned to the condominium building to re-canvass the area, looking for witnesses who might have been in or near the parking garage during the time of the shooting. They hadn't fared well. Only a meth head loitering outside the building claimed to be a witness, and after a few questions it had become clear he was just looking for some cash. They'd also gone to Mike Perry's home to discuss the current cases he and Nate were working, in hopes of identifying someone who might have posed a threat. Mike had been red-eyed and disheveled, smelling of whiskey and clearly grieving. But no one had stood out to him—at least no more than the next perp. No one had made any overt threats.

"Any leads?" Adam wanted to know.

Ryan shook his head. "I thought we had one, but it didn't pan out."

He'd gotten Nate's phone records from the wireless carrier. Nate *had* received a call in the timeframe Ryan had seen him outside the precinct, but the number was a dead end, traced back to a payphone in the downtown's Fairlie-Poplar District. He'd asked Mike about it, but he knew nothing about the mysterious call or any disagreements Nate might have been having with anyone. As much as he wanted to spare her, Ryan knew he would have to interview Kristen Weisz next. Perhaps Nate had confided in her about something he felt he couldn't share with his partner.

Nate's files were in Ryan's vehicle. He planned to pore over them to come up with a list of arrestees—both recent and past—who might be worth looking into.

"Where's Mateo?" Adam asked.

"He went home to spend time with his family. Thanks for meeting me."

"Not a problem." Adam took another sip of beer, his lips quirking up in a grin. "You *are* buying, right?"

"Hi, Ryan." He looked up. Molly, one of the bar's waitresses, stood next to the table. Her normally bright smile was missing. "We're all so sorry to hear about Nate."

"Yeah. Me, too."

"They're having the wake here on Wednesday night, after the funeral. Just police. Frank's closing the place down," she said, referring to the bar's owner. Frank was a retired officer himself. "What can I get you?"

"I'll have one of those." Ryan indicated Adam's beer. "And a club sandwich."

"Coming up."

Adam waggled his near-empty bottle. "Bring me another, Mol? And some chips with queso?"

She nodded amicably and tossed her long, blond hair over one shoulder, turning and heading back toward the kitchen. Adam made a point of admiring her retreat.

"You're not ordering a meal?" Ryan asked, adding, "I mean, with me *buying* and all."

"I've got a dinner date in a few hours. A girl from my gym." He gave his brother a pointed look. "I take it you *have* heard of dates?"

Ryan pressed his lips together, not liking where he knew the conversation was headed.

"Maybe you should try having one yourself."

He met his brother's stare. He expected to see a teasing light in Adam's eyes, but his expression was hard. "It's been nearly a year, Ry. Just forget her, all right? You need to stop acting like a dead man."

He didn't respond. Through the window, Ryan could see the Fountain of Rings inside Centennial Olympic Park. It was late afternoon, and children ran and splashed in its sprays, taking a reprieve from the sweltering heat. He recalled bringing Tyler to the fountain on a summer's day much like this one. He and Lydia had both been off from work, and they'd packed a picnic lunch, part of a *staycation* inside the city. His chest tightened as he stared out. Tyler had always loved water, had never had any fear of it.

"I might as well be talking to one of the barstools," Adam grumbled. "Why *did* you want me to meet you?"

Ryan thought about what to say. He didn't want to spread unfounded rumors or create undue fear, but Adam was his little brother. Their father had died in the line of duty when Ryan himself was barely a teenager, and in many ways he had raised Adam as much as their mother had.

"Look," he said, lowering his voice. "It's merely

speculation at this point, but there're some similarities between Nate's murder and the shooting of an off-duty police officer six weeks ago—"

"The rent-a-cop at the package store on Howell Mill."

"Same type bullets. Both guns probably had a silencer. The MO's similar, too." Ryan frowned, thinking of the newest thing they'd learned. Nate's shield was missing. It hadn't been among his personal effects.

"What does this have to do with me?" Adam asked.

He sighed. "Nothing, really. I just want you to be careful. Wear a vest—"

"I do when I'm on duty. Or at least most of the time. It's like, what? Ninety outside? You try wearing one in this heat and chasing a perp down some alley."

"It's protocol, and I *have* tried it," Ryan reminded. "I wore a uniform for four years."

Adam had always been an adrenaline junkie, which was why he'd stuck with patrol for so long. It was where most of the action was. After high school, he'd gone straight into the military. There had been no talking him out of it. After two tours in Afghanistan, he'd worked in counternarcotics special operations in Costa Rica before returning to Atlanta, completing college and joining the force.

"Just do what I say for once?"

Adam rolled his eyes.

"Beers for the Winter boys." Molly reappeared at their table bearing two bottles and the chips and queso Adam had ordered. She laid a hand on Ryan's shoulder and smiled at him. "Your food will be right out."

Once she'd moved to another table, Adam grinned, his dimples deepening as he dunked a tortilla chip into the gooey cheese. "Hey, what about Molly? She likes you. It's pretty obvious. She's always asking about you. If you're looking to get back in the saddle …"

Ryan shook his head, irritated.

"What?" Adam wanted to know. "On the hot scale she's at least a nine, maybe a nine and a half—"

"Then why don't you ask her out? She's what? In her mid-twenties? She's too young for me, and she's more your type, anyway."

Adam raised his hands in defense. "Sorry, all right?" His dark eyes grew somber. "I just want my brother to stop hanging on to a life that doesn't exist anymore."

"I'm not hanging on to anything."

It was Adam's turn to sound annoyed. "Yeah. You keep telling yourself that."

His words stuck with Ryan as he made his way to his parked vehicle a little more than a half hour later. The sun had dropped in the sky, allowing the tall city buildings to provide some shade, although it had little impact on the humidity. Heat roiled from the interior of his black Ford Explorer as he climbed inside. Adam meant well, *he did*, but Ryan knew he was angry with Lydia. He didn't like the way she had shut down on him after Tyler's death, or that she'd been the one to finally walk out of their marriage.

Deep down, he knew Adam had a point about him needing to move on with his life.

On the Downtown Connector, he took the exit for

Freedom Parkway and the Jimmy Carter Center, traveling under the covered bridge and past a row of old warehouses toward Inman Park. Containing Victorian-style cottages, Craftsman and Arts and Crafts bungalows interspersed with contemporary lofts, the historic urban neighborhood was in the midst of revitalization. Ryan and Lydia had bought the house before Tyler was born, and they'd spent nearly all their free time renovating and repairing the single-story home that was nearly a century old. Even now, a few projects remained.

As Ryan pulled onto Blue Willow Lane, his stomach did a small somersault. Lydia's Volvo sat on the street in front of the house. Parking in the single-car driveway, he extracted the cardboard box of Nate's files from the SUV's rear, then walked up the front steps onto the covered porch and went inside. Lydia was seated at the breakfast table with Tess Greene.

"Lydia's here," Tess announced to Ryan, smiling brightly as she pushed her long, silver braid behind her back. Active and vibrant although well into her sixties, Tess leased the small studio apartment over the house's detached garage. She also did some housekeeping for Ryan in exchange for a reduced monthly rent.

"I see that." His heart beat a little harder as his eyes held Lydia's.

She indicated the plastic baggie on the table in front of her, which contained syringes. "I brought insulin and needles for Max. They were in my backpack last night, but I forgot to give them to you. I put the insulin in the fridge."

As if on cue, the tabby's yellow eyes peered over the table's edge. He sat on Lydia's lap, purring like a motorboat as she stroked his fur.

"Thanks." Ryan walked to the butcher-block counter and heaved the heavy cardboard box onto it.

"We're having sweet tea," Tess said. "You want some?"

Ryan clasped the back of his neck. His dress shirt was damp from the day's oppressive heat, and the beer at McCrosky's hadn't done much to relieve his thirst. He removed his shoulder holster and laid it with the gun still inside next to the box of Nate's files. "Yeah. That would be nice."

Tess rose and went to get him a glass. She wore black leggings and a blue smock top splattered with paint. Tess was an artist, although she sold most of her paintings and drawings at flea markets and festivals, or in the funky shops in Little Five Points, as opposed to one of the upscale galleries in Buckhead or downtown. Ryan also suspected the former hippie indulged in a little weed, and he ignored the faint smell like burning rope that sometimes wafted across the yard from Tess's apartment. Although Tess hadn't moved in until after the divorce, she'd gotten to know Lydia during her occasional visits to the house.

"Lydia," Tess fretted as she stood at the refrigerator, her eyes on the window over the table, "there's a wasp in here."

The wasp buzzed and bumped against the pane, angrily trying to find a way out. Lydia remained perfectly still, appearing unfazed, although Ryan knew she was probably recoiling internally. The insect's presence caused a dart of apprehension to sail through him, too. Lydia was highly allergic to bees of any kind. A single sting could send her into anaphylactic shock.

"Don't move," he instructed. He picked up the copy of *The Atlanta Journal-Constitution* from the table. Rolling it up, he used it to smack the wasp, which dropped to the black-and-white tiled floor.

"I knew the *AJC* was good for something," he said cynically, a cop's joke.

"Thanks." Lydia watched as he stepped on the wasp to ensure it was dead, then scooped it up with the paper and tossed it into the wastebasket.

"Do you still carry your EpiPen?"

"It's in my purse."

Tess handed Ryan his tea. She'd placed a slice of lemon in it, which floated on top like a yellow wagon wheel.

"Well, I'm going to get on upstairs. Ryan, there's a load of clothes in the washer. Don't forget to move them into the dryer," she said, rinsing her glass and placing it in the dishwasher. "Lydia, honey, good to see you again."

Ryan heard the door in the foyer close as Tess went onto the porch and made her way down the steps, leaving Lydia and him alone. Outside, a soughing breeze—rare on a sunny, summer day—jostled the wind chimes that hung from the bungalow's rafters. Max leapt from Lydia's lap and went to investigate something in another room.

"I like the flooring in the sunroom," Lydia said, breaking the silence as she crossed her bare legs. She wore sandals, khaki shorts and a blue scoop-necked top.

"Tess showed you?"

She nodded. Ryan was proud of the work he'd done. He'd sanded away the layers of dark varnish to reveal the warm heart of pine panels original to the house, working on it on his days off. It served as a distraction.

"I guess you saw her painting then, too. It was a gift."

She smiled softly. "It's not half-bad."

Ryan leaned against the counter, sipping his tea. It seemed strange to see her again, twice within twenty-four hours. "Mateo and I are taking the lead on the investigation into Nate's murder. I've been working today, actually."

"I wondered." Lydia looked at his white dress shirt and dark trousers, his gold detective's shield clipped to the belt at his waist. "You're not exactly dressed for a Saturday."

She stood then, folding her slender arms over her chest, and paced slowly around the kitchen, her eyes seeming to take in the changes Ryan had made since she'd moved out. There weren't too many—a hanging copper pot rack, a stained-glass panel above the window over the sink. Ryan had bought the latter at an antique and salvage shop in the city's Castleberry Hill arts district and trimmed it to fit the space. He noticed Lydia had stopped her pacing at the kitchen's arched threshold, not braving the hallway that led to the two bedrooms that had been theirs and Tyler's.

"Is there any new information?"

"Not really." He indicated the cardboard box he'd brought inside. "Those are Nate's case files. I'm going through them tonight, looking for someone—anyone—we might need to talk to."

Looking at the box, Lydia bit her lip. "Be careful, all right?"

He knew what she was thinking. That if one of the people in Nate's files was the shooter, he would likely feel threatened by another detective showing up and asking questions. Leaving his glass on the counter, Ryan walked to where she stood, deciding to ask what had been on his mind pretty much nonstop since the previous evening.

"Are you seeing Rick Varek?" he asked softly.

She looked up at him, surprise in her brown eyes. "Why would you—"

"Because he approached me last night at the hospital." Ryan shrugged, trying to sound nonchalant, although he wasn't certain he was pulling it off. "He made a point of telling me that you and he had become *good friends*. I got the impression he wanted me to know it was more than that."

Lydia released a breath, her expression telling. "Ryan, I ..."

He stepped a little closer. "You have a right. It's just that I don't like being blindsided by something like that."

"I'm sorry." She closed her eyes briefly. "Rick had no right to tell you."

He felt a pain in his chest. "So you *are* together."

"No." She shook her head. "I mean, we've been out a few times, but it's been casual. Dinner out, mostly. We talk about work."

Ryan pressed his lips together to keep from asking the question that was nearly choking him. *Have you slept with him?* He swallowed down the hurt and jealousy. "He's a little old for you, isn't he?"

"He's fifty. That's not that old."

It was growing later in the day, making the sunlight entering the room softer and more diffused. Lydia looked beautiful standing there in it, her complexion porcelain and her dark hair framing her face. Ryan suppressed a sigh. He realized if it weren't Varek it would eventually be some other man who wanted to claim her. He'd better learn to deal with it.

She pushed her hair behind her ear in an almost nervous gesture. Then she walked back to the table and reached for her purse. "I should get going."

Ryan shoved his hands inside his pockets, watching as she placed the bag's strap over her shoulder and turned to face him. He didn't want her to go, and he guessed his query had made her uncomfortable.

"Nate's funeral is Wednesday," he said. "Are you going?"

"I have to work. I might be able to get someone to trade shifts with me, though."

He nodded, understanding the often-inflexible schedules of ER physicians. "There's a wake being planned at McCrosky's that night. Police only. You're welcome to come by after your shift if you can't make it to the funeral. You're still considered part of the family."

"Thanks. I might." She sounded sincere.

Lydia touched his arm, her fingers lingering for a bare moment, and then left the house. Eventually, he heard her car start up and pull away from the street curb. For several long seconds, Ryan stood in silence, listening to the steady ticking of the grandfather clock in the foyer. Then taking the cardboard box from the counter, he moved it into the sunroom, which contained cushioned rattan furniture and a desk he used for the glut of paperwork that came with his job. He would grab a quick shower and get started.

A wall made almost entirely of windows provided a view of the bungalow's rear flagstone patio that was surrounded by a fence of low shrubs. Dogwoods and a massive, red-leafed Japanese maple shaded the area. Ryan crossed his arms over his chest, looking just beyond the backyard. A neighbor's swimming pool caught the sunlight, its water dappled with gold.

He felt a familiar, dull ache fill him.

Following Tyler's death, the pool had remained covered by a black tarp. But a few months ago, the former residents had sold the house. A new family had moved in and reopened the pool. Ryan hadn't met them, and he had no idea whether they were unaware or insensitive to what had occurred on their property. He wondered if Lydia had seen it uncovered.

The lump in his throat grew larger.

He would gladly give his own life to bring Tyler back.

He'd been so focused on completing an investigational report that chilly January morning. He hadn't heard the mudroom door opening, hadn't noticed their sweet little boy had slipped out.

Belly knotted with guilt, he stared out at the

tranquil-looking water until his cell phone rang. Clearing his throat, he dug into his pants pocket for the device, answering it.

"Ryan, it's Darnell Richardson. I hear you and Mateo are taking the lead on Nate's case."

"Yeah." Ryan squeezed the bridge of his nose.

"I'm not sure whether to offer my gratitude or condolences." He added, "Look, I've got some information for you. I checked out John Watterson's vehicle today, like you asked. Brand new Honda Accord that's collecting dust now in his mother's garage. The poor woman got it all cleaned up but says she can't bear to sell it."

He paused expectantly. "Thought you might want to know there's a big key scratch on the driver's side."

Ryan felt a small jolt.

"Do you know if Watterson's shield was missing after the shooting?"

"No." Darnell sounded puzzled. "I didn't ask."

"That's all right. I'll find out."

"What're you thinking?" Darnell asked. "Gangbangers?"

Ryan glanced at the cardboard box. "I think it's a good place to start."

CHAPTER FIVE

———◖●◗———

SOMEONE HAD PLACED a single rose on Nate's desk, a gesture marking the sense of loss that hung over the zone five precinct. It lay on the paper blotter amid the brown stains of coffee rings and nearly illegible notes Nate had made to himself while on the phone. Nearby, paperwork threatened to overflow his plastic in-box. Ryan leafed through the forms and memos even though he'd already gone through them after the briefing on Saturday, searching for something that might stand out.

There was also a framed photo of Kristen on the desk. He felt a tug of emotion.

Around him, the bullpen bustled with activity, some of it related to the investigation into Nate's shooting, the rest focused on the dozens of other cases that screamed for attention. Ryan himself had three open homicides, now four including Nate's.

"Hell of a start to a Monday," Mateo commented over the shrill of a ringing phone. Looking at Nate's desk, he shook his head and sipped from a mug of coffee, his third that morning. "I keep thinking he's going to show up here, bitching about the traffic on Peachtree."

Ryan had checked with the zone two detectives who'd caught Watterson's murder—unlike with Nate, his shield had been accounted for. He'd been buried with it, in fact. Regardless, Ryan still believed the key scratches on both cars suggested some correlation. But in case his theory was wrong, he wanted to cover all potential avenues.

"Did you get hold of Hoyt and Chin?" he asked, referring to another pair of detectives.

"Yeah. They're on their way to talk to Leo Moore and his PO."

He'd identified Moore and a handful of others from Nate's files over the weekend. Ryan had been searching for new arrests and pending indictments requiring the detective's testimony, as well as older enemies possibly looking to settle a score. Leo Moore fell squarely into the latter category. Nate had arrested him for Schedule 1 drug possession with intent to distribute five years earlier, before he'd been partnered with Mike Perry. Moore had a long rap sheet, and word was he'd threatened Nate outside the courtroom at his hearing. According to the Georgia Department of Corrections, he'd been released from prison six weeks ago, which in Ryan's mind was good enough reason to talk to him.

Done shuffling through the in-box, he turned, meeting Mateo's evaluating gaze.

"Why do I get the feeling you sent Hoyt and Chin to see Moore because we've got bigger fish to fry?"

"We're going looking for Quintavius Roberts."

"Great," Mateo grumbled. "Can we try to keep the tally to one dead detective?"

Quintavius Roberts was the leader of HB2, Atlanta's most notorious street gang whose turf extended from the edges of the downtown to the shabby neighborhoods bordering the Braves' Turner Field. Its illegal activities, primarily drug trafficking and car theft, kept it in continual conflict with law enforcement. The keyed vehicles— Nate's and Watterson's—suggested the possibility of gang involvement, since such vandalism against police was a common HB2 initiation rite.

What Ryan wanted to know was whether the initiation requirements had been upped a few levels to murder.

A short time later, he sat at his desk returning a phone call from a prosecuting attorney in the Fulton County DA's office when he heard Captain Thompson's gruff bark.

"Winter." An older, African American bear of a man with a smoothly shaved head, he motioned Ryan to the corridor. Ryan wrapped up the call and met him.

"Nate's wife is here to pick up his things. She asked for you."

Ryan nodded. Yesterday, he'd called the relative's house where Kristen was staying, but had been told she was at the funeral home finalizing arrangements. "Where is she?"

"I put her in interview room two."

He headed through the lobby, then down the precinct's corridor to the second room with a glass-panel observation window, pausing outside it. Through the blinds he could see Kristen, arms hugged around herself as she slowly paced. A cardboard box sat on the table. Ryan already knew what it contained since he had been through Nate's locker, as well. As the investigation's lead, in fact, he'd been the one to give the okay for the items' release.

This wouldn't be easy. He took a breath and entered.

"Kristen," he rasped as he embraced her. She clung to him for a long moment, then pulled away and wiped her eyes. Her auburn hair was uncombed, and her face appeared to have aged a decade in the space of a few days.

"My brother-in-law told me you called. I'm sorry I didn't call you back, but I wasn't up to talking."

"That's all right," he said gently. "We can talk now. Why don't you have a seat?"

He pulled out one of the chairs and waited for her to sit down. "Could I get you some coffee? Or water?"

When she refused, Ryan sat at the table across from her. "I'm sorry to have to do this, but I need to ask you some questions about Nate."

"I understand. Oh ..." She opened her purse and removed a cell phone. "Steve said you asked for this."

She handed it to him. Although the wireless carrier had turned up little in Nate's phone records, Ryan still planned to look through the device's personal address book and calendar.

"I'll get it back to you," he promised. "Did anything seem out of the ordinary with Nate lately?"

She shook her head. "No."

"Any unusual hours?"

"Nate was a cop. All his hours were unusual." She sniffled softly.

"What about phone calls?" Ryan was thinking of the heated exchange he'd heard Nate having on his cell the day before his murder. "Did he receive any unusual calls at home? Maybe a discussion or argument you overheard?"

"I don't recall anything. Nate ... tried not to bring police work into our home life. It made me nervous." Kristen shook her head sadly. "I was always afraid of something like this happening."

Laughter erupted in the hall. Several uniforms conversed as they went out to the rear, fenced-in compound where the patrol units were parked, unaware that a grieving widow, one of their own, was within hearing range. Ryan waited for them to pass before speaking again. "There's a scratch on Nate's car. A pretty big one on the driver's side. Do you know how long it's been there?"

"I haven't seen his car in days. I haven't been down to the garage since ..." She halted, her lower lip trembling. Ryan knew she had been the one to find Nate when he hadn't come upstairs. Her hands fluttered nervously on the table as she composed herself. "I-I don't recall a scratch, so it must've been recent. You know how Nate was about that car. He would've mentioned something like that. Does it have something to do with what happened?"

"We're not sure." Mike Perry hadn't known about the scratch, either, leading Ryan to believe it had been made sometime just prior to Nate's murder.

"You're not treating this like an attempted robbery, are

you, Ryan? You think someone was lying in wait for him in the parking garage. They took his *shield*. He was killed because of his job."

Her eyes filled, and he reached for her hand.

"It's a strong possibility, Kristen. We're looking at every angle." After he'd run through his remaining questions, not learning much else, he rose. "I really am sorry to have bothered you. Do you need a ride?"

"My sister's waiting outside." Wearily, she pushed herself up from the table. "I just want you to catch who did this. Nate always thought you were a good cop. He'd be glad it's your case."

The praise fell heavily inside him.

She paused, her expression reflective. "We were married almost twelve years. Our last words to each other … they weren't good ones. Nate was always so busy, and I was angry because he was late to take me to a concert at Chastain Park. Josh Groban. I'd had tickets for weeks …"

She shook her head, her voice cracking. "That all seems so silly now. I really *did* love him."

"I'm sure Nate knew that," Ryan offered solemnly.

"I wish we'd had a child, you know? We talked about it for a long time, but neither of us was sure."

As he held the door for her, she stopped and looked up into his face. Her bleary eyes searched his.

"How did you get through it?" she whispered. "Losing Tyler?"

Ryan swallowed, unsure of what to say. He recalled his lowest point, how bad things had been. Sometimes the feelings of self-recrimination were still enough to drag him under. But Kristen seemed to be grasping for some small piece of insight, of hope. Finally, he said, "You keep breathing and try not to die along with him. Nate would want you to keep living, Kristen. He'd want you to rebuild your life."

He escorted her to the bullpen for the remainder of Nate's things. The noise faded into silence as they appeared. Several of the detectives approached to offer their condolences.

Kristen wept when she saw the framed photo of herself on Nate's desk.

It was early afternoon, a game day, and people were out on the streets surrounding Turner Field. Vendors sold Atlanta Braves souvenirs from folding card tables while scalpers brandished tickets as they loudly promoted their wares to the crowds headed into the stadium. On the sidewalks, men held cardboard signs advertising makeshift pay parking lots on nearby church and business properties.

"Giants are in town," Ryan mentioned absently from the passenger side of the Chevy Impala. He was still thinking about Kristen Weisz.

"It's sold-out. Should make the scalpers happy." Mateo braked at a crosswalk to allow game-goers to pass. He added dryly, "I don't suppose Quintavius might have air-conditioned box seats? We could talk to him here over a Guinness?"

Ryan gave a wan smile but kept his eyes on the road. "Wishful thinking."

As they left the stadium area and went deeper into the outlying neighborhoods, he was aware of the increasing prevalence of gang tags. Spray-painted on the concrete walls of the underpass, on the sides of timeworn buildings and rusted metal Dumpsters, they were territorial markings meant to intimidate. The HB2s had more than a hundred in its ranks and pretty much ruled the area. Those who lived here kept quiet out of fear and also out of a distrust of police. Ryan peered at the urban scenery as it rushed past. Two gang members had shown up in Nate's files as recent arrests, but one was still in lockup, unable to make bond, while the other had been remanded to state prison a week ago for breaking parole. While that meant neither was the shooter, the arrests might have been the catalyst for putting a target on Nate's back, he rationalized.

Several minutes later, their car turned onto the mostly residential Purvis Street. Quintavius ran a legitimate business as a front, but everyone knew he still spent most of his time around his old neighborhood. Mateo decelerated as they neared a row of shotgun-style houses that were at least a century old. A mom-and-pop convenience store sat adjacent to the homes, and a young black male, probably no more than ten, leaned against its cinderblock wall. Seeing the sedan, he straightened and darted quickly across the street and into one of the houses.

"Pee Wee made us," Ryan noted, using gang terminology for those too young for membership but who were still used as lookouts or runners to transport drugs. The kid had gone to warn whoever was in the house that the cops had arrived.

"Don't look at me," Mateo deadpanned as he parked against the curb and cut the Impala's engine. "White boy like you probably sticks out in these parts."

As they exited the car, Ryan scoped out their surroundings. They were here to talk, not serve an arrest warrant, but that didn't mean they would be welcome. Opening the gate to the chain link fence that enclosed the house's grass and dirt yard, they began traveling up the crumbling concrete walk to its raised porch. A wiry, dark-complexioned male in his mid-twenties came out before they reached it, however. A blue bandanna—the gang's street color and an indicator of membership—was tied over his scalp. Ryan recognized him as Warren Rucker, also known as Pooch. The innocuous street name was deceiving as he had already served a stint in prison for armed assault.

Pooch recognized them, as well, because he crossed his arms over his chest and scowled. "Detectives Winter and Hernandez. Unless y'all got a warrant, you can stop right there."

"Now don't be like that, Pooch. We're just here to see Quintavius." Mateo squinted up at him through his sunglasses.

"Social visit, huh? Well, he ain't here."

"Then where is he?"

"Went down to Miami for a little R&R."

Ryan wondered if that was true. Pooch was a hard-core

member of the HB2s and rumored to be among the next in line for leadership should anything happen to Quintavius. He wouldn't put it past the thug to attempt a coup at some point. "Then you'll have to do. Want to come down off that porch?"

Pooch eyed them with a mix of animosity and suspicion, then took his time in joining them in the yard. Ryan noticed someone peeping out at them from the shotgun's upstairs window.

"All right. Now what y'all want?"

"The HB2s still have a thing for keying cop cars?" Mateo asked.

Pooch nodded to the Impala. "Yours looks all right."

"That one's not the problem. It's city issue. Thing is, we've got two dead cops, both of them with key scratches on their personal vehicles."

The gang member made a scoffing noise. "So the *murder police* are here, asking if we did it?"

Ryan spoke. "Officer Watterson was killed a month and a half ago outside a package store, Detective Weisz on Friday night. He was off duty and in the garage of his own building."

"Heard someone lit Weisz up." Pooch smirked, his eyes cold. "Damn shame."

"But you don't know anything about it?"

"Nope."

A dog barked inside the house—a big one, judging by the sound of it. Ryan shifted his stance, tamping down an urge to run Pooch into the precinct for the hell of it.

He was pretty sure if they patted him down, they'd find something of interest. But instead he said, "I think you *do* know. Maybe you've got some recruits running around looking to earn their stripes—"

"Young bloods," Pooch interjected, playing along.

"So they bag two cops and leave key scratches behind to mark them as gang hits. Something like that would boost your street cred and move you up the ranks fast," Ryan wagered. "Maybe they saw an opportunity and even took an APD shield to flash around as a souvenir."

Pooch gave a derisive snort. "You got some imagination, Detective. *Like I said*, I don't know nothin' about it. Your boys gettin' smoked ain't on us."

"Then the scratches on both cars are purely coincidental," Mateo clarified, sarcastic.

"Could be." He shrugged and added, "Besides, if you had any real proof, you'd be makin' arrests instead of just coming 'round here fishin'. Am I right?"

He paused as a delivery truck roared past. "You want my take, though? All right, here it is. Weisz pissed somebody off. He got into somebody's fuckin' business and got himself erased. That's just part of the game, yo, and what they call a *teaching lesson*."

He looked pointedly between the two detectives.

"It's no game," Ryan warned.

"Am I crying over Weisz, Detective Winter? The answer's *hell no*. Couldn't happen to a better pig. And I ain't never heard of any Watterson, not that I give a rat's ass about him, either. But I'll say it again in case you're hard of hearin'. It ain't on us."

The midday sun beat down, causing little shimmies of heat to float up from the street out front. Ryan's eyes locked with Pooch's. He'd had enough of his bravado. He took a step closer and lowered his voice. "A word of advice. Unless you want the heat turned up on your operation, if one of yours did this, you'd better turn him over."

He felt Mateo's subtle nudge. Ryan looked back up at the porch. Three more gang members, shirtless, their chests tattooed with *HB2*, had appeared at the door's threshold. One of them held a snarling pit bull on a heavy chain leash. Several more bangers now peered at them from the windows. They were outnumbered.

"Tell Quintavius what I told you," Ryan emphasized, pointing a finger before he and Mateo turned to walk away. "*He's* a businessman, and it's a business decision. He'll know what to do."

Pooch's eyes narrowed, indicating he'd caught the slight.

Cops always kept a round in the chamber of their weapon while in the field. On guard, Ryan felt the weight of his gun in his shoulder holster as he and Mateo got back into their vehicle. In the distance, sirens wailed as police squad cars raced off to somewhere deeper inside the district.

"Well, that was fun," Mateo muttered, starting the engine. He shook his head. "You got a death wish?"

Ryan merely grunted, falling silent as they pulled from the curb. It rankled him that he hadn't been able to get a better read from Pooch. And he was far from the first punk who'd threatened him.

"So, what? You're still thinking the shootings are gang related?"

"I don't know. But right now it's the best hunch we've got."

They went past a community center, a beautiful old building that was still well cared for and looked out of place in the run-down neighborhood, nestled between a pawnshop and tenement homes. Mateo cranked up the Impala's air conditioning, which was fighting a losing battle against the humidity.

"If you're serious about turning up the heat, Narcotics might be able to come up with a warrant for that shotgun they use as a clubhouse." He glanced over at Ryan, his eyes hidden behind the dark tint of his sunglasses. "But if we come back here, we do it with a freakin' platoon."

Ryan didn't disagree. And in the meantime, they had others to look at with regard to Nate's murder. Until they had something more concrete, he couldn't afford to go down a rabbit hole with the key scratches, in case they really did mean nothing at all.

His cell phone rang. He retrieved it from his pocket and answered, rubbing his forehead with two fingers of his left hand as he listened to what the caller had to say. Once he'd disconnected the phone, he filled in Mateo.

"That was Hoyt. Leo Moore alibied for Friday night. He was at a church social with his girlfriend. The minister can vouch for him being there."

"Moore in church." Mateo gave a cynical shake of his head, acquainted with the ex-con's history. "He's damn lucky he wasn't struck by lightning."

Ryan wasn't finished. "Ballistics are back, too. The striations on the bullets used in both homicides are a match."

Impressions left on bullets fired by handguns were unique, like fingerprints. No two firearms' were exactly alike, even if they were of the same make and model. Regardless of the car keyings, it was unarguable proof the two murders were connected. The same weapon had been used to kill both Nate and Watterson. Which meant it was either the same shooter, or the gun had been passed around.

Mateo frowned hard. "What Darnell said in the parking garage about it being open season on cops? I hope to hell he's not right."

CHAPTER SIX

IT WAS WEDNESDAY night, and the bar inside McCrosky's was packed. A few officers remained in their dress blues despite the time that had passed since the late-afternoon funeral. Nate had received a full honors police burial, including fifty squad cars that had escorted the hearse to the cemetery outside the downtown. His heart heavy, Ryan had offered condolences to Kristen afterward. She'd appeared drawn and pale, surrounded by family.

Ryan no longer wore his police dress coat, which he had removed in the tight crowd. Around him, everyone was talking about Nate, relaying war stories and speculating about his murder.

Appearing beside Ryan, Adam nodded toward Mike Perry, who sat with several other detectives, including Darnell Richardson. A bottle was being passed around the table. "How's Mike doing?"

"He and Nate were close." Ryan watched as Mike drunkenly knocked over his shot glass. "He's going to need help getting home."

With a nod of agreement, Adam took a sip of his beer. "You know the saying about these things. The only one who won't have a hangover tomorrow is the deceased."

Nate's family had been invited but hadn't come. Ryan figured their absence was for the best, as the gathering following a police burial often devolved into rowdiness as mourners hid their sorrow in laughter and drink.

"What's the latest?" Adam asked. Two days had passed since ballistics had concluded the same gun had been used in both homicides, information being kept from the media but already circulating inside the APD.

"I reviewed Watterson's arrest records to see if any of his collars were a match to Nate's. They weren't." Nor had Watterson busted any of the street gang since its turf was outside his beat. Still, that wasn't keeping Narcotics from trying to get a warrant together for the Purvis Street property.

"What about Nate's cell?"

"No one in his personal contacts or call log stood out." Tiredly, Ryan massaged the back of his neck. It had been a long day, beginning with more fruitless visits to Nate's prior arrests. He'd also made a court appearance for another case before driving to the cemetery. Nate had been buried on a verdant hillside, the tranquil resting place a contradiction to his brutal death. Ryan hoped he was at peace.

Finishing his beer, Adam indicated the lukewarm one Ryan held. "I've got a dead soldier here. I'm going for another. Want one?"

"No, thanks." He didn't feel much like drinking. As

Adam worked his way toward the bar, Ryan scanned the crowded room. Mateo had departed a short time earlier, but most of the other detectives from their precinct were still here.

Lydia hadn't come by.

He tamped down his disappointment and moved to an alcove to check his voice mail. As he finished listening to several messages, including one he chose to ignore from a reporter, a gruff male drawl reached him over the barroom noise. It was impossible not to overhear.

"C'mon, babe. You too good for me or something?"

A young, blunt-faced cop from Ryan's precinct, Seth Kimmel had been sitting at one of the more unruly tables near the restrooms. Molly had been waiting on them, and although Ryan didn't know what had transpired, Seth had apparently gotten up and followed her from the table.

He gripped her arm, stopping her.

"I'm just foolin' around with you. Lighten up—"

Wringing free, Molly retreated into the corridor that led to the kitchen. Seth went after her, encouraged by the hoots and catcalls coming from the cops at his table. With an inward sigh, Ryan placed his bottle on a nearby display case that held framed police photos and mementos. He'd never liked Seth, who was a walking cliché of the over-muscled cop with an attitude, and the rough way he'd grabbed the waitress bothered him. He felt duty-bound to follow.

Shouldering his way through a group cloistered in front of one of the bar's flat-screen televisions, he turned into the exposed-brick hallway. Seth had Molly cornered, his arm braced against the wall at her shoulder. He moved each time she did, blocking her escape.

"Leave me alone, Seth—"

"Just give me a chance, Mol." He leaned closer, sliding a hand onto her waist.

"*I mean it.*" She pushed at him.

"You heard her," Ryan said, making his presence known.

Seth slid him an annoyed glance. "Relax, Detective. We're just having a private chat." Undeterred, he returned his attention to Molly.

Ryan approached and laid a firm hand on his shoulder. "Give it a rest, Kimmel, all right? She said to back off—"

Seth's temper exploded. Knocking away Ryan's hand, he shoved him back a step. Ryan shoved in return. The cop took a wild swing at him, barely missing his jaw, but Ryan grabbed the man's extended arm and with a sudden, hard twist, pinned it behind him, putting pressure on his elbow and hoisting him face-first to the wall. Seth struggled and spewed curses. He was a big guy—larger than Ryan—but the uncomfortable position his arm was in and Ryan's body weight bearing down on it restricted his movement.

"Go back to your table or leave. I don't give a damn which," Ryan ordered, irritated. He let go and took a step back.

Seth wheeled, his face beet-red under his bristled crew cut, ready to fight. But the arrival of others who had heard the commotion—Adam and Darnell included—kept the confrontation from getting more physical. Breathing hard, Seth pointed a finger. "Watch your goddamn back, Winter."

"Bitch," he spat at Molly before pushing through the men and stalking away.

Darnell gave a low whistle as he stared after him. "Damn. Is Kimmel drunk?"

"I'm going with just stupid." Ryan couldn't believe he'd actually thrown a punch at him. He was glad he had kept up with the APD's hand-to-hand combat courses, which weren't mandatory for detectives. But Seth was an oversized, well-trained brute, and Ryan also knew he had gotten lucky. Ryan wondered if the rumors about his steroid use were true. *Roid rage.* It would explain the aggression.

He turned to Molly. "You okay?"

She nodded, appearing a little shaken as she pushed her long, flaxen hair behind her. She wore jeans and a low-cut McCrosky's T-shirt. "Thank you, Ryan."

"I'll ask Frank to put a different server on his table." *Hopefully an ugly male one*, he thought. Molly retreated to the kitchen as Ryan walked with the others back into the bar. Seth glared at him from his reclaimed seat. He made a mental note to discuss his behavior with Captain Thompson, who appeared to have already departed for the night.

A short time later, Ryan watched as Darnell took Mike outside to get him into a cab. He figured he'd get going soon, too.

"On the house." He turned to find Molly next to him. She grinned and held out a beer. "It's your brand, right?"

"Thanks." Ryan accepted it, although he hadn't been planning to have another.

"I really appreciate what you did tonight."

His curiosity winning out, he bent his head closer to hers and lowered his voice. "So what was that all about?"

She sighed. "Seth's been asking me out. I like cops or else I wouldn't work here, but I don't like knuckle-dragging assholes."

Ryan couldn't help but smile at her bluntness.

"He won't take no for an answer. He was showing off in front of his buddies, saying crude things, putting his hands on me and telling them I liked it." Her eyebrows pinched together as she spoke. "I took him down a few notches so he followed me, trying to prove a point to them, I guess."

Ryan had heard some of the others talking about Molly in the way that men do. Tall and long-limbed like a model, she had the sun-kissed look of a California girl, where she'd lived before moving to Atlanta, if he recalled correctly. She was young but definitely attractive, as Adam had already pointed out. He glanced around the bar. Seth was still here, although he'd moved to the pool tables in the far corner. He leaned against the wall while one of his buddies racked balls for a game. His flat eyes remained on Ryan, however. Molly talking to him now was probably only adding fuel to the fire. "Do me a favor?"

"Absolutely."

"Don't leave by yourself tonight. I don't want Kimmel

following you out to pick up where he left off. Someone can make sure you get to your car."

He had rolled up the sleeves of his blue dress shirt, and Molly laid her fingers on his forearm.

"I take MARTA, actually, but I could still use a walk to the station," she suggested almost shyly. Her green eyes were vivid under long lashes. "We've never had a chance to get to know each other, and you really *were* my hero tonight."

Ryan realized he was being flirted with—not the first time since his divorce, although he'd never quite gotten used to it. He tried to form a suitable response, but his thoughts fragmented as Lydia emerged from the crowd. He hadn't seen her come in, and he gave a hoarse greeting, surprised.

"I know it's late," she said uncertainly. "But I ... wanted to stop by."

Her gaze shifted to Molly, who still stood close although at some point her fingers had slipped from his arm. Ryan cleared his throat and made the introduction.

"You're the ex-wife." Molly extended her hand and smiled. "I've heard some of the guys mention you. So you must've known Nate?"

Lydia replied that she had. The three engaged in small talk until Ryan indicated the bottle he held. "Thanks again for the beer."

"Sure ..." Molly took a step back. "Well, I should get back to work. Ryan, I'll let you know when my shift's over."

He gave a small nod. Once she had departed, he

returned his attention to Lydia. He guessed she had seen Molly's hand on his arm. If she had, she didn't mention it.

"It's been awhile," she said as she looked around the space. "But everything looks pretty much the same."

Ryan thought of the countless times he'd met up with Lydia here after work—when they were dating and later, after they moved in together and got married. "You know Frank. He's not a big fan of change."

As if on cue, Frank called to her from behind the bar, then came around to envelop her in a warm hug. A few others strolled over to say hello. Ryan stood nearby as Lydia talked with his peers. She wore a summer cardigan over a pretty sundress, as well as heeled sandals instead of the flats she normally sported after a long ER shift. Her newly shortened hair appeared sleek and glossy under the tavern's recessed lighting. He wondered, a little painfully, if she'd been out on a date.

"I'm glad you came. It means a lot," he said sincerely, once it was the two of them again.

"I'm sorry I didn't make it to the service." She glanced at Molly, who was a dozen feet away clearing a vacated table. "And I don't want to keep you from anything—"

"Stay for a while?" he asked on impulse. Although some of the force had begun to disperse, the ones who remained were getting more boisterous. Someone—Pearson, a detective from zone three—had begun a pretty decent acapella rendition of *Danny Boy*. But instead of it having a lulling effect, several in the crowd were lifting drinks and toasting to Nate's memory. "I mean, you came all the way down here, right? We can go out on the patio."

She hesitated, her soft-brown eyes looking into his, then gave a nod of agreement.

The terrace had been crowded earlier. But as the evening waned, Frank had apparently stopped the outside service to cut down on wait staff. The tabletop hurricane lamps had been extinguished, although the scent of candle wax still hung in the sultry night air. They were the only two taking advantage of the twinkling downtown lights. Lydia had requested a glass of wine, while Ryan had left his beer inside, instead opting for coffee.

"You're still drinking caffeine at night."

He smiled faintly as he sipped from his mug. "It's a cop thing. We build up a tolerance. Ask Mateo."

Lydia sighed in memory. "He still keeps a coffee IV hooked to his arm?"

"In your occupation I think it's what they call a central line."

Their lighthearted conversation eventually faded off into silence. Placing his mug on a table, Ryan allowed himself to study her profile as she stared up at the tall CNN Center building that loomed at the edge of the park's commons, the cable news logo a familiar object in the downtown sky. Beyond it, the twenty-story SkyView Atlanta Ferris wheel—the latest tourist attraction—made a slow revolution, a lit disk against the night.

"It's been a tough day," he confided.

"I'm sure," she said seriously, her eyes meeting his again. "Is there anything new?"

He told her in confidence about the ballistics report tying Nate's and Watterson's murders together. She looked concerned. "So someone could just be going around shooting cops?"

"Internal Affairs is conducting its own investigation. The GBI's involved, too. Unless they can find something improper both men were involved in, it's a possibility."

"*Be careful*, Ryan."

It was the same request she'd made at the bungalow that past weekend, something she had also said to him each morning when they had been together. His heart squeezed at the realization of how much he missed hearing her say that. Other cops had their St. Michael medallion, but his talisman had always been Lydia's appeal that he return home safely to her and Tyler. A recollection of the three of them here on the patio having dinner—Tyler, still a chubby-cheeked infant at the time, happily chewing on animal crackers—tightened his throat. For several moments, they simply stared at one another, until she bowed her head.

"I found someone to take my shift this afternoon," she confessed. "I went home and I got dressed, but I ..." She shook her head, her voice fraying. "I just couldn't go ... I'm sorry."

Ryan felt the sluggish beat of his heart. He was suddenly grateful she had spared herself from another funeral. For him it had been painful, but for Lydia he could see that even with seventeen months since Tyler's death, it was still far too soon. Being there would have only reawakened agonizing memories—the similar setting, many of the same people in attendance. He took a step closer.

"Maybe it's better you didn't," he offered gently.

"It's not. I should've been there for Kristen." She sounded angry with herself. "She was there for us—"

"She'll understand. You can call her next week." Tentatively, he clasped her upper arms, wanting to touch her but half-expecting her to pull away. Instead, she laid her fingers against his shirtfront. Ryan swallowed thickly.

Her delicately arched eyebrows knitted together as she frowned. "I ... don't understand myself sometimes. I'm an ER doctor. I see death every day—"

"Lydia," he murmured, hushing her as he searched for something he could say to make it all right. As if anything could ever be right for either of them again. But he paused at the figure standing in the threshold of the patio doors. The lights in the tavern's interior silhouetted Molly's frame. Reluctantly, he dropped his hands, and Lydia took a self-conscious step away from him, fixing her gaze elsewhere.

"Ryan? I'll be ready to go in about ten minutes. I just need to split my tips with the other staff and clock out."

"All right," he rasped. He looked again at Lydia once the waitress had departed. She'd moved farther from him, forced her usual composure back into place.

"I don't remember Molly," she said casually. He figured she'd jumped to conclusions. Ryan recalled how he'd felt finding out about Rick Varek.

"She's new here, sort of. Maybe three or four months."

"She's pretty." Her eyes met his for a bare, searching second, and then she reached for the satin clutch she'd placed on the patio ledge. "And I really have to be going. I've got rounds at six thirty in the morning."

"Let me walk you to your car." He felt there was more to be said between them.

"You're making a habit of that," she pointed out, forcing a smile. "It isn't necessary—"

"It's late and this isn't the safest area at night. But wait here a minute? I need to take care of something."

She sighed softly but gave a faint nod. Ryan went inside and spotted Adam, who sat at the bar with two others watching ESPN and snacking on pistachios, apparently in no hurry to go home. "Do something for me?"

"That all depends," Adam said tersely. "Does it have to do with Lydia showing up?"

He had noticed his brother hadn't come over to say hello. "She knew Nate. And for the record, I *invited* her—"

"I guess she left the surgeon at home tonight." Adam cracked another shell and shook his head at him. Ryan regretted having mentioned Varek. But he'd blurted it out Sunday night when Adam had come by the house to do his laundry.

"Do you want to help or not?"

"All right," Adam sighed. "What?"

He'd already looked around the bar and no longer saw Seth Kimmel. He might have left, but Ryan didn't want to take any chances. He asked Adam to wait for Molly near the kitchen and make sure she got to the rail station without interference.

He didn't seem displeased with the assignment. "Sure. But if you ask me, you're missing a real opportunity."

"I didn't ask." Bracing his hand on Adam's shoulder in thanks, he headed back to the patio but slowed as he neared its doors. He could already see it was unoccupied. Deflated, he walked onto it anyway, knowing in his gut she'd slipped out rather than going into the bar to wait for him. Lydia had an independent streak a mile wide. He figured Molly's statement about when she was getting off from work had left a lot open to interpretation, too. His ego had kept him from setting her straight. Only her empty wine glass remained. Its rim bore the faint smudge of her lipstick. The goblet sat on one of the bar's paper napkins, anchoring it against the breeze that had begun to pick up and hinted of an approaching rain.

I'm fine, Ryan. Good night, she'd written with an ink pen on the paper. He wasn't so sure, and he wondered if he could still catch up to her, or even in what direction she might have parked.

But a voice inside him said to just let her go.

He stared briefly out over the park in resignation. Then he went into the tavern's vestibule and took his navy dress coat from a row of wooden pegs behind the hostess desk, deciding to leave things as he had with Adam seeing Molly to the station. The barroom noise floated around him. Folding the coat over his arm, he stepped out onto the sidewalk. Thunder rumbled, the air sticky and warm, and a pitchfork of lightning lit the distant sky. The storm was moving in from the west.

The downtown's Luckie Marietta District was a walkable community of restaurants and bars, although there was currently little foot traffic due to the late hour and impending rain. Passing the church-turned-music venue known as The Tabernacle and reaching the street where he'd parallel parked, Ryan stood at his SUV, fishing inside his pants pocket for his keys. At that same moment, his attention was drawn to the street corner. A shadowed figure wearing an oversize hooded sweatshirt pulled over his head despite the heat stood there. It was too dark, and he was too far away to see his face, but he appeared to be watching Ryan. He turned and disappeared onto a side street as an APD squad car rolled past.

Getting into his vehicle and starting the engine, Ryan made a U-turn and went in the same direction, his curiosity piqued. The first raindrops hit his windshield as he drove up Spring Street.

The sidewalk was abandoned. Whoever it was, was gone.

CHAPTER SEVEN

—))•●•((—

*Y*OU'RE A COP. *Stay calm.*

He called out again, turning in a circle to view all areas of the compact backyard. His breath fogged in the biting cold.

Find him.

Still calling as he paced farther out, he scanned the line of shrubbery marking the property's border. Brown, dead leaves blanketed the bushes' tops. He searched for a flash of blue pajamas against the iron-gray morning. A small head of unruly dark hair, a hand covering a giggling mouth. Tyler loved to play.

Not the time for it, buddy.

"*This isn't a game,*" *Ryan called loudly, a growing unease inside him.* "*This isn't hide-and-seek. Come out now.*"

Everything in the small room remained the same. The twin big-boy bed with its cheerful patchwork quilt, toys arranged on shelves and piled high inside a painted chest. A mobile of rocket ships floated in midair, although the nightlight that projected stars onto the ceiling had burned out months ago.

Tired of chasing sleep, Ryan often ended up here.

He had never been able to pack up Tyler's things, instead maintaining a connection to him through those items that proved his existence. In this place, he could almost hear his raspy little laugh, could still smell the warm vanilla scent of his skin. Throat thickened by the memory, Ryan became aware of another heavy roll of thunder overhead. A storm—the second tonight—moving across the city.

It was what had originally awakened him from his troubled sleep.

Absently turning one of Tyler's stuffed animals around in his palms, he wandered to the room's blue-curtained window. Through it he saw lights burning in the small apartment over the detached garage. Chest bare, wearing only pajama bottoms, Ryan peered out through the rain at the soft glow.

Tess kept late hours, or early ones, depending on how you looked at it. A station wagon parked on the street with Florida tags indicated she again had an overnight guest. Ryan had seen him before, a silver-haired gentleman who came through town every few months.

Good for her, he thought.

No one should be completely alone.

For a time, he stood in this too-quiet place and watched the downpour, again grappling with whether he'd done the right thing in not going after Lydia last night. Ryan had believed—God, he had hoped—that giving her the freedom she wanted would allow her to begin healing. That distance from him and their crushing tragedy would let her start over, somehow.

But after her rare openness with him at the bar and the fragility she had allowed him to see, he wondered now if that was simply what he had wanted to believe.

Maybe no one ever really recovered from this kind of loss.

Somberly, he took a last look around the room before placing the toy back against the pillows and closing the door behind him. Returning to his own bed, he lay down again, for a time staring at the high white ceiling. Then he turned on the room's television, still restless and unable to sleep. His alarm would start ringing in another hour or so, anyway.

He'd begun flipping channels, looking for something besides infomercials and *Law & Order* reruns, when his cell phone vibrated on the nightstand. He'd turned off the sound for Nate's interment. In his profession, calls late at night and in the early-morning hours weren't unusual, but they rarely brought good news. Reaching for the phone, he squinted at its screen in the TV's silvered light.

"Yeah." Despite his time awake, his voice sounded rough from disuse.

"I just heard from Narco," Mateo said. "A CI gave information on a meth shipment being housed at the Purvis Street property. It arrived last night. They roused a judge out of bed an hour ago to sign the warrant."

Adrenaline kicked in. Ryan sat up, dislodging an

offended Max from the spot he'd taken on the coverlet. Their plan was to piggyback off the warrant. A drug bust would provide the opportunity to get inside the house and identify possible evidence. If they were supremely lucky, they'd find the gun used in both murders. Already, he was walking toward the shower. "When?"

"Gangstas like to stay up late and party, right? The strike team wants to get the drop on them, hit early while the bastards are still snug in their beds."

Ryan heard Evie's sleepy voice in the background. Mateo spoke to her in hushed Spanish, then returned to the call.

"Bring your Kevlar, amigo. We strike at the ass-crack of dawn."

DEA agents had begun referring to Atlanta as the "new Miami" due to its growing repute as the central hub for drug trafficking along the East Coast. And while Hispanic cartels were becoming predominant, urban youth gangs still thrived in the trade, as well. A confidential informant had offered knowledge of the shotgun being used as a temporary stash house, until the methamphetamine could be processed and distributed.

It had stopped raining, the first hint of daybreak casting the decaying street in a grainy haze. Boots thudded softly over wet concrete as SWAT officers crept onto the property and around the sides of the old house to seal off possible exits. Keeping low, Ryan moved cautiously forward, in-step with Mateo and several Narcotics detectives charged with bringing up the rear once the specialized team had entered. Humid air filled his lungs. He wore sneakers, jeans and a T-shirt, his gold detective's badge on a chain around his neck and his Glock held ready. Like the other plainclothes, his vest marked him clearly as APD.

Above him, four of their men had climbed noiselessly onto the porch. Outfitted in riot gear, the unit's lead gave the signal to commence. The no-knock warrant would hopefully allow them to catch the occupants off guard.

"Police!" Two blows with a battering ram, and the door flew open. Officers burst inside. Ryan advanced with the swarm, its ranks flowing to the left and right of the shotgun's narrow interior, more men ascending a rickety staircase to a second level. The house jolted to life. Shouts and the sounds of scurrying feet filled the rooms. The piss-colored light that had been on in the first floor went out as occupants scrambled.

In front of him, Mateo laid hands on a fleeing male—probably no more than sixteen—grabbing him by the back of an oversize athletic jersey. "Where're you goin'?"

He shoved him face-first to the interior's peeling wallpaper. Ryan stepped in to help, holding the combative youth in place until Mateo could bring his arms back and snap handcuffs on his wrists. They laid him stomach-down on the floor. The kid cursed at them, his right cheek against the filthy carpet runner.

"You got him?"

"Yeah, go. You have anything that'll stick me?" Mateo

barked, straddling the teenager as he prepared to check the pockets of his baggy jeans for weapons.

Ryan moved past, heading up the stairs toward the commotion on the second floor. Halfway up, the sharp pop of gunshots above him sent electricity tingling over his skin. His back against the paneled stairwell, gun gripped in both hands, he hastened his climb to the top. The second floor was poorly lit, as well. A SWAT officer on the landing stood over a bare-chested, tattooed male who lay sprawled on the battered wood flooring. A high-powered flashlight held by another of the officers illuminated a mortal wound to his skull and a gun on the floor near his hand. Blood bloomed beneath his head, his eyes staring blankly upward. Ryan recalled him as one of the gang members who'd come out on the porch with the pit bull two days earlier.

Around him, other gangbangers were on their knees, handcuffed. The first of them was yanked up and escorted down the stairs.

"All rooms clear," an officer in back announced loudly. Ryan holstered his gun.

"We got six. The ones you see here and two more in back," Sam Jankowski, a muscled ex-Marine and the SWAT team leader, told him. "Same number downstairs."

"Any of ours hurt?"

"Manning took a shot to the vest." He wore a communication device in his ear, enabling him to converse with other team members. "They've got him lying down. He should be all right. Paramedics are on the way." He nodded to the dead body. "So's the ME."

The gun on the floor near the thug's hand wasn't the make they were looking for. A SWAT officer went about its careful removal from the area for safety purposes.

"Is Pooch here?" Ryan directed the question to one of the kneeling gang members. So far, he hadn't seen him. The kid screwed up his mouth indolently, refusing to speak.

"Fuck you," another, more vocal, arrestee intoned.

He was met with a sharp jab in the shoulder blades from one of the SWAT team. "Shut up."

"That you, Winter?" Antoine Clark, one of the senior Narcotics detectives, called to him from a rear room.

Ryan pushed through the officers controlling the scene and went down a thin hallway with a floor slanted by age. Raucous barking coming from outside indicated the pit bull was chained up somewhere behind the house. He entered a back room that contained an assortment of weapons—eleven handguns, an assault rifle—as well as a cardboard box full of most likely stolen iPhones and small bags containing pills. A bare bulb hanging from the ceiling by a cord emitted a filmy light. He noted the Smith & Wesson 9 mm, what they were looking for, among the handguns. Ryan felt a flare of hope, although it would be up to ballistics to determine if they had the murder weapon.

"Know what that is?" Antoine pointed to stacked cases of beer on a card table. A tall, lanky African American who had played basketball at the University of Georgia in the mid-eighties, he also spearheaded the APD's gang task force. He was an expert in the street trade.

"Beer?"

"Liquid meth—dissolved in water to disguise it for transport in beer bottles—or tequila bottles, if it's coming out of Mexico."

Wearing latex gloves, he pulled out one of the bottles and peered at its contents through the amber glass, his forehead wrinkling in concentration. "Oh, yeah. That's what we've got here. And those pills are Oxycodone, already divvied up for sale on the street."

"Some arsenal." Mateo gave a low whistle as he entered and checked out the assortment of weapons. Spotting the nine mil, he exchanged a victorious glance with Ryan.

"I'll give Forensics a heads up." Mateo dug into his pocket for his cell phone, then glanced sharply upward at the heavy tread of feet in flight. "What the hell?"

All three men withdrew their weapons and aimed them upward in case shots were fired by whoever was above them on the roof. Ryan called out, alerting the SWAT officers.

"There must be a way up," he yelled. "Look for a loose panel in the ceiling!"

In his peripheral vision, he saw something large fall outside the room's single window. He spun toward it as something else plunged past. *A human form?* The window exploded, and he ducked, instinctively covering his face in reaction to the roaring discharge of a gun.

He rushed to the shattered window. One of the gang members lay on the ground below, writhing in pain. But the other one was on his feet and moving. They'd jumped from the roof—a daredevil stunt—a nearly thirty-foot drop their escape route. Ryan recognized the one running. Pooch, wearing only jeans. He clenched a gun in one hand as he looked back over his shoulder. Unbelievably, he'd managed to fire into the room on the way down.

"Antoine's hit!" Mateo yelled behind him.

On the ground, an officer advanced from the property's rear, shouting orders to drop the weapon. Pooch began shooting, and the officer dove for cover behind a line of overflowing trashcans. Knocking away the remaining glass and leaning out the window, Ryan took aim. He fired and missed, but succeeded in drawing Pooch's attention away from the pinned-down cop. Scowling up at him, he swung the gun's barrel in retaliation and released several rounds. Ryan jumped back, bullets splintering the wooden window frame an inch from his head.

The gunfire had set off a car alarm, which shrieked amid the chaos, joining forces with the canine's frenetic barks. At the same time more footsteps sounded overhead, indicating the way up to the roof had been found.

Pooch had taken off like a jackrabbit through a narrow alleyway formed by the pressed-together backs of ramshackle row houses on Purvis and the adjacent street. Ryan had a rapidly deteriorating view of him. But it still wasn't light enough, the shot too risky with civilians inside the thin-walled homes. With a curse, he yelled to the SWAT officers who were now outside swarming the yard. "Through the alley!"

He turned from the window, breathing hard.

"I'm okay," Antoine said through gritted teeth, although

he didn't look it. He sat on the battered hardwood floor, eyes closed, his back against the wall and blood staining the shoulder of his navy APD windbreaker. Mateo was on his knees beside him, trying to assess the damage.

Moving his Glock from his right hand to his left, Ryan went to the room's threshold, calling down to the floor below. "We need paramedics up here, now! Officer down!"

When he turned again, Mateo's eyes were on him, his hands pressed over Antoine's wound. His partner's face paled.

"Goddammit. Ry ... you're hit, too."

Only then did he become aware of the blood trickling down his forearm.

CHAPTER EIGHT

————◀)•●•(▶————

LYDIA CONDUCTED ROUNDS inside the ER with Amanda Jeoung, one of the third-year residents. The early hour was made apparent by the shallow light entering through the plate-glass windows they passed in the corridor.

"Caucasian male, early seventies, I'm thinking. No ID and refuses to give his name," Amanda rattled off in her usual efficient manner as they prepared to enter one of the curtained exam bays. She wore horn-rimmed, cat-eye glasses that nearly overwhelmed her fine features. "Paramedics brought him in after 9-1-1 received reports of a man in front of the Capitol building wandering in traffic."

An elderly man with a thinning comb-over sat on the edge of the exam table, muttering to himself and jiggling one leg in obvious agitation. Lydia looked over his chart on her electronic tablet.

"Sir, can you tell me your name?"

"He's been going on about aliens watching him,"

Amanda said under her breath. "And I don't mean the *illegal* kind."

He appeared too well fed to be an addict, and his clothes were reasonably clean and in good condition, probably ruling out homelessness, Lydia thought. He'd also had a recent shave. *He belongs to someone.* Considering the time, she wondered sympathetically if he'd been out all night. She attempted to examine his eyes with a penlight, but he recoiled and batted her hand away.

"Are you on any medication, sir? Is there someone we can call for you?"

He pointed a finger, his faded eyes narrowing at her. "You're one of them, aren't you? Doe-eyed little thing. You don't fool me!"

He began an angry diatribe against the government. Repressing a sigh, Lydia dropped the penlight back into the pocket of the lab coat she'd pulled on over her scrubs, a barrier against the hospital's too-cool air conditioning. "Wait here, sir, all right?"

Amanda followed her out as she gave instructions. "Altered mental status, possibly dementia with paranoia. Get Psych down here for a consult and check with the police to see if anyone's reported a missing person fitting his description. Then try to get a CBC and chem seven. In the meantime, give him five milligrams of Lorazepam to calm him down—"

Amanda startled as a tray inside the bay crashed to the floor. The man's railing grew louder.

"Dr. Rossman," Lydia called, halting the burly male

resident as he went past. "Drop what you're doing and give Dr. Jeoung a hand with bay two. She's going to need help."

She returned her attention to Amanda. "Who's next?"

"Bay four, an MVA victim. Minor fender bender, but he's complaining of neck pain. Paramedics put him in a cervical collar that hasn't been removed yet—"

"Dr. Kelley's available. Get him to have a look?" Lydia's gaze had fallen on the farthest of the bays. Its curtain stood partially open, revealing a woman who sat huddled on an exam table. She was in her early thirties, strikingly pretty and well dressed, her blond hair pulled into a long ponytail. Lydia recognized her. Elise Brandt.

"Mrs. Brandt?" she said, entering the bay and closing the curtain behind her. Lydia had treated her a few months earlier for a fractured wrist. She remembered because the X-ray had revealed another, older fracture in the radius of the same arm that hadn't healed well. There had also been some suspicious bruises, but when questioned, Elise had quickly attributed her injuries to in-line skating in Piedmont Park.

She appeared pale. A bruise shadowed the right side of her jaw, which was also a little swollen, and she held one arm protectively against her midsection. She seemed nervous, avoiding Lydia's eyes.

"I'm Dr. Costa, Mrs. Brandt. I treated you before—"

"I'm already being seen by someone," she interjected tensely. "He was just here."

Lydia consulted the woman's chart on the tablet. She

noted her blood pressure was low. "An intern took your vitals. I'm the attending physician this morning."

The woman said nothing, instead twisting her wedding band, which held a large diamond surrounded by sapphires. Lydia examined the bruise on her face. It was fresh, maybe a few hours old, but she didn't think her jaw was broken. Looking at the woman's anxious expression, her instincts spoke to her just as they had the last time.

"It's a little early for skating, isn't it?" she asked pointedly, trying to get a reaction.

"I-I took a fall in the house, on the stairs," Elise stammered. "I can be so clumsy."

"Are you hurt anywhere else?"

"I think maybe I broke a rib. It hurts to breathe."

"Lie back on the gurney for me, please."

She did as requested, her movement slow and careful. Elise grimaced and bit her lip as Lydia pressed carefully on her rib cage, her hands then moving farther down her abdomen. Her belly seemed a little rigid to the touch, possibly indicating an internal bleed. It might explain the low blood pressure. "On a scale of one to ten, how would you rate the pain?"

"An eight, maybe."

"I'm going to have a look, all right?"

She caught Lydia's wrist, halting her from lifting her top. "Is that necessary? I mean … I'd rather you not."

"I need to conduct a full examination. I can have a nurse come in with us if you're uncomfortable?"

Elise finally shook her head. She swallowed heavily and

laid her hand back on the gurney, staring up at the ceiling tiles.

Raising the woman's blouse, Lydia felt a quiet anger spread through her. A purple contusion splotched the skin over Elise's lower right ribs, just beneath the elastic band of her bra. But there were other bruises also visible on her abdomen, their shades ranging from blue to sickly green and pale yellow. Their variation indicated they hadn't been caused at the same time. Some were days, some weeks old. When she'd last seen Elise, she had given her a protective splint for her wrist and a prescription for pain meds before discharging her. Still, she'd thought about her after she had left the ER, wondering if she should have probed harder. She should have.

Lydia lowered Elise's shirt. Her voice was gentle but firm. "I don't think you fell down the stairs, Mrs. Brandt."

The woman looked away, her lower lip trembling. "I *did*."

"Someone's hurting you. Is it your husband?"

Her voice shook as she sat up. "Please, I just need something for the pain. I shouldn't have come in. I asked not to see you again—"

"You understand I have an obligation to contact the police about non-accidental or intentional injuries—"

"Please," she repeated. A tear slipped down her cheek, and she brushed it away. "I-I just want to go home, all right?"

Lydia felt tension tighten her shoulders. It was always a difficult decision. Involving law enforcement could put the victim at greater risk from her abuser, especially if she refused to leave him. She took in the woman's expensive clothing and jewelry, her designer handbag and perfect manicure. Lydia wondered if, despite appearances, she had the resources to leave.

"I can put you in touch with a women's shelter," she offered, touching her shoulder. "Or maybe you have friends or family you could go to?"

"You don't even know who my husband is, do you?" Elise whispered.

Lydia released a contemplative breath. "I'm going to admit you to the hospital, Mrs. Brandt—"

Her eyes widened fearfully. "For how long?"

"That depends. We need to X-ray your ribs and conduct a trauma panel and ultrasound to rule out internal bleeding."

"No. I can't stay—"

Lydia lowered her voice. "If you *are* bleeding on the inside, it can be very serious. Let's just run the tests and see what we're dealing with first, all right? You can *rest* here."

Elise appeared exhausted. After a long moment, she squeezed her eyes closed and nodded faintly, again twisting her wedding rings. The large diamond glinted like fire under the fluorescent lighting.

Lydia exited the bay and closed the curtain behind her. She worked to shove down her emotion. Getting the attention of Roe, one of the senior nurses, she ordered the tests. "Have someone keep an eye on her until either Radiology or Gastro comes to take her up."

Roe had apparently seen Elise in the waiting room. "Someone beat that woman?"

Lydia felt sick. She was in need of a camera. If Elise would consent, she intended to document the injuries.

A short time later, she left the bay once again, having taken the photographs with Roe and a social worker standing by. To her surprise, Elise hadn't contested them, nor had she objected when Lydia had suggested at least talking with the police to understand her options. But she hadn't been able to stop the flow of tears or her trembling.

Lydia hoped she had done the right thing in contacting the police.

She noticed the rush of activity inside the lobby. Two ambulances were unloading out front, their red light bars mingling in the morning haze with the blue lights from squad cars. "What's going on?"

"Narcotics bust went sideways," Jamaal supplied as he rifled through one of the cabinets behind the front desk.

Thinking of Nate's shooting, Lydia felt an uneasy déjà vu. At that moment, the automated doors slid open for the gurneys being wheeled inside by paramedics. A young African-American male was brought in first, one shin splinted and his right wrist cuffed to the gurney's steel sidebar. Two police officers accompanied him. Another gurney carried Antoine Clark, a Narcotics detective Lydia knew from Ryan's precinct. His broad upper body had been stripped of clothing, and a sterile dressing covered one shoulder. He was bantering with one of the emergency workers traveling beside the gurney, however, talking trash about UGA's last basketball season. Lydia took charge, sending the arrestee into one of the rooms where a trauma team was assembling.

"Hey, Lydia."

"How's it going, Antoine?" she asked, peeling back the dressing for a look.

"Shitty is how it's going—"

"No entrance wound. The bullet grazed him pretty good," the paramedic informed her. "It's going to hurt like hell tomorrow, but it could've been a lot worse. We gave him morphine, four MGs." He twirled a finger beside his ear. "He's a little loopy."

"Narco detective with a goddamn buzz," Antoine said with a half-grin.

"We'll take good care of you," she assured him. More police were now appearing inside the lobby. She directed another of the doctors under her charge. "Get Detective Clark into suite three. Start irrigating the wound and set up an antibiotic drip."

"Your husband's bringing up the rear," Antoine called out as he was rolled away.

He'd meant ex-husband. Lydia's eyes swung to the ER doors, surprise and apprehension threading through her. What was Ryan doing with Narcotics? A uniformed officer was coming in on a gurney, an oxygen mask over his face. Not Ryan.

"Blunt force trauma. He took a shot to the vest," the accompanying paramedic said. "Good breath sounds, but he's got some bruising."

"Suite four. Dr. Gulacki, go with him."

Ryan entered with Mateo and another officer. He was ambulatory, at least—walking in under his own steam—but gauze wrapped his right forearm. Blood leaked through the white meshing.

"How's Antoine?" he asked as she reached him.

"It appears to be just a flesh wound. He's lucky." But her focus was on Ryan. She looked at his arm.

"A broken window," he explained. "I cut it on the glass."

"It looks pretty deep," Mateo commented.

A nurse called for Lydia from the room where the arrestee had been taken. She hesitated.

Ryan nodded his understanding. "I'm fine, Lyd. Go."

She wanted to stay and take care of the laceration herself, see how bad it really was. She also wanted to apologize for her disappearance last night. It hadn't been fair of her. But she'd felt awkward and out of place at McCrosky's, especially after the blond waitress had shown up on the patio, indicating for the second time that she and Ryan had plans of some kind. The revelation had both surprised and stung her, but she knew she had absolutely no right to feel that way, especially when she was seeing someone herself. She also understood she was needed with the more serious injuries. Breaking her gaze from Ryan's, Lydia waved over Rossman.

"Take Detective Winter to get his arm cleaned up. He also needs a tetanus. And he's allergic to penicillin."

✻

"We talked to her. Unless she files a complaint, there's not a lot we can do," the young police officer said, giving Lydia an apologetic shrug.

She glanced at the closed door of Elise Brandt's hospital room. Ian Brandt, her husband, had charged into the hospital a short time earlier, creating a scene at the admissions desk and demanding to see his wife. Lydia had been busy with another patient, but she'd heard about the commotion. "You can't keep him out of there?"

"No, ma'am. Not if she doesn't want us to."

Seavers was imprinted on the officer's brass nameplate. Lydia didn't know him, although she'd seen his field-training officer a few times in the past. The older cop had already gone down to the cafeteria, shaking his head and calling their involvement a waste of time.

"She's insisting she fell down the stairs," Officer Seavers recounted. "She asked us to leave."

Lydia frowned. "I have photos of her injuries. Those weren't caused by a tumble down some steps—"

"They'll be evidence if she changes her mind about filing charges."

She knew the *if* was a pretty big one. Apparently, any courage Elise Brandt had mustered had quickly died at her husband's unexpected arrival. Frustrated, she shoved her hands into the pockets of her lab coat. There was no sound coming from the room. She wondered what was going on inside.

"If you don't mind, Dr. Costa, I need to meet up with Officer Kirkpatrick."

Lydia thanked him halfheartedly and remained rooted in place as he got onto the elevator. The doors closed, and for several moments she stared at the grouping of potted plastic plants that served as décor in the hallway, trying to decide what to do. A nurse pushing a medicine cart traveled past. She couldn't let this go. Lydia's teeth worried the soft flesh of her lower lip, then she went over to the room. She didn't knock before entering.

Elise lay in bed, clad in a hospital gown and an IV drip attached to the inside of her forearm. She looked away from Lydia, affixing her gaze to the wall. Ian Brandt sat in a chair beside the bed, holding his wife's hand. He was a big man, well dressed in an expensive business suit, sporting a goatee and raven, slicked-back hair.

"I wanted to see how you're doing," Lydia said to Elise. She picked up the chart attached to the foot of her bed and glanced over it, leafing through several pages.

"Who are you?" Brandt wanted to know.

"I'm Dr. Costa."

"You're her treating physician?"

"Mrs. Brandt has been transferred to Dr. Waslow, one of our gastroenterologists." She didn't flinch from his hard stare. "I admitted your wife in the ER."

His jaw appeared to tighten as he let go of Elise's hand and sat up straighter. Challenge laced his voice, which she had noticed held a very faint accent, something she couldn't quite place. "Do emergency doctors usually make room visits?"

Lydia didn't respond. She continued to focus on the chart, not liking what she read there.

"Since this *Waslow* hasn't been here yet, you can sign the papers. I want my wife discharged immediately," he demanded. "She would prefer to be at home in her own bed where she'll be more comfortable."

Lydia tamped down the dislike radiating through her. She spoke with forced patience. "Mrs. Brandt presented with pain in her upper abdomen and shortness of breath. A CT scan indicated a broken rib and blood leaking into her diaphragm. While the leak may resolve on its own with bed rest—"

"As I said, she can get that *at home*."

Her chin lifted. "We're keeping her here for twenty-four hours, for observation and intravenous administration of a painkiller. If the bleeding gets worse or doesn't clear up on its own within that timeframe, there may be a need to cauterize the area laparoscopically. I'm sure you wouldn't want to further risk her health by taking her out of here."

Brandt glared at her. Elise sniffled softly and rubbed a hand over her eyes.

"She's staying." Touching her shoulder, Lydia gentled her voice. "I want you to call me if you need *anything* at all, all right?"

She didn't expect a response nor did she receive one. Still, she laid her business card on the nightstand and with a last hard look at Brandt, walked out. She wanted him to know someone was watching. Her back rigid, she had just pushed the elevator button when she heard his voice.

"Dr. Costa."

Lydia turned. Brandt stalked toward her. "You're the one who called the police."

"This is the second time I've treated your wife in three months. Her injuries—"

"Are of her own causing." He waved a dismissive hand, a gold Rolex glinting on his broad wrist, and sighed heavily. "I know how all this must look. But Elise is alone while I'm at work, and what she didn't tell you is that she drinks too much and takes pills. She has blackouts and doesn't remember half the things she does."

No alcohol or drugs had shown up in Elise's blood panel. Lydia felt anger bubble inside her.

He consulted his watch, frowning. "I'm missing an important meeting because of this. The housekeeper called and said Elise wasn't feeling well and had taken a cab from the house. I had to call the taxi service to find out she'd come *here*, of all places."

Lydia understood what he meant. A *public* hospital. She clenched her jaw as her composure broke. "Those injuries weren't caused by a fall, and *you* know it."

Brandt stilled, his eyes narrowing.

"Do you understand why she came to Mercy, not one of the private hospitals? She didn't want you to know she'd gone for treatment." Lydia pointed at the closed hospital room door. "She attempted to file as an *indigent*. You tell me why a wife would be hiding the fact that she needs medical care from her spouse. You came looking for her because you were worried someone would notify the police about her injuries."

His tone grew indignant. "I don't like what you're implying—"

"I'm not *implying* anything. You're abusing her, and she's too afraid of you to do anything to stop it."

The usually bustling corridor was empty for once. Scowling, Brandt took a step closer, invading her space and towering over her. Lydia felt her mouth go dry. Despite the expensive clothes, he suddenly looked more like a menacing street hood. His lips curled back in cold amusement as his eyes flicked up and down her body.

"Shame. All that pretty ruined by dumpy hospital scrubs and a snotty attitude."

Her face grew hot. "I'm a doctor in this hospital—"

His voice lowered further. "I don't give a damn who you are. You should learn to mind your own business."

"And *you* should be in the back of a patrol car."

Lydia felt a hard tremor, but she refused to back down. Rage swam in Brandt's eyes. She understood Elise's fear—clearly—in that moment. The elevator bell rang and the doors opened. She turned and stepped onto it. He didn't follow, but his punishing stare remained on her until the doors closed again. Only when the elevator began its descent did Lydia allow herself to breathe. She could hear her blood rushing in her ears.

She wanted, needed, a drink. Her frayed nerves

screamed for one. But her shift wasn't over until six, a long time away.

Had she done the right thing by reporting the injuries to the police? Uncertain, Lydia rubbed a hand over her eyes. Her hope had been that their presence would give Elise a sense of security so that she might be more willing to file charges. That plan had failed with Brandt's arrival. She thought of the moral precept drummed into every medical student.

Primum non nocere. First, do no harm.

It was possible she had just made everything worse.

Reaching the main floor, she exited the elevator. Ryan stood in the ER lobby with Mateo and a handful of other police, plainclothes as well as uniforms. Upon seeing her, Ryan approached.

"How's Antoine?" she asked.

"Stoned and feeling no pain. He's in a room. They're keeping him overnight. His wife's in with him now."

She looked at his bandaged arm, the sterile gauze fresh. His T-shirt sleeve only partially concealed the familiar tattoo on his upper bicep. It created an involuntary, heated memory inside her that she hadn't been prepared for.

"Dr. Rossman doesn't have your light touch," Ryan said. "Four sutures. No muscle damage, though."

"Good." She nodded weakly, glad for some optimistic news.

Looking at her, his blue eyes filled with concern. Gently, he took her arm and guided her out of the flow of traffic. "Hey … what's wrong?"

He knew her that well, apparently. The confrontation with Brandt had rattled her. She still felt like gelatin on the inside. But she shook her head, not wanting to involve him. "It's nothing. I had a disagreement with a patient's family member, is all."

Ryan searched her face but didn't push, understanding patient confidentiality. "You were supposed to wait for me last night."

His tone was more questioning than accusing. She looked away from his steady gaze, not wanting to point out that he'd appeared to have made plans, and she hadn't wanted to get in the way. She wondered again if her confirmation that she was seeing Rick Varek had spurred him to start dating. If so, she should feel happy for him. "I know ... I'm sorry."

"The downtown can be dangerous at night, Lyd. Do you still carry your pepper spray?"

He'd given it to her several years earlier, after a nurse on the night shift had been mugged outside the nearby rail station. He had insisted she carry it.

"Do you ever stop thinking like a cop?" Tilting her head at him, she sighed softly. "I keep it on my key chain, which was in my hand ready for business all the way to my car."

A faint smile touched his lips. "That's my girl."

The familiar endearment drove a spear of pain through her. He apparently realized what he'd said, because the levity faded from his eyes, but his gaze still held hers.

Seeking a change of subject, she asked, "Why were you with Narcotics? Did it have to do with Nate?"

He kept his voice low. "We had a hunch a street gang might be behind the shootings. Narco had a search warrant, so Mateo and I and a few others from Homicide went along. We're hoping a gun confiscated in the raid will be a match."

Ryan nodded to several officers who spoke to him as they filed out. Mateo remained, although he'd busied himself at a vending machine in the patient waiting area, probably to give Ryan and her time to talk. Lydia could see him, fishing in his jeans pocket for change.

"When will you know?"

"We're waiting on the ballistics. We've got a rush on it. Probably later today."

His shoulder holster was missing its weapon. Lydia's stomach fluttered. "You fired your gun."

"I missed, unfortunately. Regardless, I'm out of the field until I'm cleared."

As a detective's wife, she had learned the protocol. Crime scene forensics would study bullet trajectories, including the ones that hit bodies. Bullets and casings would be matched to weapons so they had a solid account of who had fired and from where. It was a necessary legality. Police work had a set of rules, as well as a culture all its own.

For some reason, she thought of Ryan's formal police dress coat, having seen it hanging in the vestibule as she'd left McCrosky's the previous evening. Several others had been there as well, but she'd immediately recognized his among them, knowing by heart the exact number of stripes on its sleeve indicating years of service, knowing every commendation pin, every bar. Her fingers had briefly brushed its fine wool as she exited, the nostalgia created by the tavern, the other officers, affecting her.

"Casualties on the way," Jamaal alerted from the desk. "Two window washers fell off scaffolding onto a ledge below. Broken bones and a possible skull fracture. We're going to need a translator."

"How far out?" Lydia asked.

"Five minutes."

"I'll let you go." Ryan took a step back. Mateo now waited for him on the ER's covered portico. He was visible through the glass doors, pacing and drinking a can of Red Bull.

"More caffeine?"

Ryan shrugged. "In his defense, we've been going at it since five this morning." His eyes turned serious again. "It hasn't been under the best circumstances, but it's been good seeing you these past few days, Lydia."

She felt a dull ache in her chest.

They stared at one another for several moments. Then Lydia watched as he went through the automated doors, sidestepping a gurney being rolled inside. Looking at him as he joined Mateo, she noted the broad width of his shoulders and his lean, jean-clad hips.

The overhead intercom paged Dr. Varek to the surgical wing, hurtling her back to the flurry of activity surrounding her. She turned in time to see Ian Brandt walking through the lobby. He was headed out, apparently, but he hadn't gone out the main hospital entrance. Instead, he'd made a point of coming through the ER. His obsidian eyes pinned hers, making her mouth go dry again.

"Stay the hell away from my wife," he ordered in passing.

CHAPTER NINE

"GUESS WHO I pulled over on Peachtree last night," one uniformed cop said to the other as they passed through the precinct bullpen, their voices carrying. "Janet Jackson."

"No shit? What for?"

"One of her headlights was out."

Ryan saw Mateo look up from his paperwork and roll his eyes despite the snickering around the room. It was an old joke.

Outside, a wash of eggplant and mauve had replaced the previously blue sky as day faded closer to evening. Detectives had begun to filter out while uniforms working the night shift were assembling for roll call. Ryan peered between the window blinds as he completed his phone conversation. Watching the last of the downtown's extended rush hour, he sat on the edge of his desk, handset tucked between his shoulder and ear. Ballistics had come in on the nine mil.

"Not a match," he said as he hung up. There had been

no silencer on the firearm, something he'd hoped had meant nothing.

"Damn," Mateo muttered. "It's still a good bust, Ry. Two kilos of meth and other drugs, not to mention a dozen guns."

But it hadn't gotten them any closer to identifying Nate's killer.

The sound of a door being closed hard caught his attention. Seth Kimmel had exited Thompson's office. He shot a lethal glare at Ryan before stalking into the corridor, apparently aware he had been the one to speak to the captain. Ryan didn't care. He'd had the reprimand coming. Mateo rose from where he'd been seated at his desk and walked over. He had heard about the altercation.

"I hope Thompson gave him a formal write-up and not just an ass-chewing."

Ryan grunted his agreement. Word was that it wouldn't be the first one in Kimmel's file. There had already been civilian complaints about discourteousness and excessive force.

"As long as you're cowboyed up again ..." Mateo indicated the firearm that had been returned a short time ago and now lay in an open drawer of Ryan's desk. "Want to make a last call?"

"Where?"

"Old Fourth Ward. Lamar Simmons just walked into The Copper Coin. The bartender sent me a text. He's holed up with a bottle and two of his *ladies* in the back room."

Simmons was a person of interest in the case of an

eighteen-year-old prostitute strangled and left in a Dumpster behind Philips Arena. A known pimp, he had been lying low, and the two detectives wanted to talk to him. They had suspected he'd show up eventually at one of his regular spots and had put the word out.

Considering the news regarding the confiscated nine mil, Ryan figured they might as well make progress somewhere.

"Let's go." He got to his feet and returned the Glock to his holster. Since he'd had to wait for clearance following the Purvis Street raid, he'd had no choice but to spend most of the day riding a desk, completing forms and working tips by phone. He had cabin fever. On another sour note, they'd learned the shotgun house couldn't be connected to Quintavius Roberts, since its deed belonged to the deceased grandmother of one of the lower-ranked gang members. Quintavius was safe unless the kid implicated him, which was doubtful. Pooch had made a clean break as well, so far evading capture. But with the seizure, the HB2s had lost a serious amount of revenue potential.

"How's the arm?" Mateo asked as they walked out to the parking lot in the encroaching dusk.

"I'll live."

They stopped as Kimmel's squad car wheeled past. He gunned the powerful engine and squealed its tires as he used its light bar to cut through the traffic on Baker Street.

"Dickhead," Mateo grouched.

As they reached the Impala, another unit pulled up beside them in the busy lot. Randall Kirkpatrick, a veteran cop who was serving as FTO for one of the rookies, sat behind the wheel, his much younger charge in the passenger seat. Ryan and Mateo spoke to them as they got out.

"Heard about the raid on Purvis," Kirkpatrick said. "Bangers jumping off roofs and shooting on the way down. That's some real Spider-Man shit."

"You know it." Mateo opened the Impala's driver-side door.

"Hey, Winter, you still on decent terms with your ex?"

The query took Ryan by surprise. "Yeah."

"Good for you. I can't stand mine. You might want to give her some advice, then. Stay out of Ian Brandt's business."

Cars horns blared on the adjacent street. The name was unfamiliar. "Who?"

"Entrepreneur—a skeezy one," Mateo supplied. "I saw an article on him a few weeks back. The paper was kissing his ass like it does every pseudo-celebrity in *Hotlanta*."

Kirkpatrick nodded. "That's him. He has legitimate businesses—recording studios that cater to the hip-hop crowd, fancy restaurants and a slew of commercial real estate investments. But he also runs a few enterprises the city looks the other way on—Suede and a few other titty bars. He's connected, and he contributes *big* to local politicians, some of the more corrupt ones, if you know what I mean. The down low is that he's got underworld ties—drugs, money laundering, not that he's ever been locked up for it. He's not someone to mess around with."

Ryan frowned. Suede was a new adult entertainment lounge. It had a growing reputation as a hot spot as well as a magnet for trouble, including prostitution and drugs. "How's Lydia involved with this guy?"

Officer Seavers spoke. He was a P2, a boot, in the second phase of his probation period. "We went to Mercy Hospital this morning to check out a spousal-abuse situation. It turned out to be Brandt's wife. She refused to file charges. Your wife—I mean, your ex—was pretty worked up about it."

Brandt must be whom Lydia had gotten into a confrontation with at the hospital. "*Was* the wife abused?"

"She was banged up pretty good." Kirkpatrick lifted his uniform cap and scratched his graying head before replacing it. "But like the kid here said, she denies her husband's responsible. Insisted she fell down the stairs, which the good doctor wasn't buying. You know how it is. If the wife won't ask for help, it's none of our business."

He traded good-natured insults with another cop headed into the precinct, then returned to the conversation. "Anyway, I thought you'd want to know."

"Thanks."

Kirkpatrick and Seavers departed. Overhead, lights flickered on around the fenced-in compound. Ryan processed the information, the air around him holding the odor of exhaust fumes from the street.

"You want to go back in?" Mateo asked. "Look this guy up?"

Ryan understood the law regarding domestic violence. But he also knew Lydia's sensitivity to it. Such cases in the ER had always been particularly upsetting for her, reopening wounds from her past. Her mother had been a victim, her father's verbal and physical abuse coloring much of Lydia's childhood until Nina Costa had finally left him, taking Lydia and her younger sister, Natalie, with her. He imagined the run-in Lydia probably had with Brandt. Still, duty called. "Let's get to Simmons before he drops off the radar again. I'll check Brandt out when we get back."

Inside the car, Mateo's voice was tentative as he started the engine. "You and Lydia are talking these days. That's good, right?"

Ryan grimaced as he used his injured arm to secure the seat belt. "It's just the situation—Nate's murder, the trip to the ER this morning. It's been throwing us together."

"But it's a start."

He didn't respond, instead busying himself with looking for the antibiotic prescription he had put in the glove box, something he'd get filled at the all-night pharmacy on the way home. Still, he was aware of Mateo's lingering gaze on him as they pulled from the lot.

Partners became close by necessity. Aside from Adam, Mateo knew him better than anyone, knew just how hard he had taken Tyler's death. While Lydia retreated to New Orleans, Ryan had returned to work not too long after, seeking refuge in the job's routine as soon as the on-staff shrink would clear him. He had believed it was the only way to hold himself together. But he'd also known Mateo had served as something of a babysitter for him, making sure he was stable and focused enough not to endanger lives.

The truth was, he'd been a mess.

Mateo had put up with a lot. But he was also a husband, a father … he'd understood. An empty feeling inside him, Ryan shoved the located prescription into his jeans pocket. The police scanner on the dashboard crackled to life, the provided code indicating a public nuisance complaint farther down on International. Something for the uniforms to handle.

"She still cares about you, man." Mateo hung a sharp left, passing through the tail end of a yellow light at the intersection. He glanced over at him, his expression earnest. "She'll come around. Evie thinks so, too. You've both been through the worst kind of hell, but you belong together. Anyone can see that."

Ryan let go of a sigh, staring out through the windshield. Adam knew. Mateo might as well, too.

"She's seeing someone," he said quietly.

There really was no response Mateo could give. With a soft curse, he accelerated the car.

The interview with Simmons had taken longer than anticipated, the pimp's uncooperative attitude earning him a trip to the precinct. And while his alibi was sketchy, there currently wasn't enough evidence to hold him. Two hours later, he'd swaggered out onto the sidewalk, accompanied by his defense attorney. The two women he'd been with at the bar had been waiting for him out front. Ryan's gut told him Simmons was guilty as sin, although proving it would be another matter. Nor did drug-addicted prostitutes rank high on the overworked department's priority list. But LaShonda Butler had a heartbroken mother who wanted answers. He didn't plan on giving up.

He thought of the nine mil from that morning's raid that hadn't been a match.

He didn't plan on giving up on Nate, either.

At the moment, however, he sat at his desk in front of the computer. Mateo was gone, the lights lowered around the building's interior, and only one other detective remained, absorbed in his own paper load. The background check was unauthorized, but Kirkpatrick's warning about Ian Brandt had been on his mind. As an ER doctor, Lydia was no stranger to confrontations with patients or their families, but it was pretty clear she'd been upset by the exchange.

He found nothing on Brandt in a criminal history check in the National Crime Information Center database. But moving to its Protective Orders files, Ryan located his name twice. Two women had filed restraining orders against him, one not too long ago in Atlanta and another in Boca Raton five years earlier. Not good news.

Closing out of the database, he conducted a general Web search that generated a landslide of hits. Interspersed with the PR and marketing spin, including Brandt's participation on several entrepreneurial and nonprofit boards, Ryan found what he was looking for. According to several articles, Brandt had been named in local investigations on two separate occasions—one related to money laundering and one an assault, but he could find no mention of actual arraignments. Not that it mattered. He had been a cop long enough to know that cash and connections, as well as highly paid attorneys, could often make such things go away.

A short time later, he turned off the monitor, hoping Lydia's involvement with Brandt was done. If the wife had refused to file charges, her entanglement should end there.

It was nearly ten. He said good-night to the remaining detective and walked out through the lobby. Adam stood talking with a clerk at the reception desk. He was in uniform.

"What're you doing here?" Ryan asked.

"Transfer from my zone to yours. Background check at a traffic stop showed three active warrants. You have a detective here with dibs on the guy. I'm just waiting on papers." He hitched a thumb toward the hall that led to the restrooms. "And for my partner."

Adam noticed Ryan's bandaged forearm. "What happened?"

"A disagreement with a window. I lost." Ryan filled him in on the raid, including their failure to locate the murder weapon.

"Tough luck," Adam said seriously. He shifted his stance to allow two officers escorting a struggling arrestee to pass. The handcuffed male shouted obscenities. Adam shook his head as he accepted the transfer papers from the clerk. "It's a full moon. The nut jobs are out."

"Any interference getting Molly to the station last night?"

"It was late so I just gave her a ride home."

Ryan raised his eyebrows.

"We had another beer at her place and hung out. Could've been you, man." He changed the subject. "Hey, there's a group of us getting together to watch the game on Saturday night. You in?"

Ryan thought of his caseload. Uniforms worked assigned shifts while detectives generally worked around the clock. "It depends. I'll let you know."

Adam's partner exited the restroom. Nodding a greeting to him, Ryan watched as the two officers departed through the precinct's front doors. Then signing out at the desk, he walked to the rear compound to his SUV. After stopping at the all-night pharmacy to fill the prescription, he took Peachtree to Ponce de Leon Avenue, known to the locals as simply Ponce. The street was a mishmash of older deteriorating buildings interspersed with new loft condominiums and strip malls. Ryan traveled up it a couple of miles, going past the newly renovated Ponce City Market before turning right onto North Highland Avenue and into Inman Park. Reaching his house, he pulled into the single-car driveway. The anesthetic used for the sutures had worn off hours ago, and his arm throbbed. He was dead-tired, he realized, recalling just how little sleep he'd gotten the previous night.

Parking under Tess's unlit apartment window, he went up onto the bungalow's front porch and, using his key, inside. The security system wasn't on—not unusual since Tess detested any type of electronics and typically left it off after she'd done housework around the place. Sure enough, she'd been here, he noticed as he dropped the pharmacy bag onto a table in the shadowed entry. She had left a note there, letting him know she'd fed Max and given his insulin injection.

He's too fat. Don't let him talk you into feeding him again, she'd written in her flowery script. But the cat was nowhere around.

Walking into the dark living room, Ryan called to him, sliding off his shoulder holster with his gun inside it and laying it on the sofa. Reaching for the lamp on the end table, he froze at the metallic sound of a clip dropping into a chamber. His blood iced as the tip of a gun barrel pressed behind his right ear.

"You've been so worried about two dead cops," a guttural voice said. "Almost like you knew you'd be next."

CHAPTER TEN

RYAN RECOGNIZED THE street-hardened rasp. Heart thudding, he straightened cautiously and lifted his hands to his sides. "I'm unarmed."

Pooch pressed the barrel harder. "You think I give a fuck?"

Eager to get payback for Antoine's shooting, the police had issued a BOLO—a *be on the lookout*—for Pooch following that morning's raid. Patrol cars had been scouring parts of the city where he was known to frequent. Ryan wondered how long he had actually been *here*, waiting for him.

Tess. He felt a wave of dread. She had been in the house. "There was a woman—"

"That your momma?"

"No. She cleans the place, that's all—"

"Too bad. I like the idea of *Detective Winter* being a momma's boy." Nudging Ryan forward with the gun barrel, Pooch steered them away from the porch light filtering in through the front windows. Out of view of possible passersby on the street. Ryan looked around for some sign of Tess, hoping the note meant she had come and gone without incident. He didn't want to think of Pooch confronting her.

The pressure left his skull. "Turn around slow ..."

He obeyed. Gun trained, walking backward, Pooch scooped up the holster and weapon from the sofa and tossed them out of reach. His eyes glinted like fire in the shadows. "Good as your word, huh, Winter? Had Narco rain down hell on us. Turned up the heat like you said you would. I got some advice for you, Detective. Never confuse a single defeat with a *final* one."

Throat dry, Ryan met Pooch's hard stare. "Narcotics was coming for you regardless. They've been waiting for the opportunity. The meth shipment gave it to them."

"See, I think you had a little more to do with it than that." He gripped the gun sideways, obviously enjoying the control he held.

Tension tightened Ryan's chest. If he could distract him, he could make a run at him, but his rational mind knew it would almost certainly result in a lethal gunshot. "So what do you want, Pooch?" he asked calmly, despite the adrenaline pumping through him.

The other man's mouth stretched into a sneer. "What I *want* is to watch your brains explode all over that wall!"

Still, he didn't pull the trigger. Instead, he made a show of taking in the place. He walked a few steps before sending the lamp on the end table crashing to the floor. Picking up the framed family photo that had been next to it, he looked it over. "This your old lady? Your kid?"

Ryan's jaw clenched. The thug's hands on the treasured image burned at him.

"I asked you a question!" Still pointing the gun, he took a menacing step closer, his raised voice echoing off the high ceiling.

"It's my ex-wife."

"Ex, huh? Couldn't keep her satisfied? Bet I could." With a leering grin, he threw the photo. Ryan flinched as it missed him by inches, hitting china and glass items on the bookshelf and sending shards spraying. Pooch tilted his head, his raw-boned features hardening. "What? You ain't gonna beg me? Plead for your life?"

Staring down the weapon's barrel, Ryan felt his lungs squeeze. Still, he spoke the truth. "You're here for a reason. If it's to kill me, then my begging isn't going to change that. But the cop you shot? He's going to be okay. You take me out, and it's a whole different story."

Pooch closed in like a predator, the powerful handgun now aimed at Ryan's face. His heartbeat thrashed in his ears. He battled the urge to raise his arm in self-defense, a natural but pointless instinct. Few survived gunshots to the head at close range. No one would want to. Nerves crackling and stomach sour, he prepared to make a grab for the gun. At least he would go down fighting.

"How 'bout we do this nice and slow, *Detective*?" Smiling coldly, Pooch flicked the gun's barrel like a laser pointer. "One to the knee, one to the gut. You can *feel that* for a while before I put one in your head. I can make it last for hours—make a *sandwich* in your goddamn kitchen while you lie on the floor and bleed. You don't want to beg for your life, motherfucker? How 'bout I make you beg *to die*?"

He was close enough now that even in the darkness Ryan could see his bloodshot eyes, their sclera threaded with veins. Spittle flew from his lips as he continued railing at him. It was time.

Heart clenching, he sprang forward, grabbing Pooch's arm and forcing it up. The gun fired into the ceiling as the two men struggled for control. Ryan's dress shoes slipped on the wood flooring, giving Pooch's elbow the opportunity to jab him hard in the ribs. He staggered, catching himself against the hunt table just as the gang member backhanded him with the gun's barrel. Jagged pain shot through his skull. He went down, sprawling. His vision blurred.

"Lucky for you, it ain't up to me." Pooch hovered somewhere above him. "You hit the lottery, asshole. Quintavius is pissed, but he's gonna let you live."

Ryan listened through the encroaching haze, the floor tilting.

"*Jewel Magill.* That's why you're still breathing. But Quintavius wants you to understand one thing." He punctuated his words. "We ain't killed no cops, you hear me? *Yet.* Now step off this."

Ryan attempted to right himself, but a hard kick to his side sent him back down. Spit hit the back of his neck. He heard the thud of fleeing feet and a door opening in the house's rear. By the time he'd regained his equilibrium enough to pull himself up, tires screeched outside. Ryan stumbled to the window, but the car had already disappeared down the tree-lined street.

"Tess!" he called into the silent house. He checked the rooms one by one, finding only Max in an open closet, hiding from the intruder. The feline's yellow eyes blinked at him. Pushing aside dizziness, Ryan ran outside. Shouting Tess's name, he'd gotten halfway up the stairs to her apartment when he heard her voice in the driveway below.

"Ryan, what on earth?"

Relief threaded through him as he went back down. She wore a red tunic with gold beading over her leggings. Stacks of bangle bracelets clinked as he clasped her upper arms.

"Where were you?"

"The Inman Drip," she said, referring to a nearby coffee shop. "They had a poetry reading—"

"Did you see a car?"

"No. I took the back way." Like many in-town dwellers, Tess didn't own a vehicle. She pointed to a gap between the garage and hedges bordering the neighbor's yard. Although the neighborhood was returning to gentrification, crime remained a problem, and he had warned her about using the unlit route in the dark. Ryan grimaced as he felt the side of his head. He wasn't bleeding, but a painful lump had formed. His side ached from Pooch's kick.

"Child, are you all right? What happened to your arm?"

He didn't answer, instead digging his phone from his

jeans pocket. Holding up one hand in a silencing gesture, he made a call to 9-1-1, identifying himself with his badge number and explaining to the dispatcher what had just occurred. But without a car description, apprehension was unlikely. The vehicle had gone left on the main road, he knew that much from the sound. It had probably taken Boulevard to the nearby interstate, already slipping from the area.

Ryan felt a growing uncertainty. Quintavius had gone to a lot of trouble to assure him the HB2s weren't involved in the shootings. Along with their failure to match the confiscated nine mil to the homicides, he had to open himself to the possibility that the key scratches weren't a connection to the gang. Just a dead end he'd been blindly chasing.

"That was a *gunshot* I heard instead of a car backfiring," Tess fretted, her face pale as he disconnected the call. "This is all my fault. You've told me time after time to reset the alarm—"

He shook his head. "Then he would've been waiting for me outside."

Jewel Magill. Ryan knew the name. She'd been a public schoolteacher, a decent woman brutally beaten and shot dead during a home invasion. After a two-day investigation, he'd made the arrest, one of his first after being promoted to detective. That had been years ago, before he'd been partnered with Mateo. He wondered what connection Quintavius had to her.

Regardless, she was the reason he was breathing right

now. Pooch had gotten the jump on him. He was damn lucky to be alive.

*

Lydia pointed the bungalow out to the cab driver, paid the fare and emerged under a violet blanket of night. Passing the darkened squad car that sat on the street, she went up the ivy-edged brick steps and onto the porch with its two-seater swing. She felt fuzzy from the wine she'd been having but Tess had called, relaying what had happened and asking her to come since Ryan had stubbornly refused medical care. She'd been in her pajamas, but had quickly redressed and called for a cab.

The door opened before she could knock. The two uniformed officers who exited greeted her politely as they went past, one of them calling her by name. Stepping inside, Lydia's pulse sped up at the destruction—the scattered glass and fallen plaster. She looked up at the hole that indicated the bullet's path, suspecting it had already been pried from the ceiling and taken into evidence.

"Where is he?" she asked as Tess entered the room.

"He went to take a shower. Thank you for coming, Lydia. He'll have my hide for calling you, but he needs someone to look at him."

"You did the right thing," she assured her as Max rubbed against her ankle.

"The crime scene people have come and gone. I've been trying to clean up, but Ryan wanted to talk to the officers in here alone." She shook her head, glancing around in dismay at the mess. "In my day, criminals tried to *avoid* police. They didn't come looking for them. He doesn't think anything was taken except for some cash—thank goodness for the security box."

The box she referred to was in the master bedroom closet. The small safe bolted to the floor was where Ryan had kept his service and backup gun safely out of Tyler's reach, as well as important papers and a few irreplaceable items.

They talked for a few minutes, until Tess twisted her hands together and released a tired sigh. "Well, now that you're here, I'm going up to paint for a bit. It settles my nerves. Let Ryan know I'll take care of all this in the morning."

"Good night."

"I'd tell you not to surprise him in there, but it's nothing you haven't seen before." With a wink that belied the stress on her features, she patted Lydia's arm and exited the house.

Lydia watched from the window until the other woman was safely up to her apartment, then closed her eyes and ran a hand over her face. Blinking to clear her head, arms crossed over her chest, she wandered to the hall's threshold. The master bedroom door was closed, and she could hear the faint rush of water behind it, coming from the en-suite bathroom. She knew she should call to Ryan to let him know she was here, but instead she remained silent, her eyes fastening on the other closed door.

She felt a familiar ache.

When she had made the decision to move out, Tyler's bedroom had remained untouched, as if he might somehow return to them. She had carefully avoided it in her visits since. Lydia had no idea if it was empty now, if Ryan had finally packed away his clothing and toys.

Guilt tightened her throat. It was something else she had left him to deal with alone.

Biting her lip, swarmed by bittersweet images, she retreated to the kitchen to look for a broom.

She had just risen from her knees, where she'd been sweeping up broken glass and plaster, when Ryan spoke her name. Hands shoved into the pockets of his jeans, his hair damp, he had on a shirt, but it was unbuttoned and untucked, revealing hard pectorals and a sprinkling of chest hair. He clearly had thought Tess had left and he was alone.

"Tess called you," he said apologetically. As she put down the dustpan and came closer, he clasped the back of his neck. "Damn it. It's late. That wasn't necessary."

"She said you refused paramedics."

"I didn't need them. It's not that big of a deal." He indicated his bandaged arm, scowling faintly. "And no offense, but I've had my share of being poked and prodded for one day."

Looking at him, Lydia pressed her lips together. "Well, as long as I'm here, why don't I have a look at you? I promise I'll keep the poking and prodding to a minimum."

Her eyes locked with his until he finally released a sigh of resignation and went to sit on the sofa. Tess had provided her a rundown of his injuries on the phone.

Sitting beside him, she ran her fingers carefully through his hair, locating the swollen area on the side of his skull. "Did you lose consciousness?"

"No."

"Any dizziness or nausea?"

"Some dizziness, but it's gone now." He seemed edgy and preoccupied. Extracting the penlight she'd brought with her from her purse, she asked a few questions to check his concentration and memory as she examined his pupils. They appeared to be of equal size and reacted well to light.

"Mind if I have a look at your side? Tess said you were holding it."

Releasing another breath, he turned slightly toward her and opened his shirt further. Lydia scooted closer, aware of the peculiarity of their situation. There had always been a strong physical attraction between them. Despite her medical training, she had an involuntary response to the familiarity of his broad chest, the flat stomach rippled with strength. She examined the still-forming bruise below his ribs, noticing his flinch when she pressed against it.

"I'd like to get a CT and an ultrasound as a precaution." She reached again for her purse and the cell phone inside it. "I'll call ahead and go with you so you won't have to wait—"

"Lydia." Ryan's fingers encircled her outstretched wrist, halting her. She straightened, instant heat swirling low in her belly at his touch. His features were mere inches from hers.

"*I'm fine.* I don't need any of that, honey," he emphasized in a low voice, seeming not to notice the once-familiar endearment. He studied her. "Have you been drinking?"

Lydia felt her face heat at the unexpected inquiry. He must have smelled it on her breath despite the mint she'd had, or picked up on some other tell.

"I was ... out," she lied, self-conscious. She stopped herself from making up something more elaborate and added a little defensively, "I'm not on call."

Releasing her wrist, he clenched his jaw slightly. "Then I'm even sorrier Tess called you and ruined your night."

Embarrassed, she wondered if he had noticed her physical response to his closeness, as well, whether it had been as evident as the buzz she'd believed she had been so expertly hiding. Rising from the couch and searching for a change of subject, she asked, "How did he get in?"

"Tess had been here and didn't reset the alarm. He broke a window in the mudroom and reached through it to open the door."

"He's someone you arrested?"

"He shot Antoine Clark this morning."

Lydia felt a rise of nerves as she made the connection. "He's part of the gang you've been looking into in connection with Nate's murder."

"The job's still the job, Lyd," Ryan reminded tiredly as he touched the lump on his scalp. "His street name's Pooch. He came here to convince me the HB2s aren't involved. I've already talked to Mateo and told him to be on alert, but I think he got his message across here."

She frequently saw the gang's tatted-up members—as

well as their victims—as patients inside the ER. Bullet and knife wounds were common. "Do you believe him?"

Sitting forward on the couch, Ryan picked up their family photo that lay on the coffee table. Broken glass spider-webbed over the image. He put it back down, frowning. "We weren't able to find a match among the guns confiscated in the raid. That doesn't prove innocence—the weapon could've been stashed somewhere else—but I'm having my doubts. I was following a hunch. I might be sending us in the wrong direction. Wasting time."

He stood and paced, frustrated.

"You've had a long day, Ryan." Moving closer, she touched his bandaged arm. He'd gotten the gauze damp, and the pad underneath it probably needed changing. "Those sutures were supposed to be kept dry for twenty-four hours. Dr. Rossman gave you home care instructions?"

He shrugged, his features hard. "I needed a shower. The son of a bitch spit on me. I wanted to scrub my skin off."

"Do you still have the first-aid kit? I can redress your arm. You're probably sore, and it's going to be difficult doing it yourself."

He agreed with a sigh, indicating for her to follow. A weighted silence hung between them as they passed the closed door to Tyler's room.

Ryan led her into the master bedroom. The tasteful neutral tones and large, antique sleigh bed they'd once shared hadn't changed. Lydia couldn't help it—she wondered if other women had been in the bed since her departure.

The adjoining bathroom was still humid from his shower. It was an add-on completed during the renovations, as they had desired a larger bathroom than the one in the hall that was typical of a 1920s bungalow. Constructed of white tile and gray sandstone, with vintage wood vanities and an oversize shower, it had been a serene place to unwind. They had also done more than relax here. The intimate memories she'd tried to dodge in the bedroom confronted her again, and she flashed on an image of their lovemaking in the large stall, her legs wrapped around Ryan's hips and her back against the cool tiles as he thrust into her, water jets raining down on them. The recollection of hard muscles under wet, sleek skin, his mouth on hers, shallowed her breathing.

Searching for a distraction, she bent to retrieve the white tin of household medical supplies from under the vanity. Placing it next to the basin, she rummaged through the gauze and sterile dressings, hydrogen peroxide and antibiotic ointments. Lydia froze as her fingers landed on the small box of adhesive bandages. The carton with cheerful cartoon characters on its front had caught her off guard, squeezing her heart. Standing behind her, Ryan silently placed a hand on her shoulder. Lydia found her breath again and concentrated on her task.

A short time later, as she used scissors to remove the gauze from his arm, he spoke. "I hear you had a run-in with Ian Brandt."

Examining the sutures, she pressed her lips together,

thinking of the two officers from the hospital. "I'd forgotten cops gossip like a bunch of old women."

"Steer clear of him, Lyd."

Anger seeped through her as she carefully dabbed at the sutures with a hydrogen peroxide-soaked cotton ball. "He's beating his wife—"

"Hey." His tone was firm, drawing her eyes up to his. "I *mean* it. The guy's bad news. Let it go. We both know in our jobs—"

"Some things are out of our control," she finished on a sigh.

It was a wisdom they'd reminded each other of often, after a long and depressing hospital shift, after a particularly grim crime scene. It was why emergency workers so often ended up together, married to one another. They each understood the job. Lydia dropped the cotton ball into the wastebasket. Glancing up at him again, she felt her chest tighten at the concern on his face. After everything that had happened between them, he remained dutifully protective of her.

"Why are you so nice to me?" Her voice trembled faintly, her question heartfelt. "When I … I haven't always been the same to you."

At her question, his blue eyes darkened, emotion seeming to travel over his features. Then Ryan's hand rose to her face, his thumb stroking over her cheekbone. Lydia's heart thudded, her throat going dry as they stared at one another. She wobbled a tiny bit when he removed his touch.

"You shouldn't be driving, Lydia," he admonished.

She felt another stain of embarrassment creep over her skin. "I … didn't. I took a cab."

He frowned. "From where?"

She didn't respond, not wanting to lie to him a second time but also not wanting him to know the truth—that she'd been at home, drinking alone. She imagined his pity and disapproval, and she didn't want that from him. Instead, she focused on redressing the wound with a new sterile pad and gauze.

"Were you with him tonight?" he asked when she was done, causing her to look back up at him. Small lines of tension had formed around his mouth, his eyes. Lydia stood magnetized.

"No," she whispered.

A voice at the front of the house broke the charged silence enveloping them. Adam. Ryan let go of a soft curse. With a sour feeling in her stomach, Lydia trailed him from the bathroom.

"I heard what went down—" Adam halted upon seeing them in the bedroom doorway. His eyes slid from Lydia to Ryan, his jaw hardening. "What's *she* doing here?"

"Adam," Ryan warned.

Adam hadn't come over to say hello the previous night at McCrosky's, although Lydia had witnessed his cold stare before he'd turned his back on her. Nervously crossing her arms over her chest, she said, "Tess asked me to stop by since he wouldn't go to the ER. He's fine, by the way."

"Is that your diagnosis or his?"

"His," she replied, aware of the animosity in his eyes. Adam appeared intimidating in his uniform. He looked so much like Ryan—similar features, the same tall, lean build. It was like a photo negative, one brother lighter haired and blue-eyed, the other a darker, more mysterious version. Ryan had always been protective of his younger brother, but Lydia knew where she was concerned, their roles reversed.

"You've been showing up a lot lately," Adam pointed out, a subtle bite to his words. "This past weekend here at the house, last night at McCrosky's and now here again. *Just like old times.*"

"Where's your partner?" Ryan interjected.

"Outside in the unit."

"Everything's fine here. You can get back to him and finish your watch." The phone rang from the bedroom. Ryan didn't appear happy. "I have to take that."

He gave Adam a stern look before leaving. Lydia took it as her opportunity. She lowered her gaze and said, "It's good to see you, Adam. If you'll excuse me, I need to call a cab."

Escaping past him to the living room, she removed her cell phone from her purse and contacted the taxi service. But as she gave the street address, she became aware of him watching her from the hall. Once she'd disconnected, he walked to her.

"What the hell are you doing?" he demanded in a low, harsh voice.

She sighed. "I've already explained—"

Adam jabbed a finger back toward the hallway. "He lost Tyler and then he lost *you*. It's taken everything he has to get through this."

Lifting her chin, she felt a stab of pain. "We *both* lost Tyler—"

"That's right," he said tightly. "But you didn't pull your own child out of a pool and perform CPR on him until the paramedics showed up. And you don't wake up every morning knowing he's dead because you let him slip out of your sight for a few minutes."

She swallowed and clenched her jaw.

Adam's voice roughened. "I was here for him when you weren't, Lyd. I saw him tear himself apart. And I can promise you that as much as you blamed him for what happened, he blamed himself a thousand times more."

Lydia pressed a hand against her stomach as his gaze raked over her. "You've had no problem moving on, but now that he's finally started pulling it together without you, you're back to mess him up again, is that it?"

His shoulder radio crackled to life. With a muttered curse, he responded to the dispatcher, letting him know he and his partner were en route. Walking to the door, he shook his head. "You're good at leaving, Lydia. Go back to New Orleans ... or to your goddamn surgeon. And you smell like booze."

For several long moments after the door had closed behind him, she stood motionless, eyes burning and face hot.

Ryan located her a short time later on the porch.

"Sorry. I had to take that call." He stood next to her, bracing his forearms on the railing. Confederate jasmine grew along the nearby brick wall. "A fugitive unit thought they'd cornered Pooch in a rent-by-the-week hotel near the airport. I stayed on the line long enough to find out they had the wrong guy."

"How're you feeling?" she asked, subdued.

Ryan shrugged, watching as a fat moth flew circles around the streetlight. Beyond it, the tree limbs hung heavy with wisteria. "I've got a small headache, is all."

She felt a dull thud inside her own skull. "If the pain persists or worsens, you need to see a doctor immediately. Promise me, Ryan."

He straightened, frowning as the cab pulled in front of the house. "I was going to drive you home."

She forced a small smile, her eyes not quite meeting his. "It's after midnight. I couldn't let you do that."

His sigh held anger. "Adam jumped you. What did he say to you?"

"Nothing he wasn't completely right about," she admitted quietly. She touched his arm. "Good night."

She went down the stairs and climbed into the cab's rear. As it pulled away, she dared to look back. Ryan remained on the porch, his features shadowed, watching her departure.

"Where to, miss?" the cab driver asked in a heavy Indian accent.

Regret tightened her throat. Lydia provided her Buckhead address.

CHAPTER ELEVEN

LOOKING AT HIM, *his face appeared ashen, the once-faint lines deeper and making him seem older than his thirty-six years. Shoulders slouched under his dress shirt, tie loosened at his throat, Ryan stood in the dying sunlight seeping in through the kitchen windows. Around them, casseroles and Bundt cakes brought by well-meaning mourners filled the counters. The low, respectful buzz of conversation wafted from the living room, the voices of her mother and sister among the others.*

"When?" he managed to rasp, seeming dazed.

"Tomorrow ... with them." Lydia's eyes burned from too much crying, not enough sleep. She tried to speak, her words faltering, and tried again. "They've already booked my seat."

Ryan swallowed, his own reddened eyes glazed with fresh pain.

"I've already told the hospital."

He nodded in silent acceptance. "For how long?" His voice trembled.

Hands wrenched together, she glanced away. "I don't know."

"I said, are you all right, miss?"

Lydia looked up, the cab driver's question pulling her back to the present. He studied her from the rearview mirror.

"I'm fine." She sat up straighter to prove she really was.

"You're quiet," he commented as he drove. "Me, I like to talk to stay awake."

He continued elaborating on his work habits as the light ahead of them changed on busy Peachtree Street, flashing from green to yellow and then red. They came to a stop in front of the Fox Theatre, its minarets and onion domes making it look like an opulent mosque among the city buildings if not for the neon marquee advertising an in-town Broadway musical. Lydia watched absently as people wandered the sidewalks, hopping between the still-open restaurants and bars.

"You're from here?" the driver inquired once the cab started up again, still attempting small talk. "Atlanta?"

"Not originally," she responded quietly. "I grew up in New Orleans."

"Ah, *The Big Easy.*" He blew his horn at a jaywalker. "I ask that question all the time—*where are you from?* People work here, they visit here, but they're never *from* here. Do you work?"

"I'm an ER doctor at Mercy Hospital."

His eyebrows rose in the mirror. The information seemed to impress him.

"My son goes to Georgia Tech," he said proudly. "He's in the honors program, studying to be an engineer."

Lydia congratulated him. He chatted on, his monologue eventually fading off into white noise. Instead it was Adam's harsh words she heard echoing inside her.

You're good at leaving, Lydia. Go back to New Orleans ...

She closed her eyes against the justifiable wrath that had been in his voice. After losing Tyler, she *had* needed her mother and sister. But Lydia flinched inwardly at the hard truth. She had also needed to be away from Ryan. It hadn't been possible to look at him without seeing traces of their sweet little boy in his features, without questioning how he could have let the unthinkable happen. Without blaming him. Devastated himself, guilt-stricken, he hadn't fought her decision to return home.

Her abandonment of him seemed so callous to her now, irrational and inexcusable.

A short time later, they reached the cluster of beautiful old churches in Buckhead referred to by the locals as Jesus Junction. Lydia felt a thick tangle of emotion upon seeing the backlit stained-glass windows, the statue of Mary outside the All Saints cathedral. Where Tyler had been christened. Where his funeral mass had been held. She felt a pining ache where she had carried him in her womb. He had been taken from her so suddenly that sometimes it seemed she had only imagined him, imagined loving someone so much.

Much of the weeks following his death remained foggy to her. She'd been inconsolable. Ultimately, she had spent ten days at Tulane Medical Center in New Orleans, diagnosed with an acute emotional collapse, something no one but her mother and sister knew about. At Lydia's plea they'd closed ranks around her, still reeling themselves from the loss of their grandson and nephew. Ryan was aware of the grief counseling but not the hospitalization. She'd begged them not to tell him, not wanting to see him and knowing he would come.

It had been another way of shutting him out.

Weeks later, when she'd finally stabilized enough to return—to her job at the hospital, to him and their too-quiet house—there was a strain in their relationship, a distance between them that couldn't be bridged, although admittedly Ryan had tried. Tyler had been their soul.

She was aware of the staggering statistics, how many couples don't make it through the loss of a child.

A short time later, the cab pulled in front of the towering condominium building, its smoky glass sides glittering with the reflection of city lights. Paying the fare, she went across the plaza and, using the security code, into the lobby. It was late, the concierge already off duty for the night. Surrounded by marble walls and flooring, a chandelier sparkling overhead, she pushed the elevator button to go upstairs.

Once inside her unit, she went into the kitchen, laid her bag on the counter and checked her voice mail. There were two hang-ups, as well as a message from Rick, calling to say he had been thinking about her and that he was looking forward to the upcoming weekend. Lydia sighed tiredly. She had forgotten about the hospital gala on Saturday. Rick had asked her to attend with him weeks ago, had made certain she was off the ER schedule. There would be no getting out of it.

Now that he's finally started pulling it together without you, you're back to mess him up again, is that it?

What was she doing? She ran a hand over her eyes, knowing Adam was right. It had been her choice to let go.

Not wanting to think anymore, her emotions too sharp, Lydia counted the hours before her shift the next day, making sure there was adequate time for the sleeping pill's sluggish effects to wear off. She took it. A thickness in her throat, she poured a glass of wine from the open bottle on the counter, too.

She carried it with her to the bedroom to undress.

CHAPTER TWELVE

———— ◗•●•◖ ————

"JEWEL MAGILL WAS Quintavius's aunt," Ryan said as he entered the bullpen. Shrugging out of his suit jacket, he draped it over the back of his chair, the late-afternoon sun slanting through the window behind him. He'd been tied up in court again for most of the day—the same murder trial as Wednesday, called back after a continuance for cross-examination. Mateo looked up at him from his computer screen.

"I had someone at the newspaper check the archives." He sat behind his desk. "Magill's maiden name was Roberts. The obit listed Quintavius as a surviving nephew. He was around fifteen at the time."

"Six degrees of separation." Mateo removed the glasses he needed for computer work and rubbed his eyes. "Thank God for that, right?"

Reaching to his stacked in-box, Ryan felt the tenderness in his side, a memento from his confrontation with Pooch the previous night. He wondered if they'd seen the last of him, considering the growing bounty on his head. "Any luck with the transactions?"

They had secured both Nate's and John Watterson's credit card records, hoping to find a commonality—perhaps some locale both men had frequented—since they'd been unable to identify any crossover in their arrest logs. Mateo had been comparing the line items while Ryan was in court.

"*Nada*, but I have more to go." Returning the glasses to his nose, he studied the computer screen. "Nate left one mother of a paper trail. Six credit cards. Who needs that many? He put pretty much everything on plastic, right down to convenience-store purchases. On the other hand, Watterson appears to have had a cash-only policy. Only a handful of credit transactions in the six months prior to his death—less than seventy total."

Which meant even if there *was* a connecting physical location, it might not be apparent. Ryan frowned. "Keep looking."

"Chin and Hoyt are helping with the last of the names from Nate's files." Mateo handed a folder to an admin clerk who'd come by for it. "We're scraping the bottom of the barrel by now, but they said they'd call if anyone raised a flag. How'd it go in court?"

The case was a robbery-turned-homicide in Grant Park that had occurred five months earlier. As the senior arresting detective, Ryan had been subpoenaed to testify. "Unless the DA's office blows it, we're looking at a murder one conviction."

"Hope they don't let him plea down."

Ryan would be glad to see the perp—a violent repeat offender—permanently off the streets. But the testimony had taken time away from his current investigations, particularly Nate's. The first forty-eight hours were critical in solving homicides. Statistically, the majority of closed cases had suspects identified within the first twenty-four. With Nate, they were at a solid week.

Impatience gnawing at him, Ryan had picked up the handset on his console to reach Chin for an update himself when Mateo snapped his fingers. "Shit, I almost forgot. You probably haven't heard since you've been in court all day."

"Heard what?"

"Kimmel. He's on suspension pending an internal investigation. As of last night."

Ryan put the receiver back down.

"He pulled a car over on the Fourteenth Street ramp— failure to yield or something. There was an altercation that ended with him Tasering the hell out of some guy."

"What did the dash cam show?"

"I don't know. Thompson's not talking, and Kimmel was riding alone since he's still between partners. But the civilian had to be hospitalized, and he's screaming police brutality. The news stations are requesting the video."

Ryan glanced at the closed door to the captain's office. Normally, he took such allegations with a grain of salt, but he knew firsthand Kimmel was a ticking bomb. He went back to trying to reach Chin.

"Hold down the fort," he said a short time later, standing and retrieving his coat as Mateo returned from the break room.

"Chin and Hoyt like somebody?"

"Unfortunately, no. But since I'm free now, I'm going to take one myself. Leonard Salyers."

Salyers had been an illegal bookmaker who at one time had a dozen corner bookies working for him until he'd been the target of a Vice sting led by Nate. After being released from prison, he'd opened a small auto repair shop on Clairmont Road. Salyers was low on their list since he'd been out for two years and had kept out of trouble, but they were running out of names.

"Want me to come with you?" Mateo asked. "Salyers used to be a tough customer."

"What you're doing's important. I can handle this alone."

Stepping outside, the June heat hitting him like a furnace as he pushed through the precinct doors, Ryan battled discouragement. In the past week, they'd canvassed the area around Nate's condo building three different times, interviewed more than fifty perps from his files and conducted a raid in search of the murder weapon. None of it had panned out.

He thought about last night and Lydia, too. It didn't help with his mood.

There was another stop he planned to make after he saw Salyers.

*

The repair shop had appeared legit, with vehicles on hydraulic jacks, mechanics in overalls speaking rapid Spanish and Salyers himself under the hood of an antiquated Mercedes when Ryan arrived. The grizzled ex-con had professed no sorrow over Nate's death, but the grease stains under his fingernails indicated he was immersed in his new career. He'd also had an alibi for the night of the murder. His daughter had been giving birth at a suburban hospital north of the city.

There were details to verify, but Ryan's gut told him another name could be ruled out.

Driving on tree-lined Clairmont, he checked in with Mateo, who was on the interstate fighting the early-evening exodus from downtown, on his way to a birthday party for his seventy-year-old mother. Ryan ended the call when he reached the small ranch house on Candler Street that Adam rented. Located on the perimeter of Agnes Scott College in Decatur, it was leased to him by the women's university at a reduced rate since it encouraged having law enforcement nearby. Adam hadn't returned his call from earlier that day, and it appeared now that he wasn't home.

Ryan knew he wasn't on duty and suspected where he could find him. Making a U-turn, he headed toward Decatur's town square, which was bordered by century-old brick buildings that housed funky music venues, restaurants and bars, many of which were just coming alive for the weekend. Spotting Adam's open-air Jeep, he parked in the last available spot.

His brother was nothing if not predictable. If he wasn't on duty, he came to Ocho's on Friday nights for beer and Mexican food.

Dropping coins into the meter, the air heavy and warm, Ryan shouldered his way into the open courtyard at the restaurant's rear. Already, the patio teemed with people. Small white lights hung overhead from a massive oak tree, and several tables had dogs sitting underneath, on leashes held by their owners. The area was known for its canine-friendly atmosphere.

Adam stood with a group near the bar. Ryan recognized several of them as officers from his brother's precinct. Wearing jeans and a golf shirt, Adam held a beer bottle, his back to him.

"Hey," he said, surprised when Ryan appeared. Adam introduced him around. "You want a beer?"

"No, thanks ... Actually, I want to talk to you," Ryan said once the others had directed their attention elsewhere. "In case you didn't pick up on that from the message I left on your cell."

Adam frowned. He still wore sunglasses, although the sun had already retreated from the sky, leaving in its wake a fading wash of robin's-egg blue.

"What did you say to Lydia last night?" His tone must have told Adam this wasn't the place for their conversation. He walked from the courtyard with Ryan following. They moved to an alley on the restaurant's side.

"I knew she'd go crying to you," Adam grumbled.

"She didn't cry to me about anything. But I could tell she was upset when she left. You said something to her, and I want to know what."

With a jerky motion, Adam took a pull from his beer. "I'm just trying to look out for you, all right? She doesn't need to be coming around again—"

"That's none of your business," Ryan cut in sharply.

Adam took off his sunglasses, disbelief hardening his expression. "The *hell* it isn't. You're my *brother*. I know how bad things got." His voice roughened. "I walked in on you the night she left for New Orleans, or have you forgotten that, too?"

Ryan nearly winced, his face heating as Adam continued.

"Let me remind you. You were just sitting there on the floor in the dark with a bottle of whiskey and your gun beside you."

He hadn't forgotten. The recollection of Adam kneeling next to him, his hand on his back as he wept, hardened his gut. He'd done his best to stay strong for Lydia, but with her departure, he had come apart. The empty house, his grief and guilt ... it had been too much. Adam had taken vacation time to stay with him.

"I don't want to talk about this," he said tightly. Shoulders hunched, Ryan shifted away, but Adam blocked him, his face inches from his.

Adam lowered his voice. "I know how much you loved him ... *we all did*." He paused heavily, pain in his eyes. "But what happened was an *accident*. It could've been Lydia with him that day, but you never would've run out on her. No matter how much you were hurting, you would've done everything in your power to make sure she got through it. And you sure as hell wouldn't have punished her by getting on a plane and leaving."

Adam's jaw clenched. "I keep hoping one day you'll move on, Ry. Let her go. Get out of that house with its goddamn ghosts—"

"I appreciate your concern, *I do*." His heart hurt at Adam's fierce loyalty. He placed his hands on his brother's shoulders. "You don't have to worry about me. But just cut Lydia some slack, all right? She's … still more fragile than you think." He wished he could make Adam understand. "That's all I came to say."

Ryan dropped his hands. Adam frowned at him, seeming on the verge of a rebuttal. But instead he released a resigned sigh. "Whatever. I just don't want to see you hurt more than you've already been. Or putting your life on hold another damn minute for her."

"Nothing's on hold."

Adam appeared doubtful. He looked off to the courtyard. "If we're finished here, I've got a date who just showed up."

Ryan followed his gaze. A pretty redhead had joined Adam's group at the bar. She tossed her hair over her shoulder and lifted her hand in greeting. Adam nodded back. There was no denying his brother got around. But he was young and single. Ryan supposed he had been like that once.

"Who's this one? Another girl from the gym?"

"This one's different," Adam said, actually sounding serious. "Her name's Rachel. She's a kindergarten teacher. I met her awhile ago at a youth field day when they asked some of the cops from my precinct to volunteer. She made me work for it, man. I'd pretty much given up on getting her to go out with me, and then she finally texted this morning … Hey, if we're good, why don't you stay for a beer?"

He shook his head.

"C'mon. A big-time homicide detective might impress her." He indicated Ryan's bandaged forearm, visible with the sleeves of his dress shirt rolled up. "You can play up the wounded-hero thing. Put in a good word for me."

"I'm not going to horn in on your date."

"I'm not offering to share her," Adam said with a grin. "It's kind of a group thing tonight, anyway. We're just hanging out. Who knows? You might actually have some fun for once. You can prove to me nothing's on hold."

They'd begun walking back to the patio when Ryan's cell phone rang. He returned to the alley to take the call as Adam went on without him to meet his date. A sick feeling speared through him at what he was told over the airwaves.

Returning to his vehicle, acoustic-guitar music wafting from one of the bars, he called Adam's cell to let him know he wouldn't be staying, after all. There must have been something in his voice, because Adam said, "Christ. There's another one, isn't there?"

He felt the gathering tension in his shoulders worsen. Climbing into the SUV, he placed the mobile strobe light on the dashboard.

"Keep that information to yourself for now."

Before he could be asked more questions, Ryan disconnected the call.

CHAPTER THIRTEEN

C ORPORAL MATTHEW BOYCE had been based out of the APD's zone six precinct, thirty-two years old and recently divorced. Ryan had learned he'd been scheduled to take the detective's exam next week.

"Poor bastard," the uniformed first responder uttered, still clearly shaken. He waited nearby as Ryan knelt beside the corpse, the ME's office having finished its examination. Anger and sympathy tightened his throat. The bluish-green pallor of the head and neck, the near-absence of rigor mortis and odor of early-stage decomposition, like rotting meat, indicated death had occurred some twenty-four hours earlier. Looking over the body, Ryan pressed the back of one latex-gloved hand against his nostrils in an attempt to block the stench.

"God rest his soul," the officer intoned.

Three entrance wounds were visible through Boyce's blood-caked T-shirt. They were in his residential garage, a single-car structure with concrete flooring and windowless walls. It sat slightly behind the small house in the Maplehurst neighborhood, not far from the restaurant Ryan had just departed.

Small cones marked the shell casings on the floor. Controlled chaos was everywhere—forensics techs going about their jobs, the ME's wagon backed up to the open garage door. Other grim-faced detectives with jurisdiction were there as well, while just beyond the yard, officers kept out curious onlookers.

"Who made the 9-1-1 call?" Ryan asked, noticing a news van as it rolled to a stop out front as he stood.

The officer pointed to a bulky, new-looking house squeezed onto a parcel lot across the street. "Neighbor noticed the garage door had been open since the previous evening. Thought it was unusual and came over to see what the deal was."

Ryan regarded the residence. Dwarfing the Victorian-era bungalows on the street, it was what in-town preservationists snidely referred to as a McMansion. Desirous of the convenient location, the wealthy bought up smaller houses indigenous to the area, tore them down and put up their oversize dwellings.

"Neighbor's the CEO of a software company. He's pretty upset. Indicated he'd had words with Boyce when the house went up, but they'd smoothed things over recently. Said he liked having a cop across the street."

"He didn't hear shots last night?"

"No. Said he was home, too. I'm thinking a silencer?"

Ryan didn't respond. "I'm going to want to talk to him."

"He's expecting it. We're running down an address for the ex-wife, too."

He took another look around the small, neat garage. There was a workbench with tools in one corner and an older model Subaru Forester that belonged to Boyce. The driver-side door hung open, although the interior light had since died out. A deep key scratch ran along the vehicle's side. Ryan made sure the CSI photographer had gotten shots of it. Both the car and adjacent wall were splattered with blood.

It appeared Boyce had exited the car and been immediately confronted by the shooter. Based on the sneakers, T-shirt and sweat pants he wore, as well as the duffel bag in the car's passenger seat, it looked as though he'd gone for a workout after getting off shift. One of the detectives on the scene from Boyce's precinct had already indicated the deceased had signed out around seven on Thursday night and hadn't been scheduled for duty on Friday.

Stepping carefully around the body, Ryan reached into the vehicle for the duffel. Placing it on the hood, he sifted through the contents. Boyce's gun, Kevlar vest and uniform—shirt, pants and shoes—were tucked inside. Ryan extracted the navy, short-sleeved shirt, feeling a quiver in his stomach. The badge that should have been under the officer's nameplate was missing, the cotton torn as if someone had ripped it off in haste.

They had the key scratches, the same as the other two shootings. And it appeared Boyce's badge had been taken like Nate's. Was it possible the shooter just hadn't had the opportunity to obtain Watterson's?

Or taking souvenirs was part of an evolving MO.

It appeared more and more likely that Pooch was telling the truth and these weren't gang hits. Ryan tasted bitterness in the back of his mouth. He had handled a case like this only once before, and it had turned out to be a truck driver targeting prostitutes downtown. Not men and not police.

"If you're done, Detective, the ME's office needs to transport the body."

"This bag and its contents go into evidence," he said to the forensics tech who approached as he replaced the shirt. "I want it sealed. I'll sign for it once you're done. And I want the interior dusted for prints. Go over this vehicle with a fine-tooth comb."

The tech nodded and took over. Ryan stepped away, a heaviness inside him as two jump-suited workers came forward with a black body bag. Although Ryan hadn't known the slain officer, the murder still felt deeply personal. He spotted Mateo at the end of the driveway, pacing and talking on his cell phone.

"I don't have any more questions. You can go back out now," Ryan said to the responding officer, who was still taking in the scene with a dazed look. Ryan exited alongside him, both men avoiding dried blood on the slab floor. Outside, the sky had darkened and the warm night air carried the scent of honeysuckle. It was a sharp contrast to the putrid confines of the garage.

"You think he was followed here or someone was waiting on him?" the officer asked.

"I don't know." Ryan didn't want to speculate. He

stopped to tear off the latex gloves and paper booties covering his shoes, tossing them into a nearby receptacle.

"Do *we* need to be worried, Detective?"

Again, he didn't reply. The media hadn't yet speculated on a link between the recent police shootings, so far treating them as isolated incidents. But with a third one now so soon after the second, Ryan figured it wouldn't be long—probably tonight. He had no doubt word was already spreading through the department's ranks, something evidenced by the increasing number of police who were joining the neighbors outside the crime scene's cordoned-off perimeter. Gathering the team, aware of the tense atmosphere, he instructed officers to start a door-to-door canvass of the neighborhood to determine if anyone had witnessed anything, including unfamiliar cars parked on the street a night ago.

He frowned as another news van appeared. Seeing his approach, Mateo completed the conversation and disconnected. Arriving after Ryan, he'd been called away from the immediate scene by an incoming call.

"Thompson," he indicated. "Nate is still our case, but this thing's going wider, pronto. The chief's on his way here now. The department's forming a task force and calling in a GBI profiler. We've got a meeting at noon tomorrow."

Ryan nodded, unsurprised. "Safety protocol?"

"It's going to be reviewed with all officers in morning briefings." Mateo scratched his throat, a habit that usually meant he was riled up and antsy. "You saw the shell casings. Looks like the same type of gun again. No first shot from a distance to take him down this time, though. All three bullets were delivered up close and personal. What do you make of that?"

"He's developing confidence. Either that or Boyce knew him and didn't realize his intent."

"We can keep looking for a connection between the victims, but Thompson says the GBI thinks we have a serial killer on our hands, targeting cops at random."

Ryan stared back at the garage. There were nearly two thousand officers in the metro area.

"Fucking bloodbath in there," Mateo muttered, following his gaze. He squinted against the mobile lights set up around the driveway. "I was glad to take the cap's call for once."

"How's your mom?"

"It's her seventieth birthday. She wasn't happy about me being called away. Evie's going to push the sangria and put her to bed before the late news. She worries too much already."

Raised voices outside the barricade captured their attention. Ryan figured the man trying to gain entrance was Boyce's partner. Wearing civilian clothes, he flashed a badge and shoved against the stationed officers, trying to get past.

"Let him in," he called, dreading this. They spoke briefly to him, asking some questions, then accompanied him to view the body. Ryan laid a hand on the officer's shoulder as he broke down upon seeing the deteriorating corpse. His own heart hurt.

A short time later, he and Mateo pushed through the horde of media, ignoring questions tossed at them. They walked across the street to the towering home of the software executive who had alerted 9-1-1. As they did so, Ryan observed metal tracks embedded in the asphalt, ancient and rusted with age. They were rails that had once been used for streetcars nearly a century ago. They could still be found in some of the older in-town neighborhoods.

Mateo stepped over them as they went onto the sidewalk in front of the house's manicured lawn.

"Simpler times, man," he said.

The gun used to kill Matthew Boyce was a match to the other homicides, something that had been revealed at the Saturday task force meeting. The news had sent anxiety through police gathered there.

The meeting now over, Ryan sat at his desk inside the precinct, going through the other forensics reports that were still filtering in via e-mail. He rubbed his eyes hard enough to see starbursts. His day had begun with the autopsy on Boyce at seven a.m. He had observed it in hopes of hearing firsthand any evidence gleaned from the body that hadn't shown up in the precursory examination. He had attended Nate's, too, despite his personal connection. Both times, however, he had come away with nothing of use.

"Food trucks are in the park," Mateo announced, entering from the corridor. He tossed a brown paper bag to Ryan. "I hooked you up—Cuban, hold the pickles."

Ryan realized he hadn't eaten in hours. "Thanks."

"Anything new show up since I've been out?" Mateo unwrapped his own sandwich at his desk.

"The duffel from Boyce's car was missing something else. A department-issued stun gun. Boyce checked it out a few days ago."

His partner's eyebrows rose. Ryan figured he was wondering the same thing he was. What did the shooter want with it?

"Forensics are still coming in. They lifted a half-dozen prints on and inside the car besides Boyce's, but none matched the exemplars in the IAFIS," Ryan said, referring to the national fingerprint and criminal history database. Without a match, it meant the prints were basically useless unless they had a suspect in custody.

"What about the duffel?"

"No discernible prints. Nylon's not a good canvas."

While the investigation into Watterson's death seven weeks ago had been out of their control, they'd checked Nate's vehicle for prints inside and out, too. A receipt inside the glove box indicating he had recently had the car detailed had diminished the potential for finding anything useful, however.

They ate for a time in silence until Mateo asked, "So what do you think of Danielson's theory? Not that he could limit it to just *one*, mind you."

Ryan caught the cynical edge to his words. GBI Special Agent Joe Danielson was a trained profiler who believed the victims had been selected at random. He'd speculated to the task force that the unsub—Bureau shorthand for unknown subject of an investigation—held an extreme grudge against police for some perceived injustice. As an alternate theory, he'd also suggested the unsub could have even attempted to enter law enforcement at some point but failed, fueling a desire for comeuppance.

"Does our perp just *hate* cops or does he secretly want to *be* one?" Mateo pondered around a mouthful of ham and roast pork. "If we go with the whole hating cops thing, we've narrowed it to nine-tenths of the population. No problem, case closed."

"We haven't given Danielson much to go on," Ryan pointed out.

Five pairs of detectives, all six precinct heads and several members of the department's upper ranks, as well as representatives from the GBI, had attended the task force meeting. They had more hands on deck now, although Ryan and Mateo were still identified as the primaries in Nate's— and now Matthew Boyce's—shootings. The gathering had been tense. In addition to the homicides' specifics, there had been discussion about media protocol and police safety, with a new mandate that no officers were to be on patrol alone.

Of course, Ryan had pointed out that none of the men had been shot while on official duty. Watterson had just gotten off a moonlighting gig and gone to his car in an isolated location, while Nate and Boyce had been returning home for the night. It appeared as if each had been carefully stalked, with the perpetrator knowing the men's patterns and lying in wait for them at the safest place and time. This was the problem he had with Danielson's random-victims theory.

Whatever the homicides were, they didn't seem to be impulse shootings. This wasn't some perp just driving around in a car looking for a cop to take aim at.

Still searching for some connection between the dead men, Ryan placed the three homicide reports on the computer's split screen in front of him as he ate.

"You ready?" Mateo asked a short time later. He gulped the last of his soda.

"Yeah. I'll meet you out back." Ryan tossed the sandwich wrapper into the receptacle and stood. They were headed to the Dunwoody town home where Boyce's ex-wife lived, although the interview was mostly a formality. She wasn't a suspect. She'd been with her new boyfriend and his two sons the entire night of the murder. Still, she might be able to give some insight into Boyce's private life, his habits. She'd been notified of the death by uniformed officers the previous evening, but had been told to expect detectives.

Ryan walked to the police-only restroom, which was combined with a large locker area and row of shower stalls. Briefly, he peered at his reflection in the mirror above the basins, aware of the faint lines fanning out from his eyes and tension bracketing his mouth. He'd come in to wash the Cuban's stickiness from his hands, but instead he splashed cold water on his face. He'd been reviewing the crime scene photos from last night on his computer, as well. Matthew Boyce's corpse, the bloody garage—all of it was burned inside his brain. Nearly a repeat of what had happened to Nate a week ago. He thought of Kristen and his promise to her that he would find Nate's killer.

When he turned off the faucet and opened his eyes again, he saw Seth Kimmel's reflection in the mirror. He stood about six feet behind him. They were the only two in the room.

Ryan reached for a paper towel.

"Heard you got your ass kicked by a banger the other night." Dressed in civilian clothes, Seth smirked. "Have to give those homies a free pass next time they're on my turf."

Ryan took a deep breath and held it in, then turned to face him. "What're you doing here, Kimmel? I thought they put you on leave for that Taser stunt."

"Dash cam shows the truth. Asshole punked off to a cop and paid the price. I'm going to be cleared, so my union rep says to enjoy the paid vacation. I just came by to get some things from my locker." He swaggered closer. "I haven't forgotten I owe you."

Irritation lanced through Ryan. He was in no mood for Seth's bullshit. "Then why wait? I'm right here."

"You'd like that. Me taking another swing at you here in the house where all your buddies can pull me off and Thompson can extend my suspension." His voice lowered menacingly. "*Know this*, Winter. When I'm ready for payback, you won't even see me coming."

Ryan gave a mirthless smile. "Thanks for the heads up."

"And *good policing* on bringing in Weisz's shooter, by the way. Now there's another one of us down. With you on the job, I better start sleeping with my vest on and one eye open."

Ryan crumpled the paper towel he'd used and tossed it

into the receptacle. Seth was baiting him, hoping he would be the one to initiate another physical confrontation. He brushed past, headed out.

"'Course, from what I hear, you've got a history of letting your own die on your watch."

Ryan halted, a stunned heat sweeping through him.

He had accepted that his co-workers knew of his personal tragedy. A handful of them, detectives themselves, had even heard the recording of his anguished poolside call to 9-1-1. Police weren't special. The case had been investigated like any child death.

Shoulders rigid, he forced himself not to turn around. Seth was scum.

"I don't know who on the desk let you back here, but it's a violation of policy," he said hoarsely. "You have two minutes. Get your things and go or I'll escort you out myself."

Chest burning with anger, he walked out.

CHAPTER FOURTEEN

—————)•●•((—————

THE HOPE GALA took place annually under a massive tent at the Atlanta Botanical Garden. The black-tie event was the hospital's largest fundraiser, and the city's upper crust made up its attendees. Socialites, business executives and politicians mingled with the hospital's board and administrators, while a live band played and servers poured champagne.

Lydia stood outside the tent with her cell phone pressed to her ear. She was checking on a patient, an elderly woman with stage-four cancer who had been in the ER on multiple recent occasions, including last night. Lydia had admitted her and started the paperwork to request her entrance into hospice. She'd grown fond of Phyllis Holt, with her sweet face and kind words despite the PICC line in her arm and constant medical procedures. There was little doubt she wouldn't last much longer. Lydia wanted to get her status. Phyllis had no family to care for her, and the last thing she needed was to be discharged and sent home alone.

After waiting on hold for nearly ten minutes, she

received confirmation the woman had been accepted. Disconnecting the call, sad for Phyllis's final days but grateful she would have support, Lydia slipped the phone back into her purse. But instead of returning inside, she remained in the quiet solitude.

Admittedly, the evening had been lovely so far, the lavish gardens and dinner, as well as the limousine ride Rick had arranged. But no matter how hard she tried, her thoughts kept straying back to the news.

Another officer murdered.

Lydia had come off two twelve-hour shifts, determined to lose herself in her work. She hadn't listened to the Friday late-night news, instead falling into bed in exhaustion. Off for the weekend, she'd also slept in that morning and had learned of the latest shooting only as she made coffee in her kitchen with the television on. She hadn't known Officer Boyce, but that was little consolation. Media broadcasts were now speculating a serial killer was targeting police.

Ryan had been briefly visible on last night's footage from outside the latest crime scene, which seemed to be on a perpetual loop on the television screen. She'd wanted to call him, but Adam's harsh criticism had stuck. Lydia had kept her distance.

"There you are." Rick approached, emerging from the darkness in an elegant black tuxedo. He came to stand beside her, taking in the gardens with their ground-lit stone paths and reflection pool. "It's serene here. Hard to believe we're still in the city."

He peered upward, and Lydia followed his gaze to the

twinkling skyscrapers visible over the conservatory's domed roof. Self-deprecatingly, he added, "Well, maybe not *that* hard to believe."

He nodded back to the tent. "Serene isn't the word for in there. Had enough, have you?"

Lydia felt bad for her lengthy absence. But Rick had been immersed in conversation with a philanthropist who gave regularly to the cardiac wing, so she'd taken the opportunity to slip out. "I just needed to make a call."

"But you're having a good time? I know you've been distracted by the police shootings."

They'd talked about the latest homicide during the limousine ride.

"It's been a wonderful evening," Lydia assured him. She wore a beaded chiffon evening gown, drop earrings and high-heeled sandals.

"I'm glad. I have to be here because of my position, but you being here with me has made it more pleasure than business."

Self-conscious under his gaze, she nervously tucked her hair behind one ear. But Rick reached for her hands and drew her closer. Lydia's stomach flip-flopped uneasily as he lowered his head and kissed her. She closed her eyes and complied, disappointed that she felt no stir of desire.

"That's something I've wanted to do for a long time," he said afterward, looking into her eyes. "And as much as I'd like to do it again, we should get back. We're receiving some large contributions in there. The more the alcohol flows, so does the ink on checks."

His hand low on her back, he guided her inside the air-conditioned tent and into the milling crowd. Elaborately set tables dotted the interior. A sea of small white lights hung from the ceiling, under which couples danced on a parquet floor. At the urging of a photographer covering the event, they posed for the newspaper's society page.

Rick never drank, but he got her another glass of champagne, then led her to their table and pulled out her chair. What Lydia saw froze her in place.

Ian Brandt—in a crisp tuxedo, raven hair slicked back from his broad forehead—stood twenty feet away. He was in conversation with several of the hospital's upper-level administrators, but his dark eyes pinned hers.

"You know him?" Rick spoke into her ear to be heard above the music.

"He's … the husband of someone I treated in the ER." Although her voice was calm, Lydia's pulse rushed as she lowered herself into her chair. She hadn't noticed Brandt until now, and she wondered where he'd been during the event. Turning her head, she looked discreetly around for Elise but didn't see her. She knew she had been released from the hospital the day before.

"Well, you must have made a big impression." Sitting beside her, Rick looped one arm around the back of her chair. "He just presented a check for fifty thousand dollars."

Lydia had heard the applause while she'd been outside. Her stomach sank now at the reason. Brandt continued to spear her with his obsidian gaze, then dismissively, he returned his attention to the others.

*

Fortunately, no confrontation had occurred between Lydia and Brandt. He'd ignored her for the remainder of the evening, while she had taken care to keep on the opposite side of the tent.

She walked now with Rick in the tide of departing guests, traveling along the path through the rose garden. But as they were supposed to turn right toward the parking lot and their waiting limousine, he veered in the opposite direction. Capturing her wrist, he tugged her past a large sculpture and behind one of the tall arbors hung heavily with blooms.

"Rick," she scolded, her heels sinking in soft grass as they slipped farther away from the others. "What're you doing? There's a sign back there that said to stay on the path—"

He pulled her to him and kissed her again, this time more hungrily than before. Lydia tried not to stiffen in his arms, keenly aware of their romantic surroundings. She fully understood how she *should* feel, and she told herself to try, at least. She heard the voice of her sister, Natalie—ever the free spirit—telling her to loosen up.

It's only a lay, Lydia. Sex can do a body good.

His hands slid over the curve of her bottom, and she closed her eyes more tightly, trying hard to garner some lightning strike of desire. But after a moment, she gently wedged a hand between them, separating herself and breaking the kiss before things got more out of control.

Rick searched her eyes in the grainy shadows, breathing hard. "What is it?"

She felt a flush stain her skin. "It's just ... we shouldn't be back here."

He released what sounded like a sigh of impatience, although his voice was gentle. "We've been seeing each other for a while now, Lydia. And I've been taking this slow, haven't I?"

"Rick," she begged softly, not wanting to discuss it here.

"I know what you've been through, and I've been doing my best to give you the time you need, to wade in slowly—"

Interrupted by an electronic staccato, he frowned.

"My phone," he said apologetically, digging into the inside pocket of his jacket. "That's the hospital's emergency tone. I'm being texted." His brow furrowed as he read the screen. "I'm being called in."

Lydia smoothed her gown, shamed by the relief she felt at the disruption. "I thought you weren't on call tonight."

"I'm not, but Beau Wilkins is experiencing a possible MI."

Lydia blinked. A myocardial infarction. A heart attack. Wilkins was head coach at the University of Georgia and a football legend. He was also seventy-two years old. "How bad?"

"I'm waiting on a patch-through from the paramedics. He's being airlifted from a weekend fishing expedition in Tallulah Gorge. I'll need to meet the helicopter."

She understood. Rick was on a prestigious list of specialists to be called in case of high-profile emergencies.

While at Mass Gen in Boston, he'd performed open-heart surgery on an Academy Award-winning actor and placed a stent in the heart of the vice president of the United States.

"This wasn't how I'd hoped the evening would end," he said. "I'm sorry."

"Don't be."

As they returned to the path, he placed his arm around her shoulders. "I'll have the limousine service drop me off at the hospital and then take you home."

A short time later, they slid onto the backseat. As the chauffeur closed the door behind them, Rick turned to her. "I remember the first time I saw you, Lydia. I'd just agreed to take the position here. You were in scrubs, your hair in a ponytail, shouting out orders and wrestling a patient." A smile curved his lips. "She had a good forty pounds on you."

Lydia remembered. The patient had been high on bath salts, something they'd been seeing more of, and the ER had been filled to capacity. It hadn't been an ideal situation for meeting the new head of CT.

"I knew I wanted you then," he whispered.

Rick's phone rang again as the chauffeur entered on the driver's side. He answered, switching instantly to business mode. Judging by his side of the conversation, it was the patch-through to the paramedics en route by helicopter to the hospital's roof. Even as he asked questions and gave instructions, Rick's fingers played possessively with hers on the seat. Her throat felt tight. She had expected that sooner or later, he would become more insistent. That he would want a physical relationship to grow from their friendship. It was only natural.

A short time later, the limousine rolled to a stop in front of the sprawling downtown hospital building.

"We *will* continue our discussion," Rick promised, voice low. He brushed a quick kiss against her cheek and got out. She watched him stride toward the main entrance like James Bond on a mission.

As the limousine started back into motion, Lydia felt a growing despondency.

Before Ryan, she had never considered herself overtly sexual. She'd been too serious and hardworking, too focused on her medical training and student loans. She had believed passion was something she wasn't capable of, not really.

Involuntarily, her mind flashed to their very first coupling. Ryan's mouth on hers, his hands pulling her sweater over her head, his body trapping hers against the inside of her apartment door as her trembling fingers struggled with the buttons on his shirt. The heat between them had been immediate. Intense. Even later—even with the mundane arguments that married couples had, the stress of two high-pressure jobs and then a child to rear—their physical mating had always been a regular, carnal need. But all that had ended with their loss.

She hadn't been touched intimately by anyone since they had come apart.

Her lack of arousal with Rick frightened her. She wondered if that part of her had died, too.

A short time later, the chauffeur opened the passenger

door in front of her building. Lydia got out and, using the pass code at the main entrance, made her way into the lobby. It appeared barren, the lights on the chandelier lowered and the concierge already off for the night.

Walking toward the elevator, she realized she'd been wrong about the lobby being uninhabited. A lone figure huddled on the settee under an oil painting in the far corner. A woman. She sat outside the halo of a nearby lamp, casting her hair and features in shadow. But Lydia's pulse began to thrum with realization. Had the concierge let her in before leaving?

Elise Brandt stood and limped closer. Her flaxen hair was flat, her eyes sunken and face pale. Fresh bruises were visible on the slim column of her throat. Lydia's medical training kicked in. She went to her.

"You said if I needed anything ..." Her voice trembled. "Please help me, Dr. Costa."

CHAPTER FIFTEEN

———◀)•●•(◀———

DUSK HAD BEGUN to settle over the city. Entering the pass code to the gated parking lot behind her building, Lydia waited for the arm to lift and drove inside. She'd gotten off the interstate and gone directly to the grocery to purchase coffee and a few other staples, as well as enough produce to make a salad for a late dinner. Fortunately, there hadn't been too many shoppers on a Monday night.

The past two days had been long ones.

Parking, she got out and opened the Volvo's trunk for her canvas shopping tote. Hefting it over one shoulder, she reached inside again for her overnight bag. But the deep voice that called her name startled her, causing her to leave it there. Lydia quickly snapped the trunk closed and turned.

"This is a private lot. What're you doing here?" she demanded as Ian Brandt approached, hoping the stern question masked her unease. A glance around told her they were alone.

"Where's my wife?"

Brandt had apparently emerged from the black Lexus sports coupe with dark-tinted windows. Its driver-side door hung open, the engine left running. Lydia knew how easy it was for a second car to slip inside the lot before the sluggish security arm went back down. Building management had warned tenants to be alert. Had he followed her in and, preoccupied, she hadn't noticed? Or had he been here already, waiting for her? Either way, the speed with which he had traced Elise to her was unnerving.

"I want to know where she is. *Now*," he demanded with narrowed eyes.

Shoving down her fear, she answered coolly. "I've no idea. I did hear she was released from the hospital last Friday—"

"Don't lie to me," he snapped. He wore linen slacks and an expensive-looking dress shirt left open at the throat, revealing dark chest hair. "She's been gone since Saturday night."

"Did you try tracking her through the taxi service? That seemed to work for you before."

Brandt's lips flattened at her sarcasm. "You're playing a dangerous game."

"I'm not playing anything." Lydia lifted her chin despite her racing pulse. "And you need to leave."

"You *know* where she is." The faint accent she'd noticed before had thickened in his anger. "She took your business card with her."

"So? That doesn't mean anything—"

"I put it in a locked drawer of my desk. She pried it open. The card's *gone*," he nearly growled. A vein stood out on his forehead. "Elise doesn't have any friends or family. She's not smart enough to disappear on her own. You're the only one who would ..."

He stopped short, shoving a hand through his black hair.

Help her? Lydia wanted to finish his statement but bit her tongue this time. Of course Elise was alone without anyone to help, she thought, anger temporarily overriding her trepidation. Brandt had cut her off from everyone.

"I was at the gala on Saturday night with Dr. Varek, the hospital's head of cardiothoracic medicine," she pointed out. "*You saw me there.* So unless you're suggesting he's a co-conspirator in whatever it is you're accusing me of—"

"Where've you been the last two days?" he interrupted. "You didn't show up for work today. You haven't been around *here*, either. I'm no fool. It's no coincidence my wife dropped off the face of the earth at the exact same time."

The fact he'd been attempting to conduct surveillance on her sent a shiver across the back of her neck despite the muggy heat. Still, Lydia looked at him with defiance. "Where I was is none of your—"

She gasped as he roughly grasped her arm, escorting her from the rear of the car and backing her against the passenger door where they would be less likely to be seen by anyone looking out from the building's windows. Her purse and shopping bag fell to the asphalt as she struggled to wring free of his grip.

"Get your hands off me!" she cried, panicking.

He let go but still stood too close, towering over her with legs planted wide and blocking her escape. Her voice, when it finally emerged, shook despite her best attempt. "I'll call the police."

Her phone was inside her purse, which now lay at her feet. Brandt's leering smirk felt like a knife pressed to her throat. Lydia wore shorts, wedge sandals and a sleeveless top. But his eyes on her made her feel exposed and vulnerable, nearly naked, as he leaned in closer. His hot breath, smelling of spearmint gum, fanned her face. "And it would take what? Five minutes for them to arrive? Three if you're lucky and there's a patrol car nearby." His voice lowered. "Lots of things could happen to you by then, *Lydia.*"

The threat coursed through her veins.

"Where is she?" he demanded again, his fist slamming onto the Volvo's roof hard enough that she jumped.

"I-I can't help you!"

"You all right, Dr. Costa?" Franklin, the building's concierge, called from a short distance away. An older, genteel man with café au lait skin, a reed-thin frame and gray hair, he'd apparently just come outside with a bag of trash for the Dumpster. He stood under the building's rear portico.

Brandt backed off at Franklin's arrival. He pointed a finger. "If you know where she is, you're going to tell me."

Lydia watched as he returned to his car. He sped from the lot once the gate opened to release him. She was trembling, she realized, the metallic aftertaste of fright like bile in the back of her throat. She knelt to gather the items that had rolled from her shopping bag.

"You know that man, Dr. Costa?"

She glanced up. Franklin no longer had the trash, and he held her runaway can of tomato paste. She felt thankful he'd appeared when he had and that Brandt hadn't seen the suitcase in her trunk. The last thing she wanted to reveal to him was that she'd made a trip out of town. It would only stoke his suspicion.

"Yes," Lydia managed to get out. Rising, she took the can and returned it to her bag.

"You all right?"

She gave a faint nod. "I'm fine."

"He was in the lobby asking questions about you yesterday. And about that blond woman who was waiting on you Saturday night."

Her eyes shot to his. "You let her in?"

"No, ma'am. But I went through the lobby's security tape after he left, since he was insisting she'd been here. He showed me her photo and said for me to call him if I remembered anything. Slid a hundred-dollar bill across the desk and told me there was more where that came from."

He frowned, peering off in the direction the car had taken. "I didn't take it. I told him to leave the property."

Apparently, some kindhearted tenant must have let Elise into the lobby after Franklin had already gone home for the night. Lydia knew a hundred dollars was a lot of money to him. He was already working well past retirement age. She opened her purse, grateful. "Thank you for your discretion. Let me give you something."

He shook his head. "You've been good to my wife and me, Dr. Costa. You help people who're hurting, and I figure that woman needed your help, too. She sure looked like it on the tape. Whoever comes to see you, that's your business alone."

Franklin had asked for Lydia's assistance that past winter when his wife, Callie, had become severely ill. Their insurance was minimal, and initially she'd been sent home from her doctor's office with nothing more than pain medication. Lydia had interceded, calling in favors to make sure she was seen by the proper specialist, had the right tests performed to diagnose the reason for her persisting pancreatitis.

"If he comes back—"

"I'll bounce him right out," Franklin offered fiercely, despite his slight build and advanced years. He patted her shoulder, concern in his eyes. "He was trespassing back here. I can call the police and file a complaint."

Security cameras were posted in the building's lobby and in the rear parking lot. Ian Brandt had no doubt been captured on the footage, but so had Elise. In fact, there was probably video of her leaving with Lydia in her car in the very early hours of Sunday morning. She considered asking Franklin to find the footage and erase it, but she didn't want him to do anything that might get him into trouble with the building's management. Nor did she want to further raise Brandt's ire by pressing charges.

Lydia shook her head. "No. I'd prefer to just drop the matter."

The surrounding twilight had deepened. They went inside the building with Franklin insisting on carrying her shopping bag into the lobby. She would have to come back to her car for her suitcase later, and that was only if she was certain she wasn't being watched.

Upstairs in her unit with the door closed and locked behind her, Lydia went into the kitchen and heaved the shopping bag onto the counter. The vegetables had provided some padding, so none of the jarred or bottled items appeared broken. Brandt's intimidation hung over her, but she still believed she had done the right thing. She had lost any appetite for dinner, however.

And Brandt had been wrong about Elise. She *had* been smarter this time, sneaking away from their Tuxedo Park mansion through the bedroom window so the live-in maid hadn't noticed. She had walked to a bus stop and taken three transfers around the city before disembarking ten blocks from Lydia's building.

When she couldn't locate Lydia at the hospital, and when the answering service wouldn't provide her personal numbers, Elise had found her home address using her cell phone's Web browser. Then she had turned off the phone and thrown it away before stepping onto the bus.

Brandt had promised to kill her if she ever sought help again, Elise had tearfully divulged as Lydia examined her fresh injuries. He'd beat her again as punishment for calling in the police, an act that Lydia herself had been responsible for. Fresh guilt speared through her. Brandt had warned Elise that if she ever again considered having him arrested—if he couldn't get to her, one of his men would. Elise had finally made the decision to leave, but Lydia hadn't been able to persuade her to file charges. Instead, with a haunted expression, Elise had haltingly told her about what had happened to Brandt's first wife.

Lydia had been sickened.

She'd found the only solution the frightened, battered woman would agree to. She had driven Elise to New Orleans—to safety—under the veil of darkness, an eight-hour trip by car. No bus or airline reservations to leave a trail. Lydia had returned alone.

Nerves frayed, muscles stiff from the long drive, she opened a bottle of pinot noir from the wine rack. Pouring a glass, she contemplated the winking light on the phone console. The luminescent digits indicated six messages. Instead of hitting the voice mail's *play* button, she picked up the handset and scanned its caller ID, noting that three of the messages were apparently from Rick. He had been calling her cell phone as well, so she'd finally picked up on the drive back from New Orleans and assured him everything was fine, telling him only that she'd been called away by an old college roommate having a personal crisis. The lie had been a necessary deflection. Still studying the screen, she noticed two more calls were listed as unknown. With a twinge of unease, she wondered if the mystery caller had been Ian Brandt. She skipped over Rick's messages and went to the next two, but they were only stretches of silence culminating in disconnections.

The most recent message was from Natalie, left less than a half hour ago. Although Lydia had hugged her good-bye just that morning, she felt her heart constrict at the sound of her sister's voice.

"I tried calling your cell, but you didn't answer. I just wanted to let you know everything's fine," Natalie said, being purposefully vague. "Happy birthday again, big sis. I hope your gift arrives on time. I sent it to the hospital since that's where you are practically twenty-four/seven."

Not knowing she would be seeing Lydia that weekend, Natalie had already mailed the present. She didn't need it—seeing her sister and mother had been gift enough. After she had gotten Elise settled in, after she had grabbed a few hours' sleep, they had spent the remaining time together. Lydia sighed tiredly. She would turn thirty-seven tomorrow, but felt much older. Rick was insisting on taking her to dinner after her shift to celebrate, but she planned to beg off, unprepared to revisit their interrupted conversation from Saturday night.

But sooner or later she would have to.

Lydia took the wine with her, heading to the bedroom to shower and change. She hoped the hot water would scrub off the feel of Brandt's hands on her. The suitcase could stay where it was. She halted in the living area as the phone jangled, causing her stomach to flutter. Picking up the handset from an end table, she once again peered cautiously at the screen.

The familiar number soothed her. She answered, unable to resist.

"Happy birthday, Lyd." Ryan's voice wrapped around her. In the background, she could hear the faint chatter-over-static coming from the police radio in his SUV.

"My birthday's not until tomorrow," she reminded, feeling her spirits lift a bit.

"I know. I thought I'd beat the rush." He paused. "I wasn't sure you'd be home."

"I'm here. I was just thinking of going to bed early." Lydia realized she hadn't been privy to the local news since Saturday. Elise's situation had dominated the past forty-eight hours. "I've … been out of town. Is there anything new with the case?"

He updated her, although what he said didn't seem to offer much hope. There were still no real leads, compounded by a growing sense of paranoia among police. Ryan sounded tired.

"Did you know Matthew Boyce?"

"No," he said on a heavy sigh. "But he's still one of ours. Three men down, Lydia."

"I know," she said softly.

"I was thinking of your thirty-first the other day," he said, changing the subject to lighter fare. "That trip we took to Rosemary Beach."

Lydia remembered. It had been a magical week, still early in their marriage, even before Tyler. They had reveled in warm sun and sandy beaches, delicious seafood, long, luxurious naps and scorchingly hot sex.

"You remember that little antique shop? The one with all the sea glass and chandeliers made from Mason jars?"

She smiled to herself. "I remember the proprietor flirting with you. He wasn't too happy when I came around the corner."

"I *was* out antiquing. It was an honest mistake."

Closing her eyes as he talked, Lydia envisioned Ryan's even features, recalled the hard strength of him. She felt a sudden yearning to be with him, to feel *safe* again. Despite her outward bravado, Brandt's appearance at her building had shaken her. She wanted to confide in Ryan about Elise, but could not. He would be worried as well as angry. He'd warned her to stay out of it. She wouldn't add to his problems. Lydia fervently hoped Brandt would eventually give up the trail.

"I could use some Rosemary Beach right now," she said wistfully.

"It's been a tough day for you, too."

"Off the charts. Are you on your way home?" she asked, hearing a police code with an accompanying downtown street address being relayed over his radio.

"I'm headed that way. I followed up on a lead with Mateo tonight—which turned out to be a waste of time—then went to McCrosky's for a beer and some dinner. Hopefully, I'll get a few hours' sleep and start over tomorrow."

"Sleep well," she wished him.

"Lydia ..." He paused again, and she waited in the

charged silence. But then he simply rasped, "I just wanted to call and wish you a happy birthday. You deserve it."

She swallowed past the lump in her throat, her heart beating dully as she thanked him and said a subdued good-night.

She had made her choices. It was wrong to feel like this.

Long after the call had ended, she stood with her refilled wine glass in hand, staring out pensively through the window at the glittering cityscape.

Sometime later, the ringing phone woke her from a sleep that had been deepened by the comforting pinot. She'd been drifting in and out of dreams, filmy sequences of herself with Ryan, with Tyler, their lives together displayed to her like favorite, timeworn snapshots. Groggily, she reached for the handset on the nightstand. Her mumbled salutation was met with a hushed abyss that put her on instant alert, followed by three gut-punching words.

"Bitch. Fucking whore."

"Who is this?" she asked hoarsely, her heart climbing into her throat as she sat up.

The line went dead.

CHAPTER SIXTEEN

―――――⟫•●•⟪―――――

"JESUS. CAN I go now?" Jimmy Branford sat across from Ryan and Mateo in the precinct's interview room. Heavyset, with an acne-scarred face and prematurely balding head, he wore his uniform—navy pants and a wrinkled navy shirt with *Dogwood Mall Security* emblazoned on its back. A mobile radio was clipped to his utility belt that holstered a baton but no gun. Shoulders hunched, he regarded the detectives with narrowed eyes. "The mall opens at ten. I'm late for work, thanks to you."

Ryan wanted to tell him to shut up, but the discussion had gone on long enough. They'd have to kick him. He rose from the table, signaling Branford's release. "If we have other questions, we'll be in touch."

Branford grunted. With a scrape of his chair and an acid look, he slunk from the room.

"So?" Mateo pressed once they'd escorted him down the hall. They watched as he shoved through the lobby's glass doors and disappeared onto the sidewalk.

"He's not our guy."

"You sure? If looks could kill, we'd both be getting zipped into body bags about now."

Branford's name had been culled from the APD database. They'd brought him in because he fit the Bureau's profile—a police academy reject now working in pseudo law enforcement as a mall cop. He'd also performed community service for a prank 9-1-1 call several years earlier, something Ryan wondered if the mall's management knew about. Based on their questioning, it seemed clear Branford had a chip on his shoulder about his failed attempt at a police career, but Ryan didn't think he had the aptitude for murder. His slovenly appearance indicated laziness, and he'd been largely uncommunicative instead of confrontational, something he would have expected from a man out to prove his superiority over police. If anything, he seemed slow.

They had interviewed five others with similar backgrounds since the task force meeting on Saturday.

"If you like him for it, we'll put a flag on him and confirm his whereabouts on the nights of the shootings." Ryan checked his watch, hoping the rest of Matthew Boyce's credit card records would arrive soon. They'd filed a motion to compel with the court since one of the card companies had been lagging, citing consumer data confidentiality laws. He had accepted responsibility for going through the transactions, still not giving up on his conviction that there had to be some connection between the victims that went beyond their occupation. He planned to compare Boyce's charges against the other two deceased officers. Already, they had learned there were no crossover arrests.

Boyce's funeral was tomorrow. Returning with Mateo to the bullpen, Ryan was aware of the tense buzz inside the precinct. Plainclothes and uniforms were talking about wearing Kevlars off duty and carrying second weapons. He worried the paranoia could cause someone to overreact out of fear. There had been a rise in requests for backup even for simple events like traffic stops.

"Beautiful," Mateo grumbled as they sat down, jerking his chin toward the glass-walled briefing room. "We knew it was coming. All hail the asshole. Kimmel's back."

Seth stood inside the room with the captain and several others, once again in uniform after being cleared by Standards and Protocol. It had turned out the complaining civilian had a rap sheet in another state, effectively tarnishing the validity of his claims with the media. A nervous-looking rookie fidgeted beside Seth, probably his new partner. Seth smirked at Ryan through the glass. Jaw tight, Ryan ignored him and focused on his computer screen, checking his e-mail. Still no credit card records. He looked up again a short time later, overhearing Mateo's side of a phone call that had just come through.

"We hit pay dirt on Lamar Simmons," he said as he hung up. "He put one of his girls in the hospital last night. She's had enough and claims to have information on LaShonda Butler's murder."

Rising, Mateo grabbed his suit jacket. "She's at Mercy. C'mon. At least we can make headway somewhere."

Ryan glanced to the bullpen's large erasable board that held the names of homicide victims, the red marker they were written in identifying them as unsolved.

He figured Lydia was working today. He had phoned her last night, something he'd vowed not to do after seeing the photo of her with Varek while flipping through *The Atlanta Journal-Constitution*. The unexpected image in the society column—taken at a fancy fundraising event, the surgeon's arm around her—had hurt. He had gone for a long run afterward, trying to blow off some steam, but all he'd done was nearly give himself heat stroke in the record temperature. Still, in a weak moment Ryan had called to wish her happy birthday, wanting to hear her voice. He hadn't planned on seeing her today, not wanting to intrude on any plans she'd made. Mostly, he didn't want to know if she would be spending her birthday with Varek.

The prospect of finally nailing Simmons offered some consolation, at least.

"Let's go," he said, standing.

It was a large hospital. He could avoid her if he chose.

Tuesday morning in the ER had been a busy one that showed no signs of slowing down.

"Fracture with a bisection of the femoral artery," Ravi Kapoor called out as he burst through the lobby doors in front of Lydia. He straddled the patient, the bloodied gurney pushed by two EMTs. His gloved hands kept pressure on a gauze-packed wound above the unconscious woman's left knee.

Lydia kept pace alongside the gurney, viewing the outcome of an MVA—a motor vehicle accident—on the Downtown Connector. Although the woman's features were concealed by an oxygen mask, she appeared young, no more than mid-twenties. Her leg was badly mangled. "BP?"

"Eighty over fifty," another of the paramedics supplied. "Tachycardic with a heart rate of one-thirty."

Not good. Inside the suite, Lydia went about instructing the rapidly assembling team.

"We need another nurse in here!" someone yelled.

"There's no time for a cross match. We've got O-neg, three units. Get that IV set up now!" Lydia pinned her gaze on one of the male residents as the gurney was being positioned. "Course of action, Dr. Massey?"

He hesitated. "Push two liters of fluid, then administer norepinephrine bitartrate to get the pressure up."

"Not yet." Lydia slipped on her safety glasses. She could feel her own pulse take flight. "That's going to increase hemorrhaging. A shunt will temporarily restore blood flow around the injury—"

"If she doesn't code first," he pointed out.

Lydia's jaw set with determination. "It's the best way to save the leg and get her up to the OR, stat."

The IV line was in. Keeping an eye on the heart monitor, she rattled off orders, knowing the plan would go rapidly south if the patient became unstable. She felt butterflies in her stomach. Massey was right. With an arterial laceration, even with the transfusion she was at risk of bleeding out if they spent too much time attempting to save the limb, but they had to try.

Ravi removed his hands from the gauze, and a resident took over for him in a single motion, maintaining pressure on the packed dressing. He climbed down from the gurney. "The kid's coming in another rig, Lydia. They were still trying to extricate her when we pulled out."

The radio had advised of the particulars—rear-end collision with a rollover. First driver dead at the scene, the second car with two victims: a mother and child. Lydia ignored the stab of emotion as she made the incision above the injury, carefully clamped the artery and went quickly to work, inserting and connecting the tubing.

Ten minutes later, the patient on the way up to the surgical ward, Lydia tore off her bloodied gloves and headed to the ER's front. At nearly the same time, the red lights of the arriving second ambulance stained the vestibule walls.

Reaching the automatic doors as they slid open, her heart twisted at the blond ringlets visible at the head of the gurney. The child had been placed in a cervical collar and had a spine board between her body and the gurney padding. Lydia recognized the paramedic as Lynn Reed, a tall, large-boned woman with a nose ring and red hair shorn into a crew cut.

"Six-year-old female with recent loss of consciousness," Lynn relayed tensely. "She was talking to us when we pulled in and just blacked out."

Jogging beside the gurney, Lydia made a visual assessment. "Was she restrained?"

"In the backseat in a safety chair that wasn't properly attached. It came loose in the crash. No discernible physical injury, but her speech was slurred, and she was complaining of a headache. Vitals still in the normal range."

Lydia rolled her fist vigorously over the center of the child's chest, attempting to wake her. "Can you hear me, sweetheart?"

No response. She stopped the gurney long enough to pry open one eye and then the other. She frowned at the uneven dilation. "We've got a blown right pupil. Let's go."

Lydia called to a nurse at the desk as they hurried past. "Let Neurology know we're on our way up for a CT scan and don't want to wait."

As the elevator opened, she heard her name. Abe Solomon, the ER chief of staff, approached briskly from the hall, the tails of his white lab coat flapping.

"Hold the elevator," he ordered.

The paramedic had entered at the head of the gurney, pulling it inside with her. Lydia pressed the button to keep the doors from sliding closed.

"What do you have?" Solomon asked as he reached them.

"Six-year-old with possible craniocerebral injury from an MVA," Lydia said.

"Step off, Dr. Costa. Dr. Rossman will take it." He called the resident over.

"I've got this," Lydia stressed. Her protective instincts

had kicked in. "The mother's in the OR. She has an arterial laceration with significant blood loss. I'd like to stay with her—"

"Dr. Rossman." Solomon eyed the resident sternly over the tops of his bifocals. Rossman had initially hung back at Lydia's objection, but he pushed past her with an apologetic shrug. She stepped from the elevator, frustrated.

"She's seizing!"

Lydia whirled. The child convulsed on the gurney, her thin limbs going rigid and her head jerking off the pillow. But Solomon's hand on her arm barred her from getting back onto the elevator. He called for another of the attendings, who quickly joined the others, and the doors slid closed.

Anger and embarrassment tightened her throat. It wasn't the first time she had been pulled off such a case. "I can handle a child emergency. If you don't think I can do my job—"

"I have full confidence in your abilities, Dr. Costa. If I didn't, you wouldn't be in my ER." He cleared his throat, looking pained. "A word in my office? There's a matter we need to discuss."

Clearly, it wasn't a request. With a sense of dread, Lydia asked a passing nurse to try to find relatives of the mother and child. Her back rigid, she followed Solomon down the hall.

*

Solomon's office was a large, corner space with floor-to-ceiling windows and a view of the adjacent university campus. He instructed Lydia to sit in one of the leather wing chairs while he took the seat behind his desk, its top crowded with neat stacks of papers and medical journals, as well as family photos. She waited for the reason she had been brought here.

"How are you, Lydia?" Inside his office, his tone had softened, and he'd switched to a first-name basis.

"I'm ... fine."

"I understand you changed schedules with Dr. Haan yesterday due to an emergency? Is everything all right?"

Feeling deceitful, Lydia repeated the lie she had given Rick. "The emergency wasn't mine. An old friend from college was having a crisis, so I took the day off."

At his evaluating gaze, Lydia pulled in a slow breath. "What's this about, Abe?"

Removing his glasses, he sighed wearily and tossed them onto his desk. "There's been a complaint about you. Ian Brandt claims you've been counseling his wife on matters outside your specialization."

She wasn't all that surprised.

"Not a *formal*, filed complaint, mind you," he added, attempting to soften the blow. "But he did contact one of the board members he's on good terms with to express his upset. As I'm sure you know, Mr. Brandt's a recent, substantial contributor. The board member called me."

LESLIE TENTLER | 193

Lydia stood from the chair and paced.

"I know about Elise Brandt being in the ER last week. That you contacted the police—"

"I went by protocol."

"Although Mrs. Brandt assured you she wasn't a victim of domestic violence."

"*I went by protocol*," Lydia repeated. "Any time an injury appears to not be accidental, it's my responsibility to contact the police. That's the requirement within the state."

"It's not a hard mandate," Solomon reminded. "Unless it's a child, or a disabled or elderly person, it's up to the treating physician's discretion."

Lydia tried to rein in her frustration. "Elise Brandt's being *abused*. She's been here twice now with suspicious injuries. She gave indications that led me to believe she would be willing to talk to the police."

"But, ultimately, she didn't file charges." He rubbed at the red marks the glasses had left on the bridge of his nose. "As a physician, that's where your involvement should have stopped. Did it?"

Fuming, Lydia didn't answer.

"Mrs. Brandt disappeared over the weekend and took a large sum of money with her. According to Mr. Brandt, his wife has substance-abuse problems, which is why he's desperate to find her. He's afraid she may use the money to purchase drugs and harm herself. He's convinced you know where she is. Do you?"

"No."

"And if you did?"

She didn't reply. Solomon's mouth pressed into a hard line.

Lydia shook her head in disbelief. "Brandt *beats* and terrorizes his wife. I can't believe you're condoning—"

"I'm not condoning *anything*." Solomon's face had reddened, and he appeared a little angry himself. "But I *am* looking out for the best interests of this hospital, which is *my* job. Bart Rosedale—the owner of Southern Food Distributors—sits on our board and contributes a great deal of money through an annual endowment. He insists Brandt's a good businessman. He has a contract to supply his clubs. And to his knowledge, no complaints have *ever* been filed against Brandt by his wife."

Lydia gnawed at her lip. "So what happens now?"

A long moment passed before he said, "I told Bart I'd talk to you, and I have. I'll assure him you know nothing about Elise Brandt's disappearance. And I'll hope to hell that's true."

"Thank you," she said softly.

"You're a damn fine ER doctor, Lydia. One of our best. But in the future, refer cases like this to a social worker, where they belong, and back out of it. Personal involvement will wear you down. There's a *reason* we have to stay objective."

She felt guilty for the concern she saw in his eyes. Lydia recalled how caring Abe had been following Tyler's death. He had been the one to approve her request for an extended leave of absence, the one who had promised her she would still have a job whenever she was ready to return. She hated the situation they were placed in.

"Bart Rosedale might think he knows Brandt, but Brandt's not a good man," she said. "The hospital shouldn't be accepting money from him."

"Put your business hat on, Lydia. We're a large public hospital that barely manages to operate in the black. Hell, more often than not, we *don't*. The reality is, we can't afford to pick and choose our contributors. The devil himself could show up here with a check on the end of a pitchfork, and we'd cash it. It's just the way things are."

He pushed himself up from behind the desk, signaling the end of their conversation. Walking her to the door, he opened it for her. "Happy birthday, by the way."

He had most likely seen the ridiculously large bouquet of roses Rick had sent to the ER. Thanking him, Lydia departed through the corridor toward the elevator. Once she was out of his sight, however, she stopped in front of the windows overlooking the covered passenger bridge between the hospital and university and tried to collect herself. She hadn't been aware of Elise having anything with her but a small duffel containing clothes. If she *had* taken money from their home, Lydia figured she deserved it. Maybe it would help her start a new life.

But Lydia herself had fallen into a black hole she couldn't climb out of. She'd crossed a line where Brandt was concerned. She just wondered how far he was willing to take this. Last night, after the obscenity-laden phone call, there had been two more calls, although both times she answered, no one spoke back. Her caller ID had listed all of the calls as unknown.

Arriving inside the ER a few minutes later, she noticed the activity had finally slowed, part of the daily ebb and flow. As she went to the patient-tracking board to review the ever-changing log of which physicians were treating which cases—a diabetic with a skin ulcer, a suspected cardiac arrhythmia—Roe walked by.

"Any update on the mom and child?" Lydia asked, noting that a cystic fibrosis patient waiting on a lung transplant was in bay three. She'd gotten to know her well over the past year.

"Mother's still in surgery, but she's hanging in there. We found the husband. He's upstairs with the little girl. Neuro's running tests to determine the severity of the TBI."

Traumatic brain injury. Lydia felt a heaviness inside her.

"Do you have a break soon? There's birthday cake in the lounge. Some of the interns have been eyeing it, but I told them hands off until you were ready."

"Thanks, Roe," she said, appreciating the effort. Lydia wasn't in the mood to celebrate, but there was no point in ruining it for everyone. She glanced at the wall clock. "If things stay slow, maybe in fifteen minutes?"

"I'll alert the hungry bastards." Roe nodded to a ledge behind the admissions desk that held various files and parcels. "There's a package that came for you, too."

A brown shipping box sat next to Rick's roses. Natalie's gift. She'd been hinting it was something special, piquing

Lydia's curiosity. Her sister had a knack for selecting unusual presents from the shops in the French Quarter.

She went to the carton, which bore her name and the hospital's address on a typed label. Borrowing scissors from a desk drawer, she used its blades to slice through the cardboard, then removed the smaller box inside, wrapped in pretty teal paper. The box felt rather light. Knowing Natalie and her libido, it was probably some barely-there piece of lingerie.

She removed the satin bow and opened the lid. Lydia's heart dropped into her stomach. She threw the package to the floor and scrambled backward.

Wasps.

Dozens of them.

Most appeared dead, but a few crawled over the tissue paper inside the box while the heartier ones lifted to the air in angry, buzzing flight. The corpse of a small mouse—tongue hanging out, abdomen ripped open—lay amid the bloodstained tissue. Skin prickling, Lydia quickly checked her wrists and arms. She hadn't felt a sting. With a startled cry, she brushed one off her scrub top, instantly realizing the foolishness of that reflexive move. She'd left the EpiPen in her lab coat in her locker.

"What the hell?" Jamaal exclaimed, returning from break.

"Get that out of here!" Roe ordered, rushing over. Lydia grabbed someone's jacket from the back of a chair and tossed it to Jamaal, who threw it over the wasps remaining inside the box. Cursing, he stomped on several more creeping along the floor tiles.

"You stung, Lydia?" Roe asked, eyes wide.

Lydia's breath came in cramped waves. She couldn't be certain since her body had launched into fight-or-flight mode, but she felt none of the immediate symptoms—the dizziness, the profuse sweating, her throat swelling closed.

"I'm okay, I think," she said unevenly.

"Call security," Roe instructed Jamaal.

Lydia laid a hand on his arm, stopping him. "No."

"Lydia—"

Despite her quivering muscles, she shook her head. "Don't call them."

CHAPTER SEVENTEEN

RYAN RECOGNIZED VANESSA Parks as one of the women who'd been waiting for Lamar Simmons outside the precinct the night he had been brought in for questioning. She'd told them Simmons had cut her with a broken bottle and busted two of her ribs for refusing a john. Vanessa wanted retribution. Eyes bright with anger, she'd revealed from her hospital bed that she had been a passenger in his car the night he dumped LaShonda Butler's body.

An addict herself, it was questionable whether Vanessa would make a credible witness, but at least they had enough now to charge Simmons with murder. Exiting the room alongside Mateo, Ryan carried her written statement.

"You see the tracks on her arm?" Mateo asked. "She'll recant as soon as Simmons hooks her up again."

"Or after he threatens to do to her what he did to LaShonda." Despite his time in Homicide, Ryan hadn't numbed to the violence. Vanessa's injury was gruesome, the cut running nearly from her right eye to her jaw. But it also wasn't lost on him that she had been blasé about the murder of eighteen-year-old LaShonda. She'd revealed what she knew only when it would benefit her. As they walked down the corridor, a uniformed officer exited the elevator.

"No one goes in except medical staff," Ryan instructed him, indicating the room they had just left. "Simmons is a light-skinned African American, late thirties, six-foot-two with a snake tattoo on his neck. Be on watch."

"You got it, Detective."

They could keep Simmons away from Vanessa while she was here. Afterward, they would have fewer options.

"I'll start the paperwork for the arrest warrant," Mateo said as the officer took a chair outside the room. "The real bitch will be finding Simmons to serve it."

"Even if we can't locate him, he's going to show up here eventually."

With a grunt of agreement, Mateo dug into his pocket for his cell phone. "Let's get a plainclothes on the floor, too."

Ryan turned when someone called his name. Roe Goodman, one of the senior ER nurses, came toward him, her stethoscope bumping against her chest. She wore brightly patterned medical scrubs. They had known one another for years. He left Mateo to make the call and met her. "Roe."

"Lydia must've called you, after all." Appearing relieved, she shook her head, her short dreadlocks swinging. "Thank the Lord. I've been worried that woman's lost her mind."

"What're you talking about?"

Her mouth fell open slightly. "You're *not* here about the wasps?"

"I'm here taking a statement from a witness." Concern filled him. "What about wasps—was Lydia stung?"

"She's fine. She had a scare, is all." Roe hesitated. "She isn't going to like me telling you, but that's just too bad. You need to talk to her, Ryan. Find out what's going on. Someone sent her a box of wasps this morning, wrapped up like a present."

Surprise and anger hardened his stomach. "Did she open it?"

"She thought it was a birthday gift from her sister." Roe frowned, rubbing absently at her arms. "There was a mutilated mouse inside, too."

Lydia had made enemies in her job just as he had—junkie patients she'd denied drugs to, thugs with knife or bullet wounds she'd notified the police about. But his mind shot directly to Ian Brandt. "How'd it arrive?"

"Dropped off this morning. Security cameras show some greasy-haired kid leaving it at the front desk in the main lobby. The receptionist's new and didn't ask questions. She just accepted it and let him go on his way." Roe laid a hand on his arm, her tone confidential. "Lydia didn't want security called up. I called them anyway, so you know I'm on her shit list. She downplayed it and persuaded them not to bring in the police, saying it was just a prank and to let it go."

Ryan frowned hard. *Damn it, Lydia.* "Where's she now?"

"She's got M&Ms today. How's that for a birthday?"

He was familiar with the mortality-and-morbidity briefings in which doctors reviewed cases where mistakes had been made. They were unpleasant but necessary. "How long's it been going on?"

"Over an hour now. Shouldn't be much longer."

Off the phone, Mateo came over, attuned to the seriousness of their conversation. "They're sending Washington to help out. What's up?"

Ryan gave him the rundown, still fuming over the fact that Lydia hadn't wanted to notify the police. What he wanted to know was why. Whether she'd been stung or not, the threat was real. Somebody had made an effort to find out personal information about her—that today was her birthday, that she had a severe allergy to bee and wasp venom. He took this seriously even if she didn't.

"Go back without me and start the paperwork for the warrant." He handed Vanessa Parks's statement to Mateo. It would take awhile to get the DA's approval, fill out the forms and find a judge to sign them, anyway. "I'll call the captain and tell him I need to take some lost time."

Mateo nodded. "Sure, man."

"But don't go looking for Simmons without me."

"Not a chance. Just take care of this with Lydia."

The elevator opened, and a throng of hospital visitors exited, bearing a fruit basket and bobbing helium balloons. His eyes searched the crowd. Simmons wasn't among them. As Mateo got on and the doors slid shut again, Ryan returned his attention to Roe.

"I'm going down to security to view the footage of this delivery guy. Where's the box?"

"They took it. Said they were going to look into it."

Which meant at least a half-dozen people had handled it by now. If the box had contained anthrax or a bomb, police as well as the GBI would have been everywhere. But no one considered a box of wasps to be a deadly weapon. Except him. His jaw hurt, and Ryan realized he'd been clenching his teeth.

Eyebrows clamped down, he gave Roe his business card. "Call my cell the second she's out of that briefing."

The M&M had been brutal. They usually were. Lydia had presented on one of the cases, an intestinal obstruction misdiagnosed as food poisoning, which had led to a perforation and bowel contamination some twenty-four hours later. The patient had survived the surgery to repair the fissure but remained hospitalized, fighting peritonitis, a life-threatening infection. Although the error hadn't been hers, the diagnosing resident was under her charge, and Lydia felt responsible.

Her energy flagging, she stopped in the cafeteria for coffee before heading back to the ER. As she entered, carrying the thick paper cup covered by a plastic top, Lydia felt her heart skip a beat. Her eyes connected with Ryan's very blue, very serious ones across the lobby. Upon seeing her, he'd halted in midpace at the admissions desk. She exhaled a rough breath, her intuition tingling.

Shit. Shit. He knows.

Her gaze swung accusingly to Roe, who stood behind the desk but quickly turned away, busying herself with something on one of the monitors. Ryan approached.

"We need to talk," he said tensely.

She didn't need to ask about what. He stood with his hands on his lean hips, weapon in his shoulder holster and gold shield clipped to the belt at his waist. From the rigid lines of his body and glint of hot anger in his eyes, it was clear he'd kicked into full protective mode. She hadn't wanted Ryan involved in this. With a hard glance at Roe's back, she said, "I told her not to call the police."

"She didn't. I was here on business, and she just assumed you'd called me. Which you should have. Or if you don't want me here, at least someone with an actual shield."

"Please don't make a big deal out of this—"

His features hardened, his voice lowering further. "Someone sending you a bunch of wasps *is* a big deal, Lydia. We're talking harassment at the least, if not attempted deadly assault. This isn't something you just palm off to the jackasses in hospital security."

"I appreciate your concern, but I've got this under control—"

Ryan clasped her upper arms. His stormy eyes searched hers. "Lydia, talk to me. What's going on?"

The worry on his face eroded the façade of strength she'd been holding on to for the last several days. But a series of beeps over the intercom announced a code blue. Patient in cardiac arrest.

"I-I can't talk now," she choked out, her head turning at the rush of staff scurrying to the bay with the dome light flashing above it. Ryan's hold on her tightened.

"Roe took you off the schedule for the next half hour. Let someone else handle it for once. I'm not going away, and I'm not taking no for an answer."

Marcus Gambrell—another attending on duty—rushed inside the bay. Lydia glanced at the patient-tracking board by the admissions desk. Sure enough, her name had been erased from its top.

"Just tell me you haven't had any more contact with Ian Brandt."

Reading her face, he let go of her and released a soft curse.

✱

"So tell me."

Seeking privacy, they had ended up in the physician lounge, which had been occupied by two residents clandestinely studying for boards. Both had closed their textbooks and hurried out upon Lydia and Ryan's arrival. She stood across from him as he leaned against the counter in the efficiency kitchen, his arms crossed over his chest and somberly waiting.

"He came to my building last night, asking about his wife. She's disappeared, and he thinks I'm involved."

"Are you?" he asked, faint lines of tension deepening around his eyes.

Lydia looked at the remains of her birthday cake on the counter. Then with a sigh of resignation, she told him about her journey to New Orleans with Elise. She had left her in the capable hands of the Sisters of St. Monica, a women's shelter located in an ancient Catholic cathedral a few blocks from Lake Pontchartrain. As Ryan knew, Lydia had personal ties to it. Her mother volunteered there and Natalie—an attorney who provided pro bono legal aid in the Orleans Parish—referred battered women. As a child, Lydia herself had lived at the shelter for a time after Nina Costa left her abusive husband, taking her daughters with her. Lydia trusted the sisters completely.

Once she finished her confession, she squared her shoulders as Ryan rubbed his forehead tiredly, seemingly trying to process what he'd been told. Lydia expected him to lay into her, to remind her that he had warned her against further involvement with Brandt. But instead, she saw what looked like compassion in his eyes.

"You couldn't just refer her to a shelter here? Atlanta's a big place."

"Elise was certain he would find her. He has people working for him, Ryan. And not the kind who are on an official payroll. He considers Elise his property. I promised to help her."

"She could press charges against him."

"She won't. She's too afraid." Lydia hesitated. "Ian Brandt ... had another wife. She died nine years ago in a boating accident off the coast of the Black Sea. It was ruled an accidental drowning."

"I've done some looking around on Brandt. Nothing like that came up—"

"That's because that wasn't his name then." Lydia's heart beat harder as she repeated what Elise had confided to her. "He had it legally changed eight years ago when he came into the United States. Brandt's real name is Ion Bojin. He's Romanian, although he holds US citizenship now. He was involved in drug cartels there, but he's attempted to legitimize himself—at least on the surface. He likes to consider himself fully Americanized."

She took a breath before telling him the rest.

"He told Elise what *really* happened to his first wife to keep her in line. Her name was Ruxandra. She wanted a divorce and threatened to testify against him—to tell the Romanian authorities what she knew about his operations if he didn't agree to it. He held her on a yacht, torturing her for days before finally killing her and feeding her dismembered body to sharks. It was presumed she fell overboard and drowned at sea."

Lydia felt her flesh pebble. "He'd talk about it to Elise while they were having sex, describing what he'd done to Ruxandra. She said talking about it ... excited him. He's warned that something similar could happen to her."

Ryan paced the kitchen's narrow width. "His current wife probably knows a lot about his business dealings *here*, too. Which I'm betting aren't all legitimate."

Lydia nodded faintly. She had been a police officer's

spouse long enough to know what she had relayed was hearsay, inadmissible in court. And Elise herself would never testify to what she had told her. Brandt had terrorized her into silence.

"Elise isn't a strong person," she said emphatically. "She's been beaten down for too long. She doesn't want to bring Brandt to justice. She just wants out."

"Brandt sent you the wasps."

Lydia fell silent but agreed with the likelihood.

"Did you look at the security footage, at the guy who dropped off the package?"

"I didn't recognize him." She had been taken to the hospital's security office to view the recording. The shabbily dressed man looked like anyone—a homeless person, a drug addict—who could have been solicited off the street and handed a twenty-dollar bill in exchange for delivery.

"I had the digital video file e-mailed to the precinct. Hopefully, we'll match the face to someone in our system," Ryan said. "I'm also confiscating the shipping container and gift box. Forensics might be able to pick up some prints."

Lydia had seen the unwrapped box in the security office. Tiny holes had been punched in it to allow in air. There was also a larger opening on one side that had been closed with duct tape. Probably where the wasps had been piped in. She ran a hand over her face. If she had taken the package somewhere to open it in private ... she didn't want to think about what might have happened. But she also knew Brandt was too smart to leave behind incriminating evidence.

She went to where Ryan stood. "If you can't find any proof Brandt's behind the package, there's nothing that can be done legally. You know that. I don't want to keep stoking the fire."

His scowl deepened. "So your plan is to just ignore him and hope he goes away?"

"He *will*, eventually. I was careful. He's just guessing about my involvement, and he can't trace me to Elise's disappearance. In time he'll give up and start looking elsewhere."

"You believe that," he said dubiously.

She implored him with her eyes. "You have enough going on with your job and the police murders. I don't want you to get tangled up in this because of me—"

"Let me worry about me," he said roughly.

They stared at one another. Her throat went dry as Ryan sighed, then took her fingers in his. His voice softened, although his features remained tight with concern. "Your bravery is one of the reasons I fell in love with you, Lydia. But it scares the hell out of me sometimes."

Emotion swirled inside her. Despite everything, she still felt a bond with him.

"It seems almost sarcastic to say it now, but happy birthday," he said in a low voice. "I ... saw the roses out front. They're from Varek?"

She gave a faint nod, deflating at the admission. Ryan

was a cop. He noticed everything. Not that the ostentatious bouquet was hard to miss.

He offered a weak smile. "That must've set him back. There's enough out there to open a floral shop."

He took a step away from her, and Lydia wrapped her arms around herself.

"Is there anything else I need to know about the situation? With Brandt, I mean."

Lydia thought of what Brandt had said in the parking lot of her building. If Ryan knew he'd put his hands on her, no good would come from it. There had been no bodily injury, not even a bruise, so she doubted even a simple battery charge—a misdemeanor—would stick. Nor did she mention the unidentified phone calls. Lydia feared turning this into a legal issue would create further animosity with the hospital. Ultimately, it might even require her to divulge Elise's whereabouts, especially if she had taken Brandt's money—something she was determined not to do.

Nor did she want to get Ryan further involved. He deserved to be free of her problems. Gnawing at her lip, still fervently hoping this situation would die of its own accord, she shook her head.

"No," she said softly.

Ryan looked at her. His blue eyes were serious. "You know I still care about what happens to you. I always will."

The words drove into her heart.

"I want you safe. No more contact with Brandt. If he comes anywhere near you again, you call me."

The door to the room opened. Rick stood in the

threshold, wearing scrubs, a surgical mask hanging around his neck. Seeing the two of them, he appeared surprised. "I hope I'm not interrupting? I was told I could find you in here, Lydia. I just got out of surgery and heard what happened." He walked in and stood beside her. "Detective Winter. I suppose you're here about all this?"

The two men shook hands.

"You're not interrupting." Ryan peered somberly at Lydia. "And I was just leaving."

She made a final, quiet appeal. "Please stay out of this, Ryan."

He tossed his reply over his shoulder as he exited. "Like hell."

CHAPTER EIGHTEEN

————◗•●•◖————

D ARKNESS HAD FALLEN outside the hospital
windows. Turning the corner into the corridor,
Lydia stopped short at the sight of Rick, out of scrubs and
dressed in a sports coat, slacks and tie.

The ER had been short-staffed, and she'd extended
her shift into the evening, partly out of necessity but
also as a way to wiggle out of Rick's dinner invitation,
although it had been more *proclamation* than invite. After
Ryan's departure, Rick had informed her that he'd made
reservations at The Magnolia Room for seven p.m. He
had been disappointed, even a little sullen, when she had
broken the news a short time later that she couldn't go.

Lydia had assumed Rick had already left for the night.
Upon seeing her, he straightened from where he'd been
leaning against the wall and approached.

"What're you doing here?"

"Waiting for you, of course. I checked to see when your
shift was ending." He gave an authoritative smile. "We're
going to celebrate your birthday, Lydia. Even if you're not

in the mood after this morning's shenanigans. Have you heard from Detective Winter?"

"No," she admitted. He had been on her mind, however, his parting statement worrying.

"Well, I'm sure he'll let you know if he makes progress." He glanced at his wristwatch. "Since it's a weeknight, we're in luck. The restaurant was able to accommodate the change in reservations to a later time. They stop serving in another hour, but we can make it if we go now."

Lydia had changed from her scrubs in the physician lounge, but now wore khakis and a short-sleeved top. "I'm hardly dressed—"

"We'll swing by your place for a quick change." He reached for her hand.

"Rick ..." Lydia gently tugged her fingers free. "It's been a pretty bad day. I'd really rather just go home."

She saw his jaw tense, but he blew out a breath and nodded. "All right. If that's what you want, we'll go to your place. We'll order in from that Indian restaurant you like, put on some music and unwind. But you shouldn't be alone tonight." He lowered his voice. "Solomon's right about your needing to leave patients' personal lives alone. We're *healers*, Lydia, not counselors or policemen. That's not our jobs."

She felt her face heat at the scolding. When Rick had pressed, she'd told him a little about the situation with Ian Brandt, although she hadn't revealed her true involvement in his wife's disappearance.

"Before you get cross, lecture over," he said lightly. He

stepped closer, his hands stroking her upper arms with a familiarity that created a small knot in her stomach. "Now that I think about it, maybe a night *in* won't be so bad. Maybe I can help take your mind off things?"

Lydia hadn't forgotten Rick's words in the limousine—eventually, they would talk about taking their relationship further. And by further, he meant sex. She couldn't fault him for that, and she felt remorse for putting things off, *for stringing him along,* as her mother would say. But what had happened at the gala had given her a realization. Despite her best attempt, she didn't feel anything for Rick beyond friendship and a deep respect for his skill as a surgeon. Lydia had tabled that reality due to the crisis with Elise, but it was time she dealt with it. It wasn't fair to him otherwise.

"You ... don't understand." She hesitated before clarifying softly, "I'd like to go home *alone.*"

The vertical line between his eyebrows deepened. "Have I done something?"

"No," she assured him, voice pinched. "Not at all. This is about *me.* I'm ... just not ready for this."

His posture grew rigid. "I take it you're talking about more than tonight."

Lydia's pulse kicked up a beat. Surgeons had egos. They had to in order to make the life-and-death decisions they did daily. She knew that what she was telling him, no matter how gently delivered, was a blow.

"I don't believe this." He let out a small laugh as he dragged a hand through his peppered hair. "You're actually breaking up with me?"

Guilt filled her, but she looked him in the eye. "I'm sorry, Rick. Truly. But I … I don't think we should see each other outside of work anymore. It's just that we're at different places in our lives. We want different things—"

"Exactly what is it that you *want*, Lydia?" His face had taken on a perturbed flush. "Because I've been trying like hell to figure that out for a while now."

"Rick—"

"I've done everything right, haven't I? I've been sympathetic and patient about your personal tragedy. I've wined you and dined you at the best places in town. I've stood around like a fool, in fact, waiting for you to get on with your life."

Lydia blinked at his harshness. "Please believe me. The last thing I want to do is hurt you, but I needed to be honest—"

"Is this about your ex-husband?" His pained eyes also held a jealous glint. "Did I walk in on something this afternoon? Because I got the distinct impression I was intruding."

She swallowed hard, the question hitting close to home.

"No," she said, shaking her head. "It's about me."

"This is absurd," he muttered nearly to himself. There was silence as he studied her. Then he paced a few steps and drew in a calming breath before speaking. "You're upset about this morning, is all. You're overtired and not thinking clearly—"

"I am thinking clearly."

"We'll talk about this later."

"There's no need. And I *am* sorry, Rick."

He stared at her, the cords in his neck standing out against the collar of his dress shirt. Then in a show of outrage and hurt, he shoved through the double doors that led to the elevator vestibule, leaving her standing alone. Lydia waited in the corridor, giving him time to depart before making her way out. She attempted to quell the shakiness she felt. Rick's outburst only added to the sick feeling she'd been carrying around inside her.

Is this about your ex-husband?

She closed her eyes. These recent interludes with Ryan had confused her. She'd begun questioning every decision she had made in the wake of Tyler's death. She had been the one to let go, to want out, unable to see past the grief that shrouded their marriage. Uncertainty and a sharp regret tightened her throat.

She had no right.

Her thoughts racing, Lydia went down the elevator and made her way out of the hospital. But as she reached her deck of the parking garage, it occurred to her that she should have asked hospital security to walk her out, especially in light of that morning's events. Despite the humid heat, Lydia felt a chill on her skin, aware of her shadowy surroundings as she walked to her car. She stopped once, certain she heard the faint echo of footsteps behind her. Rick? She looked around but saw no one. Her nerves were on edge, she knew that, spiking her imagination. Still, her fingers searched inside her backpack for the key chain that also held the slim canister of pepper spray.

She picked up her pace. Reaching the Volvo at nearly a jog, Lydia hurried into its interior and locked it, then quickly started the engine and pulled out.

As the car went down the ramp to the next level, she thought she glimpsed the closing of a door in the stairwell.

CHAPTER NINETEEN

———◗•●•◖———

NURSING A BEER as he sat at the desk in the sunroom, Ryan continued studying Matthew Boyce's transaction records received late that afternoon from the credit card company. Tired of staring at a computer screen, he'd printed them out and taken them home, had spent the last two hours comparing them against Nate's exhaustive records and the smaller number of charges they had for John Watterson.

So far, nothing.

Back and shoulders stiff from the work, he stood and went to peer out the window into the dark, his thoughts spearing off in a dozen different directions.

They had arrested Lamar Simmons after receiving a tip on his whereabouts, a surprisingly easy collar. But Ryan had received no similar gratification with Ian Brandt. Riding on a tide of anger, he had gone to his offices in an upscale high-rise on West Paces Ferry. Ryan had flashed his shield and demanded to see him, but had been told by the receptionist that *Mr. Brandt* had caught a flight to New York and was away on business until the following afternoon.

The likelihood Brandt had sent Lydia the package festered. Not that Ryan could back up that theory with evidence. Brandt's prints were on file from a previous arrest—one for which the charges hadn't stuck—but they hadn't been a match to any of the ones on the packaging. In fact, none of the prints they'd lifted had been in the system. Undeterred, Ryan planned to have a face-off with Brandt when he returned tomorrow.

Absently, he took a pull from his beer. His mind still clung to his conversation earlier that day with Lydia. Touching her had been like a match on tinder for him, and he'd had to tamp down his defensiveness at Varek's arrival. Ryan wondered if he would ever be fully okay that she was with someone else.

Suppressing a sigh, he went back to comparing the line items at his desk.

As the mantel clock in the living room chimed the hour, he heard the front door being unlocked and opened. Familiar footsteps on the hardwood flooring told him it was Tess.

"You shouldn't be out by yourself this late," Ryan reminded sternly, looking up from his work as she passed the sunroom. She carried his dry cleaning, his formal police coat covered by a clear plastic bag that advertised the twenty-four-hour service.

"Oh, pooh. I'm an old woman and poor as a beggar. No one's interested in me. Besides, you need this for tomorrow, and I walked by the cleaners on my way home."

It was one less thing he would have to do tomorrow, at least. Ryan planned to attend Boyce's burial out of respect, and to be there among the plainclothes watching the mourners, looking for anyone who stood out. Unsure of the reason, maybe just because it was on his mind, he said, "Today's Lydia's birthday."

Tess stood in the room's threshold. "Did you see her?"

"Not intentionally. I was at the hospital on business."

"You ought to be taking her out to dinner," she admonished. "Not sitting here, still in your work clothes and frowning hard enough to make your eyebrows hurt."

It was true he was still in his dress shirt and pants, although he'd discarded his tie along with his weapon and shoulder holster.

"We're *divorced*, Tess," he pointed out. Feeling a tightness in his chest, he added, "And I'm pretty sure she has plans tonight."

Tess draped the dry cleaning over an armchair and came closer. In the desk's lamplight Ryan could see the crow's feet fanning outward from her eyes, as well as the faint web of wrinkles bordering her lips that were pursed in a serious expression. The long hair, worn loose tonight—as well as a pair of dangling, pyramid earrings—were her only vanities.

"Bad things happen to good people. And what happened to you and Lydia ... I can't imagine anything worse." Shaking her head, she looked off down the hallway. "Just seeing the closed door to that room, the photos of the three of you ... that sweet little boy ... it breaks my heart every day. I can only imagine what it does to the two of you."

Lungs constricted, he focused on the papers in front of him.

"*Listen to me*, Ryan. The only good thing that comes with age is wisdom, so I'm going to lay some on you, all right? Learn from my mistakes. Life goes by too fast. Don't spend it without Lydia if you still love her, and don't tell me she's seeing someone else. That's just an excuse. You need to fight for her, tell her it's time to come home and try again."

"It's not that simple," he said finally, aware of the hoarseness in his voice. He blinked away an image of Tyler—laughing, playing with building blocks in this very room. An aching guilt slipped over him.

Tess came around to his side of the desk. She laid a hand on his shoulder. "Most things worth fighting for *aren't*. Don't wait until it's too late." After a moment, she cleared her throat. "I've said my piece. Now I'm going to hang up that uniform in the closet, mooch a couple of beers from your refrigerator and go on up. Good night, honey."

Ryan remained contemplative long after Tess had let herself back out. With a burning sensation in his stomach, he wondered if Varek was with Lydia right now.

He returned to the distraction of the credit card transactions. A short time later, however, he sat up straighter in his chair. Two of Matthew Boyce's charges had taken place on separate dates at a nightspot near the Georgia Dome. He'd seen the place in Nate's records, as well, having remembered it because it seemed an unusual place for him to go. Rifling through the separate stack of papers that comprised Nate's transactions, he searched for it again. It took awhile to find it, but there it was.

Not wanting to wait until tomorrow, he grabbed his weapon and shield and left the house.

The Grindhouse was a music club located in a renovated factory building, with multiple floors connected by concrete stairs. It smelled of stale beer and sweat, although the stench didn't appear to hurt its popularity—it was packed for a weeknight. Young adults and slightly older hipsters were pressed together in the shadowy, cavernous space where Ryan spoke with the club's manager.

"If their credit cards say they were here, I'm sure they were, but I don't remember them," he said, speaking up to be heard above the noise as he handed back the photos of Nate and Matthew Boyce. He had shaggy grunge hair and multiple facial piercings. "As you can see, we draw a big crowd. Live bands seven nights a week."

Ryan felt the heavy throb of bass coming from the floor above them. "Security cameras?"

"Parking lot only. It's a digital system, set for auto-erase every seven days to save on media storage," he said with a disinterested shrug, looking off to the bar area. "Sorry."

Which meant any relevant footage had already been erased.

"Am I keeping you from something?" Ryan asked, irritated. "Because we're talking about two dead police officers, both of whom were here in the weeks prior to their murders. Officer Boyce was here twice in May, Detective Weisz on June third."

The manager's brow wrinkled. "Were they on some kind of undercover assignment?"

"Should they have been?" Ryan inquired pointedly.

"This has been all over the news, Detective." The manager nodded toward a large-screen television over the closest of several bars. "I'd like to help you out and say I remembered either of them being here, but I don't."

"I'm going to show the photos to your wait staff."

"No problem. We follow the rules, by the way. No one under twenty-one and no drugs."

As the man excused himself, Ryan peered into the rather offbeat crowd. Boyce was younger, so it might not be out of the realm of possibility for him to drop by to catch a band. But for the life of him, he couldn't visualize uptight, conservative Nate coming here unless he was on the job.

You do that and I'll fucking kill you.

Nate's threat to whomever had been on the other end of the phone call that day still gnawed at him. The venue was dark and crowded, but there were also places for private conversation, he had noticed. There was a chance Nate had been meeting a CI here. Informants typically chose the meeting locales, places where they were comfortable. They had looked at Nate's known informants, but Ryan wondered now if they should look harder.

Some time later, he went back out onto the sidewalk. None of the wait staff had recalled Nate, although one—a brassy-haired female with nipple rings visible through her thin top—thought maybe Boyce looked familiar. But she had been unable to remember anything else, including whether he'd been there alone.

Removing the APD placard from the dashboard, Ryan started his vehicle and pulled from the curb, disappointment filtering through him as he drove. But as he approached the intersection near the massive Georgia Dome, a particular ten-code on the police scanner broke through his thoughts.

Wanted suspect sighted.

His grip tightened on the steering wheel as he listened to the details.

Civilian reported sighting of suspect in June twenty-third police shooting ... black male, mid-twenties, witnessed entering an abandoned building at Cutler and Bard. Bearing a gang tattoo on right upper arm, dressed in jeans, white underwear shirt and blue kerchief ...

Pooch.

After he'd shot Antoine Clark, Pooch's face had been on the news along with the offer of a reward for information leading to an arrest. The area the police dispatcher had identified was a haven for crime, particularly prostitution and drugs. It was also within Pooch's comfort zone. Ryan was less than a mile away.

On impulse, he took a left against the light, cutting deeper into the urban jungle. The streets on this side of the Dome declined quickly, with buildings deteriorating into more run-down structures in the space of a dozen blocks. Traffic thinned as he passed a free clinic and MARTA station, then a row of increasingly shabbier storefronts.

Ryan's SUV halted just down from the building that had been a department store decades ago, before such businesses had moved north to the tony Buckhead community. The name *Schreiber's* still remained on its sun-faded stone front.

Reaching for his cell, Ryan called in a code to announce his arrival. No units were here yet, although he knew crimes in commission took precedence over a possible sighting, and uniforms working this beat typically had their hands full. Exiting the vehicle to have a careful look around, he became aware of only two others on the street—a pair of youths a block away who appeared to be dealing drugs to passing cars. He blew out a tense breath, keeping a low profile and walking around to the building's rear with his gun drawn. A door there stood ajar.

His blood iced at the female shrieks he heard coming from somewhere inside.

There were still no approaching sirens, although Ryan reasoned that units could be on their way covertly with lights off, just as he had done. He'd planned to wait for backup, but the urgency of the cries tugged at him, raising the hair on his arms.

There was no other choice. He slipped into the building's interior.

Glock poised in front of him, heart beating hard, he inched down a dark corridor before reaching doors that led into an abandoned showroom. The wails he'd been following echoed off the walls of the vast space, making it difficult to obtain their originating location. Moving warily, his senses heightened, he felt the crunch of glass from broken-out display counters under his shoes. Although the street-level windows had been boarded over, he was able to make out grainy shapes due to the dim glow leaking from a skylight several floors above. Punched-through sheetrock and trash strewn around indicated vagrants were using the building for shelter. Hearing a noise, he spun and trained his weapon on shifting shadows in one corner. Several human forms—apparently junkies there for a fix—blinked listlessly back at him. None was who he was looking for. A nude, armless mannequin stood ghostlike in the shadow of an unmoving escalator that led to the second floor. The wailing—now mixed with a threatening male voice—was coming from upstairs.

Continuing to grip his gun in both hands, Ryan went cautiously up the dead steps.

Coming in view of the landing, he felt his skin prickle. The source of the caterwauling lay amid refuse, her legs clad in holey leggings and worn boots. She was sprawled out, appearing to have been knocked down, although she quickly sat up and scrabbled backward at Ryan's arrival. Even in the darkness, he could see the white shock of her uncombed hair. She was old, thin, with razor-cut cheekbones and wild eyes. The smell of filth surrounded her. Nearing, Ryan took one hand off his weapon and raised it in a silencing gesture.

Glaring, she raised a bony fist and shook it. "You get out, too! Mine! *MINE!*"

In his peripheral vision, Ryan detected movement. A second figure was fleeing deeper into the building.

"Pooch! Police! Stop!"

The figure broke into a run. Ryan repeated the order, the slap of his dress shoes echoing through the building as he chased the rapidly retreating male past empty racks and overturned shelving units. A pale slash of light from another skylight made the white underwear shirt, the blue bandanna do-rag briefly visible before darkness swallowed them up again.

Thirty yards ahead, a door flew open. Breathing hard, Ryan cursed as the figure shot at him, the flash of a gun and the explosion of sound filling the air before the door clanged closed. Anger fueling his chase, hoping like hell backup was entering downstairs, he stopped only long enough to kick the door open, jump back against the wall and, heart hammering, peek around the corner with his gun pointed before continuing on. The stairwell was dark as a cave. Ryan heard the thud of Pooch's feet gaining distance above him, no doubt headed toward the roof. Déjà vu traveled through him.

Hand sliding against the wall, Ryan felt his way blindly upward, tripping twice on the stairs until a door opening on another level provided a cleft of light before snapping shut again.

His police training told him to wait, but his assailant had invaded his home and pistol-whipped him. Spat on him. Ryan ground his teeth. The need for comeuppance won out. He wanted to be the one to slap on handcuffs and drag the son of a bitch to jail.

Gulping in a steadying breath, he shouldered his way through the door and out. Black night cloaked the sky above him. The weather-battered roof he stood on shone an eery gray in pearlescent moonlight. Rusted air-conditioning boxes and a large ventilation system cordoned off the space. The skylights' domed tops curved like the backs of whales in water. Just beyond, a figure stood in the shadows.

"Pooch!" Ryan yelled again. "Drop the weapon!"

Pooch fired—the bullet zinging off the equipment's metal—then sprinted toward the ledge. His athletic body sailed upward, legs and arms cycling as he long-jumped through the air.

He disappeared.

Ryan dashed to the ledge, breathing hard. *Shit.* Pooch had cleared the six-foot distance between the empty department store and next-door building. Already, he was more than halfway across the lower, second roof. Too far away for Ryan to get off a shot. Pooch looked back, raising his middle finger, racing on.

His lungs squeezed with the decision. Ryan couldn't believe what he was about to do. Returning his gun to his holster and backing up, he burst forward, feeling his heart jolt and hearing his own hard grunt as he cleared the space, too, dropping painfully and rolling several times on the next roof. He picked himself up in time to see Pooch making another Olympian leap toward the next building.

A scream split the air.

Winded, adrenaline shooting through him, Ryan jogged to the ledge and peered dizzily down. His gut clenched. Pooch lay two stories below, his body twisted and motionless on the asphalt. Two squad cars had in fact arrived and were now parked haphazardly on the street with lightbars flashing. An officer rounded the narrow alley's corner and crept toward the body with his gun raised, not that such caution was needed. The already pooling blood reflected the strobe lights.

Perspiring, his body hot, Ryan scrubbed a hand over his face. He wondered what Pooch had been doing here— whether he had been serving as a bagman for the two drug dealers working the street, or whether the BOLO had forced him to take refuge in the decrepit building, resulting in a turf war with the old woman who clearly considered the second floor hers.

Pulling his eyes from the gruesome scene, he turned to see several more officers now fanning onto the adjacent department store roof.

He reached for his shield. Holding it in the air, Ryan identified himself.

CHAPTER TWENTY

LATE-AFTERNOON SUNLIGHT TRICKLED through the leaves in Atlanta's affluent Tuxedo Park neighborhood. Ryan and Mateo sat in the Impala across the street from Ian Brandt's estate, which was nestled in a wooded setting a few blocks from the Governor's Mansion. The house was typical of the residences here—a gracefully aged, Tudor-style mansion with impressive stonework and veils of climbing ivy. An iron gate closed off the driveway and property.

Ryan checked his watch. Based on the information from Brandt's receptionist, it had been a relatively simple matter to check Hartsfield-Jackson's flight schedule and estimate his return.

"Strong turnout for Boyce's funeral this morning," Mateo noted above the AC's drone. "He was highly thought of."

Ryan grunted an agreement, his eyes remaining on the house as he searched for some sign of life inside it. "Six commendations. That's a lot for a kid his age."

"He wasn't exactly a kid. He was what? Six years younger than us?"

Ryan didn't respond. Maybe he just felt that much older. He still thought of Adam as a kid, too.

He'd been on the lookout in the cemetery for anyone who didn't fit—someone who appeared voyeuristic or stood out in some undefined way—but he had seen no one among the sea of midnight-blue uniforms other than those who appeared to be grieving friends or family. At least Boyce hadn't had children, Ryan thought, elbow propped against the passenger-side window as he continued staring out. Boyce's ex-wife had appeared devastated despite the boyfriend who had shepherded her into the seats in front of the rose-covered casket and open grave.

"Are we going to talk about what went down last night?" Mateo broke into his thoughts. "Obviously, you're not planning to bring it up."

Ryan shrugged. "There's nothing you don't already know. Pooch came up short on the second jump. End of story."

"It's all in the report."

"Yeah."

"Christ, Ryan." Mateo shook his head. "What the hell were you doing out answering calls like some uni? You know the mandate. No one goes out alone."

He'd been expecting this. Until now, they'd been tied up with the funeral, then a detectives' briefing with the task force—not much time for a partner-to-partner conversation. Ryan answered with forced patience. "I was following up on a lead on the shootings, all right? A ten-code with Pooch's description came through on the radio, and I was in the area. I went to check it out."

"I could've gone with you to that club last night. All you had to do was ask—"

"I didn't want to pull you away from your family. It was a public location."

"And it couldn't have waited until daylight?"

"No."

Mateo drummed his fingers against the steering wheel, clearly agitated. "Look," he said finally. "I get that you wanted Pooch. I don't blame you. But good cops are being offed. If there *is* a serial killer out there, who's to say you weren't being set up?"

Ryan made a scoffing noise and scratched the back of his neck.

"Think about it," Mateo persisted. "You already know Nate and Boyce were at that club. What if the killer was there last night and saw you? He could've called in that sighting so he could follow you there. Bagging one of the primaries on his own case would be a real trophy."

"You're really out there," Ryan muttered.

"I don't think so. Pooch has been all over the news since he shot Antoine. So our guy calls in a false sighting, knowing you're blocks away, itching to get your hands on him and likely to be a first responder. It could've been bait to get you there."

"Here's the flaw in your theory. *It wasn't a fake sighting.*" Ryan flashed on the gruesome image of Pooch's shattered skull. "You ought to use that vivid imagination of yours to write a movie script. Make some real money."

Mateo chuckled softly. Then growing serious again, he said, "You just shouldn't be taking chances like that, Ry."

Ryan sat up straighter as a dark Lexus sports coupe with tinted windows pulled onto the street. "That's him."

As the car turned into the driveway's opening gate, Mateo drove the Impala in behind it, blocking its iron jaws from closing.

"Wait here," Ryan said, getting out of the vehicle. This was between Brandt and him.

"Why? So I can't hear enough to testify against you in court?"

A dark-haired man in a well-tailored business suit emerged from the other car as Ryan approached.

"Ian Brandt?" he confirmed.

"And you are?"

He indicated the shield at his waist. "Detective Winter with the Atlanta PD."

An expensive-looking wristwatch glimmered in the sunlight as Brandt casually scratched his goatee, appearing unimpressed. "What can I do for you, Detective?"

"You can tell me what you know about a box of wasps delivered to Mercy Hospital yesterday morning."

Brandt clicked his key fob to open the coupe's trunk. A leather designer suitcase was inside it, indicating that he had, in fact, been out of town. "Wasps? That's simple. I know nothing."

"The box was addressed to Dr. Costa in the ER. You

confronted her last week when she contacted the police about your wife's injuries. You also went to her home two days ago and accused her of being party to her disappearance."

"*I know who you are*, Detective. You must be on good terms with your former wife to do her bidding. She sent you here about this?"

"I'm here because those wasps point right back to you." Fighting the desire to slap the arrogant smirk from Brandt's face, Ryan felt his pulse kick up a beat. "From where I stand, it looks like you've gone to some trouble to find out information about Dr. Costa. You're aware she was married to a cop, you know where she lives. Did the fact she has a lethal allergy to bee venom also come up in your research?"

The other man's gaze didn't waver. Despite the fine clothing, the expensive house and car, he emanated a sinister oiliness. "I'm afraid you are—how do you say it?—*sniffing the wrong ass*, Detective. Dr. Costa and I did have a disagreement, but that's hardly illegal. And as I've said, I have absolutely no knowledge of this box of wasps. I don't like your accusation."

He lifted a splayed hand in a speculating gesture. "Perhaps someone *else* sent it? You must admit Dr. Costa has an abrasive personality and an inclination to stick her nose in places it doesn't belong. A woman like that, even an attractive one, probably has a lot of enemies."

Ryan took a step closer, barely keeping his anger on simmer. "You sent them."

"And I'll tell you once more. I *didn't*." Brandt's features had hardened, his previously faint accent becoming a bit more pronounced. "Do you have some proof of this? Did you bring an arrest warrant?" He smiled like a shark. "Then step off my property."

Ryan could haul him into the precinct for an interview, but it would be no more than a harassment technique, and there was little doubt Brandt already had a top-notch lawyer on retainer to ensure he was released in minutes. Besides, his gut told him this asshole didn't scare easily. It was tempting to let him know he was aware of his background—the changed name, the drug cartel, even the dead first wife—but he didn't want it to appear that Elise Brandt had confided in Lydia, an indicator they'd spent time together. He would save it for a time when he had something more concrete. For now, Ryan delivered a warning.

"This is over. Stay away from Dr. Costa. You don't come anywhere near her again."

"I'd take care in threatening me, Detective."

They stood nearly nose-to-nose in the summer heat. Ryan felt perspiration trickle down his back. His voice lowered with meaning. "If she'd been hurt, you wouldn't be breathing right now."

Brandt smirked once again, although his dark eyes were cold.

Ryan returned to the idling car, aware Mateo now stood outside the driver-side door, no doubt poised to step in if the confrontation got physical. They both got in, and Mateo put the car into reverse, tires squealing as he backed from the driveway.

"How'd it go?"

"It went," Ryan grumbled. Large houses on park-like lawns whizzed past.

He just hoped he'd gotten his message across to Brandt.

Two hours later, Ryan exited Captain Thompson's office. He had been summoned back to the precinct via radio. It hadn't taken long for Brandt to place a call regarding his visit, and not much longer than that for the politician he was friends with to contact a higher-up within the APD. Ryan had explained to Thompson that he'd had grounds for questioning Brandt about the package, but without any incriminating evidence, he was warned to let the matter go.

"So how much shit are you in?" Mateo asked as Ryan returned to his desk.

He shrugged. "I've been ordered to stay away from Brandt."

Mateo glanced at the captain's closed door. "Thompson *knows* Lydia. I thought he'd have your back on this."

"He did." Through the window beside his desk, the previously blue sky had begun to fade, and the long shadows of adjacent buildings now stretched over the sidewalk. "This is above his pay grade. Brandt went to the top, so considering his connections, it could've been worse."

Ryan had fully expected Brandt to cry foul over his visit. Based on what he knew from Lydia, it was part of his MO. But Thompson had made it clear he'd stuck out his neck with his own superior and he expected Ryan to back off.

"Brandt must be rubbing elbows with the right crowd—and by *rubbing elbows*, I mean lining their pockets." Mateo reached for the ringing phone on his desk. Ryan was alerted to the immediate change in his tone as he spoke with whoever was on the other end of the line. "Yeah, we're on our way."

"What?" Ryan rose along with his partner. Already, they were walking, headed out.

Mateo kept his voice low as they traveled through the corridor. "Officer-involved shooting. A zone four uniform just made a distress call. Some guy surprised him as he was getting out of his vehicle in the alley behind his home. He fired."

Ryan felt his stomach sour. Paranoia within the department's ranks had been spiraling since Boyce's murder. Everyone was on a hair trigger, looking for shooters in their peripheral vision. He drew in a labored breath. "Just tell me this guy had a gun on him."

As they pushed through the double doors that led to the parking lot, Mateo shot a glance at him, his grim expression confirming Ryan's worst fear.

"The scene's a clusterfuck right now, so they aren't sure yet. But so far, no weapon."

Letting herself into her darkened condo, Lydia felt the day's tension knotting her shoulders. Her shift had been a particularly depressing one with several tough cases coming through the ER—an assault and rape victim, a teen overdose, a likely case of quadriplegia from a biking accident. All of it had been capped off by the news of Jessica Barker, the six-year-old injured with her mother in an MVA the day before.

Word had trickled down from Pediatrics. There had been complications from the surgery to relieve a hematoma putting pressure on her brain. Like most TBIs, there was little to do but watch and wait, but the prognosis wasn't hopeful.

Entering the kitchen—fatigued, her mind full—Lydia flipped on the light but stared vacantly into the room. She wasn't hungry. Instead, she thought of the Oxycontin abuser who had been trolling for drugs and threatened her when she'd discharged him without a prescription. By rote, she poured a generous glass from the open wine bottle that sat on a butcher-block cutting board. Impulsively, she gulped it down, her throat burning at the thick, heady cabernet meant to be sipped. Her eyes watered at the self-punishment, and she coughed, wiping the back of her hand over her mouth.

Taking a breath, she poured another glass.

Lydia squeezed her eyes closed.

The wine didn't make her feel better. It only numbed her.

Is this about your ex-husband?

After the incident with the wasps, after the blowup with Rick last night and his weighted question, she had come home and drunk until she fell asleep—passed out, truthfully—in bed. She'd awakened early that morning with a headache and shaky limbs. Shame heated her face. It hadn't been the first time. Lydia was unsure exactly when she had begun to self-medicate, taking it beyond a glass or two at night to sometimes a bottle. It had been a gradual thing she had somehow lost sight of.

It frightened her that she had begun depending on wine to get through the night.

I'm still functional. I plan carefully. This hasn't affected my job.

But in her heart, she knew. Her stomach tensed.

This has to stop. Before I can't stop. The drinking's getting worse.

She poured the glass into the sink. Lydia passed a hand over her face, watching as the deep burgundy stained the porcelain basin. It reminded her of blood on the ER floor. She dumped out the remainder of the bottle, too. Rinsed all of it down the drain.

Terrified by her bravado, she let a small, mirthless laugh escape. That was all the alcohol here. It had been months since she'd fallen asleep sober. It would be a long night. But she went through the unit, and while she still had her nerve, she dumped the bottle of sleeping pills into the toilet, too.

She took a long, scalding shower, made a cup of herbal tea and went to bed.

Without alcohol to dull her thoughts, it seemed that hours passed before sleep began to claim her. Lydia was drifting when the phone rang. Turning on the bedside lamp, blinking, she reached for the handset and looked at the ID screen.

CALLER UNKNOWN.

Not again. She let it go to voice mail, dread filling her as she flipped onto her side. Within the space of a minute, the ringing started anew.

She'd had enough. Sitting up, Lydia snatched the handset. "Stop calling! I've told you I don't know anything about your wife—"

"Mommy?" A small child's rasp froze the words in her throat. A little boy.

Her nape tingled as she sat up. "Who ... who is this?"

The silence crackled with electricity. " ... Tyler."

Her hand went numb where she gripped the phone. Lydia felt ice curl around her spine.

"Come find me, Mommy," the small voice begged. "It's dark here. I'm scared."

Her flesh crawled, her stomach tightening into a hard knot.

"*Who is this?*" she choked out.

More silence. Then a giggle. "Bye."

The line went dead. Lydia disconnected and tossed the receiver to the floor, drawing her legs up to herself and clasping her arms around her shins as she sat against the headboard. Her heart pounded in her ears. She wasn't insane. Tyler was dead and that hadn't been her child. She knew that.

But it had been *someone's* child. The lisping, thin voice had been real. An eeriness settled over her, and she was unable to shake the call's intent.

Brandt had gone too far this time. Calling the mother of a dead little boy … Having a child pretend to be …

She swallowed past the lump in her throat. Tears of outrage burned behind her eyes.

The strength she had mustered earlier was gone. Lydia felt a pang of regret as her body yearned for numbing solace. *Don't think like that.*

Getting up on weak legs, she checked the phone's screen to make sure she hadn't been caught in some vivid nightmare. That she really wasn't losing her mind. Two calls *had* registered. Replacing the phone on the console, her insides quivering, Lydia sat on the edge of the bed and buried her face in her hands. She was in over her head. But no matter what stunt he pulled, she angrily swore she would never tell Brandt a damn thing about his wife.

The little boy's begging had pierced her heart, though. She thought about it all the time—how Tyler had died. Alone in a cold, watery grave. Suffocating and afraid. Wanting her. It was enough to push her over the edge.

Oh, God.

She took a breath and squared her shoulders. She wouldn't let Brandt do this to her, she wouldn't …

Lydia squeaked out a cry as the phone shrilled back to life.

CHAPTER TWENTY-ONE

A FACELESS KILLER hadn't pulled the trigger this time. But a man was dead and an officer's career was over with charges likely pending, something now in the hands of the Fulton County District Attorney's office. Ryan stared pensively through the windshield in his parked SUV. His mind flashed on the same images—the panhandler sprawled on the ground, the rookie cop squatting nearby, weeping in remorse. Surprised by the unarmed beggar, he had panicked and shot.

The incident wasn't his case, wasn't being categorized with the other shootings. But Ryan still felt a guilty, persistent tug inside him.

Although he had split up with Mateo awhile ago, he'd been too wired to go home. Instead, he'd driven around the city until he had ended up here. Ryan sat across the street from Lydia's building. He had been inside it once, months ago when he dropped off some misrouted mail. Her unit was on the eighth floor, and he looked up at the line of floor-to-ceiling windows, estimating which ones were hers.

He really was pitiable. Conducting a stakeout on his ex-wife's home.

The lights in what he believed to be her unit had been off earlier, but he noticed there was now a pale glow coming from inside. Which meant she was home and awake. Ryan had left her a message earlier that day, letting her know they'd been unable to glean any evidence from the packaging used to mail the wasps. He hadn't heard back from her, and he wondered now if he shouldn't also forewarn her about his visit to Brandt.

Or maybe he was just a glutton for punishment and needed to know if Varek was up there with her.

Reaching for his cell phone, he paused uncertainly before dialing her number. Lydia answered on the second ring. The breathless, panicky way she said his name put him on instant alert. "What's wrong?"

A beat of silence. He sat up straighter in the driver's seat. "Lydia?"

"I-I got a call ..." she stammered, her voice shaky and hesitant. "I know it wasn't real! I haven't lost my mind ..."

What wasn't real? She was rambling now, words pouring out of her about twisted jokes and Ian Brandt. He felt his stomach tense, not liking where this was headed. "Lydia, slow down. Just tell me about the call."

"It was a child, a little boy." She paused, obviously struggling to stay composed. "He called me *Mommy*. God. He ... said he was our Tyler."

Ryan went still, his skin tightening with the shock of it.

"I'm not crazy! I-I know it wasn't my baby, but I ..."

She made a choking sound that speared through him. "I thought I could handle this on my own, that in time Ian Brandt would give up and all of this would just stop—"

"You're okay, sweetheart," he rasped, attempting to soothe her despite the white-hot rage churning inside him. Brandt had no children, at least none Ryan had learned about. But he probably knew someone who did. "Are you alone?"

"Yes."

He exited the SUV. "Give me the number that came through on your phone."

"I-I can't ever tell where they're coming from. They all say caller unknown—"

"There've been others?" Ryan scowled. She'd been holding back on him yesterday at the hospital. He waited impatiently for several passing motorists and then jogged across the multilane street to her building. "Damn it, Lydia. How many and for how long?"

"I-I don't know. Seven, eight calls over the last several days. But they've all been hang-ups or obscenities before. They weren't ..."

Ryan winced. He headed tensely up the stairs to the building's plaza.

"I should've told you about the calls yesterday," Lydia said apologetically. "But I got myself into this mess. Adam was right about me needing to stay away from you. I didn't want to pull you into this—"

"It's all right," he assured her as he tried the doors. "Look, I'm at your building, but the lobby's closed down."

"You're here?" She sniffled, sounding confused.

"I was in the area." An understatement. Ryan peered into the elegant interior. "Give me your pass code. I'm coming up."

She relayed it. "I'm so sorry, Ryan. I didn't think things would go this far. I know I'm overreacting, but the last few days have been … I'm not … handling this well."

"Listen to me. There's nothing to be sorry for, all right?"

Disconnecting the call, his face hot, Ryan punched in the security code and entered the lobby. He'd visited Brandt as a warning, but it had apparently slid right off his back. Maybe even made things worse. It was clear Brandt had done his homework on Lydia, so he no doubt knew about their child, too. Local media had reported the drowning, a page two story and a brief segment on the nightly news. Even now any Web search could bring it up. Ryan swallowed, feeling an ache in his throat at how undone Lydia had sounded. The thought that Tyler could be used as a weapon against her caused fury to burn inside him. He punched the elevator button.

Calm down. Be smart.

Still, Ryan clenched his hands as he waited for the elevator to reach the floor. He fantasized about having five minutes alone with Ian Brandt.

Lydia didn't know how long he'd been there, but she now sensed his presence behind her. Her body went rigid as he moved closer and carefully wrapped his arms around her, drawing her back

against his chest. Spooning her to him. Throat tight, she swiped at the tears on her face. Light shone through the windows of their home, the day cruelly sunny and warm outside.

She'd been vacuuming and found the toy dinosaur figure forgotten under the sofa. Her fingers worried its molded plastic. It had been one of Tyler's favorites.

"We'll be all right," Ryan promised against her ear, his voice earnest. Desperate. "We're going to get through this."

Lydia knew he was hurting, too. That the guilt was dragging him under. Since returning from New Orleans, she was aware of the time he spent just staring off toward the now-locked gate and covered pool, the trips he took alone to the cemetery. Still, she wanted to ask him not to touch her. Not to hold her. She felt broken inside. She wanted her own quiet death so she could be with her baby again.

"I don't want to," she whispered.

Seeing him in her hallway, still wearing his shoulder holster and detective's shield at his waist, Lydia felt a rush of relief. She didn't know what had brought him so close to her this late at night, but she was intensely grateful for it.

For a brief moment, neither said anything. Then she went into his arms. Wordlessly, he held her.

"I'm sorry," she mumbled against his chest, knowing she had already apologized, knowing he'd told her there was no need. It felt so good to be held by him, she realized with a stab of emotion. To be safe in his arms. When he finally released her, the look of concern on his features was nearly enough to cause tears to form again in her eyes.

Following her inside, he closed the door and led her to the couch, drawing her down next to him. "Tell me about the calls."

Her hands fluttering in her lap, Lydia haltingly relayed what the child had said, aware of Ryan's stormy eyes and clenched jaw. She told him as well about the repeated hang-ups and the man swearing at her.

"Did you recognize Brandt's voice?"

"I'm not completely sure, but it didn't sound like him."

"So he had someone else do it." Reaching for the handset on the console, Ryan peered at its screen, scrolling through the list of calls. Then he stood and began pacing as he used the phone.

"This is Detective Ryan Winter with the Atlanta Police," he said, giving his badge number for verification. "I need a reverse lookup on the most recent call to this number."

After a moment, he relayed the dates and times of the other calls, too. He waited for information, then disconnected.

"They all came from the same burner phone."

Lydia knew what it was. A prepaid, disposable cell phone—a tool favored by drug dealers and terrorists. By anyone who didn't want to be traced.

"Brandt's a sick son of a bitch." He bit out the words, his features hard.

Lydia was unable to stop thinking about the little boy.

He sounded like he was maybe five or six. "I know what I heard, Ryan. I was talking to a *child*. Who brings a child into something like this?"

"You said yourself Brandt has people working for him." He clasped the back of his neck. "He could be anyone's— the son of his maid or someone else on his payroll. Kids can be coached to say pretty much anything."

She slowly shook her head in disbelief.

With a sigh, Ryan sat beside her. For a time, they stared at the television screen. Lydia didn't recall when she'd turned it on, although the sound was muted. The late-night news was running a repeat of the story about the officer who had shot a homeless man behind his house, mistaking him for the killer believed to be stalking police. Lydia had first heard about it while still on-shift in the ER.

"I didn't want to add to your problems," she murmured.

Ryan looked at her, the stress in his blue eyes indicating just how much pressure he was under. But he reached for her hand, his fingers gently tangling with hers, his thumb stroking over her knuckles. The gesture squeezed her heart.

"Lydia," he scolded gently. "You're not a problem. And this *is* going to stop, I promise. For starters, we're going to get a civil harassment order, or at least try to. Tomorrow. It might not stop the calls, but it will keep Brandt away from you. If he comes within a hundred yards of you, he'll land his ass in jail."

"Just don't confront him, Ryan, all right? Despite what we both think, you have no hard evidence he's behind this.

If you just charge in and start making accusations, he'll use it against you …"

She halted as she looked at his face. "God. You already did."

Releasing her fingers, he briefly rubbed his forehead. "I'd been planning to tell you. It's actually why I called tonight."

"He made a complaint against you, didn't he?"

"Thompson took the heat, but I've been warned to back off." His voice was low. "I'm not backing off a damn thing where your safety's concerned."

Lydia fell silent, her fingers absently toying with a cushion from the sofa. She sincerely hadn't wanted to entangle him.

"I wondered where that went," he said a short time later, breaking into her thoughts.

She glanced down at her sleep shorts and the faded T-shirt she wore. The ancient shirt was from Ryan's days at the training academy, with *Atlanta PD* emblazoned on its front. She'd had little time—only his elevator ride upstairs—to compose herself. The shirt had ended up among her things when she had moved out, and she'd kept it, its worn familiarity a comfort. Lydia had put it on after her shower, had forgotten she had it on until she'd already let him inside. A heaviness inside her, she self-consciously ran a hand through her sleep-mussed hair.

"What is it, Lyd?" he urged, peering at her with concern. "You're upset, and this goes beyond an ugly phone call."

She pictured Tyler in her mind. His sweet face with twin dimples and blue eyes. The phone call had brought it all back to the surface.

"I just miss him," she whispered.

She saw her own pain reflected in Ryan's gaze. She sighed and closed her eyes.

"Lydia," he murmured, causing her to open them again. His pinched lips and lean, handsome features were inches from hers. When he spoke, his voice was a low rasp, frayed and thick with emotion. "You know I'd give *my life* to bring him back to us."

She laid her fingers on his still-bandaged forearm. "You were a good father, Ryan."

He shook his head, his voice roughening further. "If I were a good father, he'd still be here."

"Ryan," she whispered, her heart hurting for him.

They sat coupled together, Ryan with his arm behind her on the sofa's back and Lydia turned in to him, her knee touching the side of his thigh. For a long time they simply stared into one another's eyes. They had both been through so much. Ryan had fully shouldered the responsibility for what had happened, and she hadn't made it easier for him.

Her mind played over the tears and long silences, the things she wished she had never said.

Unable to fill her lungs completely, she felt her pulse beat hard in her throat as she leaned closer, lifting her hand to caress his stubbled jaw with her fingers. Ryan's eyes darkened at her touch. He swallowed, appearing so uncertain. But then, tentatively, he lowered his head and brushed his lips against hers.

She felt heat fill her. Pulling away a few inches, Ryan searched her eyes. Then he kissed her again, more slowly this time. Their mouths joined together, Lydia moved against him, her arms settling around his neck as he deepened the kiss, holding her more tightly. His hands caressed her back then slid down to stroke her waist. She'd been lost for so long, drifting in her grief. She'd stopped believing in God. Stopped believing in *Ryan*, too. But being held by him now, being kissed by him … she felt anchored again to something strong. Safe.

It was several long moments before he broke apart from her, his breathing hard and uneven.

"What are we doing, Lydia?" he asked hoarsely.

She only knew that she needed him now, more than she needed her heartbeat or air. Lydia answered by grinding her lips to his again. Ryan grunted into her mouth in response, kissing her back harder, his body hot against hers. She was half on his lap now, aware of his hardening manhood as well as the emotion swirling within her. Lydia's fingers worked at the top buttons of his dress shirt, eager to feel the warm silk of his skin.

Ryan broke their kiss again. Lydia looked at him, already feeling a slight bruise to her lips. In the lamplight, his face was shadowed and intense. Her palm lay on his chest, and she could feel the runaway thud of his heart. For a brief moment, she felt fear he would stop things, be the one of them with reason.

"Not here," he rasped. Setting her back from him, he rose from the couch and removed his shoulder holster and gun, unclipped his shield, laying all of it on the coffee table. He drew her up by her arms.

Lydia shivered as she looked into his eyes and glimpsed the raw need that shone there.

Taking his hand, she led him into the bedroom.

In the shadows, the curtains pulled back, the bed's rumpled sheets appeared silvery gray with the lights of the city spilling on them. Ryan stood in front of her, his face a study of handsome masculinity—hard jawline and full mouth, strong cheekbones and eyes rimmed with sooty lashes. A hunger shimmered through her. He pressed his body to hers. His hands were on her, touching her everywhere, then pulling the hem of her T-shirt upward and dropping it to the floor. She wore no bra.

"God, Lydia," he murmured, his lips dipping to her throat. With a small moan, Lydia tilted her head back to give him fuller access. His hands cupped her breasts, weighing them, his thumbs brushing back and forth over her hardened buds. They ached with need.

She gave no resistance. The familiarity of his hard body, this situation—Lydia felt dizzy with the carnal desire that had abandoned her for so long.

Ryan finished the work she had started, undoing the remaining buttons of his shirt and allowing it to join the discarded T-shirt at their feet. Her palms slid over his firm pectorals, her fingers splaying through the coarse sprinkling of chest hair. Lydia rose on tiptoe to kiss the broad line of his collarbone, her fingers caressing the Celtic warrior tattoo that curled around his right biceps and onto his shoulder. Then her hands were at his waist, her suddenly clumsy fingers struggling with his belt. Ryan assisted her in undoing the buckle, then stripped the leather away. His mouth on hers again, he tugged away the sleep shorts until she stood nude in front of him.

His eyes drank her in. Ryan removed his shoes and the rest of his clothing. Her breath left her lungs as, holding her by the waist, he lowered her to the bed. The cool sheets chilled her fevered skin as he followed her down, his weight on her a welcome comfort. He bent his head hungrily to her breasts, covering each of them in turn with his mouth, the stubble on his jaw abrading her and sending a hot craving through her. Lydia threaded her fingers through the soft hair at his nape, arching upward in encouragement as he sampled each erect peak, sucking her.

He lay between her legs, and she spread herself for him, writhing against his hand as he caressed her.

"Lydia," he whispered roughly. She saw him swallow in the darkness as he stared down at her. He pressed kisses onto her shoulder, her cheekbone. Impatient, Lydia's mouth sought his, and she groaned as his tongue delved in, exploring. She was half-mad with the desire to be filled, wanting him to soothe the emptiness inside her. Ryan held her hips with his hands, stilling her. Then he entered her in a single, hard stroke, causing Lydia to cry out at the shock of it.

Her body, unused for so long, stretched to accommodate

him. Lydia felt her eyes mist as he whispered endearments against her ear, telling her again that everything would be all right.

She wrapped her legs around his hips as he began to move inside her. They found their rhythm as if they had mated only yesterday, something instinctual and unforgotten between them. His slow, steady thrusts turned her body into liquid heat. For a long time Ryan pinned her to the bed and drove into her, drove everything from her mind but their lovemaking. Unsure of how much more she could take, Lydia begged him for release, but he hushed her with his mouth, his lips demanding her submission. She ran her hands over his back, her nails gently rasping over his skin as she danced on the edge of a climax. His thrusts were faster now, too, his urgency increasing.

Her orgasm shattered her, rippling around him and causing him to cry out as he came closely behind her. She felt his heat spill into her. Ryan buried his forehead against her shoulder, spent, breathing hard.

A short time later he had moved beside her, lying on his side and holding her spooned against him, her bottom pressing into his stomach and his arm draped over her. The curve of her shoulder drew his lips.

"We were always good like this," he murmured against her skin.

Lydia's toes stroked slowly up and down his shin. She felt warm and boneless in his embrace. They lay bathed in the city's glow. She cupped his larger fingers inside hers and held his hand against her breasts. Regret caused an ache inside her.

"I shouldn't have gone to New Orleans," she admitted softly in the darkness. Emotion thickened her words. "I'm so sorry for that, Ryan. It was unfair and unthinkably cruel."

She could feel his chest gently rising and falling behind her.

"You did what was right for you. I don't blame you."

"I tried to come home ..." She needed him to understand. Her voice trembled, and she swallowed. "I tried to stay. But I ... I just couldn't put the pieces back together without him."

He held her more tightly and whispered, "I know."

CHAPTER TWENTY-TWO

———————◗•●•◖———————

H E HAD BEEN awake for a while. Ryan sat on the edge of the mattress, watching as Lydia slept. She appeared vulnerable, curled up like a kitten, her skin porcelain and dark hair spilling onto her pillow. Maybe Adam was right about his masochistic side but, God help him, he still loved her, deeply.

He would die wanting her.

Bowing his head, he rubbed his hands over his face as he released a soft breath of uncertainty. He wasn't exactly sure what had happened between them last night. What it actually meant. If it even meant anything at all other than Lydia had been in need of comfort and he had been here.

If he hadn't called her, there was a real possibility she wouldn't have turned to him. That she would have leaned on Varek instead.

Sliding into his boxers and pants, he left the bedroom and went into the kitchen with its granite counters and high-end, stainless steel appliances. The clock on the range indicated it was a little after five in the morning.

Bare-chested and barefoot, he located a glass in the cabinet and ran water into it from the faucet. He gulped it down, at the same time noticing the empty wine bottle that sat next to a single goblet on the counter. Ryan couldn't help it—he wondered if Lydia had been drinking last night. If her lowered inhibitions had led to their having sex. But she had displayed no signs of inebriation. She had been shaken by the phone call but seemed entirely sober.

Seeking activity to dull his thoughts, he rinsed his glass and the goblet before placing them both in the dishwasher. Then he carried the empty bottle to the closet he suspected held the garbage.

A half-dozen more wine bottles were stacked in the recycling bin.

"Your phone rang," Lydia said, causing him to turn. She'd donned his dress shirt, her slender thighs bare as she held the device out to him. Her eyes moved to the bin, as well. A faint blush crept onto her cheeks, but all she said was, "The screen said it was Mateo. I thought it might be important."

"Sorry it woke you." Ryan placed the empty bottle on top of the others with a clink.

"Should I assume you had a few friends over?" he asked, making a point about the bin's contents as he took the phone. The pained look on her features didn't escape him. "Because I'd feel better about that."

She glanced away, changing the topic. "You should call Mateo back—"

"*Look at me*, Lyd." It took some effort for her

cocoa-brown eyes to meet his again. His voice softened. "Are you all right?"

"I'm fine. I don't even know what you—"

"You'd had too much to drink the night you came to the house," he reminded. "You were never a big drinker. I thought then that wasn't like you."

Her chin tilted upward as her arms crossed over her chest. "So you see a few wine bottles in my garbage and accuse me of being an alcoholic?"

Placing the phone on the counter, he stepped closer. She looked beautiful with indignation simmering under her skin, but he could also see the shadows in her eyes. Ryan was a trained interrogator. Her evasion tactics and defensive body language caused a small knot to form inside him.

"You can talk to me. I'm just worried about you, Lyd," he emphasized, his voice low.

Lydia sighed, seeming embarrassed. "Don't be."

He swallowed, unsure if he wanted to ask the question. "Were you drinking last night?"

This time she looked unwaveringly into his eyes. "No."

Ryan felt the hard beat of his heart as he studied her face. "I ... saw the empty prescription bottle in the bathroom, too."

She combed her fingers through her hair in an uneasy gesture. "I need them sometimes."

"Sleeping pills and alcohol are a bad mix," he scolded.

Her expression was pinched. "I *am* a doctor, Ryan. I know that."

He didn't want to leave her like this. He wanted to talk more, to drive to the heart of whatever was hurting her—this situation with Ian Brandt, the stress of her job, her lingering grief. God knew she had a lot on her. But she appeared uncomfortable under his scrutiny, and his cell sprang to life on the counter. Mateo again. It was damn early for him to be calling—not a good sign. He answered with a note of irritation, then rubbed his forehead at what his partner had to say.

"Send me a text with the address. I'll be there in a half hour." He disconnected.

"What is it?" Lydia asked.

Tension constricted his lungs. "The rookie officer who shot the panhandler last night—he's dead. The COD appears to be suicide, but Thompson wants us there due to the recent shootings."

"God," Lydia whispered, her face paling. Realizing what she had on, she said, "You'll need this."

He waited in the living room as she went to the bedroom, returning a minute later with his shirt and other clothing. She had redressed in what she'd had on last night, the shape of her small, round breasts visible through the threadbare T-shirt. There wasn't time for coffee or even a shower—he'd have to stop by the house afterward, if he could. Nor was there time to talk about last night, about what it meant.

He knew what it meant to him.

His mind flashed on an image of Varek on top of her, doing to her what he had done. It made him crazy.

"You're working today?" he asked tightly as he slipped on his shirt and buttoned it, then sat on the couch to pull on his socks.

"I'm not on until three."

"I'm going with you to file the restraining order with the county clerk's office," he said, giving no berth for argument. He slid into his shoes and tucked in his shirt, then reclaimed his weapon, shoulder holster and shield from the coffee table. If nothing else, it would serve as a message to Brandt they meant business about him backing off. "I've got some accumulated time. I'll call you as soon as I can clear a few hours."

The court set a high bar for issuing orders based on claims of harassment. It could be hard to get, especially since there was nothing solid to link Brandt to the mailed wasps or prank calls. Ryan hoped his presence might have some sway. "When Brandt confronted you in the parking lot, did he *physically* threaten you in any way?"

Reluctantly, she admitted he had. Something else she'd initially left out in hopes of this mess blowing over. Ryan pressed his lips together. "What happened?"

Lydia hesitated. "He didn't hurt me. But he grabbed my arm, and I threatened to call the police. He ... said *things* could happen to me before a patrol car arrived."

Anger restricted his breathing, but his rational side told him it was something they could use, at least. Still, the order would be only temporary, until a court hearing was scheduled. Ryan had been turning over a longer-term solution in his mind.

"Be prepared to relay to the judge *exactly* what transpired." He felt the scowl on his features. "He's not me, so maybe you'll be more forthcoming this time."

Lydia gave a faint nod, contrite.

He looked at her. Even now, her lips appeared a little swollen. He wanted to kiss her like he had last night. Hell, he wanted to carry her back to bed and make love to her until they were both incapable of thought. Until she promised they would try again. Instead, he went to her and chastely pressed his lips to her forehead, trying not to read more into what had happened between them than he should. *Old habits.* He felt her soft release of breath as she leaned into him, her fingers splaying lightly across his chest. When she looked up at him again, he saw uncertainty in her eyes.

Ryan swallowed. They would talk about last night. Or maybe they wouldn't. He didn't know where he stood, and it was disconcerting.

"I'll call you as soon as I can," he said before departing.

The deceased officer had been on the force less than a year. Todd Parham had been single, living in a rented duplex on Edgewood Avenue. His male roommate had been the one to discover the hanged body. Now late afternoon, Ryan sat at his desk inside the precinct. But the bluish corpse as it was being cut down—rigor mortis just beginning to creep in, bowels and bladder evacuated—remained on his mind.

"COD's being listed as compression of the carotid and

trachea," Mateo confirmed as he entered from the corridor, returning from the medical examiner's office. "The ME's ruling it a suicide. Toxicology won't be back for days, of course, but there were no defense wounds or scratch marks on the throat to indicate a struggle. It's looking like he did it without anyone's help."

The ruling was what they had expected, but considering the recent murders and lack of a suicide note, they'd had to be sure. Ryan gave a faint nod of acknowledgment, a heaviness inside him. He understood the weight of guilt.

"Thanks for handling the prelim without me," he said, trying to shake off his thoughts.

"No problem. How'd it go?"

Ryan felt as if he was being pulled in two different directions. He and Mateo had parted ways after leaving Parham's home, his partner working without him so he could go with Lydia to the courthouse. Ryan had called in favors to get the situation in front of a judge quickly in the busy Fulton County legal system. After what he'd learned about the troubling confrontation in her parking lot, he believed it necessary. "We got the temporary order. It's being served on Brandt any time now."

Mateo took a seat at his desk, loosening his tie. "Glad to see you're avoiding the temptation to deliver it yourself."

He would have liked nothing better, but for now he was adhering to Thompson's dictate to keep his distance. Lydia had been anxious at the courthouse, but she'd dutifully followed his instructions about being explicit with the judge. The one exception was that she hadn't volunteered her role in Elise Brandt's disappearance, only stating that Ian Brandt had accused her of being complicit because she had been the one to report his wife's injuries to the police. Thinking of Brandt, Ryan felt his jaw clench. The temporary CHO—civil harassment order— was good for only fifteen days. Following that there would be a hearing where Lydia and Brandt would both be required to be present. She would have to come clean about her involvement under oath if the judge allowed Brandt's attorney to take questioning that far.

If Ryan's strategy worked, Lydia might never have to face Brandt in a courtroom. He tucked the business card he had located in his desk drawer into his shirt pocket. He'd already left Noah Chase a message and was waiting for a return call.

There was no going back now.

Some time later, after re-interviewing two of Nate's informants to no avail, Ryan headed with Mateo down the corridor to the rear parking lot. They would catch a bite of dinner before going to talk to the remaining staff at The Grindhouse, those who hadn't been working the night Ryan had been there.

"You must've gone by your place while you were out, too," Mateo said, the heat and humidity hitting them like a steam room despite the later hour as they pushed through the doors to the outside. "You've shaved and you're not wearing yesterday's clothes."

Ryan gave him a look. "You're the fashion police now?"

"I *am* a detective. So, yeah, I noticed." Tentatively, he

added, "Did you stay at Lydia's last night? I mean, it would be understandable after what happened. Brandt's a twisted SOB to use a kid to try to gaslight her like that."

Thinking of the situation with Lydia, Ryan held out his palm as they approached the Impala. He needed to be in control of something. "Give me the keys. I'm driving."

Mateo tossed them over. "You sleep on the couch or somewhere else?"

He didn't respond until they were both inside the vehicle. Ryan started the engine, watching in the rearview mirror as he backed from the spot.

"I don't think it meant anything," he said quietly.

Mateo sounded dubious. "Just a lay for old times' sake? I don't know."

"She was emotional and needed someone, that's all."

The truth was, he had been with Lydia for several hours at the courthouse. They had talked about Brandt, the overcrowded legal system, as well as the young officer who had ended his life. But neither had brought up what had happened between them last night. He wondered if they were both going to pretend it had never happened. The thought caused a dull ache in his chest. He had parted ways with Lydia at her car, making her promise to call if Brandt disobeyed the order or if anything else occurred. She had thanked him, her soft-brown eyes seeming to search his. Then she'd briefly touched his still-bandaged arm and somberly gotten inside.

"The Grindhouse. You're like a dog with a bone," Mateo said, breaking into his thoughts. "You really think it's a factor and not just some weird coincidence? I'll admit it's an odd place, especially for Nate, but who knows what anyone does off the job?"

None of Nate's CIs would admit to using the club as a meeting place, something Mike Perry had confirmed, as well, but Ryan was undeterred.

"I mean, we were wrong about the gang involvement, apparently," Mateo reminded.

"And by we you mean *me*." Lips pressed together, Ryan felt the heat still coming off the leather steering wheel. The evening rush-hour traffic was moving like molasses as the workforce escaped the city.

"I gave Matthew Boyce's ex-wife a call while I was waiting for you to get back from the ME," he revealed. "She insisted he was a diehard country music fan. The old-school stuff. He wouldn't listen to anything else."

Mateo looked at him, the revelation making an impact. The Grindhouse was a well-known venue for some of the more *out there* forms of music—indie-rock bands with small labels, as well as metal, punk and electronica. It was a place for emos and headbangers, not off-duty policemen who were big on Waylon and Merle.

"I think they were both there to see someone," Ryan said.

CHAPTER TWENTY-THREE

"ADMINISTER ANOTHER ROUND of Albuterol with the nebulizer and check her oxygen level again in fifteen minutes," Lydia instructed the nurse. It was Sunday night, and an older woman experiencing a severe asthma attack lay on the exam table, gasping. "If it hasn't come up, page me."

"Yes, Dr. Costa."

"We'll get you breathing better, Mrs. Tegert, so you can enjoy the Fourth tomorrow," she said, laying a sympathetic hand on her shoulder.

Exiting the bay, Lydia felt her cell phone's vibration inside the pocket of her lab coat. She took it out, tension gathering across her shoulders as she viewed Rick's name on the screen for the second time during her shift. She returned the phone to her pocket.

It wasn't Ian Brandt, at least. But it also wasn't whom she had hoped.

Three days had passed since the restraining order had been served, and so far, Ryan had been right. There had been no sign of Brandt, and the phone calls had halted. Lydia had feared the order would provoke another complaint to the hospital, but Ryan had adamantly believed that Brandt would keep silent, not wanting it known that a judge had taken her concerns seriously enough to serve an injunction against him.

It had also been nearly that long since Lydia had heard from Ryan. He'd called the night of the issuance, about Brandt and what to do if the order backfired. Neither had spoken of what had happened between them. If anything, things had seemed strained.

She didn't know where to go from here.

Lydia felt old remorse constrict her lungs. She well understood she had no right to insert herself into his life again. But in her need, that was exactly what she had done.

By all accounts, he had finally been moving on without her.

As she reviewed the patient-tracking board inside the ER, Lydia chewed her bottom lip. She'd also considered that Ryan simply viewed their sleeping together as a slip-up. It could happen between two people who at one point had been in love. Ryan still cared about her—she knew that— but he'd given no indication he wanted to press one night of sex into something more.

Lydia was called back to the bay that held the asthma sufferer. This time, she administered a steroid injection in an attempt to reduce airway inflammation. Once the woman began to show improvement, she left her in the charge of a resident, attended to another two patients and then prepared to leave for the night.

Her phone vibrated as she changed clothes in the physician lounge. Rick again. They hadn't spoken since their breakup, and he had been thankfully away at a cardiology conference in Dallas for the long weekend. The tone on her phone indicated he had left a voice mail this time. With a feeling of dread, she finished dressing and retrieved the message.

"I didn't want to leave this on a recording, but you're giving me no choice," he said. "I *miss you*, Lydia. I'm sorry for the way things went on your birthday. You'd had an exceptionally bad day, and I pushed too hard."

She heard background noise on the recording—other voices, as if he was in a public place. "I'm still in Dallas, but I'll be home soon. I want to talk."

"I'm …" He cleared his throat. "Not ready to give up on us."

The message sat heavily inside her.

As she walked from the lounge with her backpack, she passed Roe in the corridor.

"You leaving, Lydia?"

"I've already signed out. I'm off tomorrow, too."

"Lucky you, off for the Fourth. But you're still working the tent tomorrow morning, right?" she asked, referring to the medic stations the hospital hosted each year at the Peachtree Road Race. Lydia had agreed to take one of the volunteer shifts for the event that attracted more than sixty thousand participants each year.

She nodded. "Tent six. Bright and early."

"I thought I saw your name on the list." Roe hesitated, her expression turning somber. "Services for the little Barker girl are being held at the Greek Orthodox on Clairmont. Wednesday at three. I figured you'd want to know."

Staring down at her hands, Lydia thanked her. Jessica Barker had been declared brain dead and taken off life support the day before. As she boarded the elevator, her mind remained on the parents and how much their situation mirrored hers.

God had a plan. He wanted that sweet child back.

There's another angel in heaven now.

Lydia thought of all the things well-meaning people had said, trying to provide comfort. Those statements had cut at her.

She wouldn't attend the service. But she would contribute anonymously to the fund that had been set up to help the family pay medical bills. It was just something she felt the need to do.

Going through the lobby, her mind heavy, she pushed through the doors into the humid twilight of early July. But instead of going toward the parking deck, Lydia began walking in the opposite direction. She couldn't help looking over her shoulder more than once. Due to the situation with Brandt, she was hyperaware of her surroundings. Thankfully, because of the holiday weekend, there were still enough people out that she wasn't alone. A block farther down, she stopped at the crosswalk and waited for the light to change.

The last few days hadn't been easy ones.

She heard Ryan's voice in her head.

I'm just worried about you, Lyd.

With a tense breath, she consulted the scrap of paper she held in her hand.

Cars slowed to a halt, and the crosswalk light sprang to life to shepherd the small number of waiting pedestrians across. Lydia hoisted the backpack's strap higher on her shoulder and continued.

She went another two blocks and then turned onto a side street, aware that the foot traffic had thinned here. A small chill traced over her skin despite the night's warmth. She looked around but saw no one following. No Ian Brandt lurking in the shadows.

Lydia stopped in front of the aged community center building. Although its double doors were solid, she could see interior lights leaking around their edges. She wet her lips nervously, a fluttering feeling inside her.

Her father had been an alcoholic.

And she herself was obviously struggling with something dark and self-destructive inside her.

As she hesitantly entered, a few among the dozen or so people seated in folding chairs turned to glance at her before returning their attention to a man up front. He was thin, with a receding hairline, and he nodded to her before continuing.

"Welcome. There's coffee, hon," a woman said, laying a hand briefly on her shoulder in passing.

Her face hot, Lydia thanked her, grateful for her kindness but not quite able to meet her eyes.

She wanted only to listen. She scraped a hand through her hair as she took a seat in back.

Cell phone against his ear, Ryan paced in the bungalow's sunroom as he listened to Noah Chase's update. A heavy darkness had fallen outside the window, enabling him to make out his own reflection in its glass. He still wore his work clothes as well as his shoulder holster and shield clipped to his waist. His phone had begun ringing as he'd entered the house and, seeing the caller's name on its screen, he'd answered immediately.

"So it's a done deal?" he asked tensely. He only hoped he'd done the right thing.

"For the most part. She's agreed to be deposed under oath. We just moved her from the women's shelter to a safe house in the Quarter. We'll be flying her up to DC in the morning," Noah said. "Your ex-wife was right. She's scared, and considering what we know about her husband, she should be. It took some hard convincing she was better off with us than the nuns."

Ryan rubbed a hand over his jaw, thankful Elise Brandt had complied. "I know you can be persuasive."

Noah chuckled. "So can the US Marshals Service. We have two of them watching over her—big, brawny sons of bitches. I think Mrs. Brandt was convinced no one can get to her without going through them. The nuns might have God's ear, but they don't have SIG Sauers on their hips."

Ryan's connection to Noah Chase went back several years. They'd worked together on a major case that had been jointly handled by local Atlanta law enforcement and the FBI. Noah had been a senior field agent then, but he'd been on the fast track and was now a deputy assistant working within the Department of Justice's Criminal Division. His law degree from Princeton hadn't hurt his upward mobility within the organization.

"She'll qualify for WITSEC?" Ryan asked, referring to the US Marshals' Witness Security Program.

"At least for the course of a trial and probably permanently if we believe any of Brandt's associates pose a danger. According to our agent in New Orleans, the preliminary interview indicates she knows plenty about her husband's activities, including eye witnessing his money laundering for sex traffickers bringing women into the country from Russia and Romania."

Ryan thought of Brandt's strip clubs and wondered if he might be more directly involved in the trafficking himself. Regardless of the threat to Lydia, placing Ian Brandt behind bars would be a public service.

"We owe you, Ryan. We have a team that's had its eye on Brandt for a while but hasn't had much luck getting evidence. If Elise Brandt testifies to what she knows, we might actually have a case."

"How quickly do you expect to move?"

"Depending on things, we should have enough for an arrest by midweek, maybe sooner. Brandt has contacts outside the States, obviously. He's a flight risk, so we're hoping bail will be precluded." He added, "You can tell your ex-wife to relax. WITSEC has never lost a witness who followed protocol."

Ryan clasped the back of his neck. "Thanks, Noah."

"Look, I'll keep in touch on this. Stay safe yourself, all right? Your *Hotlanta* serial killer made the national news."

"Yeah," he rasped, already aware. Officer Parham's shooting of the panhandler and subsequent suicide had kicked up another round of media coverage, this time focusing on the rampant paranoia among police. They talked a bit about the situation and said good night. Tossing the phone onto his desk, Ryan released a tired sigh. He'd been out late with Mateo, following up on yet another lead. But just like the wait staff at The Grindhouse a few nights earlier, it had been a dead end.

He wondered how long before they had another man down.

He clicked off the light he'd turned on in the sunroom. Dog-tired, he was ready to see this day over.

Ryan would have to tell Lydia tomorrow what he had done—if she hadn't learned of it already by then. Thinking of her, he felt the persistent knot in his stomach grow larger. He *did* want to talk to her, but he'd been giving her space, giving them both time to try to process things. And now he'd compromised her confidence by reaching out to Noah

Chase. He hoped she would see it was for the best. If things worked out, it could solve Elise's problem permanently.

And if it didn't, it could get her killed.

He had to trust that the US Marshals Service would protect her.

Ryan went to the foyer to set the security console and retrieve the day's mail that Tess always left on the small table near the front door. Afterward, he planned to grab a shower and fall into bed. But as he stood leafing through the various bills and junk mail, Max rubbing against his ankle, something caught his eye through the door's beveled glass. He squinted, his scalp prickling at what looked like a lone figure loitering in the grainy darkness a little farther down on the other side of the street.

He had already set the security system. Entering the code on the console, Ryan opened the door and quickly stepped onto the porch for a clearer view. But whatever he thought he'd seen earlier was no longer there. Still, removing his gun from his holster, he jogged tensely down the steps and waited for a car to pass before moving across the street. Senses heightened, he strained his eyes to see some movement farther down the sidewalk or in the yards of the neighboring bungalows.

Nothing. Just darkness and the steady chirp of cicadas.

He walked cautiously up and down the muggy street, keeping his gun at the ready as he thoroughly searched the shadows before finally going back inside.

It could have been anyone, Ryan rationalized, half-annoyed with himself. A neighbor out for an evening stroll—or hell, the corner fencepost with the overgrown butterfly bush moving in the breeze behind it, playing tricks on an overtired mind.

He thought of Todd Parham and what had happened.

He didn't like to think the paranoia was starting to get to him, too.

CHAPTER TWENTY-FOUR

————))•●•((————

WHILE THE PEACHTREE Road Race started each year near Lenox Square, the medical tent where Lydia was assigned had been set up farther along the route in Midtown. She had taken the rail system there to avoid congestion. She'd worked the first shift, during which she had treated two cases of heat exhaustion, a runner who had fallen and scraped her shin, and numerous blisters and pulled muscles.

Lydia was returning home, leaving the Buckhead terminal, when her cell phone sprang to life inside her backpack. Pulling it out and seeing it was Natalie, she answered, "Happy Fourth."

She stopped walking at what her sister told her, placing her hand over her free ear to shut out the noise from the exiting passengers.

"When?" she asked.

"Late yesterday. With the holiday, I just now checked my messages," Natalie told her. "Sister Patricia said a man from the FBI and two US Marshals came to talk to her in private. She packed her bag and left with them."

"She's sure they were legitimate?"

"She called the local field office and confirmed their identifications."

Running a hand through her hair, Lydia paced on the sidewalk as she listened to what little else Natalie knew. Elise had discarded her cell phone before leaving Atlanta, so she had no way of contacting her to find out if she was all right. Despite the shorts and tank top she wore, the summer heat felt suddenly sweltering. People spilled around her, some of them sporting the coveted race T-shirts that proved their participation.

"It sounds like she went voluntarily," Natalie offered. "But how did they find her?"

"I don't know." She had a suspicion, however.

"Do you think they want her to help make some kind of case against her husband?"

Lydia had been thinking the same thing. Once she finished with Natalie, she called Ryan's cell but got his voice mail. She left no message, unsure of what to say that wouldn't sound like an accusation.

In her building's lobby, she absently greeted Franklin— who smiled at her from behind the concierge desk—then went up the elevator to her unit. Unlocking her door and pushing it open, Lydia froze. Rick was inside, fussing with a basket he'd placed on her dining table. The aroma of coffee and something savory wafted in the air.

"Lydia," he said, sounding nervous. "Surprise."

Caught off guard, she couldn't keep the tautness from her voice as she closed the door behind her. "How'd you get in here?"

"Don't be angry with him, but I talked Franklin into letting me in. I knew you were working the race this morning, and I wanted to treat you." He indicated the basket. "I stopped at Henri's for freshly baked croissants—no small feat with the race crowds, let me tell you. There's also a frittata warming in the oven."

She wasn't angry with Franklin. He'd seen Rick with her numerous times and probably assumed he was playing cupid to some romantic gesture. "I thought you were in Dallas through the holiday."

"I took the red-eye back last night." He walked to where she stood, lightly touching her arms. "I couldn't wait any longer to see you, to talk to you, Lydia, and try to clear up this mess between us."

She released a tense sigh, in disbelief he'd parlayed his acquaintance with her building's concierge to get himself into her home.

"At least have breakfast with me. I've gone to a lot of trouble here, trying to spoil you."

She hadn't wanted to hurt Rick. She still didn't. But she now wondered if his ego just wouldn't accept that things were over between them. His persistence unnerved her. Removing her volunteer ID badge, Lydia dropped her backpack into a chair and lifted her damp hair off her nape. The last thing she wanted was to have another argument with him here in her condo.

"Just let me take the frittata out. Sit down, Lydia. Give me a few minutes—I'll be back with juice and coffee."

Her posture rigid, Lydia stared in frustration at the table he had already set. As he disappeared into the kitchen, she felt the slow beat of a headache begin behind her eyes. She started to trail him into the kitchen but instead went to look through the peephole when a knock sounded at the door. Her stomach flip-flopped in surprise.

"Ryan," she stammered as she opened the door.

He stood in the hall, dressed in suit pants, tie and shirt, his badge at his waist and shoulder holster on. He'd run the Peachtree in years past, but he was obviously working today.

And Rick was in her kitchen.

"I saw you tried to reach me, but I was on another call and couldn't get to you." He hesitated, shifting his stance. "I was on my way here, actually. I went by the hospital, but they said you weren't working. We need to talk—"

"About Elise Brandt?" She stepped out into the hallway with him, closing the door partway behind her.

"You already heard. I figured as much." He cupped the back of his neck. "Look, I know you feel responsible for her, but she's going to be fine, Lydia. Hiding her down in New Orleans in a women's shelter was only a temporary measure, anyway. WITSEC's a better, long-term solution ..."

He stopped speaking at the noise coming from inside her condo unit. Ryan reached past her to push the door open wider as Rick appeared from the kitchen, carrying a tray with a juice carafe and two coffee mugs. Lydia felt dread slide through her.

"Detective Winter," Rick said with a strained smile when he saw them. "Lydia and I were about to have breakfast. Brunch now, I suppose, considering the time."

Lydia's stomach knotted at Ryan's expression, aware of how the other man's presence was being misconstrued. She'd been hoping Rick would stay put until she could explain why he was here. Ryan's jaw had hardened, his blue eyes darkening. He disregarded Rick's salutation and looked at Lydia.

"I've come at a bad time."

"Ryan," she said quickly, shaking her head. "Not at all—"

"Since you already know, there's nothing for us to talk about anyway." His tone was flat as he took a step back. "It's *done*. I did what I thought was best for her and you."

He turned and walked away. Anxiety coursing through her, Lydia followed his brisk path down the hall to the elevator, calling his name. She understood how he'd jumped to conclusions—she and Rick having breakfast in her home on her day off. It looked as though they were still together, that Rick had very possibly spent the night.

"*Ryan*," she pleaded once he'd stopped in front of the elevator and pressed the button. Touching his arm, Lydia nearly felt a jolt at the upset radiating from him. "If you'll just give me a chance to—"

"I don't give a damn anymore, Lydia." He shrugged off her fingers and took the stairwell instead. At nearly the same time, the bell chimed, and the elevator doors parted. Throat tight, Lydia decided to ride it down, hoping it would be faster and she could intercept him. She felt a small panic that he would refuse to listen or wouldn't believe her. To her dismay, the elevator stopped on another floor for passengers, slowing her descent. When she reached the lobby, she glimpsed his broad shoulders exiting through the glass doors onto the plaza.

Nearly running, she caught up with him at the tiered fountain.

"Ryan! Please, just stop, all right?"

He halted, his shoulders rigid, but didn't turn around.

"I worked the race this morning. In the medical tent," she explained in a breathless rush. Her heart squeezed with the need for him to understand. "When I got back, he was here. The concierge let him in. Will you at least talk to me?"

He turned to her, his features hard. Then Ryan closed the distance between them. Lydia's neck whipped back at the intensity of his kiss. Heat emanated off his body as his lips ravaged hers. She anchored her fingers in his shirt to hold on to him, his aggression sending a hot spike of desire through her. When he finally pulled away, Ryan spoke hoarsely, his face flushed and inches from hers as he pointed back to the building.

"You tell me you have one *ounce* of the passion with him that *we* had, Lydia. I don't care if he is a goddamn surgeon." He shook his head, his eyes stormy and pain-filled. "Seeing that pompous jackass up there, knowing you're still with him even after what we—"

"I'm not with him," Lydia broke in, her pulse still racing from his kiss. "And Rick and I were *never* together, not like that. We never will be."

Her stomach fluttered at his pinched expression. "I called it off with him days ago. That's what I've been trying to tell you, Ryan. He's upstairs *without* my invitation. I was trying to figure out a way to get him out gracefully when you showed up."

His skin bunched around his blue eyes as he seemed to process that information. For a time he stared off at the line of crepe myrtles edging the property before looking at her again. He released a strained breath.

"I've been trying like hell to figure out what happened between us the other night ... what it meant to you." He swallowed hard, his voice roughening into a low rasp. "But I *know* what it meant to *me*."

The intensity of his words shook her. Lydia felt a pang deep inside her.

"It ... meant something to me, too, Ryan." She stumbled over the words, her face hot. "Something *real*."

A nearly overwhelming wave of emotion ran through her. She fisted one hand against her chest, tears suddenly burning behind her eyes. "It ... felt like coming home again, being with you. But I've made so many horrible mistakes where we're concerned. I-I feel like I don't have a right to come back into your life. Not after the way I walked out of it—"

"I'm giving you permission," he whispered fiercely.

"Don't you see?" Self-recrimination made her voice hitch inside her throat. "Adam's completely right about me, about everything I did. How I pulled away from you ..."

He simply stared at her, compassion in his eyes.

"I-I don't trust myself anymore." Her words thickened as she shook her head. "What if these feelings are wrong and it doesn't work out? What if I hurt you again—"

"Then we *tried*."

His hands reached for hers, drawing her closer. Her eyes misted, blurring her vision. Ryan leaned into her and gently tipped her chin upward, this time his lips a softer, lingering caress against hers. Her heart ached with the realization of just how much she needed him. Only the sound of his cell phone—someone sending a text—pulled them apart. Wiping at her eyes, she became aware of others around them, tenants from her building and other passersby who were out enjoying the holiday festivities along Peachtree. She and Ryan were receiving a few looks, particularly with his shield and holstered gun on display. He'd pulled out his cell phone, frowning as he stared at it.

"You have to go," she said in disappointment.

"Yeah." He squinted at her, appearing shaken himself. "We need to talk. About us."

She gave a small sigh of agreement.

"Can I see you tonight?"

Lydia swallowed hard and nodded.

They stared at one another until she filled the empty

space in their conversation, still stunned by Elise's cooperation with law enforcement.

"How'd you manage this with WITSEC?"

"I have a contact at the DOJ. It turns out Brandt's been on their radar for a while now," Ryan said. "If Elise testifies to what she knows about her husband, she could be free of him."

"And if he goes to prison, it would also remove him as a threat to *me*," she acknowledged softly, her heart constricting at his likely true motivation. "What are they after him for?"

"For starters, money laundering for an international sex-trafficking operation. There's probably more."

Lydia felt a small chill despite the heavy heat.

"Stay on guard, all right? It could still be days before they make an arrest." He peered back toward her building. "Do you want me to get rid of Varek for you before I go?"

Lydia shook her head. "I still have to work with him at the hospital. I'm hoping to get him out amicably."

"Too bad. That's something I could get into."

She suppressed a soft smile.

Ryan took a breath. "We'll go to dinner provided nothing comes up with the investigation? I'll come by around seven?"

She agreed, not asking where they were going. It didn't matter. She just wanted to be with him and talk out whatever it was they were doing. Hope flitted through her. Biting her lip, she watched as he walked down the concrete stairs that led from the plaza and out onto the sidewalk.

With the crowds that were out, there was no telling where he'd had to park.

Lydia went back inside the building, preparing herself. She felt genuinely bad for Rick, but she had to tell him the truth. It was something she'd been struggling with for a while now.

She was still deeply in love with her ex-husband.

CHAPTER TWENTY-FIVE

THEY'D DINED AT Venezia, an intimate restaurant not far from Lydia's building. It had been around for years but even with the ever-expanding Atlanta dining scene, it remained a favorite, somewhere they had gone in years past to celebrate special occasions.

Lydia stood now on her condo's balcony. A section of the Lenox Square parking lot below her had been cordoned off for the annual Fourth of July fireworks. The sidewalks and green space along Peachtree teemed with people as they waited for the show to begin.

Ryan opened the sliding glass door and stepped out.

"Is everything all right?" she asked. He had been pulled away to take a call.

"It's happening sooner than I thought." He came up beside her, bracing his hands on the balcony's railing. "They're arresting Brandt sometime in the next twenty-four hours."

She felt a rise of nerves. Thinking of Elise, Lydia stared

briefly beyond the mall to the high-rises that had begun to glimmer against the smoky eggplant sky.

"Thank you," she said sincerely. "For getting involved in this."

She saw he'd taken subtle notice of the thin-stemmed goblet she held. Lydia had refused wine at dinner.

"Sparkling water," she clarified, lowering her gaze as she hesitated, gathering her courage. "You were right. I've been drinking too much. I'm trying to stop."

At the confession, she felt her face infuse with heat. But Ryan's fingertips skimmed her jawline, causing her to meet his eyes again. The concern she saw in them touched her deeply.

"You've been through a lot, Lydia."

Her shoulders lifted in a shrug. "That's the excuse I gave myself for too long."

"And you've recognized it's becoming a problem," Ryan pointed out, his voice low as he bent his head closer to hers. "I'm here to help you. In any way I can."

She released a breath, giving a faint nod as he took her free hand in his, his thumb brushing back and forth over her knuckles.

"I meant to ask earlier. How'd it go with Varek?"

They had been occupied at dinner talking about other matters—their painful breakup and the feelings that, despite everything, still remained between them.

"He wasn't happy, but he wished me well. He said he wasn't surprised, actually."

Ryan tilted his head slightly. "About what?"

Lydia felt butterflies in her stomach as she looked at him. "That I wanted to try to work things out with you."

She saw emotion play over his features. Taking the glass she held and placing it on the small bistro table, Ryan slowly drew her to him.

"Do you remember how we used to be?" he asked.

She nodded in silence, bittersweet memories pricking her heart.

"We loved each other before we lost Tyler," he whispered roughly. "I believe we can again. We're *supposed* to be together, Lyd. We need each other to get through this life."

She caressed his shirtfront, in wonderment at the forgiveness inside him.

They'd talked, too, about the aftermath of their loss. How it had frayed what they'd once had. But this time there had been no blame, just two people seeking solace in one another. Light showered over them as the inaugural firework burst into the air with a thunderous, rolling boom, releasing an emerald starburst with spokes that spread outward into the darkening night. The pyrotechnic sizzled and snapped as the crowds below cheered.

Lydia never saw the second explosion.

Instead, her lashes drifted closed as Ryan dipped his head to kiss her. The heat from his body as he held her, his low grunt of need as the kiss slowly deepened, made their surroundings melt away. When they finally broke apart, raw desire shone in his eyes.

"I don't really care about the fireworks," he admitted, voice husky.

They both knew there were things to work out that couldn't be settled in the bedroom. But Lydia couldn't help it—she craved the physical contact, the warmth of his skin against hers. The security and thrill of being in his arms.

She led him inside.

In the bedroom, Ryan closed the curtains, creating a dark and intimate space despite the festivities outside. As he walked to where she stood beside the bed, she felt a yearning ache. Her eyes went to his mouth as he spoke.

"I've never stopped loving you, Lydia. I've felt married to you no matter what a damn piece of paper said about us."

She savored the sight of him until he pressed his lips sweetly to her forehead before gently tipping up her chin and kissing her again. Lydia wrapped her arms around his neck, her heart beating hard.

They'd lost so much time.

She watched, her breathing shallow as he slowly undid the buttons on her sleeveless blouse, shrugging it downward to her elbows and trapping her arms. Head tipped back, Lydia made a soft, mewling sound as Ryan tasted her exposed shoulder, her throat. He murmured endearments, his love for her, against her skin.

She responded by hungrily joining her mouth to his as he pushed her blouse the rest of the way down and let it drift to the floor. Ryan unhooked the clasp of her bra behind her back, his hands cupping her small breasts once the lace garment had fallen away. Lydia slid his tie free and began unbuttoning his shirt, lost in her desire. His body was so hard and male. She felt a growing urge as he toyed with her stiffened nipples while she worked, pulling lightly at them with lean, masculine fingers.

Slowly, he caressed away the remainder of her clothing—her skirt, her panties—his mouth all the while pressing kisses against her skin. Then clasping her shoulders, he lowered her to sit at the bed's edge.

Lydia's heated blood coursed as Ryan stood over her, his shadowed face somber and intense. He tugged free of his open shirt, revealing the flat plane of his stomach and broad chest, and let it fall to the floor, too. She gazed up at him before pressing her lips to the vertical trail of coarse hair below his navel that disappeared at his belt.

"Lydia," he whispered roughly, sliding a hand through her hair.

She lay back on the bed, sensations swirling low in her belly as he removed the rest of his clothing before joining her. Lydia parted herself for him, hearing her own shaky intake of breath as he slid a hand between her legs, expertly stroking her before sinking a finger deep inside her slick, moist heat. Lydia moaned, eyes closed and body arching as she ground into the heel of his palm, her desire nearly spiraling out of control. Murmuring to her, he moved his finger in and out of her in a slow, maddening rhythm, his thumb applying sweet pressure to her most sensitive spot. Ryan had always known exactly how to touch her, what to do to her. Lydia's head rocked weakly back and forth as she whispered his name.

A short time later her orgasm shattered her.

As her breathing slowed, he covered her body with his. Looking into her eyes, Ryan guided himself inside her. Lydia gasped and wrapped her legs around him.

"Ah, God," he whispered raggedly, brow furrowed and eyes squeezed closed.

He stilled before thrusting into her again, his mouth capturing hers as his strokes gentled and slowed. Lydia splayed her fingers through the soft hair at his nape. Her nerve endings stirred and tingled as he made love to her, her body responding to the erotic, unhurried pace Ryan set for them. The pleasure undulated and intensified, carrying them both on its crest until his thrusts deepened, and she felt him finally reach his own shuddering release. The heat of him spilling into her caused her to nearly climax again.

Some time later they lay together, legs tangled as the world came back to a gradual focus. The fireworks still made it sound like a battlefield outside, their muted colors filtering through the curtains. Lydia felt safe, sated, her head against Ryan's chest.

They'd made love twice now in the span of a few days. Neither time had they used protection.

She'd had a difficult time becoming pregnant with Tyler. Maintaining the pregnancy, as well. He had practically been a miracle birth. She was also older, thirty-seven now. Lydia fully expected nothing to come of it.

Pensively, carefully, she stroked her fingers over Ryan's

forearm that lay in the curve of her waist. It was no longer bandaged, and the stitches had been removed a few days ago, although the reddened, scabbed-over laceration remained.

He was right, she conceded, her throat tight.

They belonged together even if Tyler was gone. Even if there were no more children and they had only one another to make a family. There was no one else for her, either. No one else she would ever desire.

Maybe it had taken this long for her to finally begin to heal, for the scar tissue to form some measure of protection over her battered heart.

To find her way back to him.

They'd fought their way through a sea of pain and, somehow, had found their way back to one another.

"You're quiet," he observed. Tenderly, Ryan tipped her chin upward to expose her face to his. His blue eyes were like midnight in the shadowed room. "You all right?"

She sighed softly, a sense of peace falling over her. "I was just thinking about how much I've missed you. How much I've missed this."

His lips lingered against her temple.

"So what will it be? *Absolut* or absolution?"

Adam looked up at the pointed comment. He'd just taken a seat at the bar in McCrosky's, which was packed with spillover revelers from the festivities taking place in Centennial Olympic Park. He gave what he hoped was his most charming grin. "I'm not much of a vodka drinker. Maybe a beer?"

Standing behind the raised mahogany counter, a bar towel slung over one shoulder, Molly pressed her lips together in a pout. "You never called. Liar."

Adam sighed inwardly. Busted. He hadn't expected her to be working tonight. "It hasn't been on purpose. I've been taking some extra shifts, so I've been pretty wiped after hours. But I'm here now, right?"

"*To see me.*" She arched a dubious eyebrow. "And not because this dive is your favorite hangout."

With a faint chuckle, Adam lifted his palms in surrender. "Maybe I *will* go for some of that absolution? If it's still on the table?"

She smiled finally and flipped her long hair behind her.

"Since when do you tend bar, anyway?" he asked.

"Since I got back into town yesterday. I went to visit family. I've been asking to get moved off the floor, and one of the regulars quit, so Frank's trying me out. He needs all hands on deck tonight. I'll be back with your Heineken, but we're busy, so it might take a minute."

She moved on to other customers. Adam looked around, recognizing some of the usual crowd, but they were few and far between in the sea of new faces. He was aware that a uniformed officer being off tonight was tantamount to winning the lottery, since the Fourth was one of the rowdiest holidays. He snacked on pistachios that sat in a dish until Molly returned with his beer. "Thanks."

"So you *do* plan on calling me?" she asked, obviously enjoying herself.

Adam gave an affirmative nod. "Absolutely."

"Go easy on the extra shifts. You know what they say about all work and no play." With a suggestive wink, Molly ran her hand up his arm. "Hey, where's your brother tonight?"

"Beats me." He tipped the bottle to his lips and swallowed. "You know, you're always asking about Ryan, Mol. Sure you wouldn't just rather have him call you?"

Frank yelled to her from the other side of the bar. He indicated two customers waiting to be served. She rolled her eyes. "Duty calls."

Adam watched as she went back to taking drink orders. Someone in the tightly packed space jostled him from behind. Deciding to take his beer elsewhere, he swiveled the stool around and stood. Seth Kimmel leaned against the adjacent brick wall, watching him with flinty eyes. Apparently, he wasn't the only cop off duty tonight. Adam recalled Ryan's altercation with him the night of Nate Weisz's wake, as well as the reason for it. Molly. He gave the other man a cool nod of indifference and walked to one of the alcoves where a flat-screen television was blaring ESPN. The seats were full, however, so he remained standing.

It didn't take long for Seth to follow him over. He wore jeans and a T-shirt stamped with the logo of a local gym.

"Well, if it isn't the *other* Winter," he said mockingly. "What I want to know is whether you're as full of yourself as your brother."

Adam gave a casual shrug, although his eyes narrowed. "One thing's for damn sure—I don't have his patience."

"Word of advice?" He nodded to where Molly worked behind the bar. "You're not the only one sticking it into that. Better *wrap it up good*, son."

Adam bristled. So this *was* about Molly again. Seth was jealous. It was common knowledge she'd repeatedly refused his attentions. Still, he kept hanging around her like a hungry dog. It was downright creepy.

"Where I stick *anything* is none of your business. And don't talk about her like that, all right?"

Seth let out a derisive snort, the smell of liquor emanating from him. "Listen to you. She's a goddamn badge bunny, and you Winters act like she's some fair virgin to protect."

Adam's voice lowered in warning. "I've got no beef with you, Kimmel. Back off. Before I back you off."

"You think so?" Eyebrows clamped down, Seth leaned into his personal space. "Your brother—the big-fucking-deal detective—had his cronies around the night he got the better of me. But look around. There's a different crowd tonight."

Adam felt the muscles cord in his neck as his tolerance slipped another degree. He didn't want to take up Ryan's fight, but he wasn't going to put up with much more bullshit, either. This guy might be a juicehead, but he wasn't the only one in sparring shape. Not to mention, he appeared halfway to hammered.

Adam stepped so close their noses nearly touched.

"You're not dealing with a detective this time," he pointed out, shoulders rigid. "I'm on the streets like you. *I play rough.* Eight months in counternarcotics in Costa Rica put me up against some of the toughest sons of bitches anywhere. But if you still want to be stupid and take me on, we do it somewhere else."

Seth crowed, "That's what I figured—"

"*Don't* misunderstand me." Adam's words hardened. "Not here in Frank's place. But I'll go out back to the alley with you right now. And you've got my promise you won't be the one walking out of it." He let a purposeful beat of silence fall. "You in or not, big guy?"

A second of doubt flickered on Seth's blunt-featured face. He gave an inebriated wobble.

Adam shook his head. "Jesus. You're shit-faced, Kimmel. It wouldn't even be a fair fight. Go home before you embarrass yourself."

Seth's skin reddened as he glared at him. But even with the booze and steroids, he still had a few working brain cells, apparently. He tapped a finger into Adam's chest. "You know what? It's the birthday of our country. I feel like celebrating tonight. But I'll deal with you later, asshole. And that's a *promise.*"

With a last, meaningful scowl, he scrubbed a hand over his blond crew cut and retreated into the crowd.

Adam took a jerky pull from his beer bottle. It was true what their mother had told Ryan and him growing up, that bullies were all cowards at heart. Still, the exchange had his nerves crackling.

A short time later, he'd gone into the bricked corridor that led to the restrooms when he heard Molly speak to him. Adam stopped and turned. "Hey."

Reaching into her apron pocket as she approached, she pulled out his cell phone. "You left this on the bar."

"Oh. Thanks."

"Who's Rachel?" she asked with a frown.

Adam felt heat sweep over his face. Rachel was the girl he'd recently started going out with—three times now in the space of a week. He liked her. A lot, actually, and it seemed like she was into him, too. In fact, the only reason he wasn't with her tonight was that she'd planned a trip months ago with some girlfriends to Hilton Head for the July Fourth weekend.

"Just a girl," he said with a dismissive shrug.

She lit up the phone's screen before handing it to him, accusation in her eyes. Adam glanced at the text, his flush deepening.

FELL ASLEEP ON BEACH & HAD SEXY DREAM ABOUT U.

REENACT IT WHEN I GET BACK? ;-)

MISS U.

Rachel had attached a photo of herself in a bikini.

"You've got a girlfriend," Molly said in a flat tone.

Adam's chin dipped downward. He rubbed the back of his neck, displeased she'd been peeping at his phone. "It's nothing serious—"

"It *sounds* serious," she said snippily. "You made up

that stuff about working extra shifts because you've been avoiding me. I don't like being lied to, Adam."

Annoyance filtered through him. He didn't think he owed Molly an explanation. They had never even been on a date. He'd simply done Ryan a favor by seeing her home that night. Sure, they'd kissed and engaged in some heavy petting before he'd come to his senses, disentangled himself and called it a night. He *had* promised to call her, but then Rachel had finally come around.

"Look, I don't owe you anything just because we messed around. I didn't plan it this way, but I just started seeing someone, all right?" His words came out more sharply than he'd intended.

She gave him a hurt look and retreated to the kitchen, pushing through the double doors marked Staff Only. *Great.* Feeling ambushed, Adam dragged a hand over his mouth. This was turning out to be a real waste of a night off.

Returning to the main area, he noticed Seth closing out his tab at the bar. Adam hung back until he was done, although he caught the man's lethal glare as he stood and shoved his wallet into the back pocket of his jeans. Then Seth used his index finger and thumb to form the shape of a gun.

Pointing it at Adam, he cocked and fired, then strode out.

Shaking his head, Adam ordered another beer and took it to the back of the room, partially to give Seth time to clear out of the area before he exited, too. He'd already backed him down once, and with his current mood, the idea of pummeling him was becoming too big a temptation.

A short time later, he shouldered his way through the bar's crowd to the vestibule. Stepping out onto the sidewalk, he was met by the bass beat of live music coming from Centennial Olympic Park, accompanied by the booming discharge of fireworks. The park had begun putting on a display that rivaled the one at Lenox Square across town, and he looked up to see colorful pinwheels overlapping as they spread out in the black velvet night. The muggy air smelled singed from the explosives, reminding him of combat. He was supposed to meet up with some buddies who were down at the festivities but decided to just go home.

He passed through the throngs before finally turning onto Fairlie Street several blocks down. The crowds had dissipated somewhat here, with only a handful of people walking around and a small group of young adults sitting on the steps of an old building under renovation, smoking cigarettes as they talked. Despite the police shield Adam carried in his back pocket, he ignored the bottle they shared tucked into a brown paper bag. They all looked up briefly at another explosive burst of light in the sky.

His Jeep sat in an alley behind some loft apartments. He parked there often—illegal, but one of the few perks of being a cop. A small decal on the windshield alerted meter readers that it belonged to one of their own. Entering the murky passage, he dug his hand into the pocket of his jeans for his keys.

He halted at the scratch marring the driver-side door. *What the?* He felt a sudden chill of recognition.

Adam whirled.

The searing impact knocked him to the ground.

Dazed, clasping feebly at his shirt, he heard his own rasping breath and felt warm wetness on his fingers. His chest was on fire. *Help me.* But the cry remained trapped in his throat. A hooded male wearing jeans and sneakers stood inside the alley, gun raised and face in shadow. Overhead, the sky lit into pink as another rumble of fireworks echoed.

White-hot pain flattened Adam's lungs. He couldn't breathe. He tried to get up—get to the off-duty weapon he'd left in his Jeep—but his body managed only a weak flail. In his hazy vision, he saw the man moving toward him. He was tall and lanky, with pale skin and an angry, mauve slash for a mouth. Blond hair was visible under the hood.

Confusion mingled with the terror clawing at him.

It wasn't a man.

Her features were sullen as she stood over him, the grim black nozzle of the gun's silencer peering down. Pointing at him. Adam felt his world darkening. His heartbeat thrashed in his ears.

Three shots. Two up close and personal.

Her eyes glittered with tears. "You're all alike."

"Molly," he managed in a hoarse whisper. "Please, don't."

CHAPTER TWENTY-SIX

RYAN RUSHED INTO the crowded ER lobby with Lydia beside him. Fear weakening his limbs, he flinched inwardly at the police—some in uniform, some not—who were already gathering, talking in low tones under the harsh fluorescent lighting. Eyes turned toward them as they approached. He felt Lydia's fingers slip into his.

This couldn't be happening.

He forced himself to breathe as the group parted for them. Mateo came forward and clasped his shoulders in a firm grip. "He's *alive*, Ryan. Focus on that. They were able to stabilize him enough for surgery."

"How bad is it?" he asked, unable to suppress the quaver in his voice.

"We … don't know yet. It was a single GSW to the chest." Mateo hesitated, lines appearing in his face. "The paramedics think he might've been there for a while before he was discovered."

The information felt like a punch to his throat. Lydia squeezed his hand harder.

"Was he conscious when he arrived?" she asked. When Mateo shook his head, she added, "I'll go up and see what I can find out. Stay with him, all right?"

"Yeah." Mateo nodded.

Ryan squeezed his eyes closed as Lydia put her arms around his neck and hugged him hard.

"I love you," she whispered before walking briskly away.

Additional police were entering, and Ryan nodded, stone-faced, as more words of support were offered. Darnell Richardson and Antoine Clark, as well as several others he considered friends, were among the growing ranks. There were also many he didn't know, officers most likely from Adam's precinct. He saw his brother's partner, his face strained, as he came into the lobby. Ryan concentrated on remaining stoic, on trying to keep his knees from giving out on him.

"Let's get you up to the waiting room. Lydia will know where to find you," Mateo said a short time later. He was already guiding him out of the flow of police and others inside the overcrowded ER. "Evie's on her way as soon as the sitter gets to the house. She sends her love."

Mateo and Evie had been here for him before. Darkness washed over Ryan as he flashed on the day of Tyler's drowning, the déjà vu squeezing his chest. But this time it was images of Adam—in his military and police uniforms, in basketball clothes, as a dark-haired kid who followed his big brother everywhere—that tore at him. His stomach clenched, the hospital's antiseptic smells and blue corridor walls a sudden assault to his senses.

Once they were in the elevator alone and headed up to the waiting room, Ryan bowed his head and rubbed a hand over his burning eyes. Mateo leaned in awkwardly, one hand on his back.

"*Be strong*, man," he urged. "Adam's tough, not to mention stubborn as hell. He's going to pull through."

Ryan prayed that was true.

As the elevator doors slid open and they began walking, he realized they were headed to the same small, private waiting room where Kristen Weisz and her family had gathered as they awaited news on Nate. Entering, seeing the upholstered chairs and stacks of magazines fanned out on low tables, he felt physically ill.

"Tell me what you know," he said in a frayed voice.

"Task force members are on the scene—Chin and Hoyt, too. They're keeping me updated by phone. They talked to the civilian who called 9-1-1. The guy was using the alley as a cut-through when he found him. He didn't hear anything or see anyone else around. We've got men canvassing the area, talking to people and checking for security cameras that might've caught something." Mateo peered at him worriedly. "Ryan, you ought to sit. You're not looking too good."

His limbs still trembled, but he was too restless. The helplessness was suffocating. It felt better to stand and pace. Mateo went to a water dispenser in the room's corner and returned with a filled paper cup, handing it to him. Ryan accepted it, drinking down the cool liquid to ease the dryness in his throat.

"Adam was going to McCrosky's?" he asked, crumpling the empty cup.

"He'd just come from there. He had a receipt in his wallet. He was there a little under an hour, based on the time stamp. Our guys are there now, too, asking around."

"The casing's a match," Ryan said knowingly.

Mateo gave a somber nod. "Ballistics will have to confirm it, but it's our shooter. Ryan's Jeep was keyed."

His jaw ached from being clenched. He thought of his brother, wounded, lying in an alley alone.

"The shot came from about twenty feet away based on the location of the recovered casing. But what we don't know is why—"

"He didn't get a chance to finish. There're a lot of people out for the Fourth," Ryan said, the grim scenario already formed in his mind. "The shooter fired from a distance, then came in for the kill. But he got spooked by someone approaching on one of the streets and had to take off. Did Adam still have his shield?"

"I don't know. I'll find out."

The fireworks in the park would have most likely masked the already muted discharge of a silencer. Whatever it was that had scared this guy off, Ryan wanted to feel gratitude, but all he felt was a growing need for vengeance. He closed his eyes and took a breath, swallowing hard. He wondered if Adam had gotten a look at the perpetrator, if he hadn't lost consciousness immediately.

"There were some kids hanging out in front of a closed-down building nearby. One of the girls remembered Adam from an ID photo," Mateo said. "But she didn't recall anyone following him, at least no one who stood out enough to notice. Maybe our guy was already in the alley, waiting for him?"

Ryan didn't answer. He passed a hand over his face and then took several slow steps, his lips pressed tightly together. This hit seemed less planned, even impulsive. Watterson had also been in an alley, but the location had been remote, with a cinderblock wall and trees providing a shield. It had also been late at night and in a much less populated part of town. Taking Adam down in a location like that—in a downtown cut-through where he could be visible from either direction, on a holiday when the streets were busy—had been an enormous risk, suggesting the shooter was either beginning to think himself invincible …

Or he was spiraling out of control.

Mateo came closer, concern knitting his brow. "Ryan, have you reached your mom?"

Melanie Winter had moved to the Georgia coast several years earlier, to an active lifestyle retirement community where her sister and brother-in-law also lived. All of them were currently on a cruise in the Caribbean.

"Not yet." Dread pooled in his gut. He thought of the night his father had been killed on the job. Ryan had been only thirteen, Adam eight. "I'm going to wait until we know something."

Until he learned exactly what Adam was up against. He felt nearly dizzy with fear.

Blue uniforms had begun to have a presence in the hallway outside the room now, having moved up from the ER lobby. Ryan shook hands with Captain Thompson and the chief of police, as well as two others high up enough in rank to feel okay with entering the refuge of the private waiting room. As the men offered support, Ryan nodded his head numbly. Guilt thickened his throat.

He should be the one in there, bleeding, being operated on.

He should have caught this psycho.

Ryan was one of the lead detectives on the case. Had Adam been placed in the shooter's sights because of their blood relationship?

Overwhelmed, he startled at the PA system paging a doctor to the Oncology ward.

A short time later, Lydia appeared in the room's threshold as the command filtered out. Seeing her pale, worried face, he felt his heart drop into his stomach. This time, he lowered himself into a chair.

"He's in surgery now," she said as she entered. "They're doing everything they can."

"Some of the men are giving blood downstairs." Mateo moved toward the door, no doubt to give them privacy to discuss whatever Lydia had learned. "I'll be back, all right? We're all praying, Ryan."

He made the sign of the cross and closed the door behind him.

Ryan's stomach hardened as she took a seat beside him, placing her hand on his thigh and turning toward him as she spoke softly. "There's no spinal damage. But he has a shattered rib, and there's a serious injury to his right lower lung. A massive hemothorax with blood collected in the pleural cavity. The recommended course is to perform a partial lobectomy."

Lose part of his lung.

He felt tears sting his eyes. Lydia reached for his hand.

"What does that mean for him, exactly?" he asked.

"He can survive with it. He may have to get off the streets, but he can still have a normal, healthy life. It'll take some time to get his stamina back, but Adam's fitness level and age work in his favor."

Even as he nodded, he felt the hair on his arms rise. Her hesitant expression told him there was something else.

"The blood loss was … significant. They're giving transfusions." She took a tense breath. "There're also bullet and bone fragments embedded in his heart, Ryan. They have to come out. They're making his heartbeat erratic and could cause cardiac arrest."

His throat convulsed.

"Rick's performing the cardiac aspect of the surgery. I … made sure of it. He's already on his way in." She looked at him, clear-eyed and emphatic as she squeezed his fingers. "It's a complicated procedure, and he's one of the best cardiac surgeons in the country."

Ryan shook his head, uncertain. "Varek? I don't know—"

"Trust *me*, Ryan. I've already talked to him by phone. He'll do his very best, just as he would for any patient. *He's the best chance Adam's got.* He needs to be the one."

"All right," he said, his voice breaking. Lydia put her arms around him. Ryan was aware of the tears that leaked from his eyes. He felt powerless. Tyler was gone.

Adam had to live.

"I can't lose him, too," he whispered.

Lydia stood in the threshold of the ICU suite, one shoulder leaned against the doorframe. Her chest ached at the sight of Ryan in a chair beside the bed, absently running one hand over his mouth as he watched his brother. Adam remained unconscious and on a ventilator. Tubes ran in and out of him as a cardiac monitor beeped nearby, accompanying the vent's mechanical whooshing sound.

She swallowed hard, a similar scene settling over her. An image of Ryan, devastated, grasping Tyler's small fingers in the shattering quiet after the respirator had been stopped, tore at her heart.

He looked up as she came forward and laid a hand on his shoulder.

"He survived the surgery," she reminded, her voice soft. "That's something."

He gave a faint nod. Rick had spoken with both Ryan and Lydia early that morning. To his credit, he'd set aside any bruised feelings and had been a consummate professional, carefully explaining that the long surgery had been successful but the next few days were critical.

That conversation had taken place more than eight hours ago.

Adam's vitals needed to improve, and he needed to regain consciousness. The longer he remained on the vent and immobile, the risk for things like a clot breaking free or pneumonia setting in went up. As a doctor, she understood his life was in a fragile state and things could go either way.

Adam's dark, spiky lashes formed half-moons against his pale cheeks as his chest rose and fell with the ventilator's unnatural rhythm. Lydia moved closer to the bed and threaded her fingers through his hair, her throat tight.

Fight, Adam. Don't leave us.

They stayed until visitation time was up and then walked together from the suite. It would be another forty-five minutes before anyone except medical personnel would be allowed in again. Glass doors that led to a patio adjacent to the ICU nurses' station revealed a sunny day outside. It was already afternoon.

"Have you eaten?" she asked, concerned. "Tess brought some food by, which I put in the fridge in the lounge. I think she's just trying to find some way to be helpful, but I'm sure it's superior to the cafeteria's—"

"I don't want anything." Hands shoved deeply into his pockets, Ryan peered through the suite's glass window at his brother. "I'm going to the waiting room until I can get back in. There're still some of us around."

Although most of the police had left around four that

morning after Adam was out of surgery, Lydia was aware a handful remained, most of them uniforms who'd been on duty last night and had stopped by after their shifts, hoping for good news. She had seen them in the waiting room and circulating in the hallways.

"You haven't had any *sleep*, either," she pointed out gently. Ryan appeared tense and exhausted, his face pale and jaw stubbled. He still wore what he'd had on when they had gone to dinner last night. Lydia had caught a few hours in the bunk beds that were in an adjoining room of the physician lounge—used by doctors to nap between double shifts, or when a patient was too critical to leave. For a time, she'd coaxed Ryan into lying down in the narrow bed with her between visitations, but when she awoke a short time later, he was gone.

"We're here again, aren't we?" he said quietly, his eyes bleary. "Last night ... when we were together ... I thought maybe everything was finally going to be okay."

Lydia touched his arm in sympathy.

She spoke to one of the ICU nurses behind the desk as they passed it on their way out a minute later. Lydia wore medical scrubs and a lab coat, items from her locker she had changed into a short time ago. She'd found someone to take her shift that morning since she had been up most of the night.

"I'm on from one to five," she told him. "We're short-staffed coming off the long weekend, and I've had some sleep. Ryan ... I can check on Adam at every break—"

He shook his head. "I'm not leaving."

Lydia halted him. She looked into his eyes. "If *anything* happens, I can be up here in seconds. The nurses know me. They'll keep me closely in the loop. And as far as visitation goes, Adam's partner is in the waiting room. He just came back. They're close, and he wants to help. Please, Ryan. Go home for just a few hours and take a nap, all right? Have a shower and something to eat. Come back when my shift's over, and then I'll go home for a while. That way, one of us will always be here."

"I can't leave him."

"You can't keep going like this." Her voice softened in understanding. "Adam's condition could remain unchanged for a while. You have to pace yourself. He's going to need you *more* once he's awake."

He rubbed the back of his neck and released a breath.

"Have you spoken with your mom?"

"Her ship docked this morning in the Cayman Islands. She was going to try to get on the earliest flight here."

Lydia hoped they would have better news for Melanie by then regarding Adam's condition. At the thought of her arrival, however, she felt her stomach do a nervous little flip. She didn't know what her former mother-in-law's reaction would be to her and Ryan's reconciliation. Considering things, emotions would already be running high, and she knew her departure had been another hard blow for the family.

They reached the main ICU waiting area where a half-dozen police sat, sipping coffee from foam cups and talking quietly among themselves. Lydia and Ryan stood at the room's double doors. Beyond the chairs filled with people, a mounted television on the wall broadcasted the midday news. Lydia had seen the footage earlier, but she still felt gooseflesh rise on her skin.

Struggling and handcuffed, Ian Brandt was being taken into FBI custody by a half-dozen federal agents. It appeared dark on the recorded segment, suggesting the arrest had happened under cover of night. The television was on mute, but the caption at the screen's bottom was visible.

Atlanta businessman arrested on money-laundering, sex-trafficking charges.

"It went down this morning," Ryan said, peering at the screen where Brandt was being put into the back of a dark SUV. "I'm sorry. I should've told you once I heard."

Lydia ran her hand down his forearm. Adam's shooting had been the lead on last night's news, and she'd seen it on replay throughout the morning, as well. Until now, Ian Brandt had been the largest threat looming in her life. But everything now paled in comparison to Adam's fight.

"You've had other things to deal with," she said softly.

"My contact at the DOJ's been keeping me updated. Brandt was arraigned a little while ago in federal court. I don't know if the news is reporting it yet, but the judge considered him a flight risk and refused to set bail."

Lydia felt some relief, at least for herself. She knew the challenge Elise still had in front of her. Testifying against her husband, facing him in a courtroom—she couldn't imagine how terrifying that would be.

And if he was acquitted …

"He still has associates out there, Lyd. Keep your guard up."

"I will," she promised, not wanting to give him anything else to worry about. "So you'll go home for a few hours?"

He sighed, his eyes meeting Mateo's as he stepped off the elevator a little farther down the corridor. Lydia knew he'd gone home with Evie once Adam was out of surgery. He was now dressed for work, wearing his shield and holstered gun, but apparently had come by to check in.

"Talk some sense into him, Mateo? He needs some sleep," Lydia said as he reached them.

"He's hardheaded, but I'll work on it." Appearing uncomfortable, he asked, "Anything new?"

She shook her head.

"I need to talk to you for a minute, Ry." Glancing at Lydia, he added, "Before you go, I mean."

He briefly clasped Ryan's shoulder before turning into the waiting area where the others were.

"You'll call me if anything changes?" Ryan asked Lydia.

"The very second."

He studied her, his blue eyes tired. He didn't have to speak. Emotion seemed to hang in the air between them. Lydia knew he was grateful for her presence. Gently cradling the back of her neck, he drew her to him. She closed her eyes as his lips lightly brushed hers. They broke apart only at the soft claps of approval coming from the police in the waiting room.

A short time later, Lydia went back down the hall. But she didn't go directly to the ER. She still had some time before her shift, so instead she returned to the ICU. She talked to the nurse at the desk, asking that she be kept immediately updated on any changes. Then hesitating at the door, she entered the suite where Adam lay.

She felt her heart squeeze all over again. Seeing him like this—vulnerable, fragile, a machine breathing for him—was difficult. Adam was always so intense and full of life.

She knew what he thought of her. Lydia wanted a chance to somehow set things right between them.

Moving to the bed, she clasped Adam's still, cool fingers in hers, an ache inside her throat.

She hadn't prayed since Tyler's death. She'd been too angry with God and felt betrayed by her faith. But taking a halting breath, she closed her eyes now and silently asked for assistance, if anyone was listening.

CHAPTER TWENTY-SEVEN

———————◀)•●•(C———————

"SO WHAT'S YOUR take?" Ryan asked tensely as he stood with Mateo outside the ICU waiting room.

"It doesn't look good. Witnesses at McCrosky's confirm he and Adam had words last night and that Kimmel threatened him."

Ryan paced a few steps, a tingle in his chest, as his partner continued.

"Detectives went to his place—middle of the night—and no one was home. He didn't show up for his shift this morning, either."

"What about his cell?"

"No answer. We entered his apartment a little while ago under the guise of a safety check, but it was unoccupied. Vehicle's missing from the parking lot, too." Mateo scratched his jaw. "We're keeping this on the down low for now, until we know more. Ballistics are back, by the way. The gun used on Adam is a match to the other shootings."

Ryan stared at nothing for an overlong moment. Saying

he *disliked* Seth Kimmel would be an understatement, but he didn't see him as a serial cop killer.

Mateo splayed his hands. "Look, I know it's crazy, but you've got to admit Kimmel's disappearance right after the shooting is all kinds of suspicious. It's no secret he's got anger issues. Half the force hates him, and he's been passed over repeatedly for promotions—which could lead to a real grudge. If you squint hard enough, he's a sideways fit to the GBI profile."

Apparently anticipating Ryan's next question, he added, "And no, there's no nine mil registered to him, but that doesn't mean he doesn't own one illegally."

Ryan drew in a slow breath and released it. All of this was conjecture.

"It's not him," he said quietly.

"You sure about that?" Mateo persisted. "What if Adam *did* get a look at his shooter? It would explain why Kimmel's MIA. He knows Adam will identify him when he wakes up."

If he wakes up.

"We need to find him." Tired, Ryan squeezed the bridge of his nose, at least sure about that much.

"We've put a statewide BOLO out for that damn muscle car he drives."

"What about cameras?"

"No CCTV systems in the alley or access streets. Sorry, Ry."

He realized Mateo was peering at him.

"How're you doing?" his partner asked, shifting his stance to make room for a nurse pushing an EKG cart past.

Ryan sighed, not quite meeting his eyes. "I'm okay."

Mateo nodded toward the officers seated together in the ICU waiting area, Adam's partner among them. They were cloistered off from the civilians who also occupied the space. "You've got support. You can see that in there. The captain says to take the time you need."

Overwhelmed, Ryan clasped the back of his neck, at a loss for words. He cleared his throat. "Tell Evie I appreciate her being here last night. I never told her."

"She knows. She's happy about you and Lydia, too." He lowered his voice. "It's pretty obvious you guys are working things out."

Thinking of Lydia, Ryan felt his heart fill. Their lovemaking last night still tugged at him, as did her confession about the difficulties she'd been having since their split. He was worried about her, and he knew she was being strong for him now. Trying to help him get through this. He'd kissed her in front of the entire waiting room, but he didn't care—his emotions had gotten the better of him.

Ryan ran a hand over his mouth, still in disbelief about this latest hard turn of events.

Mateo gave his shoulder a light tap. "You should get going. Go home and grab some sleep while you can."

He pressed his lips together, something Mateo had said earlier jabbing at him. He should have ordered it sooner. "I want a cop positioned outside Adam's room. Can you get a plainclothes in there now?"

"Sure, but it's the ICU. There're nurses everywhere."

"You said yourself Adam could've seen his shooter."

Mateo reached into his pocket for his cell. "You're right. Better safe than sorry. All it would take is for someone to code. They're distracted and our guy goes in."

In his brother's fragile state, it wouldn't take much—a flipped switch on the ventilator, air injected into an IV line—to finish him. Ryan felt his muscles weaken at the thought. It seemed improbable in a crowded hospital, but he believed their killer was becoming bold enough to try anything. If he was going to be away for even a few hours, he wanted extra vigilance.

"Go on, Ryan. I'll keep watch on him myself until we get someone here."

"Don't get too hung up on this Kimmel thing," he warned. "I want you to treat this like it could still be anyone. Whoever you get for the detail, make sure they're watching everyone who goes in. If anyone looks like they're loitering or just seems out of place—"

"Got it." Mateo bobbed his head in understanding. "He could be the freakin' one."

At home, Ryan had drifted in and out of an uneasy sleep before finally giving up on the prospect entirely. He had showered, changed into fresh clothes and allowed Tess to coax some food into him before leaving again.

Know this, Winter. When I'm ready for payback, you won't even see me coming.

As he drove his SUV, Seth's threat that day in the precinct locker room replayed itself. But as much as Ryan himself loathed him, he still couldn't envision him as their shooter. The man's entire ego was wrapped up in the uniform and badge. He was a jerk, but he wasn't psychotic. Nor would he risk going down in the APD's annals as a cop killer.

Then where was he?

Fatigued and emotionally wrung out, Ryan passed a hand over his burning eyes and admitted he wasn't entirely sure about anything anymore.

The spired brick buildings of Agnes Scott College soon appeared on the SUV's right. A short time later, he turned onto Candler Street. The small ranch house Adam rented, nestled farther back among tall pines and other trees, came into view. Pulling into the driveway, Ryan cut the engine and sat inside the vehicle, his posture loose as he stared blindly out. He felt powerless not being part of the hunt for Adam's shooter, but he also understood why he had been temporarily removed from the case. Still, he'd come by here on his way to the hospital to look through his brother's belongings, hoping to find something that might tie him to the other victims. Some clue as to why he'd been targeted among the hundreds of metro officers.

The thought that Ryan himself might have been the reason due to his role in the investigation sat in his stomach like a stone.

Taking a tense breath, he exited the vehicle. Then digging the extra key Adam had given him from his jeans pocket, he stepped onto the porch, unlocked the door and went inside.

The house's quiet hit him hard. It was as if Adam no longer existed.

Don't think like that.

With a heavy heart, Ryan glanced around at the evidence of his brother's bachelor lifestyle. The living area was sparsely decorated, and clothes, as well as a Kevlar vest, were strewn on the couch. Athletic equipment, including several basketballs, a pair of high-tops and a gym bag, had taken root in one corner. An empty beer bottle sat on a coffee table amid copies of *Sports Illustrated.* Ryan couldn't help it—he briefly closed his eyes, Adam's face and voice in his head. He had seen him off at the airport for dangerous tours in Afghanistan and Costa Rica. But the sight of him tethered to a bed by EKG leads and IV lines, an endotracheal tube down his throat ... it frightened him.

Gritty eyed, he went into the kitchen. It was a notch or two neater in here, at least, although dishes were stacked in the sink. He shook his head, mustering a faint smile at Adam's characteristic untidiness.

For the second time in twenty-four hours, Ryan had a flashback of sitting next to him all those years ago, holding his small hand as their mother tearfully broke the news their father was gone.

Gone, like Tyler. Maybe Adam now, too.

Ryan felt a lump form in his throat. He had seen too much loss in his life.

Shaking off his grim thoughts, he looked around and

reminded himself why he was here. He flipped through mail on the counter, checked the phone for voice mail and studied the various notes and cards pinned to the refrigerator door with magnets. Nothing stood out beyond a recent snapshot of Adam and the girl Ryan had seen at the restaurant in downtown Decatur that night. In fact, the photo might have been taken there. He recalled her name was Rachel. In the image, Adam appeared handsome and whole, his arm around the pretty redhead's shoulders. He'd told Ryan she taught kindergarten.

He wondered if she knew about the shooting. Ryan didn't recall seeing her at the hospital.

His stomach fluttered as his cell phone rang. Reaching into his pocket for it, he checked the screen before answering.

"Did I wake you?" Mateo asked.

Ryan restacked the mail he'd gone through, deciding not to tell him where he was instead of resting. He didn't need a lecture. "No."

"I thought you'd want to know. A patrol unit just called in the plates on Kimmel's vehicle. It's parked on a side street near the Midtown MARTA station."

Admittedly, it was an odd place since it was nowhere near the officer's apartment complex on Briarwood. MARTA lines ran all over the city, including into the suburbs. "Which means he could be anywhere."

"Including Hartsfield," Mateo pointed out. "We've got units in the area, as well as men checking the transit's security cams for him. Detectives are headed down now to get the airlines' passenger logs."

"Any activity on his credit cards?"

"Nothing since the bar last night," Mateo said. "But he could've paid for a ticket with cash. You going back to the hospital soon?"

He felt a hollowness in his chest. "Yeah."

"Hang in there. I'll keep you posted."

Ryan disconnected, blowing out a breath before returning his cell to his pocket and leaving the kitchen. The ranch had a single bath and two bedrooms, one of which had been made into a home gym, with free weights and a bench press. Ryan wandered past it to the bedroom Adam used. Like the rest of the house, it was a study in his brother's special form of chaos, a contradiction to his military training. The bed was unmade, with a pile of mismatched clothing on the floor, and the top bureau drawer hung open. Ryan went to inspect its contents, then moved his attention to a duffel that lay on the bed. He unzipped it, surprised by the female clothing packed inside. A girl— perhaps Rachel—must have stayed overnight recently and left it behind.

A key chain crowded with novelty charms and discount cards lay on the bed, too, nearly obscured by the rumpled sheets. Curious, Ryan picked it up and shuffled through the items that included a tiny enameled heart, a whistle and miniature flip-flop ...

Ice water moved through his veins.

The last charm bore the logo from The Grindhouse.

Movement reflected in the bureau mirror. Ryan dropped the key chain and whirled, his hand reaching for the off-duty gun he wore holstered under his shirt.

"Don't."

Molly stood in the room's threshold, her blond hair wild and unkempt around her shoulders. Clad in a sweat jacket with the hood down and jeans, she gripped a handgun fitted with a silencer in both hands, pointing it at him. Ryan froze, his heart slamming into his ribs.

"Easy," he rasped, feeling the blood drain from his face. He slowly moved his hands out to his sides. Shock made his ears ring. "Molly ... you *know* me. Don't do anything you'll regret, all right?"

As she stared at him with a sullen expression, his mind raced. *Her* duffel and key chain. She was on her way out of town. Adam *had* seen her last night. He guessed she'd gotten into the house somehow before him. His arrival had surprised her, and she'd hidden, leaving her belongings out in the open in her haste.

There were probably things in the duffel, souvenirs, which would link her. When he had come across it, she'd had no choice but to show herself.

Adrenaline pumped through him. She'd been right there in front of them, hiding in plain sight. Female, not male. They'd ignored the credit transactions from McCrosky's since it was a given any cop in downtown had been there.

Ryan suspected why she was here now.

He spoke calmly despite the heavy thudding of his

heart. "Adam's badge was on him last night. It's not here ... That *is* what you're looking for, isn't it?"

Her eyes were wet, her mouth pinched. Molly gripped the gun harder. "Take your gun out slowly and put it on the floor. I've seen your backup through your shirt before, so I know where it is. Don't make me hurt you, Ryan."

When he hesitated, she snapped, "Do it!"

Muscles rigid, he kept one hand in view while he carefully reached under his shirt for his gun. He went onto his haunches and placed it on the carpet, then rose, his mouth and throat dry. Disbelief still tightened his skin.

"Can we talk about this?" Ryan asked gently. "Molly ... you're not well. Let me help you—"

"Why are you here?" she demanded. "Is Adam dead?"

"He's in a coma. He's in bad shape." He kept his tone even, aware showing any anger could be a fatal mistake. "Do you want to tell me *why*, at least?"

She chewed her trembling lip. "He was just like the rest of them. He used me and then he lied to me. I hope he *dies*."

His nerves zinged with electricity. Ryan took a cautious step closer, his hands remaining poised at his sides. Molly liked him, he knew that, and he hoped he might get her to let her guard down long enough to disarm her.

"How is he like the rest of them, Molly? Adam's my little brother. Help me to understand—"

"You *know* how!" Agitated, her high-pitched voice split the air. "They all want to screw me. They act like I'm someone special until they get what they want!"

Her lip curled back in disgust. "And then they go home to their stupid wives and girlfriends, smelling like sex. Like *me.*"

You do that and I'll fucking kill you.

Nate had been talking to Molly on the phone that day. She must have called him, threatening to approach Kristen Weisz. As she railed, Ryan took another cautious step closer.

"I have feelings! I'm not some whore they can just shove their cocks into and then pretend like nothing happened!"

"You're upset. You have a right to be," Ryan said soothingly. "No one should treat you like that. *No one.*"

She changed her grip on the gun to one hand, using the other to wipe at her watery eyes. He was less than five feet from her now.

"You always treated me good, Ryan. At Nate's wake, after the way you protected me from Seth ... I *thought* you liked me," she said, sniffling. "I wanted you to like me so much."

"I *do,*" he stressed, reaching a hand out to her.

Her mouth went slack. Something shifted in her expression, the vivid green irises transforming into brittle glass. Without warning, she fired. Ryan felt the impact in his side, a cutting pain that doubled him over before dropping him. His breath froze inside his lungs. Through his shock, he saw Molly staring down at him.

"You're a liar like the rest of them." Her voice was cold. "I know you're back with your bitch ex-wife."

CHAPTER TWENTY-EIGHT

P ANIC MADE HIM lightheaded. Body wet and shivering, he created a seal over Tyler's mouth and nose. Two rescue breaths. He watched the small chest lift. Then thirty compressions, fast and hard. Again.

With each press on his sternum, he made a bargain with God.

Please don't take him. I'll do anything.

Tyler lay on the concrete, his dark hair wet and skin tinged blue against his sodden pajamas. Tears blurring his vision, he stopped CPR long enough to search for breathing or a pulse. Some faint proof of life. Wiping water from his face, he screamed out hoarsely again for help.

He did the breaths and compressions, two and thirty, two and thirty—fingers numb with cold and fear choking him as emergency sirens began to wail in the distance.

In his torment, his eyes were drawn across the pool and its half-sunken tarp in the frigid water. Adam stood on the other side, watching him. He clutched Tyler's small hand.

Tyler grinned his little-boy grin and waved.

Ryan winced and pulled his head upright, the dream disintegrating at the white-hot flare of pain. Molly was on her knees beside him, pressing one of Adam's T-shirts against his side. Her long hair brushed his chest.

He must have passed out. Ryan swallowed roughly, disoriented. He sat on the floor, his back against the bed's railed footboard and his jean-clad legs sprawled on the oatmeal-colored carpet.

The metallic scent of his blood made his stomach clench.

Eyes watering, he tried to wrench away from her painful ministrations. His skin prickled as he realized his wrists had been bound to the footboard's legs with plastic zip-ties, the kind used to subdue arrestees. Whether they had been taken from his pocket while he'd been out or had been among Adam's things, he didn't know.

The carpet held a rusty trail of blood. Vaguely, Ryan remembered being dragged on his back. Which meant a through-and-through. He flinched, perspiration popping out on his forehead as she pressed another shirt into place on top of the other one.

"Your back's bleeding, too."

"I need to see the wound, Molly," he panted. "See how bad it is—"

She hushed him, her face inches from his. Late-afternoon sunlight filtered in through the window, highlighting the amber flecks in the green eyes rimmed by black lashes. She appeared calm, even serene now, her agitation gone. "Don't squirm. You'll only make it worse."

Ryan grimaced against the pain radiating in his side. Molly had already proved herself a good shot. If she'd wanted to kill him, she would have. "Listen to me, all right? I need you to call 9-1-1. You don't have to be here. You can take my SUV and go."

She sat back, staring inquisitively at him as she brushed her hair from her eyes. She'd removed the hooded sweat jacket, revealing the short-sleeved top she had on underneath it.

"I've never hurt you, Molly. You *know* that." He swallowed with effort. "I need help."

With a resigned sigh, she reached for something behind him on the bed. Ryan's blood ran cold as he saw what she held. His shield. As she studied it, her eyebrows drew pensively together.

"She's old. She's not even that pretty." Frowning, she ran the tip of a bloodstained fingernail over the gold metal. "Is it because she's a doctor?"

Ryan drew in a labored breath, closing his eyes against a wave of dizziness. He needed to keep talking, keep a rapport with her and not drift into unconsciousness again.

"What …" He wet his lips as he gathered his strength. "What do you know about Lydia?"

The feel of cool fingers sliding through his hair made him shiver, as did the closeness of her voice.

"I know *everything*. What a heartless bitch she is. How

she left you after your little boy died. She doesn't deserve you."

He forced his eyes open, recognizing the editorial. "Who told you that? Adam?"

Molly shrugged. "He didn't like her showing up, either."

She had to be talking about Nate's wake—the night Lydia had come by. Ryan recalled Molly eavesdropping on them on the patio ... as well as the hooded figure he'd glimpsed on the street when he'd gone out to his car. The one he thought had been watching him. The kitchen at McCrosky's had a rear exit. It would have been possible for her to temporarily slip outside.

"He took me home, but he was more interested in bitching about *her* than anything." With a huff, she toyed with the buttons on his shirt. "We finally started messing around, but just when things started getting hot, he made up some excuse and left. I don't think he could get it up."

She leaned closer, her intimate whisper against his ear making Ryan's flesh pebble.

"Lydia's so cold she even shriveled *your brother's* dick."

She sat back on her heels and smiled at her own joke before her features morphed into petulance again. Picking up his shield from where she'd placed it on the floor, she examined it in her palm, frowning hard. "*You* were supposed to take me home that night, Ryan. Not Adam. You *wanted* to. I could see it in your eyes and the way you were standing so close to me. The way you protected me from Seth. Everything would've been different if *that bitch* hadn't shown up."

"Different?" Ryan repeated hoarsely.

She leaned forward again to touch his face. "It was *our* chance. I have a secret … I've always had a crush on you, Ryan. I like you more than any of them. And I know you would've treated me right if you could've just come out of your shell. I kept waiting for you to make your move, but you were just too shy to go after what you wanted."

She shook her head. "The number she did on you … it hurt your confidence."

"Molly, *please*. If you like me so much, call for help. This … isn't good."

She said nothing in response. He had a rising sense he would die here.

"I pretended Adam was *you* the night he took me home. I wanted him to really fuck me. Get rough with me, you know?"

Her forehead creased faintly as she glanced to the cotton garments covering his wound. Blood—a round spot of it, the size of a half-dollar—had already begun leaking through. Ryan felt cold, his skin clammy. Anxiety traced over him. "I'm going into shock, Molly. Is that what you want?"

She pensively chewed her bottom lip. Without another word, she rose to her feet and left the room.

The zip-ties cut into Ryan's wrists as he pulled at them. He felt stupid and angry that Molly had blindsided him. That she had hidden her psychosis from a bar full of trained detectives and police. He leaned sideways, testing the strength of the bed's metal feet, then winced at the hot flash of pain the movement created. It took his breath away, narrowing his field of vision.

Don't pass out again.

Head leaned back against the footboard, he tried to console himself with the fact that he hadn't been the only one who'd been fooled. John Watterson and Nate, Matthew Boyce, Adam—they'd all been much closer to Molly than he had, apparently. He tried to picture Nate at The Grindhouse with her as his clandestine date, paying her way in and pretending to like her music so he could screw her. Ryan shook his head. He'd thought he and Kristen were stronger than that.

That lay had gotten him killed.

A trickle of sweat rolled down his temple as she returned with a few towels. His mind turned to Lydia and their too-late reconciliation, his belly knotting with regret. If he died, Ryan feared she wouldn't survive another loss.

Molly sank down beside him.

"How ... how'd you know about Lydia and me?" He grimaced, tamping down a wave of nausea as she tucked a towel behind his back. Even with the terrible pain, he couldn't stop from trying to fit the pieces together.

"I went to the hospital last night. To find out if Adam was dead. I saw you with her. *The two love birds*," she said sourly.

Ryan hadn't even seen her there.

Her tone was matter-of-fact. "You might think you can

work it out with her, Ryan, but you can't. I can hear the coldness in her voice every time she answers the phone. A woman like that doesn't change. She'll never forgive you for what happened. She only wants to keep you close so she can torture you."

His eyes were squeezed closed, but he opened them again. Apprehension curled around his spine. "You ... called Lydia?"

A faint smile played on her lips as if she was about to say something clever.

"*Tyler* called her, too."

He felt his muscles go rigid. It had been Molly making the prank calls, not Brandt.

"Who ... was the child, Molly?"

"A kid in my apartment complex. I was babysitting."

"And the man who called?"

She shrugged. "Just a date."

Ryan squinted at her, anger heating his face. "You sent the wasps."

The afternoon sunlight caught her blond hair. Molly lifted the length of it behind her head and let it fall around her shoulders. The movement might have been sexy if not for the vehemence brimming in her eyes. "I wanted her smug face to swell. I wanted to make her ugly. I bet you wouldn't like her so much then."

He clenched his teeth. "She could've *died*—"

"Then she could be with her precious Tyler."

Her flippancy hardened his stomach, just as his rage exhausted him. Ryan felt himself grow frailer as he tried to get his mind around the fact that the threats to Lydia had been about him.

"You're white as a sheet," she cooed, moving closer. *Too close.* He swiveled his head away, but she cupped his jaw and forcefully turned his face back to hers. "Don't be mad. You need your strength. You can't get so worked up about every little thing."

He thought of all Molly knew about Lydia—her birth date, her allergy to bee venom. "But how'd—"

She laid her fingers against his lips, hushing him.

"Personal information's everywhere on the Internet. You're a detective, you know that," she scolded as if she could read his mind. "I also work in a cop bar, and your friends like to talk, Ryan. Especially to a hot waitress who's *overserving* them. All I had to do was ask the right questions." Her fingernail scraped over his bottom lip. "I like your mouth."

Ryan wrenched away from her.

"Frank mentioned the allergy. He was talking about some drama on the patio before you two were married. She was a lucky woman, Ryan. But she threw you away."

He groaned, pain lancing through him as she suddenly lifted her thigh and moved to sit on top of him, straddling him intimately. The floral scent of her perfume mingling with his own coppery odor increased his nausea. His clothing was damp, his heart skittering in frantic, shallow beats. Bending her head, she pressed her lips to his throat as she undid the top buttons on his shirt. Then her mouth covered his, and he felt repulsion flow through him. Molly began to rotate her pelvis, grinding against him as she undid another button and slipped her fingers inside. Fresh perspiration covered his skin. He felt the warmth of more blood leaking from his wound with her movements. A gray mist fell over his vision.

She was going to kill him.

The electronic shrill broke through the sound of his ragged breathing. His cell phone. She must have taken it along with his shield and weapon. Based on the sound, it lay on the bed behind them. Ryan wheezed, stars exploding in his vision as she climbed roughly off him, clearly displeased by the interruption. She went for the phone.

"It's *her*," she said stonily, walking to stand in front of him.

Molly waited for the ringing to stop, then for the beep that indicated a voice mail had been left. She pressed the screen and put the device to her ear, and he saw her jaw harden as she listened to his message. Ryan's heart twisted. He longed to hear Lydia's voice, fearing it would be the last time.

There would be no 9-1-1 call. Molly wasn't leaving here until he stopped breathing. He prayed her interest in Lydia would end there, too.

Lips pressed flat, she deleted the message, then tossed the phone back onto the bed. Picking up his shield from the carpet, she shoved it into her duffel. Ryan knew in his gut it held the others, packed beneath her clothing.

The call had angered her, her gaze now cold.

"And you *did* hurt me. The night you palmed me off on

Adam so you could be with *her*. She can't even give us our privacy now, can she?"

Stepping closer, she ruffled her fingers through his damp hair. "She's looking for you, by the way. Adam died."

CHAPTER TWENTY-NINE

———————◦)) • ● • ((◦———————

STANDING IN THE hallway outside the ICU, Lydia disconnected her phone. Unable to reach Ryan by cell, she had called the bungalow's landline as well, but had spoken only to Tess, who had been there borrowing the oven. She'd told her Ryan had set out some time earlier for the hospital.

Then where was he?

She searched through the phone's contacts, located the needed number and dialed.

"Hernandez," Mateo answered curtly on the second ring. Wherever he was, Lydia could hear urban noise and conversation in the background.

"Mateo, it's Lydia." She paced a few steps. "I'm sorry to bother you, but Ryan isn't with you, is he?"

"Lydia—I didn't recognize the number. He's not here, but I talked to him awhile ago by phone. He said he was headed back to the hospital. He's not there yet?"

"No, and he isn't answering his cell," she said, faintly worried.

"Did you call the house?"

"Tess said he left there about an hour ago." At the elevator's chime, Lydia glanced to the bay a little farther down the corridor, watching as the doors opened. Ryan wasn't among the exiting passengers. "I need to locate him—"

A strain entered his voice. "It's not Adam, is it?"

"It's *good* news," she assured him. "He's out of the coma. He's still critical and isn't able to communicate yet, but they're hoping to take him off the ventilator soon."

She heard his release of breath. "Thank God."

"Ryan's mother is here now, too."

"Look, I'm sure he'll show up soon. He's pretty shook up, blaming himself for Adam being shot. Maybe he just needed some time. You know Ryan. He's probably driving around somewhere trying to get his head on straight. I'd try to find him for you, but I'm tied up here—"

A male voice interrupted. Lydia heard the term *chain of command*. She knew enough about police protocol to understand they were talking about evidence handling.

"Hold on a sec, Lydia."

She waited as Mateo gave directives. Then he stopped talking altogether, the noise around him receding. Lydia guessed he was taking the phone to a quieter area. Finally, he spoke again. "Sorry. We've got an active crime scene here."

She felt butterflies in her stomach, almost afraid to ask. "Another officer?"

He hesitated. "In an alley off International Boulevard."

Lydia ran a hand through her hair. The location wasn't far from where Adam had been found the previous night.

"Confidentially, the deceased is from our precinct and until now was a person of interest in the investigation, so we're back to square one," Mateo said. "Ryan will want to know about this. I'm going to leave a message on his phone if I can't reach him, either. When he shows up at the hospital, make sure he's spoken with me, all right?"

Shocked by what she'd been told, she agreed. "Mateo. If you reach him, please have him call me."

"You got it. As soon as I finish up here, I'm headed to where you are. I want to talk to Adam the second he's able. So will Ryan." He disconnected.

Tension tightened her shoulders. With a slow release of breath, Lydia turned off her phone—a requirement for re-entering the ICU—and returned it to the pocket of her lab coat. This wasn't like Ryan. She'd had to practically throw him out of the hospital, and even then he'd been adamant about being kept updated. Lydia thought about what Mateo had said. *He's pretty shook up, blaming himself for Adam being shot.* She knew he was taking this hard, which was all the more reason she wanted to reach him with good news.

Pushing through the wing's double doors, she nodded to the plainclothes officer who had been assigned guard duty before moving to the threshold of the ICU suite. Inside it, Melanie Winter sat in a chair next to the bed. She clasped Adam's still fingers.

"Is something wrong?" she asked, a tremor in her voice, when she saw Lydia. "He's unconscious again."

Lydia came closer and laid a reassuring hand on her shoulder as she looked down at Adam. "He's just asleep, Melanie. They had to sedate him pretty heavily so he wouldn't fight the ventilator. But he woke up on his own, and his vitals are a little better. I talked to his nurse. The doctors are going to attempt to extubate him in a few hours, so they'll start lowering his medication soon."

Relief filled her blue eyes, her face framed by a soft, pixyish cut. Her hair, still mostly a light brown, appeared sun-streaked from her ocean cruise. "So he'll be able to breathe on his own?"

Lydia smiled softly and nodded, feeling her own heart lift.

To her great relief, Melanie hadn't snubbed her as she'd feared. Instead, her former mother-in-law had hugged her on sight as if she and Ryan had never come apart. There hadn't been much time, and so far they had talked only about Adam's condition. Lydia wanted Ryan to be the one to tell her about their reconciliation, anyway; it was his place. Hope flitted through her that Melanie would be happy for them despite everything.

"Did you reach Ryan?" Melanie asked.

"No, but I left a message." Worry nagged at her once more.

We're here again, aren't we? Last night ... when we were together ... I thought maybe everything was finally going to be okay.

She recalled Ryan's telling statement, making her aware of the parallels he'd already drawn between Adam and Tyler. Lydia knew he was expecting and bracing for the worst. That he was already shouldering the responsibility for Adam's shooting. His state of mind concerned her. She had ridden with Ryan to the hospital last night, but she could take a cab back to her place to get her car.

Her shift had ended a short time ago. Lydia touched Melanie's shoulder again, capturing her attention. "Since you're here with Adam now, I'm going to look for Ryan."

Somberly, she thought of where he might be.

"You're supposed to be heroes."

His head had been leaned back against the footboard, but at her statement Ryan looked at Molly with reddened eyes. He felt a despairing anger. Her own ire apparently faded, she had returned to the room and come to sit cross-legged near him again.

Grief for Adam had distracted him. Only now did he notice she had taken the shields—sick mementos from her kills—from her bag.

"Do you know what your friend, Nate, liked?" she asked absently as she moved the badges around on the carpet, placing them in some special order only she understood. "Blow jobs."

She pushed her long hair behind her, sliding one to the grouping's center. "I sucked him off in his car a half-dozen times, probably. He'd come by after work and wait for me outside. He'd pull my hair and tell me to swallow. Men want what they can't get at home."

His face grew hot. He didn't want to remember Nate—any of them—like this. Ryan squinted at her.

"Nate …"—he drew in a painful breath—"took you to The Grindhouse."

Molly looked at him, surprised. "How'd you know that?"

When he didn't respond, she went back to her badges. "It was a good band, and I wanted to go. I promised him something special afterward. I suppose Nate figured he wouldn't know anyone there."

"You went with Matthew Boyce, too."

She gave a casual shrug. "Matt hated the place, but I still got him to meet me there twice. After that, he'd only come by my apartment …"

The reflective smile on her lips faded, her mouth tightening. "He told me he despised her. I thought with the divorce final he'd be willing to take things out into the open. But he said I'd gotten possessive and he couldn't be serious with someone who'd fucked her way through the force."

Ryan concentrated on his words, fighting lightheadedness. "Is that why you keyed their cars? Because they hurt you?"

She lifted her chin. "Men are psychos about their rides."

His mood sank deeper. What he'd originally thought to be a gang marker had been merely adolescent-level retribution. Something a spurned teenager might do to get even with an unfaithful boyfriend. Ryan felt a spasm in his back from his current position, but if he remained immobile it lessened the pain. Based on where he'd been shot, he guessed the bullet had missed vital organs. Otherwise, he'd most likely be dead by now instead of slowly bleeding out. He stared at Molly as she continued playing with the badges, a bitter taste in his mouth. A vision of Adam lying in a grimy alley, alone and mortally wounded, thickened his throat.

"But you took it beyond that," he pointed out. "The scratches weren't enough—"

Bitterness filled her voice. "They got what they deserved."

Ryan noticed it then. There were four shields. The two gold ones mounted on leather wallets were his and Nate's. The other two belonged to uniformed officers. But she should have had only Matthew Boyce's. She hadn't gotten John Watterson's or Adam's. He couldn't see the number on it, but intuition pressed down on him.

"Seth Kimmel … that's his badge."

She blinked at him in the slanting sunlight. Putting away the grim keepsakes, Molly moved the duffel aside. She sighed and unfolded her long legs, slinking toward him on all fours. "That *asshole* was the reason I couldn't get back to Adam. I ran out of the alley when I heard those kids coming. Seth was right there on the street in front of me, gunning that stupid Mustang. He saw me. He could connect me."

Ryan turned away from her as she ran a fingertip along his jaw. "Seth finally got his roll in the hay. But I don't want to talk about that anymore."

Her breath fanned his ear as she pressed closer, her voice suggestive. "Finish what we started earlier? This could be our only chance to be together—"

"That's not happening—"

"Because of Lydia?" she snapped.

"Because you *shot* me."

His physical condition didn't seem to make an impression on her. She peeled off her top that was splotched with his blood, revealing a satin bra, clearly ready to pick up where she'd left off now that her anger over the phone call had ebbed. His skin prickled as she leaned in to nibble on his earlobe, a low purr in her throat as her hand roamed his bared chest. Stomach souring, Ryan leaned away, wincing as pain speared through him. Her palm slid down to the inside of his thigh, squeezing him intimately. She was out of her freaking mind.

The sound of a car traveling up the driveway made them both freeze.

Ryan's pulse raced. His ears strained for the sound of more than one vehicle and the shuffling of heavy footsteps. Armed officers in SWAT gear. But instead, his heart began to thud as the single car came closer.

Dear God. No.

The familiar sound of the engine was ingrained too deeply in his memory. All those years hearing it pull up outside their home. His eyes watered in recognition.

Lydia's Volvo.

Rising, Molly carefully looked out between the window blinds.

"That *cunt*." Features hard, she moved to her duffel and snatched it up, placing it on the bed and shuffling through it. Ryan craned his neck, trying to see what she was up to behind him. She pulled fresh clothes from the bag. Panic made his lungs restrict.

"The door's locked," he bargained. "You want to be alone with *me*. You don't have to answer it—"

"I'm not stupid! Your SUV's outside. She knows you're here."

His breath rasped out of his body. He screamed Lydia's name, attempting to warn her away.

"Shut up!" Molly stood over him, something gripped in her hand. Ryan went cold as he realized what it was.

The missing stun gun from Matthew Boyce's belongings.

He tried to scream out another warning, but it died in his throat as she pressed it to his collarbone and held it there. Ryan's body convulsed with the charge, pain exploding inside him as his mind melted into white noise.

CHAPTER THIRTY

LYDIA HAD BEEN leaving the cemetery when Tess reached her by cell, telling her she'd noticed the extra key to the house Adam rented was missing from the peg where it hung in the mudroom.

That clue had led her here.

Parked beside Ryan's SUV, she stared out at the modest white ranch and wondered whether he'd come here to be alone. She couldn't just call here since Adam had done away with his hard line years ago. Not to mention, Lydia had tried Ryan's cell several more times, but it had gone straight to voice mail, as if it had been turned off.

I'm not intruding. I'm here with good news. Taking a breath, she turned off the Volvo's engine, also cutting off the radio station she'd had on as she drove. Getting out, she walked onto the porch and knocked. She waited, then knocked again. Her stomach flip-flopped as, a few moments later, a familiar blonde—the waitress from McCrosky's—answered.

"Lydia, right?" She smiled brightly, wiping her hands

with a dishtowel she held. "I'm Molly. We met at Frank's place?"

She nodded, caught off guard. "Of course …"

"I'm sure you're looking for Ryan. He's in back, but he's on the phone." She opened the door wider and took a step back in invitation. "You must've just gotten off work."

Lydia still wore scrubs and her lab coat. In her haste, she hadn't taken time to change. She hesitated in the heat, then hitched her backpack higher on her shoulder before stepping inside. Confusion filtered through her. Molly was the one she'd believed Ryan had made plans with the night of Nate's wake. For all she knew, they had. She tamped down the uneasy feeling she had about her being here now.

"He's in the bedroom talking with Mateo." Molly closed the door behind her. "It sounds important. They've been going at it for a while. I was just going to make some tea. Would you like some?"

"You're a friend of Adam's?" Lydia asked carefully as she followed her through the living area, aware of the other woman's tall form, clad in faded jeans and a slightly sheer, sleeveless blouse. Her flaxen hair appeared disheveled and hung halfway down her back.

"We've gone out a few times. We're mostly friends, though." They passed through the hall and entered the kitchen. Dishes were stacked in the sink, and a collection of cereal and granola boxes sat on the counter. Molly put down the dishtowel and turned to her. "You're probably wondering why I'm here, right? I live close by. Adam gave me an extra key, so I came to check on the place and pick up the mail."

She made a helpless gesture. "I'm just trying to do what I can to help, you know? I wanted to talk to Ryan, so I've been waiting for him to get off the phone."

Moving to the stove, she picked up the teakettle. "Did you want a cup?"

Lydia shook her head, her muscles tensing as she noticed the mismatched buttons on Molly's blouse. As if she'd had to redress quickly. Was it possible she had walked in on something here?

She didn't believe that. Still, her skin tingled, a heavy feeling in her stomach.

"I could ask you instead of Ryan. Is there any change with Adam?"

"We're … hopeful. His vitals are improved." Lydia took a step back toward the hall. "Excuse me. I'm going to find Ryan—"

"He's in the shower, Lydia."

Lydia turned to look at her, her lips parting at the flat comment. Molly's eyes were on her, a small, superior smile on her face. She still held the empty teakettle while water ran in the sink behind her. "He's washing the *sex* off him. He doesn't even know you're here. I'm sorry you had to find out like this. Ryan's been working up the courage to tell you."

Adrenaline raised the hair on Lydia's nape. This woman was lying. Something was very wrong. Lydia left the kitchen, her heartbeat hammering in her ears. Reaching the hallway, she called out. "Ryan—"

Something hit the back of her skull with a sickening thud, and Lydia fell to her hands and knees, her backpack slipping off her shoulder. She heard herself moan as dizziness slammed into her, making the floor tilt. The aluminum teakettle rolled on its side nearby. Molly had thrown it at her?

Warmth trickled down her neck. Fear rose like bile in her throat as several drops of blood splattered onto the carpet below her. She swayed, closing her eyes and trying not to pass out.

Was this who … was she …

"Ryan!" she screamed, her voice frail and high-pitched. Molly grabbed at her, trying to wrench her up, but Lydia twisted away, kicking her shin with her sneaker-clad foot and making her bite out a curse. Woozy, she scrambled away on all fours until a metallic sound froze her in place. Lydia had been on the shooting range with Ryan before, and she recognized the sound, her heart turning over. A bullet dropping into a chamber. Lydia felt her insides go weak. She hadn't seen a gun. Molly must've had it hidden in the kitchen. She turned her head to look at her, trying to focus her bleary vision. The gun had a long cylinder attached to the barrel.

"Get up," Molly ordered.

"Where's Ryan?" Her breath came in fast, shallow waves. "Tell me where he is!"

She cried out in pain as Molly fisted a hand in her

hair, ripping some of it out as she forced her unsteadily to her feet. Standing behind her, Molly wrapped her arm tightly around Lydia's throat and pressed the gun against her temple with her other hand. Struggling dizzily, Lydia felt more blood leak down the back of her neck.

"I should've taken care of you in that garage." Molly's hateful voice in her ear sent a hard chill through her. "I had acid to throw in your smug face. Who'd want you after that?"

Lydia felt herself nearly hyperventilating. She recalled that night at the hospital, after her fight with Rick. She'd gotten paranoid someone was following her, and she'd rushed to her car with her key chain and pepper spray in hand. The pepper spray. Lydia's heart sank. It was in her backpack. Her eyes moved sluggishly to the blue-and-white striped bag on the floor. Molly walked backward with her toward the kitchen, her forearm compressing her windpipe and the gun to her head.

Where *was* Ryan?

Molly tightened her hold and dragged her when she tried to resist. "Since you've shown up uninvited, *Lydia*, maybe we need to revisit that plan."

CHAPTER THIRTY-ONE

RYAN'S EYES FLUTTERED open. With effort, he pulled his head upright as all of it came rushing back to him. Lydia's arrival. The stun gun that must have jolted him into unconsciousness. His muscles were still numb and weak from the charge, but his heart clenched at Molly's voice coming from somewhere inside the house, indiscernible but threatening.

She had her. Lydia's terrified cries made something break loose inside him.

He fought against the zip-ties binding his wrists to the legs of the footboard. The makeshift dressing over his wound had fallen away, the stun gun's violent current apparently catalyzing the bleeding. Ryan felt lightheaded at the bright, fresh blood soaking through the lower right quadrant of his shirt.

Lydia screamed for him.

Fear clouded Ryan's vision. He had to get free. If it killed him, he had to get to her, protect her from that psychotic bitch.

Desperate, he pulled again at his restraints, causing pain that stole his breath. Perspiration rolled down his back.

Get past the panic and think. She's still alive because Molly wants to play with her. But you're running out of time.

Ryan couldn't pull his way free of the zip-ties, couldn't break them, but could he leverage the footboard off the floor just enough to slide the plastic strips down its legs to free himself? He didn't know where the strength would come from, but he had to find it. He wasn't even certain he could stand.

Craning his neck, he looked around as best he could. Molly had left his Glock on the bureau, confident he couldn't escape.

Lydia's cries pumped adrenaline into him.

Ryan braced his feet against the adjacent wall, applying his weight to the footboard as he pushed up using his back. Searing pain tore through him. He heard his own anguished groan and felt sweat pour from his body. The effort intensified the burning in his side and made more blood seep out of him.

He managed to lift the footboard from the floor—maybe a quarter inch—but it dropped back onto the carpet with a muted thud before he could slide either restraint down enough.

Ryan cursed in defeat, eyes closed and chest heaving as his head fell back weakly against the rails. He tried to find his breath as a wave of despairing heat fell over him.

He had to try again.

✳

Bewilderment and terror clawed at Lydia as Molly forced her through the kitchen entrance, her right arm wrapped around her neck like a restraint collar and the gun pressed to her temple.

I had acid to throw in your smug face.

She went rigid, grasping onto the counter's edge to anchor herself as it came within reach.

"Move, *bitch*." The pressure on her throat intensified, making her wheeze until her fingers released their hold. If this was the police shooter … was Ryan dead? Tears leaked from her eyes.

Molly continued to propel her forward until they stood in front of the oven.

"Reach out your hand and turn on the eye."

Her stomach twisted in sick realization. Molly was going to burn her.

"*Do it.*" She pressed the barrel painfully against her skull. "Or you stop breathing *now.*"

She had no choice. Lydia's fingers shook as she hesitantly reached out to the dial, turning on the gas. Disbelief sent waves of hot and cold pulsating through her.

"You're insane!" she managed to croak out, struggling.

"On high."

She did as told, her legs wobbly and heart skittering in frantic beats as she stared at the dancing circle of blue fire. Molly's hold on her throat was the only thing keeping her standing. Dread churned inside her. She didn't understand any of this—why this woman had followed her in the garage that night with the intent of harming her, why she hadn't just finished her already with a bullet to her brain.

"P-please! Don't do this—"

"Did you think I was going to make it easy for you?" Standing behind her, maintaining her tight grip, Molly rocked Lydia's perspiring body back and forth. "*Poor thing*. You're a doctor. You know how disfiguring burns can be."

Lydia moaned softly. Dizzy, she felt more blood trickling down the back of her neck.

"Don't worry. You'll see Ryan one last time. I want him to have a look at the pretty, new you."

He was still alive, then.

Lydia's hand bumped against a bulge in the right pocket of her lab coat. Her EpiPen. She'd taken to carrying it directly on her after the wasp incident.

Her blood rushed in her ears. It was the only chance she had. She wasn't going to just let herself be maimed! Gut clenching, she inched her hand carefully into her pocket, trying to gain control over her trembling fingers as Molly continued her verbal attack.

"I've dealt with women like you before." Her breath rasped against Lydia's ear. "Thinking you're better than me. That you can have any man you want. You came into Frank's place and *stole* Ryan like he still belonged to you! You threw him away until you thought he could be interested in *me*! Was that fun for you?"

"N-no!"

Gasping against the crushing pressure on her throat,

Lydia managed to flip the cap from the carrier tube using her thumbnail. Then tilting it sideways, she slid the injector out into her pocket. She tried to pull off the safety release in an awkward, one-handed move but failed, losing her grip as Molly began forcing her forward at the waist, tightening her hold on her throat even more and making it impossible to draw air into her lungs. Fresh panic set in.

"You can fight, but you're going to faint eventually, *runt*," the taller woman said, grunting with effort. "And I'm going to hold you down until I can smell your flesh cooking. *Delicious steak Lydia*."

The lack of oxygen was weakening her quickly, the circular flame growing unfocused in her watery vision. Lydia's muscles jumped under her skin, her heart squeezing. She did her best to twist her head away from the hot flame as she was pressed closer. Lydia's chin-length hair hung down. It would catch fire first. Nausea swept through her at the heat radiating onto her skin.

Her lungs screamed for air. Black spots danced in front of her eyes as Lydia discreetly removed the injector from her pocket. Gripping it in one hand, she pulled off the safety release with the other.

Molly kicked the back of her knee, nearly collapsing her face-first onto the stove. "You're going to need a closed casket, you stuck-up—"

Now.

With a burst of energy, she blindly plunged it up and behind her. Molly shoved her away with a howl.

Coughing and gasping, Lydia whirled. She'd hit Molly

in the throat. She stumbled away, knowing she hadn't been able to hold it there long enough to deliver the full dose of epinephrine. But Molly was bent over, grasping her neck, the gun pointing downward and Lydia's makeshift weapon on the floor. Lydia bolted from the kitchen, hoping she'd hit the jugular or carotid, doing damage. But the stomach-turning *thwap* of the gun's silencer a few seconds later confirmed she'd missed her mark. Wall plaster exploded near her shoulder, making Lydia cringe as she reached the crossroads between the living room and hallway.

The front door was a dozen feet away but a direct target, out in the open. Molly was coming for her. Limbs shaking, she turned sharply and, scooping up her backpack in the hall, ran into the closest room on the right. Slamming the door closed, she locked it as another bullet made splintering impact with the wood. She sobbed in terror, crouching behind a metal tower that held a set of free weights. Ryan was here somewhere, probably injured. But he was *alive*. Molly had said so. Lydia couldn't leave him.

"You fucking bitch!" Pounding on the door, Molly screamed vile threats that made Lydia's blood curdle. Jaw clenched, her breath rasping sharply, she dug through her backpack for her cell phone and key chain that held the canister of pepper spray.

Like bringing a knife to a gunfight.

Tears flooded her eyes as she willed her fear-clumsy fingers to punch the numbers on her phone.

"9-1-1. What's your emergency?"

"Please help me!" she pleaded, panting as Molly

continued her assault on the door. "I'm at a house on Candler Street. It's a white ranch with pine trees all around. There's a woman with a gun. She's shooting—"

"What's the street address?"

"I-I don't know!" Lydia's stomach squeezed at the sudden, eerie quiet in the hall. "It's two properties from the MARTA stop on the corner of Barfield. There's a black Ford Explorer and a silver Volvo parked in the driveway! Please, hurry!"

She tugged at her hair, her voice breaking. "We need an ambulance, too. There's … a police officer here. He's hurt."

"We have cars en route. Stay on the phone with me, ma'am. What's your name?"

She rocked in place. "Lydia. Dr. Lydia Costa."

"Where are you in the house? We need your location …"

The dispatcher's words faded into dust, replaced by a rising buzz in Lydia's ears. She heard a click and saw the doorknob turning. Horror washed through her. Molly had found the key.

Lydia screamed, shielding her head with her arms as the door swung open and hit the wall with a whack. Molly stalked into the room with the gun raised, her eyes glinting with fury. Sparks flew as a bullet ricocheted off the iron weights. Lydia scrambled backward on the floor, her pepper spray gripped in her hand.

She would die here. Her heart went weak as Molly stood over her, smiling coldly, the gun aimed at her face.

The booming explosion deafened her.

Lydia watched, stunned, as Molly's head snapped sideways and she dropped to the floor in a red mist, legs sprawled out, the mane of hair partially hiding her face.

"Take the gun."

Ryan's hoarse voice pulled her gaze from the body. He entered from the hallway, still in shooting stance, his steps sluggish. Lydia's heart beat painfully.

"Ryan ..." she croaked out.

His face was ashen, the right side of his half-open shirt soaked with crimson. The amount of blood frightened her. She wasn't sure how he was standing. Lydia managed to crawl timidly forward and pull the gun toward her, although there was no doubt Molly was dead. Her mouth hung open, her green eyes staring out unseeingly through flaxen hair. Lydia swallowed hard at the globs of brain matter sitting amid skull fragments.

She looked back at Ryan. She cried out as he collapsed against the wall, his back leaving a bloody smear on the way down.

"Ryan!" She went to him on her hands and knees. Her lungs squeezed as she pressed two fingers firmly against the side of his throat. His pulse was weak but existent, his breathing shallow and fast. His skin was cold. Clammy. With a sob, Lydia tore his shirt open the rest of the way and saw the hole in his side. With shaking fingers, she grabbed for a T-shirt Adam had left hanging on the bench press and pushed the cotton deeply into the puncture, then used her hands to provide direct pressure over it. She noticed his abraded wrists and the plastic cords encircling them. Her body shivered as she heard the approaching wail of sirens.

"Hold on, Ryan," she pleaded to his unconscious form, a hard ache inside her throat. Tears obscured her vision. "Please don't leave me."

A minute later, she screamed out their location as first responders entered the house.

CHAPTER THIRTY-TWO

M ORE THAN A week had passed, and while Adam was no longer in the ICU, he remained in a stepdown unit. He looked like hell, Ryan thought. Noticeably thinner and pale, with the telltale scar of open-heart surgery peeking from the top of his hospital gown.

But he was miraculously alive.

Ryan sat in a chair beside his bed, still hospitalized himself. He hoped to be released as early as tomorrow, however, and had felt strong enough to make the journey from his own room to Adam's without assistance.

"I didn't sleep with her, you know." Adam adjusted the IV line inserted into the back of his hand, then attempted to disentangle it from the other wires attached to him.

Leaning forward to help, Ryan shifted carefully, feeling the tug of sutures covering his own healing wound. For the last several days he'd foregone the standard hospital apparel, instead wearing sweatpants and a T-shirt under a robe Lydia had brought him from home.

"I don't think it mattered," he said. "She'd lost control.

In the end any perceived slight was reason enough for retribution."

Deep hollows were forged under Adam's eyes. "God. To think I wanted you to ask her out."

"She fooled everyone," Ryan reminded soberly.

"I could always tell she was sweet on you, but …" His head against the pillow, Adam appeared remorseful. "Who knows what I told her about Lydia."

They were still learning about Molly Renee Babin, including the fact that she'd departed California not long after her boyfriend there, a Los Angeles police officer, had died from an apparently self-inflicted gunshot wound. The LA coroner had ruled the death a suicide, but in light of the Atlanta shootings, the case was about to be reopened. Not that it would make much difference now, Ryan thought, other than to give his family some closure.

"What?" Adam asked.

He realized he'd been staring at his brother, still marveling at his survival. Ryan's voice roughened. "I'm just glad you're still here."

Adam released a weak huff, bluish stubble shadowing his jaw. "I still can't believe that bitch told you I was dead."

Even in his current condition, some of Adam's intensity had begun to return. Ryan wanted to tell him not to call her that, but he didn't, aware he'd had the same powerful feelings.

The APD had gained access to Molly's mental health records, which revealed that she had been treated for a persistent borderline personality disorder in California.

Perhaps even more telling, her father had been the police chief in a small town in Idaho, where Molly had lived until running away to the West Coast as a teen. Mack Babin had abused her sexually throughout her childhood, she had revealed to psychiatrists. There was some loose evidence to support her claims, although no charges had ever been filed.

In the days before her final rampage, Molly had flown to Idaho, apparently to visit her father's grave.

The headstone had been vandalized with spray paint.

Ryan wondered if Molly's fixation on law enforcement had started with the father who pretended to love her but clearly hadn't. If what she'd claimed was true, he had exploited her in the worst possible way. It was possible her vengeance on the men who failed her had been a subconscious act against the one person who should have been her protector.

Once he was released from the hospital, Ryan would be scheduled to attend a hearing in front of the department's shooting board. He dreaded it, even though he had already been told it was basically a formality. What he'd done had been necessary to save a life.

Still, he didn't take killing someone lightly.

"So when were you going to tell me about you and Lydia?" Adam asked, recapturing his attention. The heart monitor beside his bed beeped steadily, accompanying his raspy voice.

So he knew. Ryan released a breath. "When I thought

you were strong enough. I didn't want to get you worked up. Who told you? Mom?"

"She broke the news—"

"I don't need another lecture, Adam," he said quietly.

But his brother reached out from the bed and laid his fingers on his forearm. "I'm not going to give you one." He took a labored breath, still clearly in pain and dealing with reduced lung capacity. An oxygen cannula remained clipped under his nose. "You're my brother, Ryan. If I've had a grudge against Lydia, it's only because I love you, man. But I also have to believe in you and trust you're doing the right thing."

"*I am*," he stressed. Pressing his lips together, he added, "We are."

"Then that has to be good enough for me."

Ryan tilted his head at him. "So you're calling a truce in this war against Lydia?"

"Mom and I've talked a lot since she's been here." Adam didn't look at him as he spoke, instead focusing on the blanket tucked around him. "She got me to finally see how much losing Tyler affected Lydia. How she might've let her grief confuse her. She says I'm *intractable*—hell, I'm not even sure what that means—but that I need to forgive her and give you both my support."

He toyed with his hospital ID bracelet before speaking again. "Lydia and I've talked, too. Especially since I've been a captive audience here. I've listened instead of just lighting into her on sight."

"She's come to visit you?"

"Yeah. More than once."

"Then she's braver than I even realized." He had meant it as a joke, but Adam's expression remained serious.

Ryan became aware of the tension that had released from his body. So their mother had brought about this change of heart. He was grateful for the time she had been here, even though he hated that it had been under such difficult conditions—both her sons wounded, Adam nearly dying. Ryan understood how lucky he himself had been. The shot delivered at close range had passed through the muscle surrounding his abdomen. It had bled like hell, but it hadn't entered his stomach cavity, hadn't hit any vital organs.

Adam had a long road ahead of him that included at least two more weeks of hospitalization and a stint in pulmonary physical therapy to strengthen what remained of his right lung. His career as a beat cop was over, something he had just begun to accept. They had talked tentatively about him taking the detective's exam the next time it came around. Until then, once he was well enough, he'd work a desk job at his precinct. It would be an adjustment for his adrenaline-junkie brother, but Ryan knew how much worse things could have been.

"Just do me a favor?" Ryan asked, attempting to lighten the mood. "This is a big city—not south Georgia where we grew up. Stop being a cheapskate. Get a security system, even if your landlord won't subsidize the installation cost."

Based on the jimmied lock, Molly had gained entrance through the ranch's back door.

Adam smiled faintly. "Whatever, man. Not that yours did you much good with that gangbanger."

"Talk to Tess about that. They have to be *on* to work."

Both men looked up at the tentative knock on the door. The red-haired kindergarten teacher stood in the room's threshold. She had been a regular presence since returning from the beach and finding out what had happened. Ryan greeted her, rising gingerly from the chair, his palm pressed against his side.

"Please," Rachel said as she entered. "Don't leave because of me."

"I need to get going anyway." Ryan laid a hand on her shoulder as he slowly walked past. He'd begun to feel his strength waning. "Before they do a bed check and discover I'm AWOL."

"Hey."

At his brother's voice, Ryan turned.

"*You do what you need to do*," Adam said meaningfully. Rachel had moved to his bedside, and a nurse had also entered the room. "Not that you need it, but you have my blessing. Truce."

Ryan nodded.

He had begun his slow trek back to his room when his cell phone rang inside his bathrobe pocket. He stopped amid the others in the corridor—mostly hospital staff—and reached for it. Seeing the number on the screen, he took the call.

"I rang your room and no answer," Mateo said.

"I've been with Adam." He considered taking a seat

on an upholstered bench under a nearby window, but remained standing. "What's up?"

"I thought you'd want to know. Tox screen's back. It's clean. No drugs in the bloodstream or muscle tissue, including residual traces in the organs."

Which confirmed what they had already suspected. Molly hadn't been taking the medications prescribed by her California psychiatrist. She had probably been off them for a while.

"Thanks," Ryan said, finding his voice.

"How're you doing? You got your release papers yet?"

"I'm hoping for tomorrow."

They talked for another minute before Ryan disconnected the call. But as he returned the phone to his pocket and began walking again, he couldn't help it—his mind remained on Molly. He continued to grapple with the knowledge that someone who had seemed so outwardly normal had been masking such delusional thoughts and careening emotions. That she'd been capable of such predatory violence. She'd been diagnosed with mental illness, but she'd also had the cunning that spoke to some degree of lucidity. Threatening Nate from a payphone. Then stepping up a level, buying a burner phone to ensure the calls to Lydia were untraceable to her. A prepaid cell had been linked back to Matthew Boyce's phone records, as well. But Molly hadn't been as careful everywhere. A post-mortem roll of her prints had generated a match to the passenger-side door handle of Boyce's car and to the packaging used to mail the wasps to the hospital.

He thought of the men she'd been having relations with—Nate and Matthew Boyce overlapping, apparently. Where Watterson fit in, they didn't yet know. Ryan wondered how many others on the force had been with her but hadn't come forward.

Turning the corner that led to the elevator bay, he stopped to rest.

"You should be in a wheelchair."

Lydia appeared beside him, in scrubs and her lab coat. She linked her forearm with his, assisting his slow walk. Ryan guessed she was on break and had been headed up to his room when she had spotted him, inching his way along the corridor like an arthritic old man.

"I don't need a wheelchair," he argued. "I'm getting out tomorrow—"

"That remains to be seen." But her smile was soft as she looked up at him. Lydia's dark hair had been pulled into a short ponytail. Pale lip gloss appeared to be the only cosmetic she wore.

She looked beautiful to him.

"I'm guessing you've been to see Adam."

He decided not to let on that he knew about their private conciliatory conversations. "He's still got a long way to go."

She nodded thoughtfully. "He's motivated. He'll make it."

Coming to a halt in front of the elevators, she pressed the button. "I saw Melanie a little while ago—headed out through the lobby. She was going to Adam's to get some of his things and then to your place to do laundry."

"You know Mom. She's planning to stay until he's out of the hospital and able to care for himself."

The elevator chimed. Once the doors slid open, they walked inside. Lydia pressed the button. "I suspect his new girlfriend will want to lend a hand, too. I've talked to her a few times now. She seems pretty great."

"Yeah," Ryan agreed, facing her. Alone on the elevator, he tucked strands of hair that had come loose from her ponytail behind her ear. They felt soft, like spun silk. Lydia's fingers caressed his raised wrist.

"I love you," she said.

Ryan thought of what Mateo had told him as he lay in bed post-surgery. Even now it created a knot inside him. In Molly's apartment, police had found the vial of sulfuric acid she had supposedly taken to the parking garage that night, intent on harming Lydia. Ryan wasn't sure what had spooked her from her mission, but he thanked God for it.

He also wondered again if Lydia hadn't simply become the target for the pent-up jealousy Molly felt regarding women who had what she didn't. Love. Only with Lydia had Molly acted out—not with Kristen Weisz or Boyce's ex-wife. If it was true Molly considered him special, then Lydia's appearance at the wake and his focus on her had quite possibly been the tipping point.

Placing a finger under her chin, he gently lifted her face and joined his mouth to hers. They broke apart only when the elevator's bell chimed, announcing they'd reached his floor. But as the doors opened, he slid his fingers through her hair again and searched her soft-brown eyes.

"I'm *fine*, Ryan," she murmured, apparently reading his thoughts.

But was she? He worried about how this most recent trauma had affected her. She had taken to sleeping in the recliner in his hospital room when she was off-shift, instead of going home. Lydia insisted it was because she wanted to be with him, but he worried it was also because she was afraid of being alone.

"Let's get you to your room," she said, walking with him, her arm once again offering support.

"I heard from Elise Brandt," she revealed once they'd entered Ryan's room. Someone—an orderly or some other hospital attendant—had remade the bed in his absence. He stopped in front of the bureau topped with flower arrangements and cards, looking at her.

"The US Marshals allowed her a call, and it was me. She sounds *strong*, Ryan. She wanted to thank me—thank both of us—for everything we did."

He had been the one to tell Lydia it had been Molly, not Brandt, behind the wasps and calls. But it didn't matter. Ian Brandt was a dangerous man. He'd killed and abused, engaged in felony activities. He deserved to be imprisoned. They had helped put Elise a step closer to freedom. There was no trial date yet, but Ryan hoped the ultimate outcome would be justice.

He watched as Lydia turned down the bed. The way

she had stood up repeatedly to Brandt, her quest to rescue Elise—it all spoke to her bravery.

As did the makeshift weapon she had plunged into her captor's neck.

Thinking of the torture Molly had attempted, Ryan's lungs squeezed. He'd learned of it only after reading the transcript of the statement Lydia had given police.

"Let's get you into bed." She returned to him. "You look tired, Ryan. I swear it's like talking to a brick wall, but you're overdoing it …" She must've seen something in his expression. "What's wrong?"

Throat tight with emotion, he said, "Just that I don't want to waste another minute of our lives."

For several moments, Lydia peered up at him, her gaze liquid and questioning as her fingers lay against his chest. She shook her head. "I still don't understand." Her words held a faint tremor. "The amount of blood you lost, how long you went without treatment. You should've been in hypovolemic shock. You pushed the limits of endurance when you got free—"

"I *had* to get to you." The pad of his thumb caressed her cheek. It was the only explanation he had. "Nothing could keep me away."

Ryan pressed his lips to her forehead.

EPILOGUE

————— ◗•●•◖ —————

FOUR MONTHS LATER

"ARE YOU SURE about this, Tess?" Lydia asked as the two women stood in the sunroom of the Inman Park bungalow. With the cooling weather, the leaves on the Japanese maple visible through the large window had finally begun to turn a rich burgundy.

"Oh, he won't be any trouble. And I've gotten attached—that's why I suggested it to Ryan." Tess flipped her long braid over her shoulder as she bent to scratch Max's head, eliciting a throaty purr from the feline. "This old-timer's set in his ways. He likes his old haunts."

"It *would* be easier for him," Lydia conceded.

Tess smiled. "I'll consider him a housewarming gift."

A thud coming from outside attracted their attention. Lydia walked to the side window to see Carl Buchwald in the driveway, moving boxes from the back of his open station wagon. Silver-haired and large-framed, Carl would soon be the house's new owner. He'd already begun storing some of his things in the detached garage, since he had closed on his home in Florida and would be staying in the small upstairs apartment with Tess until the house was vacant.

"I still can't believe he was your high school sweetheart. After all these years."

"Turns out he might've been the love of my life." Tess had come to stand beside Lydia. "I just didn't know it at the time."

Tess had revealed the identity of her regular male guest after learning of Ryan and Lydia's plans. She and Carl had been briefly engaged after school, but she'd broken things off when he had enlisted in the Army. She hadn't wanted the life of a military wife. He had moved on, married someone else and had three daughters. Tess had never forgotten him, however. Carl had first contacted her a little over a year ago, some time after the death of his wife, Beth. After the military, he'd had a successful second career in insurance. He had bought the bungalow outright, and at Ryan's asking price. According to Tess, they had been talking about taking their relationship to another level—getting a place together—for a while.

"He's going to be closer here to his youngest in Spartanburg. She has two grandbabies. And I'm going to have a bigger place."

"And a *roommate*," Lydia reminded, shaking her head in wonderment. "If there's a wedding, we're going to want to know."

Tess chortled good-naturedly. "Oh, I doubt that'll happen. For now, we're just going to enjoy ourselves shacking up. It makes Carl feel naughty. Us old folks have to get our thrills where we can." She touched Lydia's arm, growing serious. "I'm sure going to miss you both, honey."

Thinking of the impending move, Lydia felt butterflies in her stomach. But it hadn't been an impulse decision. It was something she and Ryan had discussed at length. When the opportunity had opened for Lydia at a smaller regional hospital in Asheville, North Carolina, they'd taken it as a sign. The hospital had been accommodating, working to help speed along Lydia's license to practice from the North Carolina Medical Board. Ryan had in turn put in for a transfer to the Asheville Police Department. Compared to Atlanta, the force was a fraction of the size, but the city was growing, and the department had an urgent need for someone with Ryan's level of experience in homicides.

The city's slower pace was something they both desired.

Lydia's orientation for her new job would begin three days from now, on Monday, and Ryan would join her after his tenure with the APD was completed in another week.

She had mixed emotions about the move, but those emotions included hope. They were leaving Atlanta, but leaving together. It would be a fresh start.

"The same could be said of you," Tess pointed out, breaking into her thoughts. "You should let *us* know of any wedding plans."

Absently, Lydia touched the simple, platinum band on her left hand. Ryan had begun wearing his ring again, too, although they hadn't exchanged vows or made anything official on paper. Perhaps in time they would. For now, their focus was on simply being together. On building a new life. The rings were more a statement of what was in their hearts.

So much had changed over these last months, Lydia thought once Tess had gone outside to give Carl a hand.

Lydia had begun talk therapy again. Dr. Sarah Rosen had been a godsend, someone to help her more fully come to terms with Tyler's death as well as her dependency issues that had spiraled from it. They had also spent time working through the trauma of Molly Babin's attack. With the pending move, Dr. Rosen had referred her to a new counselor in Asheville, urging her to continue with therapy at least until she was settled into her new job and home. Lydia had also taken up meditation and yoga.

She still struggled, but she felt stronger than she had in a long time.

With Ryan's support, she had stopped drinking completely, believing it the best course for her.

They had spread their off-work time between the bungalow and her condo, until she had found someone to sub-lease. Since then, they'd been here in this house that held so much of their lives.

Arms crossed over her sweater, Lydia looked around the sunroom with its high walls and beamed ceiling—the good bones of the old house—before wandering down the wainscoted hallway. She stopped at the door to Tyler's bedroom, which stood open.

Ryan had taken the afternoon off. He knelt on the floor in front of the blue-painted chest of drawers, unaware of her presence. His back was to her as he slowly removed clothing from inside it—little-boy shirts and pants, underwear and pajamas. They'd been going through Tyler's things together, deciding which ones to donate to charity, to a child in need, and what to keep. She watched, a dull ache inside her as he held one of the items to his face, his shoulders lifting under his shirt as his lungs expanded. Lydia knew he was searching for some left-behind trace of their child.

Tyler would always live in their hearts.

She came inside. Ryan rose and turned to her, placing several pieces of clothing onto the pile they had created.

"I ... thought we'd want to keep that," he said quietly, nodding to a stuffed animal that lay on the bed. The rabbit's synthetic fur had been worn smooth by fondling and repeated machine washings. Tyler hadn't gone to sleep without it at night. The bittersweet memory pricked her heart.

"He always loved it," Ryan rasped, a wash of pain in his blue eyes.

With a small nod of agreement, Lydia picked it up and carefully placed it in one of the packing boxes with the other keepsakes—myriad photos, Tyler's christening gown, a sweater Melanie had knitted for him, some of his favorite toys.

"Did you really give Max away?" she asked a few moments later.

As Ryan shoved his hands into his jeans pockets and moved closer, she sighed. "It's the right decision, probably," she said. "Tess adores him, and he'll be spared the stress of getting used to a new place. It could also be awhile before we have a permanent address."

"He *did* come with the house," Ryan reminded. "We found him in the backyard after we moved in."

For now, they'd rented a loft apartment in downtown Asheville, near the hospital in a renovated factory building in the heart of the city's arts district. Located on the fifth floor, it was within walking distance of shops and restaurants, and the balcony had a stunning view of the Blue Ridge Mountains. Once they were both settled in their new lives, they would begin looking for a house, possibly in the nearby, quaint town of Woodfin.

They'd also talked casually about living higher up in the mountains, in some cabin with a running stream on the property and an outdoor fireplace on the deck.

Removing his hands from his pockets, Ryan tangled his fingers with hers. "So we're really doing this?"

Lydia released a nervous breath. "I hope so. It's a little late to back out now."

His expression grew serious. "This is going to be *good* for us, Lyd."

This starting over *was* both exciting and terrifying. But they wanted a new place where they weren't constantly reminded of their loss. A new town, with new people, could hopefully offer that.

But there had been so many good, precious memories here, too.

"I've been looking around," Lydia said, wistful. "We did

so much work here, Ryan. You, especially. You really put your heart into this place—"

"My home is wherever you are." He touched her face, seemingly aware of the emotions barely contained under her surface. She leaned into him and kissed him softly, her arms around his neck.

Once her lips left his, she took a step toward the boxes. They still had a lot of work to do before she left for Asheville. Part of their furniture had already been sent to the new apartment, while the rest would be temporarily put into storage once Ryan officially turned the house over to Carl late next week.

"Have you talked to Adam?" she asked.

"Yeah. We're still a go for tomorrow night."

Although Ryan would be in town for a while longer, Adam and Rachel were planning a going-away party for them both, to be held the night before Lydia's departure. They'd reserved a large room at Ocho's, the Mexican restaurant in Decatur. All the usual suspects would be there—Mateo and Evie, Darnell, Antoine Clark and his wife, as well as Roe, Abe Solomon and a half-dozen others from Lydia's workplace. Rick Varek had also been invited, and although he'd declined, he had wished them well. He was now dating a nurse in Oncology.

"Have you figured out how Adam's taking all this?" Lydia asked. He and Ryan had always been close, and Adam's injury had only strengthened that bond.

"He's his usual stoic self. He says Asheville's only a few hours away, so expect him to visit often."

Lydia smiled. "I'll consider myself forewarned."

"I'll miss him. No one to use up my laundry detergent and raid my refrigerator." Although his tone was sarcastic, Lydia knew being separated from Adam was the one hesitancy he had.

"He's going to be fine, Ryan." Lydia touched his arm.

After an eight-week medical leave, Adam had spent the last two months working the front desk at his precinct house. But he had regained his strength and appeared to be recuperated. He and Rachel had also grown more serious, becoming nearly inseparable when neither was working. The injury, his brush with death, seemed to have matured him.

He was scheduled to take the detective's examination next month.

They went back to their task of sorting clothing, talking about Tyler and sharing precious memories as they sat on the floor together. After a while, however, Ryan stood once more and offered his hand to Lydia, helping her up.

"You okay?" Concern was visible in his eyes.

She released a breath, but nodded. This was hard for them both—going through Tyler's things. The move necessitated it, but it was also necessary for them to let go. Looking at Ryan, she thought of the old proverb: *A shared joy is a double joy; a shared sorrow is half a sorrow.* Their eyes held until she went into his embrace, laying her head against his chest as he wordlessly held her. But with her sadness, she also felt an abiding love.

She felt fortunate for their second chance. *For him.*

A short time later, he cleared his throat and released her, his hands gently clasping her upper arms. "Let's take a break from this, all right? I think we both could use one."

Lydia took a last look around the increasingly sparse room. Then they walked from it together.

"Brandt's trial has a start date," he confided in the hallway. "December fourth."

Lydia felt her stomach flip-flop. "When did you hear this?"

"Noah Chase called while you were out with Tess."

The two women had gone to the home improvement store on Ponce for more packing items—boxes, tape, labels. Lydia's mind went to Elise. She was living somewhere else now, most likely in another state and under a new name. But she would have to resume her former identity when she appeared to testify. Lydia doubted she would ever see or talk to her again, but she hoped the best for her.

"Let's get you into a jacket. It's cold out," Ryan said as they entered the living room. He reached for her coat that hung on the hall tree. "At least as cold as it gets in Hotlanta in early November."

They'd heard earlier that week that Asheville had already gotten its first snow. It had been only a few inches, but the thought excited Lydia. Growing up in New Orleans, she'd never even seen a snowfall until a college ski trip.

"Where're we going?" she asked as he held her coat out for her and she slipped her arms inside it.

"Piedmont Park."

"We'll have to take the car," she pointed out as Ryan

slid on his leather jacket. "We could just walk to Goldsboro Park right here in the neighborhood—"

"Piedmont's beautiful in the fall." Looking at her, he appeared handsome in the fading sunlight filtering in through the large windows, his features even and his eyes a smoky blue. Ryan gave a small shrug. "It ... could be our last time."

A slow realization spread through her.

He had asked her to marry him there—in the gazebo overlooking Lake Clara Meer—all those years ago. Lydia remembered it like some hazy dream. It had been approaching twilight, and the downtown cityscape had just begun to glow, reflecting in the water's mirrored surface. The park had been busy that night, but their surroundings, the people, had faded away until it was only them.

Looking up at him, Lydia's fingers laced with his.

"Piedmont it is," she said softly.

ACKNOWLEDGMENTS

THANK YOU FOR taking the time to read FALLEN. My readers are the reason I write and I'm so appreciative of your ongoing support.

A very special thank you is owed to Angelita Ritz, R.N., who has more than thirty years of nursing experience, including twenty-five years spent inside the ER. Angelita, you were invaluable to me in the depiction of medical scenes and use of terminology, and I cannot thank you enough. You were a fantastic beta reader, as well. I am also deeply grateful for the work of Joyce Lamb, who edited this book, and for critique partners Michelle Muto and Kelly Stone. Michelle, thank you for helping guide me through this next step of my writing journey. I'd also like to thank my agent, Stephany Evans of FinePrint Literary Management, who has always believed in me.

Finally, thank you to my husband, Robert, for your love and for encouraging me to always keep writing.

ABOUT THE AUTHOR

LESLIE TENTLER IS best known as the author of the Chasing Evil Trilogy (MIDNIGHT CALLER, MIDNIGHT FEAR and EDGE OF MIDNIGHT). She was named as a finalist for Best First Novel at ThrillerFest 2012 for Midnight Caller, and as a finalist in the 2013 Daphne du Maurier Awards for Excellence in Mystery and Suspense for Edge of Midnight. She is also the recipient of the prestigious Maggie Award of Excellence.

Leslie is a member of Romance Writers of America, International Thriller Writers, The Authors Guild and Novelists, Inc. A native of East Tennessee, she currently resides in Atlanta.

If you enjoyed reading Leslie's work, please consider leaving a review, however short. Of course, simply telling others you enjoyed this book is also sincerely appreciated. Word of mouth is the best promotion.

Visit Leslie and sign up for her newsletter at
www.LeslieTentler.com.

OTHER WORKS BY LESLIE TENTLER

Midnight Caller
Midnight Fear
Edge of Midnight

Made in the USA
Middletown, DE
02 November 2014